RIVEN

Sarah Bryant

Proudly Published by Snowbooks in 2012

Copyright © 2012 Sarah Bryant

Sarah Bryant asserts the moral right to
be identified as the author of this work.

All rights reserved.

Snowbooks Ltd.
email: info@snowbooks.com

www.snowbooks.com

British Library Cataloguing in Publication Data
A catalogue record for this book is available from the
British Library.

Paperback ISBN 9781907777639

RIVEN

Sarah Bryant

RIVEN

To all of you who helped make Scotland my home.

Acknowledgements

A number of people deserve thanks for helping me make this book what I wanted it to be. First, Clare Whittaker and Carol Christie for being my critique group – I miss you guys! Carol again for helping to streamline my dodgy Scots. Elaine Di Rollo for reading whatever I hand her and always criticizing honestly. My husband Colin for all of his patience & support. My children, Finn and Nuala, for bearing with me when five more minutes turns into an hour. Laura Erel for her commentary and also for being one of my first and most faithful fans. John Purser for explaining Gaelic plurals. And last but by no means least, the team at Snowbooks for doing what they do, and doing it so well!

Who shall say that Fortune grieves him,
While the star of hope she leaves him?
  Robert Burns

PROLOGUE

She couldn't stop crying, though she couldn't remember what she was crying for. She only knew that something had been taken from her, something so vital that she didn't think she could ever be whole again. And though a part of her wished that she could remember what her tears were for, another part of her knew she couldn't bear that memory.

But she did remember weeping like this once before, for years beyond count. She remembered a bottomless pool filled with her tears. But that had been in the poisoned paradise she'd forsaken. Here, her tears ran down her face, like a human's, and like those mortal tears they disappeared into the long, indigo grass, leaving no trace.

Sometimes, one or two of the angels came and tried to comfort her. There was one with ropes of white hair and a silvery aura, who smiled and moved with a dancer's grace. There was another with an aura of fire, and green eyes hard and bright as gems, who spoke of inevitability and sacrifice.

11

There were others, too, who came less frequently. All of them talked as if her silence were a vessel they were determined to fill. Their words fell away like her tears, lost in the grass.

But the one who came oftenest never spoke at all. He had black hair, black eyes, but an aura like a summer sunset. Sometimes he came with books, and sat by her silently, reading. Sometimes he brought musical instruments, and played them with a skill that told her he'd practised them, not just relied on his innate power to make them do his will. Sometimes he brought little gifts – a shell of a heartbreaking blue, a handful of velvety moss, a speckled feather. Things from the place she dared not remember. She left them where he laid them, at her feet.

On the day he finally spoke to her, though, he didn't place his gift with the others. Instead, he knelt in front of her and offered her something on the palm of his hand. It was a tiny, empty, cut-glass bottle with a cork stopper.

"I thought that this might help you," he said. His voice was musical, but then every angel's voice was musical, just as all their faces were beautiful.

Nevertheless, she looked at him more closely than she'd looked at the others. There was something about him that set him apart from them. Maybe the sympathy in his dark eyes. Maybe the kindness in the turn of his mouth. Or perhaps it was the fact that he would sit in her silence for as long as it took her to break it, because, somehow, she knew this with absolute certainty.

And so, surprising herself and, apparently, him, she answered, "What is it?"

"A lachrymatory. A bottle for your tears." It was the shape of a tear itself. He touched the stopper. "The tears evaporate slowly, through the cork. They say that when the bottle is dry, the grief will be healed."

"Who says this?"

"The humans who made it."

Hesitantly, she took the bottle from his hand. As her fingertips brushed his palm, a warmth passed into them and spread through her, as if he really were wrapped in a summer sunset. Her cheeks flamed. Raising a hand to them, she realized that they were dry. She looked at him in amazement.

"What is your name?" she asked.

"Lucifer," he answered.

Lucifer. Lux ferre. Light-bringer. "Thank you," she said, "but it seems I don't need the bottle after all." She offered it back to him.

"No," he said. "It's yours." He reached out and closed her fingers around it, and then, boldly, his own gold-brown ones around them. The surge that went through her then made a shadow of the first. The whole world seemed lit by his brightness. Light-bringer indeed.

But as she began to smile, the light faded. Lucifer's hand dropped from hers as black clouds rolled across the sky, and then they were no longer sitting on an indigo hill, but on the pitching deck of a boat on a nighttime sea. Lucifer's face greyed, and then melted, his form dissolving even as she reached for him, turning to liquid beneath her hands, which rolled away as she scrabbled to contain it. She shrieked his name into the howling wind, but the last glowing drops escaped her fingers, merging into the opaque water that rescinded nothing but the cracked shadow of her own face.

CHAPTER I

She was not shrieking when she woke. She wasn't even crying. But a low, involuntary noise came from deep inside her, as it did every time she woke from a dream of him, to relive the loss all over again.

Nothing in Sophie's life before Lucas had prepared her for that loss. His death didn't just devastate her, it consumed her, so that she didn't know where grief ended and she began. It turned her days to a dull, protracted ache, her nights to a horror of dreaming of him – or not. She truly didn't know which was worse: the cold reality of another night without him, or awakening from a sweet dream to an aftershock of that first, sickening thud of realization that she would never see him again.

Her only consolation then was how little time she had left to bear it. When she'd first learned that she would die on her eighteenth birthday, Sophie had been devastated. Now, a mere month later, it was almost a comfort. Of course, no one but

Michael knew about it. No one knew about the dreams, either; not even her mother, whom, more often than not, she woke to find standing over her bed, awakened by the keening, her eyes frightened and helpless.

Guilty as she felt for making her mother suffer, Sophie refused to talk about what had happened, allowing her parents to believe the story Michael had told them when they came to take her home from Ardnasheen. It was the same story he'd told to the police and the papers and the hospital that set her broken wrist. That she and her friends Ailsa and Lucas had all run afoul of a well-integrated sociopath, and she'd narrowly escaped becoming his victim. That Lucas had saved her life, but tragically drowned, along with the criminal, in doing so. That unlike Sam's, his body hadn't been found, and likely never would be. Not in that fathomless black water, full of fast currents and deep crevices.

Everyone believed his story, even Ailsa. Michael had cleaned up her recollection of that terrible night before anyone could question her, along with the blood and the remains of the Revenants who had fought Sam with Sophie. But when he'd turned to Sophie to do the same, she had flat-out refused. Every memory she had of Lucas was precious, and she meant to keep them all – even the painful ones.

"You can never talk about it," Michael had said to her, when he realized that nothing would change her mind. "You can never tell anyone what really happened."

"I'm not stupid, Michael," she'd said bitterly.

His eyes had been like an old dog's: sad and soulful and pleading. "Think about it, Sophie. It will be a terrible burden. I could take the pain away."

"You mean, make me forget him."

"I mean, you don't have to suffer."

Her answer to that had been a withering look. She could see that he was worried that she'd talk, though he needn't have been. She could never have spoken about what had happened that night, even if anyone would have believed it. There was no parallel for her grief, and no outlet. She spent both day and night curled in her bed, eating only when forced to, pinned between merciless pain and the inability to cry, believing that nothing could ever be worse than living every day without Lucas.

That was, until her parents threatened her with the hospital. With her childhood bout of therapy still fresh in her mind, Sophie got up, got dressed and began to act out her "recovery". She had her hair cut into a bob that hung just shy of her shoulders, because her mother assured her a new look would help her move on. She hid her dangerous thinness under layers of clothes. She even pretended to be enthusiastic when her mother suggested a move to Edinburgh, where the Art College had offered her a temporary teaching post after a lecturer had left unexpectedly.

"But I thought you hated Scotland," Sophie said, not wanting to alert her mother to her own dread of returning there.

Though Edinburgh was worlds away from Ardnasheen, it still felt too close for comfort.

"I hated living on a sheep farm in the middle of nowhere," Anna answered, putting a sandwich Sophie hadn't asked for down in front of her. "But Edinburgh is different. Tiny compared to London, of course, but still a city. And the art college is first rate. It's an honor to be asked."

Sophie picked at the sandwich, feeling as if her stomach were full of stones. "But what will I do there?"

"Get a job," her mother answered, with a canny look in her blue eyes and a steely practicality in her tone that told Sophie more than she would ever say aloud about the real reason for the move. "You could have a look at the university, too. Or take some music lessons – Edinburgh's a mecca for *clarsach* players."

Sophie said nothing to this. She hadn't touched her harp since Lucas died. She didn't think she ever would again. But to say so would only spark another argument. Besides, she could tell that her mother didn't really want to talk about university or music. She wanted to talk about the thing she hadn't yet said.

"Please just say what you mean, Mum," Sophie said dully.

She expected her mother to protest, to pretend Sophie hadn't guessed she had an ulterior motive. Instead, taking a deep breath, she answered, "It's time you put what happened behind you. Re-engaged with life."

Re-engage with life. It was impossible on so many levels

18

that Sophie had the urge to laugh. Looking up at her mother, though, she knew that this would lead right into hospital. "Okay," she said, and went back to picking at the food she couldn't possibly swallow.

*

A few weeks later, lying in her old bed in the new flat in Morningside, Sophie had to admit that her mother had been partly successful in her first goal, if not her second. She hadn't had a dream since they'd arrived in Edinburgh – or none she'd remembered. Nor had she woken to find her mother standing over her, and slowly, as the days passed, her mother began to lose her haunted look. More to the point, she backed off a bit in her attempts at forcing food and sympathy onto Sophie.

And, as her mother had suggested, she got a job. She didn't particularly want one, but when she saw how desperately her mother wanted to believe that it would help her, she put in an application at a coffee shop. She reasoned that it would at least make one of them feel better, and since she was going to be miserable anyway, it didn't much matter where she went about it.

On her first day of work, Sophie got up at six. Her shift didn't start until nine, but she always woke early now, even when she didn't dream. She left her bed and padded into the kitchen, cringing as her bare feet came into contact with the cold linoleum, and turned on the kettle with a hand only recently liberated of its plaster cast. When the water boiled, she filled a mug with it, and then folded her hands around it. She didn't want a drink, only the warmth of the hot porcelain.

As she held the mug, she gazed blankly out the window. The flat was on the top floor, and the view from the kitchen was an uninspiring montage of rusting downpipes, grizzled flowerboxes and soot-stained chimneys. Sophie stared at it until the water in the cup was lukewarm. Then she put the cup down on the worktop and went into the lounge.

She opened the curtains covering the big bay window, carefully avoiding her harp case which lay underneath. Anna had set up her easel in the window's flood of light, and was already at work on a blue-toned cityscape. Sophie thought she recognized a section of the Royal Mile, though she didn't know the city well enough yet to be certain. It was definitely Edinburgh, though. Not the colorful, bustling Edinburgh of Festival brochures, but the late-autumn version, where the pubs' hanging baskets were full of weeds and papery brown leaves, and the grass in the parks bent and silvered with a heavy mist that never seemed quite cold enough to turn to frost, under a sky in shades of gray. *Bereft*, Sophie thought, and wrapped her arms more tightlyaround herself, trying not to feel the ruts and ridges of her own starving body.

Abruptly, she turned from the window. She would go for a walk, to fill the time until the café opened. She pulled on clothes and boots, then an old waxed jacket of her mother's.

She walked down the four flights of stairs, let herself out into the chill grey morning and then turned south, away from the city center.

She was going to the Braid Hermitage. She'd walked past its entrance with her mother several times. Though they'd never ventured inside, something about the dark tangle of woods so close to the city had pulled at her. The streets were quiet as she approached it, aside from a few early dog-walkers. By the time she reached the gate by the old Toll House, though, she was alone.

She paused to look at the little stone house. It was the kind of place she might have wanted to live one day, if things had been different: old enough to be interesting, small enough not to be intimidating. There was no sign of life in the house, now, though, and the garden was a tangle of long yellow grass and overgrown bushes.

A flicker of movement and color at the back of the house caught Sophie's eye. She pushed through the creaking gate, onto the path that led into the reserve. At the center of the back garden she found what she was looking for. It was a small tree – a Hawthorn, she thought, though without leaves or flowers, it was difficult to tell. By the look of its gnarled and twisted trunk, it was very old. It was covered in bright strips of cloth tied to its twigs and branches, so that the tree seemed alive with multicolored butterflies. A string of little silver bells hung from one of the lower branches, tinkling softly when it moved in the breeze.

The tree was beautiful, but there was also something strange about it, as if it belonged to another place or time. *Bells ward against faeries.* Sophie shivered, remembering the similar string of bells at Niall Aiken's cottage in Ardnasheen. Niall Aiken, who had become another of Sam's victims. Crossing her arms over her chest, Sophie looked around. At this time of the morning, a London park would have been populated with runners and dog-walkers. Except for one set of footprints in the mud of the track, however, she might have been the last person on Earth.

Sophie stood looking at the path disappearing into the tangle of winter branches. For the first time since Lucas died, she felt afraid. *What for?* she asked herself. No Revenants had appeared to her since the night on the boat, and at any rate, that night had proved that they weren't to be feared. As for human threats, there was little left for her to lose.

Shaking off her hesitation, Sophie began walking briskly up the path. The burn ran sluggishly beside it, smelling vaguely chemical, as all city streams seemed to do. A couple of mallards approached hopefully when they saw her, and then went back to picking at the stream bed for food when they realized she had none to offer. Other, smaller birds flitted among the bare branches, but there was something subdued about their movements and even their chatter, as if nothing could quite penetrate the forest's early winter hush.

The footprints petered out at a shallow spot in the stream, across from a large stone house that Sophie thought must be the Hermitage that the park was named for. She stopped, looking around. There was still no sign of anyone but herself on the path. The silence felt thick, the bare trees and dark, glossy stands of rhododendron watchful. *You're being stupid,* Sophie told herself. *There's nothing here.*

And so what if there is? a smaller, deeper part of her wondered. What, after all, did it matter if one of Lucas's *síth* appeared and swallowed her whole? She'd failed to save him, and saving him had been the purpose of her human life. Everything else was killing time.

Sophie looked down the muddy bank of the burn, daring something to emerge from the water. She saw nothing but a dead white moth, spiraling in an eddy. And then, something else. A flicker of movement that didn't belong. She climbed carefully down to the water's edge and peered into the shallow pool. A rusting ring from a pop-top can glinted dimly among the pebbles. Fine green weed drifted in the current, anchored to a white stone.

Or did it? There was something slightly off about its movement, as if it were out of time with the flow of the water. And then, between one blink and the next, the stone became a face, the weed a spill of green hair fanning around it, bound with a filigree band of silver, studded with pearls. It was a beautiful face, but also terrifying, for although its features resembled a woman's, there was nothing human about it. The pallid skin was tinged blue-green, the cheekbones too sharp and the cheeks too hollow, the eyes wide and silver-white, like cracked glass.

As Sophie watched, the water woman smiled with predatory glee and reached toward her with a pale, long-fingered hand. Sophie fell back with a cry as the tips of the woman's fingers breached the surface of the stream, thin and pale as bones. She tried to push herself to her feet, but they slid on the slimy mud of the bank. She turned, engulfed now by terror, and grasped at the stones and exposed roots in the bank, dragging herself upward. Something cold and wet and strong as a vice closed around her ankle. She cried out again and kicked hard against whatever held her, and it let her go.

Sophie didn't pause to see whether she was followed. She scrambled up the rest of the bank, turned back the way she had come – and ran hard into something. She stumbled back, yelling again as she felt hands close over her shoulders. It took her several moments to realize that it wasn't any monster that had grabbed her, but a young man of about her own age.

A young man, she saw as she recovered from her initial shock, who belonged in a fashion photograph, or on the cover of the edgier type of romantic novel. He was tall and slender, with fine-boned Eastern features, long black hair indifferently tied back with what looked like a loop of electrical cable, and the bluest eyes Sophie had ever seen. He was dressed in a jumbled collection of clothes: several shirts layered under a bobbled lime-green jumper, paint-spattered jeans held up by a red necktie threaded through the belt-loops, scuffed combat boots, and a black parka. He held a half-spent cigarette in slender fingers also covered in paint, and he was asking her something.

"Pardon?"

"I said, are you hurt? Did you fall?" His accent was soft lowland Scots, cut with something more foreign, possibly Asian.

"No. It was…I mean, I was…" *What, Sophie? Seeing scary green-haired women in the water? Being chased by monsters?* She drew a shuddering breath. "I thought I saw something down there," she said, pointing toward the bank she'd just scaled. "Something…bad."

He raised his eyebrows, but he turned toward the stream. He started toward it.

"I don't think you should go down there," Sophie said.

The young man only smiled, and disappeared over the edge of the bank. He was gone long enough that Sophie began to wonder whether he, too had fallen afoul of the woman in the water. Just as she took a step forward to look, though, she heard a cough, and then he reappeared, clearing his throat.

"I didn't see anything," he said, looking at her curiously

as he dusted his hands on his trousers. They, too were paint-stained, the nails filthy.

Sophie wondered if she was losing her mind. She wondered if the guy waiting for her to answer was as much a figment of her imagination as the green-haired woman had been. Because she had to have been. No other explanation made sense, least of all that she was real. Water horses in secluded Highland ponds were one thing; *sìth* in polluted city streams were quite another. Or so she wanted to believe.

Pushing that thought away, along with any doubts about the young man's reality, Sophie said, "I'm sorry. I thought that I saw something in the water, and then when I went to look I slipped, and caught my foot on the way back up, and my imagination got going…you know, with the woods and being by myself and all…"

She knew that she wasn't convincing him, even before she looked up to see his half-smile. "Look, thank you for coming to my rescue," she said, trying to sound calm and collected, "but really, I'm fine. Anyway, I've got to go. I'm expected at work…" She was already walking away, but the man didn't move. He just stood watching her with that same, strangely knowing expression on his face. "So…well…good-bye," she finished.

"Very well," he said as she began to walk away.

Very well? she thought. *Who talks like that?* Except, of course, she'd known someone who did.

"I'll see you soon," he added. And though it was only a throwaway expression, something about his tone wasn't quite so easy to dismiss.

CHAPTER 2

Sophie had chosen the café because of the name – Brewed Awakening. It also helped that it was on Victoria Street. Although it was either a bus ride or a long walk from the flat, and there were plenty of places nearer that would no doubt have hired her, Sophie loved the little street curving steeply from the Grassmarket to the Royal Mile. It was like an afterthought, its brightly colored storefronts at odds with the gray city around it – as out of place as she felt.

The building was a narrow one of three stories, the front painted forest green, the name in gold-leaf gothic letters over the door. Sophie stopped in front of it, pulling the iPod buds from her ears. The Clash streamed out of them: she hadn't been able to listen to anything but abrasive music since leaving Ardnasheen. She stood there, still half-listening to Joe Strummer wailing tinnily that Rudy Can't Fail, consumed by something she could only think of as stage fright. Her heart beat hard and her breath quickened just thinking about opening the café door.

Get a grip, she told herself, but it didn't help. Panic had set in. She knew that she couldn't walk into the café's steamy atmosphere and pretend to be normal. Nothing about her was normal, or ever had been. She turned to go.

As she did so, though, the door opened. A woman emerged in a cloud of warm, damp, coffee-scented air. She looked to be in her forties, but she was dressed like a student, in an emerald silk sari blouse under a pair of old denim dungarees. She had coppery skin, a long black plait with a scattering of white hairs twisted through it, and large eyes of a startling green. There was a mark between them where an Indian woman might wear a bindi, though hers looked more like a tattoo. It was an indigo triangle, made up of three tiny conjoined spirals.

"Sophie Creedon?" she said, her voice low and sweet, with an unexpected Irish lilt.

"Good guess," Sophie answered.

"Brilliant! Matrika." She held out her hand, and Sophie shook it. "I'm so glad to see you again," Matrika said, ushering Sophie through the door.

"Thanks, but I don't think we've met."

"No, no, of course not," Matrika said, guiding Sophie into the café. "But I saw you when you came in to ask about the job. I told Angus, 'We must hire that girl. She has soulful eyes.'"

Sophie had to bite back a bitter laugh at the irony. Matrika

29

didn't seem to notice. She led Sophie to a table by the front window set with two large, steaming cups. She indicated the one topped with foam. "Cappuccino, dry." She smiled at Sophie's quirked eyebrow. "Question three on the application: favorite caffeinated beverage." She sat down in front of the other cup, which held something the color of tea. However, the steam rising from it smelled like no tea Sophie had ever encountered. It was smoky, earthy. Wild.

Wild? Sophie scoffed at herself as she sat down. *I really am losing it.* She picked up her cup and sipped. Then she looked at it in surprise. If it was possible for a cup of coffee to be perfect, this one was.

Matrika nodded and smiled as if she'd heard the compliment. "So, Sophie," she said, sipping her own drink, "welcome to Brewed Awakening. Apologies for the name – the place came with it, and I was informed that it was something of a cult sensation with the students, so…" She shrugged.

"Actually, I kind of like it," Sophie said.

"See? I knew you'd be perfect. It was the same when I hired Angus – I just knew that he'd fit."

"Angus?" Sophie said. She vaguely recalled the young man who'd given her the application form.

Matrika nodded. "You'll be working a lot with him. He's away on a field trip this week, but you'll meet him next Monday."

"Great," Sophie said, wondering vaguely why a guy who

worked in a coffee shop would be doing field trips. "Where should I begin?"

"There's no hurry. Sit. Finish your coffee, and then I'll show you around."

Touching Sophie's hand lightly, she stood up and retreated behind the counter to serve the lengthening queue. Sophie didn't know whether it was the warmth, the coffee or Matrika's touch, but for the first time in weeks, she felt something other than ravaged.

*

That morning, Matrika guided Sophie through her set of tasks. They were less demanding than her duties at World's End had been. She even picked up the workings of the espresso machine quickly enough that by lunchtime, Matrika could leave her to it. It was just as well, since the café was continually busy. The clientele was varied, from students to businessmen to harried-looking mothers with pushchairs and nappy bags. Matrika greeted them all with equal welcome, and an impressive number of them by name.

Finally, mid-afternoon, there was a lull. Apparently unconcerned about leaving the counter unattended, Matrika took Sophie on a tour of the building. "This bit is for the corporates," she said, indicating the tables in front with their wooden ladder-backed chairs, the white walls hung with tasteful modern art. The room was pleasant, efficient, not too cosy: perfect for a quick cup of pre-work coffee or a lunchtime meeting.

"Back here's for the mums." She led Sophie through an archway and into a room whose small, leaded-glass windows looked up at the castle. It was furnished with soft, shabbily pretty, mismatched furniture, low tables, and old fruit crates full of toys and games and coloring supplies. Framed children's drawings hung on the walls. A log fire crackled in an ornate Victorian grate, which had been painted silver and supplied with a safety cage.

Matrika went up the stairs in front of Sophie. They emerged into a large room with plum-colored walls, flooded with light from more leaded glass windows lining the front wall. "And this is for the children," she said. "Children" apparently meant people Sophie's age or a bit older, several of whom were sitting on the velvet-upholstered couches, floor cushions covered in Rajasthani embroidery and giant beanbags. Along one wall was an aquarium full of bright tropical fish. The opposite one had a long trestle table lined with computers. It was exactly the kind of place that Sophie would have loved, when she was still in a mood for that kind of thing.

"It's great," Sophie said sincerely.

"The kitchen's through there," Matrika said, pointing to a door at the back. "But I do the baking before we open."

"All of it?" Sophie asked, thinking back on the display cases full of pastries and cakes.

Matrika smiled. "With a bit of help from Angus, and the occasional student during the Festival or New Year or graduation weekend. Now, I'll show you the Eyrie."

"The what?"

"Where I go when I'm tired of being sociable. Consider it a break-room."

Matrika headed for the final flight of stairs, which had a sign over it reading "Employees Only". It was so narrow that Sophie's shoulders brushed the sides. She was wondering how Matrika had ever got it past Health & Safety, when they emerged from the dark stairway into Sophie's idea of paradise. The room was in the attic of the building, its wooden beams exposed. There was an arched dormer window in each wall, all with a broad, cushioned window seat below them. Another long trestle table stood in the middle of the room, lined with ladder-back chairs. And every inch of available wall space was covered with bookshelves.

"You like it?" Matrika asked, looking at Sophie speculatively.

"I love it," Sophie said, looking out one of the windows at the sea of slate roofs and soot-stained chimneys and television aerials.

Matrika smiled. "I thought you would."

Sophie glanced at her. "Really? Why?"

"You seem a thoughtful kind of a girl." She considered Sophie for a moment, her head slightly to one side. "Sad, though." Sophie waited for her to ask why, and Matrika grew leaps in her estimation when she didn't. Instead, she turned to one of the bookcases and called, "Freyja!"

There was a movement on the top shelf. A large cat stood, stretched and then looked down at them. It was like a miniature lion, its long coat a magnificent red-gold color, its unblinking yellow gaze both intelligent and untamed. After studying them for a few moments, it leapt soundlessly onto the table, walked past Matrika and then sat down in front of Sophie, looking up at her inquisitively. She couldn't help smiling as she reached out and stroked it.

"That's better," Matrika said, watching her. "You have a lovely smile."

Freyja lifted a delicate paw and touched Sophie's hand, as if asking a question. Sophie picked her up and the cat settled into her arms, purring gently. Her fur smelled sweet and wild, like a pine forest after rain. The sense of peace that had sprung to life that morning with the cup of coffee spread further into Sophie.

"She's beautiful," she said, stroking the cat's head. "What breed is she?"

Matrika shrugged. "That's anyone's guess."

"Isn't she yours?"

"She isn't anybody's. She wandered in on the day I opened the shop, and she's mostly been here since."

"Mostly?"

"She takes herself away now and then - rather like me, actually. I think it's why we get on. No ties."

"You don't come from Edinburgh," Sophie said. This was obvious, but she was uncertain how else to ask Matrika about her background without sounding rude.

Matrika smiled, and sat down on the edge of the table. "No. India, to begin with. Ireland most recently."

"How did you end up in Edinburgh?"

Matrika shrugged, looking out the window. "Things became…complicated," she said after a moment, though she seemed uncertain of the choice of word. "Edinburgh is easier, especially this bit. It's mostly students and tourists. No one planning to stay for long. Are you?"

Sophie looked up in surprise. Matrika's eyes were sharp and shrewd and bright. "I…well, I suppose it's up to my mum, really…"

"You seem old enough to make your own decisions."

Sophie smiled bitterly, her eyes on the rooftops framed by the window. "My track record in decision making isn't so brilliant, actually." She could still feel Matrika's eyes on her face, questioning. "I was up here already, you see. Well, not here. The Highlands. It was meant to be my gap year…" And then she couldn't make herself say anymore. She didn't know why she'd said so much already. All she wanted was to run, before she had to put words to all that had gone wrong. Before she felt compelled to explain it all to this woman she barely knew.

But Matrika surprised her again, touching her hand gently and saying, "I'm sorry."

The simple intimacy of the gesture undid Sophie's fragile composure. To her utter mortification, she burst into tears. But Matrika didn't seem fazed by it, or even surprised. She guided Sophie to a chair and sat down next to her, waiting as she wept into Freyja's thick fur. For some reason, the cat didn't protest, but nestled closer to her, which made Sophie cry even harder.

When the tears abated a bit, Matrika offered Sophie a tissue. "Do you want to tell me what happened?" she asked.

And before Sophie had consciously realized that she did, the story was tumbling out, in stammers and stilted phrases. Of course she omitted parts – even undone, she knew that to tell it all would be madness, never mind breaking her promise to Michael. But she told Matrika everything that mattered.

"They never found him," she concluded. She couldn't look at Matrika. She looked instead at her hands, stroking the cat mechanically, until Matrika reached out and stilled them, closing her own warm fingers around Sophie's cold ones.

"How long ago did this happen?"

"One month," Sophie said with a shuddering breath, "six days, and nineteen hours."

For a moment, Sophie thought that she saw anger flash in the woman's eyes. It was gone too quickly to tell. When she looked at Sophie again her eyes were soft and sad. "I'm sorry, Sophie," she repeated. "And that's not a platitude. I lost the love of my life, too. There is nothing more devastating."

"No," Sophie sniffed, "*I'm* sorry."

"What for?"

"For losing the plot like this."

"Why shouldn't you? It hasn't even been two months."

"Still, you'd think I'd have got over it enough not to burst into tears in front of a complete stranger."

Matrika shook her head. "You'll never be over it – not completely. But with time, you'll find a place for the grief. Learn to live with it. You're young, yet."

At that, Sophie nearly burst into tears again, because the one thing she didn't have was time. She managed to say, "I suppose so."

Matrika looked at her appraisingly again. "Do you believe in Heaven, Sophie?"

Sophie blinked at her, uncertain whether she'd heard correctly. But Matrika didn't make any attempt to explain. She only waited, patient as she'd been all along. Finally, Sophie said, "I suppose I do. But I'm not relying on meeting Lucas there, if that's what you mean."

Matrika rested her chin on her hand, looking out the window. Her face shone like bronze in the light of the westering sun. "Well," she said at last, "perhaps that's wise. And it would be hypocritical of me to argue with you. Still, I can't quite bring myself to believe that true love can ever be thwarted entirely. I've always felt that somehow, in some way, he and I will be together again. No doubt the same is true for you."

Sophie knew better, but she also knew that it would be ungrateful of her to say so, when Matrika had been so kind. "Maybe you're right," she said, but when Matrika looked at her, Sophie had the impression that she wasn't fooled.

For a moment, Sophie thought that the woman was going to ask her something else, but then Matrika gave a slight shake of her head and said, "I hope that you find peace, Sophie."

"So do I."

"I'm glad you came to us."

And Sophie realized that she was, too.

Chapter 3

Sophie hadn't much liked the constant, windblown rain in Ardnasheen, but at least it had been definitive. By comparison, Edinburgh rain seemed sullen, drizzling stickily from low, brooding clouds, its dampness creeping through the stone walls and roof slates to infect everything. Even when the rain stopped, the city felt damp to her, permanently gray and drooping.

It was raining when she got off work at the end of her first week at Brewed Awakening. It was five o'clock, and she was meant to walk up to the art college to meet her mother, but she loitered for a long time at the door of the café, unable to make herself go out into the dank evening.

"Here," Matrika said, pushing a hot paper cup into her hand. "This will ward against the dreichest of dreich." Matrika liked to throw Scots words at Sophie, because they often made her smile.

"Dreich?" she asked, taking the cup gratefully. The steam smelled sweet and spicy.

"It means that," Matrika said, pointing outside.

"So why didn't they name this place Dreichburgh? It isn't very Eden-like, as far as I've seen." Matrika smiled, and Sophie took a sip of the drink, which was every bit as delicious as it smelled. "What is this?"

"Massala chai. It's been fuelling the subcontinent for millennia."

"I can see why," Sophie smiled. "Thank you." Matrika nodded and went back to wiping the counter, shooing Freyja off of an empty cake stand where she was devouring crumbs and drips of icing. With no excuses left, Sophie tightened the pulls on the hood of her raincoat, slung her messenger bag across her back and stepped out into the night.

The streets and stone buildings looked slick and oily. The air didn't seem cold at first, but Sophie had been in Edinburgh long enough now to know that its chill was deceptive, working its way into her slowly, until it was impossible to shift. Sighing, she sipped her tea and began walking down the hill toward the Grassmarket.

She passed the gaudy fronts of the shops and tourist pubs, crossed the street and walked past Armstrong's with only a quick glance. Once, the cavernous vintage clothing store would have been paradise to her. Now its flamboyant window displays were only one more reminder of all that was wrong in her life. There was nobody to dress up for, no place to go, and hardly any time left for it even if there had been.

She passed a hotel, a few small antiques shops with their outer doors shut for the night, and then turned up the narrow close that led between a youth hostel and a nursery school. The close was dark at night and usually deserted, but it was a lot faster than going all the way around by Lady Lawson Street. Still, Sophie walked quickly, keeping her head down.

She was past the nursery school and almost onto Heriot Place when she saw them. It had been so long since the last time she'd seen a Revenant, and so much had happened, that at first she couldn't quite believe that they were real. But they didn't shift, and after a few stunned moments Sophie had to accept that her eyes weren't deceiving her.

There were three of them, two women and a man, huddled like urchins on the far side of a wide puddle. Their hair was ragged and their skin beginning to disintegrate around their milky eyes, which were fixed on the water at their feet. The man looked up briefly, caught Sophie's eye, and then pointed at the water.

Sophie took a reluctant step toward the puddle, and she, too, looked into it. At first she saw nothing but the reflection of the Revenants' silvery-blue, spectral glow. Then the glow began to shift and flicker, to take on color, changing from blue to green to gold, threads of light running along the water's ripples like a windblown cinema screen. She crouched down to get a better look, and abruptly the colored lights stopped moving. They swelled, joining together, forming a picture.

It took Sophie a long moment to make sense of it, and several more to believe what she was seeing. Because there was no denying or mistaking that it was Lucas. He was sitting cross-legged on a bed, leaning up against a wall that seemed to be made of solid stone. The wall was bare, but the bedclothes were ornate, glinting with gold and colored gemstones. He was dressed in peculiar clothes: an old-fashioned suit of threadbare black velvet, too big for him by several sizes, its hems frayed and torn. He wore no shoes or socks or shirt. His hair was a bit longer than Sophie remembered it, its black waves matted and streaked with something white. A fine gold chain ran from within the jacket, along the counterpane and on out of the picture, so that she couldn't see what, if anything, it attached to.

"Lucas…" she said, unaware that she'd spoken the word aloud until he turned to her. She dropped her cup with a cry and reached out, her fingers hovering over the image of his face and tears springing to her eyes. "Oh my God, Lucas, you can hear me? You're *alive?* How? Where?"

For a moment his eyes met hers. They looked sad and hollow and infinitely old, exhausted in a way that told her he had suffered, and perhaps was suffering still. But there was no recognition in them, only a confusion that knifed straight into her.

"Lucas, it's me!" she pleaded, but he looked away again and resumed his unfocused stare. Sophie plunged both hands into the puddle, but she came up with nothing but dirty water than ran through her fingers. Worse, the picture was gone, as were the Revenants which had showed it to her. However she scrabbled, she couldn't feel anything but grit and the pitted rounds of old cobbles. However she searched, she saw nothing now but the faint reflection of her own face. At last she fell still, soaked and weeping, and wondering if she'd finally lost her mind.

"What is it with you and water?"

Sophie leapt up, shedding tears and mud. Once again, someone was standing on the far side of the puddle, but he wasn't a Revenant. All she could make out was a dark figure, lumpily nondescript, and the red glowing point of a burning cigarette. Nevertheless, she knew exactly who it was.

"What are *you* doing here?" she demanded.

"Says the girl trying to swim in a puddle." He stepped into a patch of light from one of the windows above. He was dressed much as he had been the day at the Hermitage, though this time he had the hood of his coat pulled up against the sullen drizzle, and an old army satchel slung across his back.

"I wasn't trying to – " Sophie began angrily, but she stopped when she realized she could offer no more explanation for her strange behavior than she had the first time she'd met him. "I…lost something."

He cocked an eyebrow. "Ever thought of keeping to dry land? It's easier to keep track of things."

"Wow, there's some wonderful advice," she snapped,

annoyed at him for disturbing her mid-breakdown. Mostly, though, she was angry at whatever twisted part of her mind had offered her Lucas and then snatched him away again.

After a few moments, at the end of which the guy from the Hermitage was still standing studying her, she said, "So what *are* you doing here?"

"Practicing."

"Practicing what? Stalking?"

"That's a bit dramatic, don't you think?"

"Honestly, I don't know what to think. It's twice now I've run into you in creepy, deserted places."

"Edinburgh's small," he said. "No doubt people cross paths all the time. Besides, it has more than its fair share of creepy, deserted places."

"Honestly? This is just coincidence?"

He shrugged. "Think what you like." He dragged on the cigarette, and then began to cough – the kind of deep, rattling cough that usually belonged to smokers who'd been at it far longer than he could have been.

"Those things'll kill you, you know," Sophie said dryly.

"So will walking dark alleys at night."

"Whatever. I've got to go." She turned away, and then stopped short when he said, "I'll walk with you."

"Thanks," she said warily, suddenly, keenly aware of the intensity of his gaze, "but I'm fine. I'll go the long way around, and I promise to avoid all bodies of water." She began to back away.

He sighed. "If I had it in for you, don't you think I'd have made my move while you were weeping into the puddle?"

"Is that meant to fill me with confidence?"

He flicked the cigarette butt into the water, where it sizzled and then sank. "Listen," he said, looking her straight in the eye, "Edinburgh isn't the worst city in the world, but no city is a good place for a girl to walk alone after dark. Especially one as accident prone as you seem to be. So, please, let me walk with you." He said it as if he were unused to saying "please".

"I don't even know you."

He leapt across the water in one long, graceful stride. Sophie took another step back, and then felt stupid when she saw that he was offering her his hand to shake. Reluctantly, she took it. His grip was firm, and warm, and weirdly comforting. "Rive," he said.

"Seriously? That's your name?"

He smirked, shook his head. "What, were you brought up by wolves?"

"Socialists, actually. So your name's really Rive?"

"Why would I lie about it?"

"Got a surname?"

"Rive."

"Right, then…nice to meet you, Rive. I'm Sophie Creedon."

45

Rive raised his eyebrows. "Would one of those Socialists be Anna Creedon?"

"Good guess," Sophie said. "Do I want to know how you know my mum?"

"I don't," he answered, "but I love her work. The college is lucky to have her."

Sophie had to smile. "I suppose I should have known."

"That I know of your mother?"

"That you're an art student."

Rive looked down at himself, then up at Sophie, with a wry half-smile. "And here I was, thinking I passed as a toff."

Hesitantly, Sophie smiled back. Then she shuddered violently. She didn't know whether it was from cold or delayed shock or both.

"Here," Rive said, and began to take off his coat, but Sophie waved it aside.

"It's alright," she said. "I'll be fine once I start moving."

"Let's go, then." They splashed back across the puddle and on up the close. After a few moments silence, Rive said, "So, what did you lose?"

"Pardon?" Sophie asked.

"In the puddle. You said you lost something."

"Oh." She thought of Lucas's tired eyes, empty of recognition. For a moment, she couldn't think of anything else to say. But she could feel Rive's eyes resting on her. There was something too calm about his look, as if he already knew the answer to his question, and was more interested in how she would react to it, than how she'd answer.

"Something important," she said at last, avoiding his eyes. "I thought I saw it…but I was wrong." *Or was I? Is Lucas really alive somewhere, chained in a stone cell?* To deflect that train of thought, and Rive from asking any more about it, Sophie said, "So if it isn't stalking, what *were* you practicing here?"

Rive gave her an inscrutable look. After a moment he said, "I'll show you."

They'd reached the top of the close, where it turned into Heriot Place. The turreted silhouette of George Heriot's school rose up against the reddish sky, like an ancient fortress. Rive walked a bit farther, until they came to a smaller building, similar in style to the school. Rive stepped into a shadowed angle of the wall, and beckoned to Sophie. There were still lights on in some of its windows, and by their diffused glow, she thought she could make out something on the brickwork. Reluctantly, she moved closer. They were letters, she saw – elegant calligraphy, rendered big and bold as graffiti, spelling "Riven."

"This is what they assign at the art college?" she said.

"This is purely recreation," Rive answered.

"Can't you get arrested for writing on walls?"

He shrugged. "Only if you get caught."

There were a few moments' silence, and then Sophie asked, "So what does it mean?"

"Rent. Torn. Rive-d."

"Cute. But I meant, why did you write that, and not something else? Is it just a play on your name, or is it some kind of socio-political statement?"

She was being sarcastic, but the look he gave her was serious, even appraising. "Ask me that sometime when you know me better."

Sophie couldn't decide what she thought about that answer. Rather than dwell on it, she changed the subject. "You don't sound like you come from here."

"It's a fusion accent," Rive answered. "Scotland-via-Tokyo-via-Athens."

"Seriously?"

He smiled. It made him look younger, less intimidating. "I come from what you'd politely call a multicultural family."

"So how did you end up here?" Sophie asked.

"The family's what you'd politely call a bit of a mess."

"Oh," Sophie said. She knew enough about messy families not to pry into that confession.

They walked on, passing the car park on Keir Street, the communal gardens behind a quadrangle of tenements, and then they turned right onto Lauriston Place. There the pavements were brightly lit and full of people: doctors and nurses from the hospital, students from the art college and university, even

48

some uniformed kids from the school. Traffic whizzed by in both directions. It felt to Sophie like emerging into another world.

"I'll be fine from here," she said. "Thank you for walking with me."

Rive smiled ironically at her. "Is that a dismissal?"

"Of course not," she answered, irritated. "I just meant you can go back to stalking hapless girls or defacing property, or whatever you were planning to do with your night before I interrupted."

"Don't apologize. It was…a pleasure." He said the last part much as he'd said "please" earlier.

Sophie gave him a dubious look. "Well then your social life must be even less exciting than mine. Anyway, thanks." She turned toward the art college, just as Rive called, "Wait!" She turned back, suddenly dreading whatever he was going to say next.

But she never would have guessed: "It is."

"What is?"

"Boring. My social life. Running into you will probably be the highlight of my evening." Once again he said it speculatively, as if it surprised him.

"Um…I'm flattered?"

"Sorry, that came out wrong. What I meant to say was, I don't know many people here. So maybe you'd like to get together sometime? I mean, properly. There's this place on

Victoria Street, Brewed Awakening – twee name, great coffee – " Sophie groaned. "You know it?"

"I work there."

Undaunted, he smiled. It was unexpectedly sincere. "Well then, maybe sometime during your break…?"

Sophie looked at him for a moment. She didn't know whether it was his admission that he was lonely, or the one about his troubled family, or simply the fact that he'd been there for her twice when no one else was, but she felt a sudden softening toward him.

"Okay," she said. "Sure, that would be…" *What?* she thought, abruptly at a loss. She didn't want Rive to think she was interested in a relationship, if that's what this invitation was about. She didn't even know whether she wanted to be his friend. She couldn't imagine meeting him at the cinema, or introducing him to her mother; if nothing else, there seemed so little point.

But she'd already agreed. "So, do you have a phone number?" she asked.

"I don't have a phone. But I know where to find you. I'll see you soon." He gave a nod of the head that was almost a bow, oddly foreign and formal. At the same time, Sophie saw her mother hurrying toward them, her blond hair coming down from its perpetually unraveling knot as she tried to fasten her overly-full bag. Sophie had to smile at her endearingly constant state of chaos.

"That's Mum now," she said, "I'd better go."

"Take care, Sophie," Rive said. "And stay away from puddles."

"Right," she said. He began to cough again as she turned away. Its rumble followed her, along with the feeling of his eyes on her back, all the way down the road.

CHAPTER 4

"Who was that?" Sophie's mother asked as she caught up with her. "And why are you soaking wet?"

Knowing that her mother hated her taking the shortcut through the close, Sophie said, "Ah…it was a puddle."

"And the boy?" she asked, shaking her head.

"He's called Rive," Sophie answered as they walked toward the bus stop. "He sort of…came to my rescue. Actually, he goes to the art college."

"Oh?" She'd said it to assure her mother of his suitability as a walking companion, but when she saw her mother's look turned speculative, Sophie wished she'd kept her mouth shut. Matchmaking for her daughter was one of Anna's favorite activities, and had been Sophie's least favorite, even before Lucas. "What's his subject?"

"I don't know."

"He must be a first year – I haven't seen him in any of my classes. You'll have to introduce me."

"It's not really like that."

"Oh?" Anna asked, clearly disappointed.

"I mean, I only just met him myself. It's not like we're friends or anything."

Anna walked in thoughtful silence for a few moments, and Sophie guessed what was coming next. She braced herself, and then, sure enough: "Sophie, you really ought to give people a chance. I know that you've been through a difficult time, but you can't shut everybody out forever because of it."

"I'm not shutting anybody out," Sophie said, trying not to get angry. "But I'm not going to just throw myself at the first boy who comes along, either."

"I don't mean for you to throw yourself at anybody," Anna said, exasperation creeping into her tone. "But when somebody reaches out, you could at least try to respond. Like that girl Ailsa, the one who keeps phoning – "

"I can't talk to her," Sophie said, too quickly and sharply. She couldn't seem to make her voice behave. "Not yet."

"But it's been over a month since you left Ardnasheen," Anna insisted. "At some point, you're going to have to begin to move on – "

"Mum, don't," Sophie said.

"I'm sorry, love, but I think you need to hear this. I know that you liked that boy – "

"Lucas," she said. Her mother never seemed to want to

speak his name, as if she blamed him for dying and making Sophie miserable.

" – but you were only together a few weeks," Anna plowed on. "Honestly, how involved could you have been?"

Sophie looked at her mother, feeling furious and weary and defeated all at once. There was no way to make her understand, no words to explain what she'd had, and lost. "I'll phone Ailsa," she said at last.

"Oh, please do, Sophie," Anna said, so clearly relieved that Sophie immediately felt guilty for being angry at her. "The poor girl sounds desperate to speak to you. Her boyfriend was involved too, wasn't he?"

Sophie couldn't make herself speak. She nodded once, almost imperceptibly.

"Well, maybe it would do the two of you good to spend some time together. Talk about it, work it through. Why don't you ask her down here for a weekend?"

Sophie had to suppress a hysterical laugh when she pictured Ailsa in the flat, the two of them weeping into their cups of tea. She wasn't angry at her anymore; she wasn't afraid of a confrontation. More to the point, she knew that her silence must be hurting Ailsa. But she simply could not imagine what she would say to her.

Likewise, she had no idea how to answer her mother. And so she was deeply grateful when the bus pulled up to their stop,

packed nearly to bursting, precluding any further conversation
– at least for the moment.

*

A couple of hours later, Sophie sat on her bed, staring at
her phone. Her mother had reminded her of her promise to ring
Ailsa twice during dinner, and again when she was clearing
up. Sophie knew that she would stop short of actually standing
over her to make sure that she did it, and thankfully, she wasn't
the kind of mother who would put a glass to the door, or even
hover in the hallway in hopes of hearing something of the
conversation. But nor was Sophie the kind of daughter who
would be able to lie to her about it. She would have to make
the call.

Taking a deep breath, Sophie flicked through the list
of contacts on her phone, and stopped on the number for
Madainneag. At this time of night on a Friday, Ailsa would be
working. She could leave a message, if the ancient answering
machine hadn't run through its tape. Then she'd have done
what she said she would do, without having to have any
difficult conversations. Feeling slightly better, Sophie pushed
the button.

To her horror, Ailsa answered on the first ring. "Oh my
God, Sophie, I am *so glad* you phoned!"

Sophie had been so certain that she wouldn't answer, that it
took her a long moment to think of something to say. "How did

you know it was me?" she asked finally, wincing at how stupid it sounded even as she said it.

"Caller ID. Mum bought a proper phone and had it run up to my room. It was the only way she'd let me stay here, after…"

There was a long silence, during which it seemed to Sophie that she could actually hear the seconds passing. Finally, she said, "I…I'm sorry it's taken me so long to phone you back." She thought of, and rejected, a long string of excuses, settling in the end on the truth. "I just didn't know what to say."

There was another long silence, and then Ailsa let out a breath. "To be honest, I didn't know, either. I just…I needed to make sure you're alright. As alright as you can be, I mean, given everything."

Sophie leaned back on her bed. After the first awkward silence, she'd begun to relax. Hearing Ailsa's voice was unexpectedly comforting. "I guess I am. I mean, I got a job, if that counts."

Ailsa chuckled. "It counts if you show up. Is it another pub?"

"A café. It's alright, actually. The owner is quite laid-back, and the hours are sane, at least compared to World's End." She paused. "What about you? How come you aren't at the pub?"

"Ruadhri got a new girl after you left. It's her shift tonight."

"So all of the…you know, what happened…it hasn't hurt his business?"

"Hardly," Ailsa said, her voice acidic. "It's done wonders for it – for the whole village."

"What do you mean?"

"Disaster tourists."

"Pardon?"

"Oh, you know – the tourism equivalent of those people who chase after ambulances, hoping to see a crash. They read the story in the newspapers I guess, and they want to see the place for themselves. They've overrun the village."

"That's creepy," Sophie said. *And difficult to picture.* Ardnasheen had become a ghost-town in her mind, as if it couldn't still exist and function without Lucas in it. But of course, that was ridiculous. Most of the people there hadn't even known him. Realizing how little his death must have meant to them brought her close to tears again.

To stem them, she asked, "How's the new girl?"

Ailsa's tone warmed. "She's a laugh, actually. Mad as a hatter. Of course, she's no you, but it's better than living in this fusty dump by myself."

Sophie smiled sadly. "You didn't want to move out?"

Ailsa scoffed. "I'd like nothing better. But with all the tourists, the housing situation is worse than ever. It was live here or give up the job, and I can't afford to do that. Not yet, anyway." There was a long pause, and Sophie wondered whether Ailsa had other reasons to want to stay. Whether it

57

would be as difficult for her to leave as it would be for Sophie to go back.

As if hearing the thought, Ailsa said, "I miss you, Sophie. And I just want to say – "

"Don't," Sophie said quickly. "There's no need."

"Of course there is. I acted crazy, and I know that what happened is as much my fault as anyone's."

"Ailsa, really – "

"Hear me out, Sophie. Please."

Sophie shut her eyes, and waited.

"I know you think I should have listened to you about Sam. But the weird thing is, I *did* listen. When you told me what he tried with you that night, I believed you. I thought he was disgusting. I never meant to go out with him, and I *definitely* never meant to do it behind your back. But somehow, when he asked, it all changed. I just…I couldn't say no. I wanted him. I can't pretend that I didn't. But it was like it wasn't *me* wanting him…like there was some other thing going on, something pushing me…"

She trailed off. Sophie felt tears slipping down her cheeks. "He was like that," she said. "Persuasive. I don't blame you. I never did."

"But *I* blame me," Ailsa said softly.

"Don't. Please, don't. You couldn't have stopped him, not once he'd decided what he wanted – " Abruptly, she stopped speaking. She hadn't meant to say so much. She hoped it wasn't too much.

After a silence, Ailsa confirmed her fears. "There was more going on than I knew, wasn't there," she said.

"Ailsa, I don't – "

"It's okay. You don't have to tell me. I just…it would help me to know that it wasn't all my fault."

Sophie's tears were flowing faster. She gave up trying to sound like they weren't. "It wasn't your fault at all," she said. "You were a means to an end for him. Nobody could have held out, once he decided on them."

There was another long pause. "That almost makes me feel better," Ailsa said at last. "Except that *you* held out, didn't you."

Sophie drew and then let out a shuddering breath. "That was different."

"I know it was. And I hope, someday, you'll trust me enough to tell me why."

Sophie couldn't make herself answer that. "I'm glad we talked, Ailsa," she said instead.

"So am I. Good-night, Sophie."

"Good night." Sophie closed the phone, and then shut off her bedside lamp. She turned over, pulled up the duvet, and cried herself to sleep.

*

That night Sophie dreamed, but not of Lucas. Instead she lay in frigid darkness, under what seemed to be a slab of stone until, with great effort, she managed to move her hand through it. She realized then that it was water, and she knew with sudden dream-certainty that she lay at the bottom of the sea. Struggling, she managed to move a fraction of an inch, but the effort tired her to the point of exhaustion, and despair.

Then, just as Sophie began to lose consciousness, something warm and living touched her hand. It was both smooth and bristling, tough like leather, yet pliant. It pushed into her palm like a dog's muzzle. A moment later it slipped away, and then something was closing over her, like a heavy bag that melded to her skin where it touched her, squeezing and prodding her into a different shape. It didn't quite hurt, but the sense of her body being tugged into a different form was enough to make her scream. Or to try: because, when she opened her mouth, no sound came out.

A moment later she forgot her fear as the terrible pressure lifted and dispersed, and she found that she could slip through the dark water as easily as a fish. She tried to look down at her body, to see what the doggy creature had done to her, but it was too dark to make out any more than a shadow. The creature's nose brushed against her again, and then several others, touching her as if in greeting. Shadowy bodies slipped through the water beside her own. But they seemed to be growing less shadowy. A gentle green light began to glow around them, growing brighter as they descended. At last, Sophie could see the creatures that swam with her – they were seals. She had a moment to wonder what it meant, when the others abruptly stopped swimming.

Looking down, she saw why. What had seemed to be abstract shapes in the green glow had come into focus as a vast city, over which Sophie and the seals hovered. There were faery-tale turrets and pointed spires, crenellated walls and streets made of smooth, square stone. She saw gardens and outdoor markets, parks with strange, spindly trees and beds of softly tufted flowers. There were people too, tall and graceful, with pale, regal faces and long hair that rippled as if on a lazy wind, in every shade of blue and green. Their clothing flowed around them, glinting with precious metals and stones that reminded Sophie of the bed on which Lucas had sat in her vision.

But there was no time to consider what that might mean. One by one, the seals around her were dropping through a gate, intricately wrought from what looked like pure light, and opening upwards, like a trap-door. At last, only Sophie and the seal that had changed her were left. It looked at her. Something about its eyes was strange. After a moment, Sophie realized that they were green rather than dark like the other seals', with a round dark pupil. Human eyes.

The seal gave her a gentle nudge. Sophie looked down at the city for another moment, and then she swam through the gate. As soon as she was through, the water was gone, as well as the restrictive seal-skin. Instead she was wearing a gossamer-fine dress the color of a tropical lagoon, studded with glittering gems. She drifted down through warm air, coming to rest gently in one of the gardens she'd seen from above.

A moment later, a young woman drifted down beside her. She didn't look like the other people on the park's web of paths. Their hair flowed in shades of blue and green, while their eyes were black from lid to lid, without a hint of iris or rim of white. The girl beside her had long, black hair and eyes as green as spring leaves. They were the eyes of the seal that had guided her, but Sophie no longer thought they looked human. Their intensity reminded her of the angels'.

"Welcome, Sophie," she said in a soft, musical voice, with a gentle smile.

"Welcome to where?" Sophie asked, dazed.

"Key-Ys."

"What is that?"

"The city of the depths. Dahud's city."

"Who is Dahud?"

"She is Queen."

Sophie considered this for a moment, and then asked, "Why am I here?"

The girl's smile faded a little. "You came for your heart's desire."

Sophie shook her head. "I have no heart's desire. There's

nothing that I want except…" All at once, her heart beat wildly. She grabbed the seal-girl's hands, half-noticing as she did so that they were covered up to the elbow in intricate, spiraling symbols, like an Indian bride's henna tattoos, except that they were a deep blue. "He's here? Lucas is really alive?"

The girl didn't answer. Instead, she reached into the lush grass and plucked something from its midst, pressed it into Sophie's hand. Sophie looked down, her mouth open to demand answers. But when she saw what she held, she shut it again, her throat full of tears as the hope she'd thought was dead flickered back to life.

In her hand was a spray of bright blue forget-me-nots.

CHAPTER 5

Sophie opened her eyes, her head full of confused images. A faery-tale city, seen from above. Black eyes without whites. Her bones warping to the shape of a different body...she shuddered.

It was still dark, and the green numbers on the digital clock said 3:49. She felt exhausted, as if she'd just run for miles rather than awakened from a dream. Her muscles and joints ached as if they really had been wrenched out of position. Slowly, she pushed herself to sitting. It was only then she realized that her hair was damp. She touched a strand of it to her tongue, and tasted salt.

There was also a strange, sweet smell in the room; almost, but not quite, familiar. With a quivering hand, she reached for the bedside lamp and turned it on, and then sat back, stunned. Her bed was strewn with forget-me-nots, covering her like a quilt. For a few moments she couldn't think. Then, gradually, the dream began to come back to her, and as it did, the hope

64

that had sparked when she saw Lucas in the puddle took hold of her, and began to burn.

Sophie gathered the flowers into her lap, trying not to let herself believe their evidence, because she knew that to lose Lucas again would finish her. But holding the bunch of flowers, looking into their yellow-and-blue eyes, she couldn't believe anything else. Somewhere, somehow, Lucas was alive.

For a long time, Sophie couldn't think beyond the magnitude of that. But as the first rush of elation began to seep away, the doubts crept back in. Clearly, he wasn't simply waiting for her in the house at Ardnasheen. Whatever had happened to him, wherever he was, was far more complicated than that.

She tried to remember the details of the dreams and visions. The place she'd just come from, the city beneath the sea, was called something that sounded like Car-ees. Sophie pulled out her music notebook, opened it to a blank page and wrote the word with a question mark beside it. Then there was the woman with the cracked-glass eyes, who she'd first seen in the Hermitage burn. By the pearl-and-silver crown, Sophie guessed she must be the queen the seal girl had spoken of. She had called her something that sounded like David. Sophie wrote that down, too. Then there was the seal- girl herself. Was she one of the selkies Lucas had told her about in the Angel Cave? She wrote "selkie", and another question mark. And then, Lucas. The stone room, the gold chain, the eyes, empty of recognition…

Trying not to think about that, Sophie began to sketch the things she'd seen as best she could. When she'd put down all that she remembered, she was left with only one possible conclusion. Lucas was somewhere in that city beneath the sea. But he was likely a prisoner and, what was worse, he didn't seem to know her. Unless she could find her way to that city and make him remember, he was as lost to her as he'd been before.

Sophie went to the desk and retrieved her laptop. She opened a search engine, typed in "Carees" and came up with a list of pages offering career advice. She tried a few alternate spellings, with no more luck. After that she searched futilely for "Queen David", and even tried looking through lists on the mythological pages that came up when she entered "Sea Queen". None of them made any reference to a green-haired, silver-eyed water woman.

Sophie shut the computer and sat watching dawn push grey fingers into the dark beyond her window, trying to think of a way forward. As far as she could tell, the mysterious city in her dream had little to do with angels. If the seal girl really was a selkie, then she was also one of the *sìth* – the faeries – which was, once again, something far removed from angels and aeons. Something that Sophie knew very little about, other than what Lucas had told her and a couple of harrowing encounters with less-than-friendly specimens.

Frustration and exhaustion fuzzed her head, along with

what she suspected were the beginnings of a migraine: a block of silver spots, swimming at the edge of her vision. Sophie swallowed two tablets from the bottle of ibuprofen she kept on the bedside table, and then laid her head on her folded arms, trying to make the spots fade and her mind work.

Outside, the birds were beginning to sing. The sound made her think of Suri's cemetery. She wished that she could ask Suri for help, but she hadn't dreamed of her since the time Suri had warned her against reading the *Book of Sorrows*. She didn't know whether Suri had abandoned her on purpose, or if she'd somehow been forbidden to contact Sophie since then; neither option was particularly comforting.

Then again, Suri wasn't the only angel she knew, or the only one who'd helped her. She couldn't believe she hadn't thought of it before. Reaching for her messenger bag, she dumped its contents onto the floor, grateful that she'd been too depressed to clear it out. She sifted through the detritus of receipts and small change and tissues until she found what she was looking for: a battered business card, printed with the name "Michael Halyrude" and a phone number.

She sat down on the bed, punched in the number on her mobile, and sat listening to it ring. She'd counted six, and was beginning to give up hope, when somebody finally picked up. There was a clatter, a curse, and then a groggy Irish voice said, "Hello?"

"Hi, Michael."

"Who is this?"

"Sophie – Sophie Creedon."

He sighed. When he spoke again the Irish accent was gone, replaced by the strange, unplaceable lilt that always ran beneath the angels' chosen accents. "Do you have any idea what time it is?"

"I thought angels didn't sleep."

"We don't," he said irritably. "But occasionally we like to rest, or meditate, or listen to silence instead of the incessant demands of humans."

"Look, I'm sorry, but I really need to speak to you."

"Why?" he asked, suddenly sounding worried. "Has something happened? Has someone been asking questions?"

"No, nothing like that. But yes, something's happened." She took a deep breath, wishing she didn't sound so shaky. "Michael – I think Lucas is alive."

There was a long silence, and then a sigh. "Sophie, you saw Azazel stab him through the heart and throw him into the sea."

"I know. But I never saw his body."

"Listen…I know that this is difficult for you, but you're going to have to accept that he's dead. He couldn't possibly have survived that fall into the sea, paralyzed with poison and bleeding as badly he was."

"I'm not asking your opinion," Sophie said sharply. "I'm

telling you that I have evidence that he survived, and I think he's in trouble. I need you to help me find him."

When Michael answered, he no longer sounded condescending or worried, though he didn't sound any happier. "What do you mean by evidence, Sophia?"

Now that she had his attention, Sophie didn't quite know how to explain it to him. In the end, she decided not to try – either he'd believe the truth, or not. "I've seen him," she said.

"What? Where?"

"In a – " she stopped herself just short of saying "puddle" and finished, "a vision."

"A vision?" He sounded dubious again.

"Come on, Michael, you're an angel. You should be all about visions."

"Very well," he sighed. "What happened in this vision?"

"He was dressed in strange clothes, and he seemed to be in a stone room. He had a chain attached to him, that looked like it was tied off to something. And he looked at me. He *saw* me."

There was a long pause. "Is that it?" Michael asked at last.

"No," Sophie answered, deciding that she might as well go for the gusto. "I've also seen a woman with green hair and freaky silver eyes, and people who can change into seals. I think they're *sìth* – selkies, or something like them. They live in a city under the sea, called something like Carees. And I think that's where Lucas is."

There was another long pause. At last, Michael said, "Even if there's any truth in these visions, I can't help you."

"Why not?" she demanded.

"Because angels avoid the *sìth,* and they avoid us…a tacit non-aggression pact, if you like. But as it happens, Sophia, I don't think that these *are* true visions."

"Then what are they?" she cried, and then winced, hoping her mother hadn't heard. In a lower voice, she continued, "Believe me, I'm not delusional."

"I know that. But you are grieving, in a way that no mortal could ever understand." He paused, and then continued gently, "The offer still stands, you know. I could take all of it away."

"No," Sophie said coldly. "I don't want to forget him, especially not now."

"But Sophie – "

"No!" she hissed. "I know that he's alive, and if you won't help me find him, I'll just have to do it on my own!"

She thought that he would push her further, but he only said, "Very well," again. Then, just as she was about to say good-bye, he said, "Sophia, have you met anyone down there?"

The question took her aback, and put her on her guard. "Of course I've met people down here."

"I mean, anyone special."

She gave an incredulous laugh. "Like a guy? Are you seriously asking me if I've got a new boyfriend?"

"No, no, of course not. I just wanted to be sure…well, that you have friends."

Although she knew that angels couldn't lie, she could tell his answer was scraping the boundaries. "I'm not quite seeing why this is relevant," Sophie said, certain now that he was fishing for some particular information. She thought of Matrika and Rive, then rejected them almost as quickly. They might be unusual, but she was sure they weren't *sith* or angels.

"I don't suppose it is," Michael said at last. "It's only that I worry for you."

"Well, thanks, Michael," she said with bitter irony. "But if you really want to help me, you'll help me find Lucas. Give me a ring if you change your mind."

Though she knew that it was childish, she hung up before he could answer, and flopped back on her pillows. She was frustrated, not only by his evasion, but because she had the niggling sense that he'd said something significant, and she'd missed it. She lay there for a few dejected moments before she realized what it was. *Paralyzed with poison and bleeding as badly as he was.* She had never told Michael that Sam's sword had been poisoned. And by all logic, she and Lucas and whoever had given Sam the poison should have been the only ones who knew.

*

On the bus ride to work, Sophie tried to think of ways that

Michael could have found out about the Queres, and not been the one to have given it to Sam. She even considered calling him back and asking him point blank, but in the end she couldn't do it. Not yet, anyway. She knew that it was pathetic, but too much had been taken from her for her to bear another loss. She wanted to believe that Michael really was what he seemed to be. Besides, she reasoned, it made little difference either way, when it was unlikely she'd be seeing Michael again.

Sophie walked up Victoria Street and pushed through the café's steam-covered door, looking forward to Matrika's calm, cheerful presence after her unsettling night. Instead, she found Angus behind the counter, and no Matrika in sight.

Sophie hadn't looked too hard at him the first time they met, but now she took a moment to study him. He had thick, dark brown hair and brown eyes, and the kind of face that looked like it should be smiling. He also had a dark tan that didn't make much sense given the current weather.

"You must be Angus," she said, coming around the counter and hanging up her bag and coat on the antique hat stand.

"And you must be Sophie," he said, with a warm smile and an extended hand.

Sophie shook it, noticing the firm grip. Her mother said you could always tell a reliable person by their handshake; not that she'd have thought Matrika would hire anyone who wasn't. "Nice to meet you," she said, tying on her apron as

Angus served a customer. When he was done, she said, "Have you worked here for long?"

"About a year," he answered. "Ever since I came to university."

"Edinburgh?" He nodded. "What do you study?"

"Archaeology," he answered.

"That sounds interesting," Sophie said, pouring herself a cup of coffee. In fact, it sounded like just the kind of thing she'd once imagined herself doing, before her life took a sharp turn for the weird.

"It is," Angus said, rearranging muffins so that the trays still looked full, though the morning rush had already taken its toll. "But it's definitely not as glamorous as everyone thinks."

"What – no unwrapping of mummies and discoveries of golden hordes?"

He smiled again, making his eyes into crescent moons. "Well put it this way: I've just spent a week in Croatia, going through an ancient Roman latrine with a toothbrush and an ice-pick."

Sophie had to laugh. "Did you find anything interesting?"

"Aside from a lot of suggestive graffiti about someone called Matella, not really."

Before Sophie could say anything else, another round of customers came into the café. After that, there wasn't another lull until after lunchtime. Then Sophie took a cup of coffee and her bag up to the Eyrie, to see if the dream's words and images made any more sense in the light of day.

Freyja was lying on the table in an oblong of sunshine, paws curled and eyes closed. However, when Sophie took out her notebook and opened it to her drawing of the undersea city, Freyja stood up, stretched, and came to investigate. She peered down at it as if she were about to make commentary.

"So," Sophie said to her, "any thoughts?"

"They're good. Are you at the art college?"

Sophie turned to see Angus standing in the doorway, holding a mug and a plate with two chocolate chip cookies on it, smiling his infectious smile.

"No," she said. "Drawing's my mum's thing. I'm on a gap year." *Or a gap hiatus-before-extinction.*

"Do you mind if I sit?" he asked.

"Of course not," she said, although she'd been looking forward to the time alone to think.

"Matrika sent these," he said, setting down the plate of cookies and sitting down across from her. He took one of them and then pushed the plate across to her, as Freyja looked on with clear longing.

"Thanks," Sophie said. She broke off a piece of the cookie and gave it to Freyja, who devoured it and then sat looking at Sophie with soulful eyes until she gave her another.

Angus observed this, and then he said, "Don't tell me you're one of those girls who only eat lettuce."

74

"Do I look like one of those girls who only eat lettuce?"

He studied her for a moment. "Yes," he said at last, "and no. You seem too down-to-earth for stupid diets. Still, you look like a bit of chocolate wouldn't hurt."

Sophie rolled her eyes, but she picked up her cookie and took a bite. It was good: so good that she took another bite, surprising herself, and making Angus smile again, though Freyja looked chagrined.

"Matrika must be the best baker in the city," he said.

Sophie shrugged. "I've not really been here long enough to say."

"So you're working in a café for your gap year?" he asked, slightly incredulously.

"It didn't start out that way," Sophie admitted. "It's…well, it's complicated. Anyway, my mum's a guest lecturer at the art college this year, so I decided to come with her when my first plan…um…didn't work out."

Angus nodded, and then pointed to the notebook, which was still lying open between them. "So what is it?" he asked.

Sophie thought about evading the question, but meeting Angus's frank gaze, she found herself saying: "It's just something I dreamed."

"Hm," he said, chewing thoughtfully on the last of his cookie.

"Hm, what?"

"I don't know, exactly. It reminds me of something, but I'm not quite sure what…"

Sophie was considering how to answer when Matrika came into the room, her arms full of cookbooks. "What reminds you of something?"

"Sophie's drawings," Angus answered, before Sophie could deflect the question. Irritated, Sophie pushed the notebook toward Matrika, who studied it for a moment before saying, "A decent rendition. But you've spelled it wrong."

"Pardon?" Sophie said.

"It isn't Carees. It's Ker-Ys." She put down her stack of books, picked up Sophie's pencil and wrote the words under Sophie's mis-spelling.

"You've heard of it?" Sophie asked in disbelief.

"Of course. It's from a famous legend."

"About what?" Sophie asked eagerly.

"A drowned Breton city. But how did you come to draw it, if you don't know the story?"

"I…I don't know," Sophie said, hoping that Angus wouldn't contradict her. "It must be something I heard about once." Thankfully, Angus said nothing. "So what is it about?"

"You can read it for yourself," Matrika said. She walked over to one of the bookcases, the hem of her long, green skirt trailing on the floor. It reminded Sophie of the sea-people's clothing. Matrika glanced along a row of titles, and then pulled down a thick volume with worn, cloth-and-board covers. She put it in front of Sophie. The faded gold letters on the cover read: *Le Barzhaz Breizh.*

"I don't know French," said Sophie.

"Which is neither here nor there," Matrika answered, opening the book to the index, "since that's Breton, which is a different language entirely. The title means 'Ballads of Brittany'. It's a collection of all of the most famous Breton legends and folk songs, with English translations, and somewhere...here!" She flipped to a page in the middle of the volume. "This is the story of Ker-Ys. It's not a particularly happy one, but then few of these old ballads are. Borrow the book, if you like."

"Thanks," Sophie said.

"My pleasure," Matrika smiled. "Let me know what you think of it. Now, if the two of you've finished your cookies, I'm afraid another footsore tour group has just arrived."

CHAPTER 6

Sophie didn't have time to look at Matrika's book until she was back at home. Her mother was out at an opening and had said she might be late. With a twinge of guilt, Sophie pushed aside the dinner her mother had left for her on a plate in the refrigerator, and took out a yogurt. She made a cup of tea, and took them both to her bedroom where, she noticed, her mother had put the bundle of flowers she'd swept up that morning into a glass of water. She was glad that her mother wasn't there, to ask for an explanation.

Sophie climbed into her bed, pulled the duvet over her legs, and opened the book to the page Matrika had marked. The title ran across the top: "The Submersion of the City of Ys."

It was written in verse. It was about a Breton king called Gradlon, who ruled a city built beneath sea level. There was no description of what the city looked like, aside from the assurance that it was the most splendid one in France. But the ballad did say that the water was kept at bay by a high wall, to which only Gradlon held the key.

Aside from laying out those facts, a lot of the ballad was given to moralizing about drinking and bad behavior, to which the people of Ys seemed given. Sophie was about to turn her attention to her yogurt when a word near the bottom of the page caught her eye. A shiver went through her as she read:

"But the lover who could that hear

Whispered in the king's daughter's ear:

'What about the key, Dahud dear?'"

Sophie raced through the rest of the poem. Dahud, the princess of Ker-Ys, stole the key to the city's sea gate while her father slept, to give it to her lover. He opened the gate at high tide, and the city was engulfed. Gradlon escaped, but Dahud was swept away. She wasn't drowned, however. Instead, she turned into a mermaid, who sat on a rock by the sunken city and sang of what she had lost. There was nothing to suggest that the city still existed somewhere under the sea, or that Dahud had stayed on as its queen. And yet, Sophie thought, too many bits of the story matched her dream for them not to be connected.

Closing the book, she went to her desk and turned on her computer. She typed "Ys" into the search engine. The first link to come up was Wikipedia. She read:

"Ys, also called Ker-Ys, is a mythical city that was built on the coast of Brittany and later swallowed by the ocean. Most versions of the legend place the city in the Douarnenez Bay."

Sophie pulled up a map of Douarnenez Bay. It was a part of the Bay of Biscay, in northwest France: in other words, nowhere near Ardnasheen. Nevertheless, she kept reading, skimming past the parts of the story that matched the ballad until she came to something new:

"Ys was the most beautiful and impressive city in the world, but quickly became a city of sin under the influence of Dahud. She organized orgies and had the habit of killing her lovers when morning broke." Sophie thought of Lucas's chain, and the jeweled bed, and then wished she hadn't. Pushing the image away, she continued:

"One day, a knight dressed in red came to Ys. Dahud asked him to come with her, and he agreed. A storm broke out in the middle of the night and the waves could be heard smashing against the gate and the bronze walls. Dahud said to the knight: 'Let the storm rage. The gates of the city are strong, and it is King Gradlon, my father, who owns the only key, attached to his neck.' The knight replied: 'Your father the king sleeps. You can now easily take his key.' Dahud stole the key from her father and gave it to the knight, who was none other than the devil. The devil, or, in another version of the story, a wine-besotted Dahud herself, then opened the gate.

"A wave as high as a mountain collapsed on Ys. King Gradlon and his daughter climbed on Morvarc'h, his magical horse, but the horse was slowed by the extra weight, and couldn't outrun the flood. Saint Winwaloe approached them and told Gradlon: 'Push back the demon sitting behind you!' Gradlon initially refused, but he finally gave in and pushed his daughter into the sea. The sea swallowed Dahud, who became a mermaid or morgen."

Sophie had never heard of a morgen. It was highlighted as a link. She clicked it, and then read through the new page that came up:

"Morgens are Welsh and Breton water spirits that drown men. They may lure men to their death by their own sylphic beauty, or with glimpses of underwater gardens with buildings of gold or crystal."

Sophie tried to remember the city in her dream. She wouldn't have said that it was made of gold and crystal; then again, she hadn't got near enough to its buildings to be sure. It had certainly been beautiful, though, and so had its people. She read on:

"The morgens are eternally young, and like sirens they sit in the water and comb their hair seductively. They are also said to carry humans down to their underwater kingdoms."

Sophie looked up from the screen, only half-seeing the lit windows of the flats across the road. Her mind was reeling. Could the city she had seen in her dreams and visions be the actual, mythical Ker-Ys? Was it ruled by this same Dahud?

If so, and if Lucas was her prisoner, then he was in serious trouble.

Sophie dropped her head into her hands. There didn't seem to be any logical conclusion except that Lucas had been taken prisoner by a morgen. He wasn't quite human, but that might make him all the more attractive to her. And if there was one thing she'd learned from the faery tales of her childhood, it was that the evil queen never lets her prisoners go – not, at any rate, without a fight.

Sophie looked up at her reflection in the window, and smiled bleakly at the absurdity – not of the conclusion she'd come to, but of the fact that she was the one who would have to do something about it. She had no idea how to get to Ker-Ys, or how to find Dahud once there, let alone how to fight her. In fact, she knew almost nothing about the mythical world to which Lucas had introduced her, except that its creatures tended to be duplicitous and deadly. She felt like crying: not from sadness or even desperation, but from the sheer magnitude of the task ahead of her. Because if there was one thing she knew, it was that she had to find Lucas and bring him back where he belonged, or die trying.

*

Sophie woke early the next morning with a strange feeling in her gut. It had been so long since she'd felt it, it took several moments for her to identify it as hunger. It annoyed her.

She'd spent the rest of the previous evening working out the beginnings of a plan, and she'd wanted to start on it as soon as possible. But her stomach was insistent. She stopped in the kitchen for a bowl of cereal and a glass of juice before she went out.

There was a rime of frost on the panes of the bay window, and so Sophie collected her blue down jacket, a hat and gloves. Then, after a moment's hesitation, she opened her wardrobe, reached into the bottom of her backpack, and pulled out the red jumper of Lucas's that had been wadded there since she left Ardnasheen.

As she unrolled it, a waft of his incense smell engulfed her. Rather than unravel her, though, it strengthened her determination. She took the dagger hidden in the center of the roll, and stuck it through a belt loop of her jeans. Then she pulled on the jumper. It was far too big, but it was also her only physical connection to Lucas; perhaps it would help her find him. She zipped her jacket over it, and then left the flat.

It was colder than she'd anticipated outside – colder than it usually got in London. Still, the sky was clear blue, and the sun cresting the tenements to the east warmed her face. She walked up Comiston Road, turning left down a side-street and left again down Braid Road. When she reached the head of the path at the Hermitage, though, she paused. The bright winter sun didn't seem to penetrate the thick canopy of tree branches, although they were bare of leaves. The bells in the branches of the tree in the Toll House garden sounded frail and lonely, barely as loud as the breeze that moved them. Once again, there was no one in sight.

Sophie thought of the cold hand that had closed around her ankle on the first morning here. She thought of Rive, appearing out of nowhere. She knew she couldn't expect anyone to come to her rescue this time. She touched the hilt of the dagger for courage, and then she opened the gate.

Sophie had no trouble recognizing the place where she'd seen Dahud before. The same white stone was there, with the same feathery, bright-green spill of weed. Sophie took the dagger out of her waistband and held it in both hands. Then she crouched down and looked into the water.

Nothing happened. The weed continued to follow the drift of the current, the water to slip over the stones. There was no sign of unnatural movement, no shifting of white stone into inhuman flesh. What, she wondered, was she doing wrong? Everything seemed to be as it had been on the day the water-woman appeared to her.

Except that this time, Sophie was looking for her. Maybe that was the problem. Sophie tried to clear her mind; to think of nothing. She rested her eyes on the stone and the weed, but she didn't stare. She even let them relax, so that her focus went hazy. Still, nothing happened.

"So what?" she said aloud, her voice sharp with frustration.

"Now you're afraid of me? Or is it only that this time, I'm not afraid of you?"

You should not speak to us like that, little girl.

Sophie gasped, looked around her even as she knew that she would see no one. She had not heard the words spoken aloud, but inside of her head, in a whispery voice that seemed to swell and ebb like waves on a beach.

"Let me see you," she said, and then added, "please."

There was a gurgling rush of sound, like a waterfall. Like laughter. Then the voice spoke again: *You should be careful what you wish for.*

"There's only one thing I wish for," Sophie answered.

The one thing you cannot have.

"Why not? Because you want him?"

Because he is ours already.

"How exactly do you figure that?"

We found him. We made his frozen heart beat again. We made his cold blood run hot.

"Name your price," Sophie said, determined not to let the water woman unsettle her.

There is no price.

"He can't be much use to you, kept against his will."

The weird, watery laughter sounded again, and then it was as if a window had opened in the water. There was none of the wavery shift of her other visions: one moment Sophie was looking at stones in a stream bed, and the next she was gazing

85

down the length of a vast hall, its pale walls shimmering with faint, iridescent color, like mother-of-pearl. Golden sconces glowed with green light, and a blue velvet carpet ran up the length of the room, ending at an elaborate throne. It was made of coral and shells and smooth, silvery bits of driftwood. An old fishing net studded with sea-glass hung like a canopy overhead.

In the throne sat Dahud. She was more beautiful than Sophie remembered, her mint-green skin lustrous as pearl, her bottle-glass hair hanging to her waist in two plaits, wound with silver wire and topped with the silver filigree crown that matched her eyes. Her gown, too, was silver, and so long that it flowed down over the steps of the throne, pooling on the floor where someone sat at her feet.

Lucas.

Sophie was suddenly afraid to look at him, afraid of what the queen's words might have meant. She forced her eyes downward. It wasn't as bad as she'd feared. He was thinner, his hair longer and matted with tangles. His jacket was gone, leaving him wearing only the tattered trousers, like a shipwrecked man. But he was Lucas, and he was alive.

The relief, however, lasted only a moment. Because it was then that he shifted, and Sophie saw a glint of gold: the chain she'd noticed in the first vision. She had assumed that it attached to some kind of manacle, or perhaps, at worst, wrapped around his neck. Now she saw with horror that it ran straight into the center of his chest, as if it had sprouted from beneath his skin.

Worse still, the queen held the other end, wrapped around her wrist like a lapdog's leash.

"Why is he chained like that?" Sophie demanded.

With a small, chilly smile, Dahud gave the chain a tug. Lucas flinched, but then he gazed up at her with rapt attention. Sophie's heart constricted painfully. "What have you done to him?"

Dahud walked her fingers down Lucas's bare shoulder and across his chest, stopping where the chain emerged. "Azazel's aim was true. Lucifer's heart was riven. We sewed it up." Dahud looked back at Sophie with disdain. "With his own heartstrings." She ran the golden chain between her fingers, holding Sophie's eyes.

"The chain...the chain is part of his heart?"

"Was." Dahud let a bit of it through her fingers. "He must have loved you well, for it to be so fine." She drizzled a coil of the delicate chain into her cupped hand, then closed her fist on it with a reptilian smile.

"That is revolting!"

"Why? He is happy."

"I don't believe you."

The queen didn't answer, but her smile widened beneath eyes feral and fierce. She turned to Lucas. "Well, pet?" she said. "Shall we show her?"

Lucas met her gaze with one of joyous wonder, and a smile that broke Sophie's heart all over again. He reached up, and the queen leaned down, and Sophie could only watch, horrified, as Lucas took the green-haired woman in his arms and kissed her. Dahud's long, pearly fingers push into his hair; his arms tighten around her. Even as the tears clouded her vision, Sophie couldn't look away.

At last, Dahud pulled back, and Lucas sank down on the dais steps with a dazed smile. "Lucas?" Sophie said tremulously.

He turned to her, his eyes wide and dreamy. He looked at her for a moment, without recognition, and then he turned his gaze back to Dahud.

"You see?" she said. "He has forgotten you. Better you forget him, too."

"No!" Sophie cried, anguished. "He would *never* forget me! You've done something to him…bewitched him – "

"He is ours!" the queen interrupted, her voice suddenly sharp and icy.

"Then unchain him," Sophie retorted, "and let me hear him tell me so."

The queen's expression grew menacing. She seemed to grow, her face changing, her cheeks hollowing and skin darkening, wrinkling, until there was nothing beautiful about her. "Do not cross us, little girl! You will regret it."

"We'll see about that," said Sophie, and she ran her hand through the water, shattering the image.

CHAPTER 7

Sophie didn't begin to cry until she was half way up the path. Then the tears burst out of her, as violent as they were sudden. She sat down blindly on the first thing that came to hand – a damp, mossy tree trunk. She was certain that Lucas was under some kind of enchantment, but it didn't comfort her. All she could think of was the way he had kissed Dahud, the dreamy ecstasy in his eyes. That, and her own utter powerlessness to do anything about it. She had come to the Hermitage believing that she would leave knowing what to do next. Now she knew even less than before.

"Well, hen?" said a spindly voice beside her.

Sophie jumped, and then swiped at the tears on her face, turning to see who had spoken. It was an old woman. She wore a dark, shapeless coat, sensible, thick-soled shoes, and she leaned on a walking stick carved with Celtic knotwork. Sophie stood up, wiping a sleeve across her face again in mortification.

"Sorry," she said. "I'm fine, really – "

The woman smiled faintly and shook her head. "I'm old enough to have heard every lie goin'. You're no 'fine'."

Sophie looked at the woman. She was tiny – shorter than Sophie by a few inches. Her hair was wispy and white, her face a web of wrinkles, her eyes milky with cataracts. And yet, her gaze was keen despite it.

"You're right," Sophie admitted, "I've been better. But I'm just on my way home now. Honestly, I'll be alright."

She went to step around the woman, and found her way blocked by the walking stick. She took a startled step backward. She hadn't even seen the woman lift her arm. It seemed impossible that she'd be able to move even half so quickly.

"I really do need to go," Sophie said.

The woman continued to gaze at her, and though Sophie was uneasy, she didn't feel quite as alarmed as she thought she should. There was something calm about the old woman's presence, something solicitous in her scrutiny. At last, she moved her walking stick.

"If you're thrawn," she said, "then I'll no stop you. But you strike me as someone with somethin' she needs to get off her chest, and I'm good at listenin'. Go on – tell me whit's wrang?"

Sophie smiled sadly. "You wouldn't believe me."

"Because it involves the sea witch?"

Sophie froze. "Who are you?" she asked after a moment.

"I'm Morag."

"How do you know about *her*?"

"Anybody would know aboot her," Morag answered with a shrug, "if they'd hauf a mind to listen."

"Listen to what?"

Morag waved her hand vaguely toward the stream. "The burn's talked of nothin' else since you first came and called her."

Sophie glanced uneasily at the roiling brown water, and then she looked back at Morag. There was something about her that reminded Sophie of the angels she'd met – a sense that what one saw of her was only a screen, hiding something more ancient and powerful than her mind could have accepted. Because of that, and because she really had nothing to lose, she spoke the exact words she was thinking: "Are you one of the *sith*?"

The old woman looked horrified. "Whisht, lass! You'll have them on us!"

"So you believe in them?"

"Only a fool denies the fae." Then she gave Sophie a canny look. "Was he one of them?"

"Was who one of them?"

"Whatever lad has got you greetin'."

After a moment to decipher the Scots, she answered, "No."

"Aye, and a good thing, too. Faery men are nothin' but trouble." Before Sophie could think of a response to that, Morag asked, "Now, what do they call *you*?"

"Sophie."

"Well, Sophie, come wi' me. I'll make you a cup o' tea, and you can tell me all aboot what he's done, this lad o' yours."

Morag turned and began to shuffle toward the road. Sophie hesitated. It was one thing to stand talking to a batty old woman out in the open, quite another to follow her home. Even if she was really just an ordinary old woman, believing in the *sìth* was hardly a recommendation.

"That's very kind," Sophie said, "but I've really got to be – "

"Tea!" the woman insisted, lifting her cane to pontificate, and wobbling dangerously.

"Alright, I'll walk home with you," Sophie said quickly, catching Morag under the elbow before she toppled. "And then I'll see if I have time."

"It's just there." Morag lifted her cane again to point toward the Toll House.

"You live there?" Sophie asked, surprised.

Morag answered with a curt nod.

"I love what you've done with the tree. The bells and the ribbons and all."

Morag smiled, but shook her head. "The clootie tree isnae my doin'."

"The what tree?"

"Clootie. Means 'cloth'."

They'd reached the garden fence. There was a small gate

92

set between two stone posts. One of them, Sophie saw, was inscribed with a symbol – three conjoined spirals, arranged to form a triangle, like Matrika's tattoo. She wondered what it meant, as Morag opened a gate and led Sophie inside. Together, they walked to the tree. As they approached, Sophie saw that there was a small ring of stones beside it, surrounding a hole in the ground. Within the hole, she could hear running water.

"It's a kind of prayin'," Morag continued, fingering one of the strips of cloth. "You tear a piece from your clothin', dunk it in the well and then tie it to the branch o' the tree. You make your prayer to the spirit o' the well. Sometimes it's done to honor the spirit. More often it's a supplication. The ailment will fade wi' the cloth, until it falls awa'."

Sophie studied the fluttering ribbons. There were hundreds of them, some bright and new, others no more than a few grey threads barely clinging to a twig. *All of them prayers.* She wondered how many had been granted.

"Who is the spirit of the well?" she asked, hoping that it wasn't Dahud.

But Morag answered, "The triple goddess."

"I've never heard of her."

"Naw – few have, anymore." She paused, looking into the well, and then she said, "She's the oldest of all deities. The maiden, the mither and the crone."

"Does she have a name?"

"Too many to count." Morag stared into the water for

another few moments, and Sophie had the impression that her eyes cleared and brightened. When she looked up again, though, they were the same milky blue as before. "Now, tea," she said.

Sophie turned automatically toward the house, but Morag stooped under the tree and began poking with her stick in the long grass. At last she found what she was looking for: a battered copper tea-kettle.

"Would you get the water for me, hen?" she asked Sophie. "If I bend down, I'll no get up again so easy."

"Of course," Sophie said, taking the kettle. "Is it...?" She glanced toward the back door of the house.

"Ach, no!" Morag said. "It's well water for me, or nothin'."

Sophie looked dubiously at the hole in the ground. "Are you certain it's safe?"

"Oh, aye," Morag assured her, brushing more grass aside to reveal the remains of a small fire. "Even the sea witch wouldnae cross the goddess."

Sophie had been thinking more along the lines of dysentery, but she accepted the assurance anyway. Kneeling down, she dipped the kettle into the well. The water was icy cold, and had none of the chemical smell of the burn. In fact, the well seemed to exhale a sweet breath of damp earth and grass, crushed fern and mint. She breathed in a few times before turning back to Morag with the filled kettle.

The old woman had managed to stir the fire to life and

erect an iron tripod over the flames, with a hook hanging from its center. Sophie hung the kettle from the hook while Morag pushed her way back under the laden branches of the tree, rummaged again in the grass, and came back with two chipped willow mugs and a battered tin box. She set the mugs by the fire and opened the box. It was full of dried leaves and blossoms and twigs. She scooped out a handful of the mixture, put it into the kettle and then, with a grateful sigh, she settled into a rusted lawn chair. Sophie sat down across from her on an upturned milk crate.

"Now," Morag said, with a keen glance that made Sophie think once again that her eyes couldn't be as poor as they looked, "you tell me about this laddie, and how he's got muddled with the sea witch."

"I wouldn't know where to begin."

"His name?"

"Lucas," Sophie said, fingering the hem of his jumper where a bit of it had begun to unravel. "His name is Lucas."

Morag nodded and smiled encouragingly. "A good name. And how did you meet him?"

"That's where it gets complicated."

"I may be old," Morag said, looking into the kettle, which had begun to give off a pungent steam that reminded Sophie of something, though she couldn't think what, "but I've no lost my wits yet."

Sophie looked up at her. "Oh, no – I didn't mean to suggest

you had. It's just that – " She stopped. Looking into Morag's calm, kindly face, her protests suddenly seemed pointless. The woman had spoken of sea witches and *sìth* – either she had experience with these things, or she was mad, and either way she wasn't likely to laugh Sophie out of the garden.

"He died," she said. "Or I thought he did. But then I began to see him. In dreams, and visions. Always in the water. I saw Dahud, too. The sea witch – or I assume that's who you mean." She looked at Morag, who nodded thoughtfully. "I didn't know anything for certain until this morning, when I saw them both, together…" Sophie wanted to tell Morag about the kiss, to ease the sting of the memory, but she couldn't make herself say the words.

Morag, however, gave her a frank look and said, "She's taken him her for her lover."

"I…I think she has," Sophie answered, trying to keep her voice steady.

"The sea witch kills her lovers," Morag said matter-of-factly.

"What!" Sophie cried.

"Aye – once a year, as teind tae the Deep."

"Teind?"

"A kind o' tax."

"Right. And the Deep…isn't that the underworld?"

"It's where the powers are that give Dahud her ain power."

"I don't understand," Sophie said, although she did. She

was hoping that Morag was mad, that she was wrong – that she would say anything other than what she seemed to be saying.

Rather than answer, though, Morag took the kettle from the fire and a tea strainer from her coat pocket, and filled the two mugs. It looked an ordinary liquid brown, but smelled sharp and sweet and earthy.

"Drink," Morag said.

"What is it?" Sophie asked dubiously.

"Herbs tae heal the heart," Morag answered, and sipped hers. Sophie did the same. The tea tasted exactly as it smelled, but better.

"Morag," Sophie said tentatively, not wanting to make her clam up again, "do you know how I can save him?"

Morag sat in silence for a time, looking at the tree. The fire whispered and cracked, the breeze rifled the ribbons in the branches, stroked the bells, and the well's spring murmured. Then, as Sophie was beginning to despair, Morag turned back to her and said, "Tam Lin."

Sophie looked up. "Pardon?"

"Tam Lin, the faery knight."

"I'm afraid I haven't met him."

"Naw," Morag laughed softly, "and you should thank the gods for that!" And then she shut her eyes. Sophie wondered if she was having some kind of spell, until the old woman began to sing. She had a mellow contralto voice that must have been beautiful when she was younger.

> "Oh I forbid you, maidens a',
>
> That wear gowd on your hair,
>
> To come or gae by Carterhaugh,
>
> For young Tam Lin is there.
>
> There's nane that gaes by Carterhaugh
>
> But they leave him a wad,
>
> Either their rings, or mantles green,
>
> Or else their maidenhead…"

What? That was a bit more graphic than the other Scots ballads Sophie had heard, and at first she thought she'd got it wrong because of the heavy dialect. As she listened, though, she realized that the story was exactly as strange and creepy as she'd first thought. It was about a wood haunted by the faery knight, Tam Lin, who demanded payment of any girl who passed through it. He would accept it in the form of money, jewellery, clothing – or, if they had none of those, their virginity.

One headstrong girl called Janet, who believed that she owned the wood as part of her inheritance, went there to pick flowers. As soon as she did, Tam Lin appeared and asked for his due. Janet, smitten with him, gave it in the latter form, and ended up pregnant. Determined not to be married off to the first taker, she went back to the wood to ask Tam Lin for help. He told her that he had once been a human knight, but one day he fell off his horse, and the faery queen caught him. She took him back to her court, where he became her favorite. But seven years had passed, and it had come the time for the queen to pay her teind to Hell, and he feared that he would be used as payment.

Tam Lin told Janet that there was a way to win him back before it happened. But it involved outfacing the faery queen, on the night of Halloween, when her power was the greatest. He told Janet to wait for them at the crossroads, where their procession would pass, and look for the white horse, which he would be riding. Then, she would have to grab and hold onto him as the faeries changed him into various horrible things, to try to get her to let go. When he turned into a burning coal, she was to throw him into the water, and he would become human again. Janet did all that he had told her, and won him back.

Morag's voice died away on a sigh of wind. Sophie sat staring at her, the ballad's weird images tumbling in her mind. "Well, lass?" Morag said after a moment.

"It seems like an awfully roundabout way of getting a husband," Sophie answered after a time.

Morag laughed. "That it was. But she loved him, more than her fear or doubt. More than her ain life."

Sophie thought for another moment, and then said, "So is that what I have to do to get Lucas back? Hold onto him while the sea witch turns him into monsters?"

Morag gave her a pitying look. "All you can be sure of, when dealing wi' the fae, is their perversity."

"What do you mean?" Sophie asked, thinking that killing

the *Each Uisge* and the *Cait Sìth* had been fairly straightforward, if not exactly easy.

"They dinnae abide by human laws. Cruelty and wit make up the better part o' their nature, and if the two of them can be joined, then so much the better."

The tenuous peace Sophie had felt as she sipped her tea faded back into dejection as Morag confirmed the enormity of her task. Apparently Morag realized this, because she reached out and put one knotted hand over Sophie's. "Dinnae despair, lass. If you love him enough, and you dinnae lose your faith, you'll find a way."

"I don't even know where to begin." Sophie said miserably.

Morag looked at her with gentle, cloudy eyes. "You could ask the goddess for help."

"What? You mean the clootie tree?"

Morag nodded. Sophie had her doubts about the tree and the goddess, but Morag had been kind to her, and she had no better ideas. "Does it matter where the cloth comes from?" she asked.

"The closer tae your heart, the better."

Sophie inspected her clothes, and her eyes stopped on Lucas's jumper. True, it wasn't hers, exactly, but it was closer to her heart than anything of her own. She tore off a few red strands of wool from the fraying hem. She got up, dipped them into the well, and then stood holding them, dripping, uncertain of what exactly to pray for. Of course she wanted Lucas back, but what good would that do her if they only had a few months together before she died, or disintegrated, or whatever happened to an aeon who'd flouted the laws of the Balance?

There was one thing, though, of which she'd been certain since she saw him in the puddle in the old town; one prayer her heart had been repeating since the dark water first swallowed him. "Please, keep him safe," she said softly, as the wind strummed the bells in the branches. Then she tied the wet wool to a spiky twig, and stepped back from the tree, turning to thank Morag. But the old woman was gone, along with the fire and the tea things, as if none of them had ever been there at all.

CHAPTER 8

As soon as she met her mother that evening, Sophie knew that something was up. At the bus stop Anna seemed preoccupied, silence replacing her usual, tangential chatter. But if she was lost in thought, it was no dreamy reverie. Even after they boarded the bus, her eyes flickered nervously between the window and her daughter, and she couldn't seem to stop playing with the rings on her fingers.

At last, Sophie couldn't stand it anymore. She put one of her hands over her mother's and said, "You're going to wear holes in your fingers doing that."

Anna smiled distractedly, pushing an escaping strand of hair into the paisley scarf that held it back. "Sorry," she said.

"Is something wrong?"

"What makes you ask?"

"Let me rephrase that: something's wrong. What is it?"

Anna sighed. "You know me too well. But it's nothing for you to worry about."

Sophie rolled her eyes. "You do know that's the one sure way to make your kid worry?" Anna gave her another halfhearted smile. "Okay, I know you aren't splitting up with Dad, since you already did that. So, let's see...you're getting married?"

"God, no," Anna said, with a laugh that was more genuine than the smile.

"Dad's getting married?"

"Not as far as I know."

"The job's crap?"

"No, it's fine. I just have a lot on my mind...the show... other things..."

Sophie gave her a long look, wondering if she was one of those other things. Wondering, too, whether telling her mother not to worry about her could possibly do any good. But the bus pulled into their stop then, and Anna almost leapt out of the seat. Sophie followed her to their flat in silence. Anna glanced over her shoulder once as she unlocked the door, as if she were expecting someone, but there was no one there.

As Sophie helped her mother make dinner, all sorts of possibilities ran through her mind. Anna had decided single motherhood was too much to cope with, and asked her father to come get her. She'd met a new man and invited him for tea, and didn't know how to break it to her daughter. Sophie's lingering depression had finally sent her round the bend, and she'd arranged for doctors with straight-jackets to come and take Sophie away…

Sophie had almost convinced herself that she was being absurd when, half way through supper, the door buzzer went. Anna jumped as if she'd been stung, and gave Sophie a furtive look.

"Expecting someone?" Sophie asked, trying to ignore the clutch of anxiety in her guts.

"Well, actually…"

"It's Dad, isn't it?" Sophie said, getting up before her mother could.

"No, love, it isn't Dad. Listen, I know that I really should have asked you first, but I knew you'd just say no."

Sophie could hear footsteps on the stairs, and the echo of voices. Girls' voices. *She couldn't,* Sophie thought, *she wouldn't…* She flung the door open, leaned over the bannister just as Ailsa turned her hopeful face upward with a tentative smile. But Sophie hardly saw it. She was looking at the girl beside her: a girl with long, white-blonde dreadlocks caught up in a loop of silver Christmas tinsel. A girl with quick, birdlike movements and a laugh like a bell.

She didn't dare believe it until the two girls rounded the final turn in the staircase, and the blonde one finally looked up. She grinned, winked one black eye and then threw her arms around Sophie, nearly toppling them both with the weight of her backpack. Sophie was engulfed in the sweet-spicy atmosphere all of the angels seemed to carry with them.

"Sophie!" she cried, her American accent stronger than ever. "I am *so excited* to finally meet you. I've heard so much about you, it's like we're friends already!" Quickly, before she released her, she whispered, "That was for your mom's benefit. Ailsa knows everything. Go with it for now, and I promise to explain later. By the way – love the hair!"

*

After one of the more surreal dinners Sophie could remember, during which Suri regaled them with stories about her world travels and ate more than any normal person possibly could, Anna shooed the girls out of the kitchen, saying that she'd do the dishes and give them all a chance to "catch up". She said this with a look so hopeful that Sophie swallowed the lecture she'd been planning about interfering with her life, made cups of tea for everyone, and ushered the girls into her bedroom.

"Alright," she said, shutting the door and leaning against it, "which one of you wants to tell me what's going on?"

"We're here to cheer you up," Suri said brightly, poking around the paltry collection of cosmetics on top of Sophie's dresser.

"And make sure you don't do anything mad," Ailsa added.

"Why would I do something mad?" Sophie asked.

"Oh, say, because your fallen angel boyfriend's been kidnapped by an evil mermaid who enjoys making unsuspecting men into love slaves before bumping them off?"

"Ailsa!" Suri cried, turning around and brandishing an eyeliner pencil. "You're supposed to be making her feel *better*!"

"Sorry," Ailsa said. "But after everything with Sam, honesty is my policy."

"So when you said she knows everything," Sophie said to Suri, "you meant *everything.*"

"Everything that I know, anyway," Suri answered, dropping the eye pencil and rummaging in her messenger bag until she found a tube of black liquid eyeliner. She turned back to the mirror and began to paint on cat eyes.

"So why did you – " Sophie stopped, realizing she didn't know how to finish the question without offending Ailsa.

"Tell me?" Ailsa said, with an arched eyebrow, looking up from Sophie's notebook, which she'd opened to the drawing of Ker-Ys.

"Well, you did seem pretty keen to forget everything when Michael offered."

"Yeah, well, he failed to mention the side effects of mind-wiping," Ailsa said grimly.

"What side effects?"

"Nightmares, for a start."

"She kept waking me up screaming," Suri explained. "See, memory-laundering doesn't actually get rid of the memory –

106

nothing can do that. It just buries it so deep you forget about it…or that's the idea. But sometimes the subconscious can't quite keep a lid on it. Do you have any false eyelashes?"

"Wow, there's a question I never thought I'd hear."

"Is that a no?"

Sophie just laughed. Sighing, Suri pulled out a tube of mascara. "Anyway, in the end I figured the truth couldn't be worse than whatever her subconscious was feeding her."

"It's not even close," Ailsa agreed.

"Plus, I've never gone in for mind-wiping. Abuse of power and all that. And it *really* pissed Michael off, which is always fun. So, yup – she knows everything."

"So how did you find out?" Sophie asked after a moment's consideration. "That Lucas didn't die, I mean?"

"Because Azazel showed up in the cemetery ranting about the injustice of it," Suri said, rummaging once again in her bag.

"Azazel's back in Heaven?"

"Sure is," Suri answered.

"But he was fallen!"

"That's why he's confined to the cemetery, with all of his powers stripped – driving me *crazy,* I might add."

Sophie's head was spinning. "Maybe you'd better start at the beginning."

"We'll even use small words and simple sentences," Ailsa said, pulling a Galaxy bar out of her backpack and dividing it among them.

"Unnecessary sarcasm," Sophie said.

Ailsa winked at her and smiled. "I learned it from the best."

"God, I love Earth," Suri said, taking the chocolate in one hand as she spread black glitter on her eyelids with the other.

"The beginning," Sophie reminded her.

"Okay, so I gave you some bad advice, yadda yadda yadda…Lucifer disappeared into the briny deep, you skewered Azazel – nice one, by the way! – and Ailsa got her mind wiped. That's when I decided it was time for someone sensible to step in."

"That being you?"

"Of course!" Suri answered with a withering look. Against all logic, her eye makeup looked amazing.

"But don't you need armor to come to Earth?"

"Yup. Which is why I'm wearing it." She pulled off one of her black wrist-warmers, exposing her slender forearm. Sophie saw nothing but white skin. "Relax your eyes," Suri said. "You can only see it when you aren't trying to see it."

"Very Zen," Sophie commented, but she let her vision relax and haze. Now when she looked, Suri's arm was covered in clear scales that shimmered with a faint iridescence. They didn't look like armor so much as a second, reptilian skin. "Holy hell!"

"Freaky, isn't it?" Ailsa asked, stirring her tea with her chocolate.

"Not as freaky as it would be if I dissociated into a million pieces," Suri answered, putting her wrist-warmer back on.

"So how did you get it?" Sophie asked. "I mean, the armor. I thought you needed permission to take it."

"We do," Suri answered. "But luckily, Ansiel at the armory owed me one. So I got the armor and then headed to Ardnasheen to tell you your honey wasn't really dead. But you weren't there, and the whole place was this shambolic mess – "

"And next thing you know, the Angel of Death is pulling pints at the world's remotest pub," Ailsa said, licking chocolate off of her fingers.

Sophie found it disturbingly easy to imagine Suri bantering with the pickled old men holding up the bar. "Why the job, anyway?"

Suri shrugged, fishing out a lipstick. "Ruadhri was going apoplectic with all the new business and no help but Ailsa. What could I do? It's an angel's duty to serve humans, after all."

"You're telling me you took a bar job purely out of altruism?"

Her lips quirked upward. "Well, that, and barmaids hear everything. I figured I might learn something useful. I mean, I knew Lucifer was alive, but I didn't know how or where. But I did know he couldn't have gone far, what with the staves and all. So I thought maybe someone local would've had a sighting." She dotted crimson lipstick on her lower lip.

"And someone did?"

Suri rolled her eyes. "Some*one?* None of the local *sìth* will talk about anything else! I got a blow-by-blow from a water horse nursing a *really* big grudge – something about her boyfriend getting tag-teamed on a mountain by Lucifer and a human girl?" She cocked an eyebrow at Sophie.

"Believe me," Sophie said, "he deserved it."

"Well, she's got a bone to pick with you. Or she did. She was the one that brought Lucifer to Dahud, so I guess maybe now she considers herself avenged."

"Oh, God..." Sophie groaned.

"Look on the bright side," Suri said, pulling her black jumper over her head and dropping it unapologetically on the floor, to reveal a perfect figure in a red satin bra, and her sigil sweeping across her back, graceful as wings. "He probably wouldn't have survived otherwise. Faery queens have ways and means the rest of us don't."

Sophie sat thinking as Suri began rifling through her backpack and then pulled out a red sequined slip-dress. The dress was sleeveless, so the ends of Suri's sigil still showed: a spiral on each shoulder.

"Not to sound ungrateful," Sophie said at last, "but back to that bad advice...last time we talked, you told me to listen to Michael and leave all of this well alone."

"Yeah, well," said Suri, "that was before I realized he was trying to kill Lucifer."

Sophie had guessed it already, but hearing it from Suri was still a slap in the face. "He gave Sam the Queres," she said.

Suri nodded and pulled the band from her hair, so the brilliant ropes fell down around her shoulders. "And called up that cat demon, and probably even the water horse, although I haven't figured out yet how he managed that…*sith* aren't biddable like demons, and angels don't usually deal with them."

"Yeah," Sophie said dismally, "that's exactly what Michael told me."

"You've spoken to him?"

Sophie nodded, furious with herself. "Called him up to tell him that Lucas was still alive."

For the first time Sophie could remember, Suri looked shocked. She paused, both hands full of tights. "Tell me you didn't."

"Well, I was having these weird dreams and visions," Sophie said defensively. "I needed to talk to someone about them, and there literally wasn't anyone else I could ask."

Suri looked at Ailsa. "I guess now we know why he took off."

"He went back to Heaven?" Sophie asked.

Suri shrugged. "All we know is he left Ardnasheen. On the morning ferry, two days ago."

"With a big suitcase," Ailsa added.

"Do you think he's going after Lucas?" Sophie asked. "Oh my God – you don't think he means to…to finish it?"

"I don't know," Suri said. "I mean, Michael's always been hard line, but nothing's as cut and dried these days as it used to be." She looked speculatively at Sophie. "What exactly did you tell him?"

"That I'd seen Lucas."

"In visions?"

"It was only one vision, then. I saw him in a puddle."

"And how did you find out about Ker-Ys and Dahud?"

"That was a dream. I didn't know what they were at first, but Matrika – the woman I work for – recognized the drawing I made of the city, and lent me a book with the ballad in it."

Suri considered this, winding and unwinding a pair of tights around her hand. Finally, she said, "It could be worse."

"Could it?"

"Definitely. Michael likes literal, so he won't believe they're true visions until he finds proof. And then, assuming he does, he'll have to decide what to do about it. That gives us at least a few days' head start." She looked back at Sophie. "Plus, if you can see Lucas, it means some part of him still has a connection to you."

"Only a part?"

"Don't worry. It'll all come back once we break him out of Ker-Ys."

"That's the plan?" Sophie asked incredulously.

"No, that's the goal. We don't have a plan yet."

"But she's been doing some research," Ailsa said hopefully.

Suri dropped the tights and reached again into her backpack, this time bringing out a fat ring-binder. She handed it to Sophie, who looked at it doubtfully. "Maybe you could paraphrase?"

"Okay," Suri said, dropping it on the bed, "so apparently, Dahud is one of Celtic mythology's nastier figures." She finally chose a pair of tights – plain black – and began to pull them on.

"So she's a faery?" Sophie asked.

"Part faery. But don't get any ideas about cold iron. It won't work on her."

"Because she's also part human?"

"No – she's also part demon." Sophie looked up at her in surprise, and Suri said, "Remember Dahud's lover – the one who opens the sea gate and floods Ker-Ys in the ballad?"

"Wikipedia said that he's the devil."

"Simplistic, but yes, more or less," Suri agreed. "He's a daeva called Abaddon. It means 'destruction'. These days he doesn't often leave the Deep – you know about daevas and the Deep, right?"

"Only a little."

"The point is this." Suri opened the binder, flipped through a few plastic sleeves full of intriguing-looking clippings, and then settled on one. It looked like a page from a medieval manuscript. It appeared to be written in Latin, which Sophie couldn't read, but it began with an illuminated letter. It was a picture of a man holding his bleeding wrist over a cup while a woman drank from it. Suri tapped the picture with one glittering black fingernail.

"Abaddon gave his blood to Dahud, and it made her part demon. The key was the price she paid for it."

"Why did she want to be part demon?"

"Because she believed it would make her immortal. She'd been sacrificing men to the Deep for years, in hopes that the daevas would give her eternal life. I guess Abaddon finally took her up on it."

"But why did he want the key? I mean, why flood the city?"

"Because it was going all holy on him." Seeing Sophie and Ailsa's incomprehension, Suri flipped through a few more pages, then showed them a medieval wood-cut of a crowd of people kneeling before a haloed man holding a cross.

"That's Saint Winwaloe," she said. "He'd come to Christianize Ker-Ys. It was happening everywhere, back then – Christianity just plowed right through the old religions. People stopped believing in their traditional deities, and so the deities lost power. Some of them accepted it as the rightful way of things. Others fought to hold onto whatever strength they could, at any cost. That meant destroying whatever the Christians made. Abaddon was one of those."

"But didn't Dahud realize she'd be left with nothing once the city sank?" Ailsa asked.

Suri smiled sadly and shook her head. "Dahud was drunk,

as usual. Besides, she'd already got the demon blood she wanted – she thought she was immortal, so what did it matter?"

"She *thought*?" Ailsa asked.

"Yes. Abaddon lied to her: being half demon couldn't make her immortal, because no creature can live with only a partial emanation."

"A partial *what*?"

"Emanation. The combination of body, soul and anima that makes a living being what it is. See, when her father pushed her into the ocean, the human part of Dahud drowned, but not the demon part. She couldn't exist as half a being, so she began to die. When she realized it, she called out to the daevas to save her. But it was the *sìth* that answered. They completed her with part of a *sìth* self: a mermaid's tail."

"So that bit of the ballad is true," Sophie mused.

Suri nodded. "Dahud has a fish's tail instead of legs. It means that she can never walk on land again, and for that she hates it. Well, also because she thinks it's hideous…not to mention making it hard to pull guys." She flipped to another print, this time a Victorian engraving of a woman recoiling in horror from the fish tail that stretched out where her legs should have been.

"She doesn't let anyone talk about it, never mind see it. But she can't forget about it, either. It drives her crazy. Well, crazier. So anyway, since she began to hide it, she's always kept a pet…a human man whom she'll enchant and keep by her, to pay homage to her beauty. To make her forget her tail. But she can never truly forget, and so, every winter solstice, she sacrifices her guy to the Deep, hoping they'll make her a full demon, with human legs."

Sophie thought of the queen's long silver skirt, pooling around the steps to her throne. Around Lucas. A cold finger traced down her back. "The teind," Sophie muttered.

Suri looked surprised. "Well, yes – that's what they used to call it."

"So what actually happens to these teinds?"

Suri sighed. "The daevas take them to the Deep. After that, no one knows. But none have ever come back."

Sophie thought about this. Then she said slowly, "These 'pets' – they've always been human?"

"As far as I know."

"So she must be thinking that it will be different with an angel. That she'll get what she wants."

"I guess," Suri said.

"And if Lucas goes to the Deep, I doubt that will do anything good for the Balance." Suri shook her head. Sophie felt ill. "So how do I find her?"

"You can't just go rushing off to challenge a half-demon sea witch thingy to a duel!" Ailsa said.

"I've killed a water horse, a demon and a fallen angel," Sophie argued.

"Dahud is more powerful than any of those," Suri said.

"That's how she made her queendom, and it's how she keeps it."

"What about this?" Sophie took the dagger from its hiding place in her wardrobe, and handed it to Suri.

"Carnwennan," Suri said with a faint smile, running a finger across the flat of the blade." Where did you get this?"

"It kind of ...appeared...when I was fighting the *Cait Sìth.*"

Suri looked up at Sophie with eyes that were oddly frank and serious amidst the glittering make-up. "Okay – if you drove this through Dahud's heart, yes, it would probably kill her. But first you'd have to get close enough, and that's the problem. A faery or a demon fights fair, mostly. Even Azazel's poisoned sword was straightforward in its way. But Dahud is subtle. If you came at her with this," Suri twirled the knife in her fingers so that it became a blur of icy light, "she'd give you one look, and you'd put it through your own heart, believing it was exactly what you'd meant to do."

"What are my options, then?" Sophie asked dejectedly, as Suri handed the knife back to her. "I just resign myself to letting her toss Lucas to Hell?"

"Of course not! But we need to find a way to outwit her. We have to take our time."

Time is the one thing I don't have. But it would do the others no good to know that. "Okay," she said, "well, I've got work in the morning, so I'd best get to bed, but we can work on this tomorrow – "

"Bed?" Suri cried. "I haven't been in Edinburgh in three hundred years. We're going dancing!"

CHAPTER 9

Sophie's mother was so overjoyed that she was going out – with two friends, no less – that she gave her twenty pounds and an open curfew, then retreated to the sitting room to paint. But when Sophie picked up her jacket and headed for the door, Suri said, "Where do you think you're going?"

"Ah – dancing?"

"Not like that, you're not."

Sophie looked down at herself: old jeans, faded blue converse all-stars and a paint-spattered London Marathon t-shirt that had once been her father's. "What's wrong with it?"

Suri rolled her eyes. "Seriously? I don't even know where to begin!" Sophie saw Ailsa hiding a smirk, until Suri turned her critical eyes on her. "And you're not much better!"

Suri steered them back toward Sophie's bedroom, then made them both sit on the bed while she rummaged in Sophie's wardrobe. Within five minutes she'd shut the door, shaking her head. "All the shopping malls on Earth at her fingertips, and the girl doesn't own one decent outfit!"

She upended her backpack on the floor, revealing what looked like the contents of a circus-performer's costume chest. She picked through the pile, occasionally pausing to hold something up for inspection. Sophie was about to breathe a sigh of relief that Suri had discarded the emerald green sequined bustier in favor of a cornflower-blue velvet skirt, even if it was somewhat shorter than what she would have chosen, when Suri cried, "And this…and these…and – ooh, yes! Perfect!"

Along with the skirt, Sophie found herself holding two pairs of tights – one silver and one black fishnet – a stretchy silver top that looked like it would barely fit a three-year-old, and a purple vest top with a rhinestone eye on the front. As she looked at the armful in despair, Suri dropped a pair of black biker boots at her feet with a self-satisfied grin.

"Um, Suri – " she began, but Suri had already turned her attention on Ailsa. With a sigh, Sophie discarded her jeans, picked up the silver tights and began to pull them on. By the time she was wearing the whole outfit, Suri had got Ailsa into a black velvet mini-dress, gold GoGo boots and purple lace tights. Suri pulled on knee-high black boots and the biker jacket with the stencil of the Celtic cross, which Sophie remembered from their dream trip to Paris.

"How did you fit all this into that backpack?" she asked as Suri approached her with the pot of glitter gel.

"And how did you have anything in my size?" Ailsa added, leaning toward the mirror to apply plum-colored lipstick. "I must have at least six inches on you."

Suri waved a hand vaguely at her backpack, which looked as full as it had when she'd tipped it out. "Angel luggage doesn't follow the same space-time rules as human luggage. Now shush, or I'll mess this up." She dabbed the gel on Sophie's eyelids, then went to work with an array of cosmetic tubes and pencils. When she finally handed Sophie a mirror, Sophie didn't recognize herself. The girl staring back at her looked moody, even dangerous. Though it was strange to see herself like that, it wasn't without a certain thrill.

Suri took the mirror back out of her hands, and gave it to Ailsa, who was similarly made-up, her long, copper hair piled in loops and twists on top of her head. "Holy crap," Ailsa said.

"No kidding," Sophie agreed.

Suri smiled. "I think we're good to go." She tossed Sophie the furry purple leopard-print jacket she'd worn in the Paris dream, Ailsa a similar one in burgundy, plus a pair of long purple gloves, and the three girls headed for the door.

"Bye Mum!" Sophie called, hustling her friends out the door quickly, in case her mother saw her new look and demanded her twenty pounds back.

"Bye girls!" she called back in what Sophie thought of as her painting voice: dreamy, distracted, possibly even unaware of what she was saying.

They hailed a cab and Suri directed the driver to the Cowgate, which was when Sophie realized she had no idea where they were headed. Ailsa apparently thought of the same thing. "If you haven't been here in three hundred years, then how do you know where to go?"

"I asked a couple of angels who were down for the Festival last year," Suri answered, meeting the cab driver's raised eyebrows with a dazzling smile and a handful of coins. "Keep the change," she said as they climbed out.

It was Friday, and the streets were full of students letting off steam. Most of them were heading for the brightly-lit bars of the Grassmarket, but Suri linked her arms through Sophie's and Ailsa's and led them in the opposite direction, deeper into the Cowgate.

The street was dark even on a sunny day, the stone walls of the medieval tenements rising up on either side like sheer cliff faces. Sophie began to feel the old, familiar unease that indicated Revenant territory. She tried not to look too hard into shadowy corners, or at the people they passed.

"Why so jumpy, Sophie?" Suri asked as they passed under the high, echoing arch of George IV Bridge.

"I'm not," Sophie said, looking up into the bridge's shadowed depths, where the bubbling voices of pigeons blended eerily with the rattle of traffic on the road above.

"There's nothing to be afraid of here anymore," Suri assured her.

"Anymore?" Ailsa asked doubtfully.

Suri nodded and continued cheerfully, "Now, a few hundred years ago, you wouldn't have wanted to be walking here alone at night. It was all cut-throats and body-snatchers then."

"Lovely," Ailsa said. "Which one are you looking out for, Sophie?"

Sophie turned quickly away from the watery glow coming from the mouth of a close across the road. She didn't know whether Suri had told Ailsa about the Revenants, but she did know that this wasn't the moment to find out. She glanced at Suri, who met her eye and squeezed her arm quickly, letting her know that she'd seen it, too.

Suri began chattering to Ailsa to draw her attention away from Sophie. Sophie crossed the street and looked into the close. Sure enough, a Revenant hovered there. It was a young one, still more or less resembling the man it had been. More than that, she recognized it as one of the ones that had showed her the vision of Lucas in the puddle. Sophie braced herself as the creature's eyes met hers, waiting for it to approach her. Instead, it gave her a long, measured look, and then it bowed its head, as if in affirmation, turned around, and walked away.

"Sophie?" Ailsa called from across the street. "What are you doing?"

"Um…what about this pub?" she said, grasping at the first excuse that came to mind. It was a dingy looking place in the block next to the close where the Revenant had appeared. "We could go here?"

Suri looked at her with raised eyebrows, miming the question that was running through Sophie's mind: *What the hell was that?*

"Yeah," said Ailsa, "if we want to get chatted up by petty criminals. Anyway, I thought we were going dancing."

"Dancing," Sophie repeated dazedly. "Right." She re-crossed the road and joined her friends. They walked for another block, and then Suri guided them up a narrow, cobbled side-street. Sophie could hear the pounding bass of the sound system while they were still fifty meters away from the lit door. By the time they reached it, the pavement was shuddering. The door looked like any tenement door, except that it was lit by two hissing gas lamps, one on either side of an antique-lettered sign reading "Lux Aeterna".

Suri sashayed right past the long queue stretching from the cordoned-off door, and flashed one of the bouncers a beaming smile. Immediately he smiled back. It looked as incongruous on his scarred and stubbled face as it would have on a bull terrier's. "Good evening, ladies," he said, his eyes running greedily over Ailsa's body. "You on the list?"

"What do you think?" Suri answered sweetly, batting her eyelashes. Looking slightly dazed, the bouncer unlatched the velvet cordon and let the three of them through. "Thanks!" Suri said, and blew him a kiss as the people on the street began to moan and protest.

"How did you do that?" Ailsa asked, as they made their way along a downward-sloping corridor whose stone walls were set with more gas lamps.

Suri grinned. "Angelic charm. But to tell you the truth, I think Ailsa's legs would have done the trick by themselves. You could have played up to him a bit."

"Please – you'll make me vomit all over this lovely outfit," Ailsa said.

The music got louder as they descended. By the time they reached the coat check, they couldn't hear each other speak. They handed their coats to the bored-looking, blue haired girl in the booth, who said something incomprehensible and handed them tickets. Then Suri led them through a churchlike archway, which let out into a vaulted stone room packed with people and pulsing with colored light, and the beat of a trance track loud enough to rattle Sophie's teeth. To her surprise, she didn't mind, though dance music wasn't generally her thing. There was something blissfully mindless about music so loud it was impossible even to think over it.

Suri took Sophie and Ailsa each by one hand, and led them toward the bar. The crowd parted in front of her easily, and Sophie wondered if that was also down to angelic charm. "What do you want?" Suri yelled at them.

Sophie looked at the array of colored bottles on the

125

mirrored shelves. Suddenly all she wanted was to lose herself. "Whatever," she yelled back, and turned to look at the crowd as Suri conferred with the bartender. With the flashing light and flailing bodies it was hard to make out anything in detail. She caught a glimpse of a girl in a shimmering bikini top with graceful, elongated limbs and hair that seemed to have a greenish tinge. Just as Sophie wondered if she was seeing it right, the girl looked at her and smiled, showing sharp, glassy, shark-like teeth. Her eyes were black from lid to lid. Before Sophie could react, she was lost among the writhing bodies.

A moment later Suri was pushing a glass into her hand, full of something fluorescent green. "Cheers!" she said, tapped Sophie's glass with her own, and then took a big gulp. Sophie sipped hers. The drink was sweet, with some kind of bite, though it didn't taste particularly alcoholic. Still, that could be deceptive, and she knew from Lucas that angels had to drink copiously to feel any effect. *Small sips,* she told herself.

They were making their way around the perimeter of the room, looking for a free table, when Sophie saw the Revenant again. This time he had the two female ones with him, as he had that night in the alley. Sophie dropped her drink; Suri caught it. Ailsa, luckily, was watching the DJ at the back of the room and didn't notice.

"Do you usually see this many?" Suri said into Sophie's ear.

Sophie shook her head. "Plus, I've seen these ones before."

As she watched, they beckoned to her and then slipped into the crowd, moving back toward the door. "What the hell is going on?" she asked.

Suri gave her a considering look, and handed her drink back. "Have some of this. I'll try and find out."

"But – " Sophie began, but Suri had already disappeared. She was looking around for her when Ailsa grabbed her arm.

"Sophie, have you *seen* that DJ?" she yelled. "He is ten kinds of hot!"

Sophie looked distractedly toward the mixing deck, and then she did a double take. *It can't be,* she thought at the same moment he looked up, pushing long black hair out of his face.

"Oh my god, that's Rive!"

"You *know* him?"

"Not very well…"

Ailsa shook her head with an ironic smile. "How do you do it?"

"Do what?"

"Attract nothing but beautiful men?"

"It's not like that," she said.

"If you say so."

"Honestly – I've only met him twice."

"Which is enough to be able to introduce me," Ailsa answered. "Come on."

Before Sophie could protest, Ailsa was dragging her toward Rive. He wasn't wearing his layers of clothes this time, but a washed-out London Calling tee shirt, black jeans and studded black boots. His arms were covered in intricate tattoos, shapes and symbols rather than words or pictures. Sophie had to admit Ailsa was right. She hadn't noticed when he'd been wearing all of the bulky layers, but now she saw that he had a model's body to go with the face – slender, but corded with muscle. He looked up from the deck as they approached, and for a moment Sophie could tell that he didn't recognize her. Then his eyes widened, and a strange, troubled look crossed his face.

"Sophie!" he said, leaning in so that she could hear him. "I didn't know you for a moment."

She glanced self-consciously at her clothes, and then back at him. "They're my friend's clothes."

"They're good," he said, but his look was equivocal.

"I didn't know you did this." She gestured to the sound system.

He shrugged. "Now and then."

Sophie was wondering what to say next, when Ailsa poked her in the back. "Ow! I mean, sorry…Rive, this is my friend Ailsa. Ailsa, Rive."

"Nice to meet you," he yelled, and then he began to cough.

"You too," Ailsa yelled back. Then, "Are you alright?"

He nodded, turning away until he stopped coughing. When he turned back, for a fleeting moment, there was a strange look on his face, almost as if he were in pain. The next moment, his expression was serene again and he was leaning in to speak

128

into Sophie's ear: "Listen, I'm off at the end of this set." So close, she could see that his cheeks were flushed, as if he'd been running hard. Heat radiated off of him, as well as something else – an invisible aura, crackling with energy. So she jumped when he spoke again: "Meet me in the Sanctum."

"What?" she yelped, as if she'd been stung.

Rive gave her a half-smile. "The VIP room."

"Oh," she said, feeling like an idiot.

"It's that way." He pointed to a low archway at the far side of the club, beside the bar, which led into a purple-lit corridor. Sophie nodded, and Rive smiled – a whole one this time, though it was tinged with something else, too. Regret, she would have said, if that had made any sense.

Sophie and Ailsa made their way slowly back across the dance floor to the place where Suri had left them. Ailsa said, "So, a hot DJ who hangs out in VIP rooms. How come you didn't tell us about him before?"

Sophie shrugged. "There's nothing to tell. I just seem to keep running into him." She knew that Ailsa wanted to talk more about Rive, but she hadn't seen any sign of Suri since she left them to investigate the Revenants, and it was beginning to worry her. "Can you see Suri anywhere?"

Ailsa stood up on tiptoe and peered out over the crowd. After a moment, she shook her head. "But she's so teeny, I don't know how I would. Anyway, I'm sure she's fine. She's probably just made ten new friends. Look, that's Rive finished. We'd better go."

Sophie looked at Ailsa, who looked toward the purple corridor with evident longing. "You go," she said, handing Ailsa her drink. She'd only had half of it, but she could already feel it going to her head. "I'll do a sweep for Suri, and then come find you."

"Oh no," Ailsa began, "I don't think – I mean, I'm really very shy…well, I am when it comes to gorgeous DJs – "

"Ailsa," she said firmly, "he's a decent guy, in his own snarky kind of way. You'll be fine."

"I'll be fine," Ailsa repeated. Then she knocked off the end of both drinks, ditched the glasses on a table, and moved toward the purple archway.

Sophie watched until she was out of sight, and then she turned back toward the corner where she'd seen the Revenants. There was no trace of them anymore – not that she'd expected any. As the new DJ began to spin a trip-hop track, the alternating colored lights switched to a blacklight that made Sophie's top and tights glow violet, and the rest of her disappear into shadow. She moved slowly around the perimeter of the crowd looking for Suri, but only halfheartedly. She knew that Ailsa was right: there had to be a hundred people on the dance floor alone. It would be impossible to pick Suri out of them.

She started back toward the purple corridor, telling herself that Suri was capable of looking after herself – more capable, at any rate, than Ailsa would be. She was passing by a row of three smaller arches, which led into a dimly lit alcove, when something made her stop. In the alcove, lit so dark a blue that it was almost swallowed in shadow, someone was moving. More than one – it was a couple, clenched in an embrace.

It was hardly an unusual scene for a nightclub, but something about the way they moved seemed off. Sophie took a step closer, squinting into the darkness. For a moment, the shadow of a hand reached up against the blue wall, the fingers grasping as a drowning man grasps at the surface of the water. Then the couple turned, so the woman's back was facing Sophie. Her blond hair was short and spiky, and her short, gold-spangled dress had a low-cut back, revealing the black symbol curling like a poison vine across her shoulder blades. She wore a metal cuff on each wrist, glinting dully in the dim light.

There was no time to think. Sophie leapt into the alcove, grabbed the angel's shoulders and wrenched her away from the man, noticing as she did so that her hands seemed to be glowing. But there was no time to think about it. The man stumbled back against the wall, his eyes terrified as he clutched at his throat, gasping for breath, and Sophie realized that she knew him.

"Angus?" she said, and then someone shoved her hard against the wall: the angel, her face ugly with fury, her dark mouth set in a snarl.

"You stupid little bitch," she hissed. "You'll pay for that!"

Sophie kicked at her with all of her strength, but the angel held on. She looked over the angel's shoulder at Angus, who was still standing there, though he no longer gasped for breath. "Run!" she cried, but he only shook his head dazedly, as if he didn't understand the word.

Now the angel was leaning toward Sophie, her mouth twisted into a smile. "Sophia, right? I've heard about you. Rest assured I feel privileged to finish what Azazel couldn't."

Sophie laughed. "You think that I'd willingly give you my soul?"

"I don't want your soul. I only want you dead."

"You don't want my soul?" Sophie repeated, trying to make sense of this.

The angel smiled. "The golden ticket back to Heaven? It's a faery tale. But the hit is real enough, and as long as I'm stuck here it helps pass the time. And him?" She jerked her chin in Angus's direction as her hands tightened around Sophie's throat. "He all but handed it to me on a platter."

Sophie's heart slammed in her chest as she struggled to breathe. But she also felt herself fill with furious hatred, and it became a kind of strength. The blue light in the alcove seemed to deepen and brighten at once. The edges of Sophie's vision shimmered like pavement on a hot day, but the angel remained solid in the center, like a target in a gun's sights. Sophie kicked out again. This time, when her boots connected with the angel's legs, they gave way. The angel fell backward, with Sophie on top of her.

Sophie moved as if she'd trained all her life for it, first kneeling on the angel's arms to pin them, then closing her hand over her throat. She pressed down, and the angel's eyes rolled back. Sophie was half-aware that Angus was still watching, and that he probably shouldn't be. She was also aware that the Revenants had come back, hovering on the periphery of the scene, watching with silent intensity. She was barely aware of them. The need in her to destroy the evil thing in her hands drove everything else to arm's distance.

She felt the angel's pulse beat hard against her fingers; she knew instinctively that it was almost finished. The next moment, there were hands on her shoulders, a voice screaming into her ear against the pounding music, "Sophie, let go! *Let her go!*"

Abruptly, the killing rage ebbed. Sophie fell back, gasping, into Suri's arms. Her strength had departed with her rage, leaving her a quivering mess. Suri put an arm firmly around her waist to steady her as the Revenants melted into the shadows.

"What are you doing here?" Suri demanded in an icy voice, and for a moment Sophie thought that she was speaking to her. Then she realized that the question was directed at the fallen angel, who was sitting up, gingerly touching her neck, her wary eyes fixed on them.

"She's no human!" the angel hissed, pointing a quivering finger at Sophie.

"Answer me, Berith," Suri said, putting herself in front of Sophie. She radiated a faint, silvery light. Tiny as she was, and despite the sequins and combat boots, Sophie had no trouble picturing her on a mountain top with a flaming sword.

Berith glared. "Clubbing – just like you."

"You know that's not what I mean!" Suri snapped. "Your territory is three hundred miles from here. What happened to your staves?"

Berith crossed her arms, flaunting the metal cuffs, and smirked.

"Tell me what happened to them," Suri said, "or I'll let her finish what she started." She nodded at Sophie, who was praying that it wouldn't come to that, as she didn't think she could raise a hand at that moment, let alone throttle a heavenly being.

Berith's smile flattened. "I don't know. They weakened, and then they shut down."

"How long ago?" Suri asked.

Berith shrugged.

"Ready, Sophie?"

"A couple of months," Berith said grudgingly. "Maybe three."

Suri took this in, her face inscrutable. At last she said, "Very well." Then, so quickly that Sophie hardly saw it, she took Berith's wrists in her hands. Berith's eyes widened in shock as her cuffs glowed with sudden white light.

"What have you done?" she asked, touching one with a finger and then pulling it back, as if it had burned her.

"What should never have been undone," Suri answered. "Start now, and you should get back to your bounds in one piece. But you'd better run."

Berith gave her a venomous look, and then she disappeared into the throng of bodies on the dance floor. Suri took a deep breath. As she let it out, her silvery nimbus faded and she looked once again like an ordinary girl. She turned to Angus. He'd dropped onto a stone bench set against the wall, his face ashen in the weird light.

"You alright?" Suri asked him.

"Oh, sure," he answered with a nauseous smile. "One minute this beautiful girl's chatting me up, the next she's sucking the life out of me, and the new girl from work is glowing blue and jumping her like some kung fu princess... yeah, it's all just an ordinary night out for me."

Sophie and Suri exchanged a glance.

"If either of you want to explain what just happened, now would be a good time," he added.

"Do you really want to know?" Suri asked him. "I could help you forget about it."

"You don't do mind wiping," Sophie reminded her.

"I don't do *involuntary* mind wiping. I mean, not unless I absolutely have to."

"Forget it," Angus said, standing up. "No one is wiping anything." He moved toward the archway, only to find Suri in front of him, her arms crossed on her chest and her face determined.

"If you don't want to forget," she said, "then we need to explain."

"I'm not so sure I want to hear it."

"Not an option. You either know the whole truth, or none of it. And believe me, if you couldn't run away from Berith, you have no hope of getting away from me."

Angus looked from one girl to the other, and then he sighed, holding up his hands. "Okay. But let's get out of here. Go somewhere where we don't have to yell."

"Deal." She turned to Sophie. "Let's get Ailsa."

"Who?" Angus asked warily.

"Don't worry," Suri said, patting his shoulder. "Ailsa is entirely human."

Chapter 10

"VIP room at the Lux," Suri mused as they walked down the purple hallway, where the music was quieter. "What did you say this DJ's name is?"

"Rive," Sophie answered.

"Hm. Haven't heard of him."

"I don't think that's his real name."

"No kidding," Suri said, and then, "Is that it?" She pointed to an iron-studded wooden door at the end of the corridor, with an angel in flight stenciled on it. Sophie shrugged, Suri knocked, and the door opened inward.

For a moment, Sophie forgot about the fight, and her freakish combat skills, and even Angus's brooding presence, as she took in the fabulously bizarre scene beyond the door. Underneath the furnishings, the room seemed to be a stone vault much like the main part of the club. However, the stark space had been transformed into a gothic fever-dream in gold and purple. The walls were draped with velvet and tapestries, the furniture was all dark, heavy antiques, the light came from flaming wall sconces and an elaborate chandelier full of real, damson-colored candles, dripping wax decadently onto the Persian carpet below.

The people who filled the room were equally strange. As Sophie scanned the crowd for Ailsa, she saw the girl with the black eyes and green hair, draped across a boy who grinned at her, showing canine teeth as long as a dog's. Another boy, this one with glittering blue skin, was deep in conversation with a dark-haired, green-eyed girl who bore more than a passing resemblance to the seal-girl from Sophie's dream of Ker-Ys. The girl saw her, smiled and waved, and then disappeared. Sophie blinked, then looked away, feeling queasy. But it didn't help. Every person in the room seemed to have some feature that was distinctly inhuman, and they shifted and blended like figures in a magic lantern.

"Don't you know anyone normal?" Angus asked Sophie, destroying any possibility of convincing herself that the fight had left her delusional.

"Yeah," Sophie said, "you." He gave her a black look. "Well," she relented, "Ailsa's fairly normal, too." She pointed toward a gilded sofa where Ailsa and Rive sat passing a bottle of champagne between them. "And Rive's standard-issue for an art student-slash-DJ. Come on." She pushed through the crowd toward them, Angus and Suri following.

Rive looked Sophie up and down when she stopped in front

of him, raising his eyebrows at her disheveled appearance. "Don't tell me – a tidal wave?"

"Crowd surfing," Angus said.

"Networking," Suri said simultaneously. They glared at each other.

"A minor mishap," Sophie said firmly, as Rive began to protest. "Honestly, I'm fine." To change the subject, she gestured to the room and added, "I thought you didn't know anybody in Edinburgh."

Rive shrugged. "I met a few people last week."

"A few?"

He shrugged again.

"I thought you two had ditched me," Ailsa said, though she didn't seem particularly upset by the fact.

"Sorry," Suri told her, "it took us a while to find each other, and then I saw someone I used to know, and Sophie saw Angus – " she gestured to him.

"From work," Sophie explained.

"Hi," Angus said with a wan smile.

"And one thing led to another, and have you got any more champagne?"

Ailsa's eyes were wide now with curiosity as she passed Suri the bottle, but she'd clearly got the message not to ask any more in front of Rive. "Sophie? Angus?" she asked, pulling another bottle from an ice bucket.

"No, thanks," Sophie said. She was suddenly exhausted,

too tired even to keep up the pretense of having fun, and the spots at the edges of her vision signaled an approaching headache. "We came to tell you we're going home. I've got work tomorrow, and I'm getting a headache."

"A headache?" Rive repeated, giving her a probing look.

"Yeah...migraines, I've always had them...a couple of tablets and I'll be fine."

Rive looked like he wanted to say more, but Suri handed him the champagne bottle and stood up, saying, "Always the sensible one, Sophie." She gave Ailsa a pointed look, and reluctantly, Ailsa stood too.

"You sure you can't stay?" Rive asked, though it was hard to tell from his tone whether he wanted them to, or was only issuing a formality.

"Yes," Suri said firmly. "Nice to meet you, Rive."

"You too," he said, and smiled at them all. To Sophie, it looked forced, and his eyes kept creeping back to her, as if he were trying to figure something out. "I guess I'll see you around."

That seems to be the pattern, Sophie thought, forcing a smile of her own.

*

"How did you say you met that guy?" Suri demanded as soon as they were out on the street.

"Rive?" Sophie said. "I don't know…I seem to run into him everywhere. Why?"

Suri frowned, her eyes distant as she turned into the Cowgate. "There's something weird about him."

"Yes," Ailsa said dryly, "he's a hot guy who I was actually successfully chatting up, and now I'll probably never see him again."

"I wouldn't be so sure of that," Sophie muttered, rubbing her head where it had begun to ache.

Suri watched her with keen eyes. "You were serious about the headache?"

"Unfortunately," Sophie answered, rifling through her pockets for tablets before she remembered the jacket wasn't hers.

"You get them often?"

"Often enough. Anyone got paracetamol?"

"Come here," Suri said, holding out her arms.

"Um…why?" Sophie asked dubiously.

Suri rolled her eyes. "Just do it!"

Sophie stepped forward. Suri put a hand on either side of her face, reached up, and kissed her on the forehead. Immediately, the pain and the spangles vanished. "How did you do that?"

Suri smiled. "Trick of the trade."

"Kind of like glowing?" Angus said pointedly. "And taking down super-powered homicidal women single-handed?"

Ailsa's petulant look turned to one of interest. "Oooh – what did I miss?"

"My question exactly," Angus said.

The girls looked at each other, and then Suri flashed him a dazzling smile. "So, Angus, do you believe in angels?"

*

An hour later, the girls were onto their second pot of watery coffee at a bolt-hole pub behind the High Street, Angus was on his third whisky, and he knew most of what he needed to know to follow Suri's description of what had happened with Berith.

"So that woman was a fallen angel trying to suck out my soul to get back to Heaven?" Angus said, in what Sophie considered a remarkably calm voice.

"Actually, I think she was just trying to get high," Suri said consolingly.

"Right…that's so much less disturbing…"

"But what happened to Berith's staves?" Sophie asked.

"I don't know," Suri answered, turning her coffee cup pensively in its saucer. "And she was telling the truth, so she doesn't know either. Maybe they just malfunctioned for some reason…although that's never happened before."

"I hear another 'or' in there," Sophie said.

"Or," Suri answered, "it might mean that something else is going down in the grand scheme. Something bigger than staves and fallen angels."

"There's something bigger than staves and angels?" Angus asked, looking peaked again.

Suri gave him a pitying look. "I'm afraid so."

"Like what?" Ailsa asked.

"I don't know," Suri sighed. "But it's not the only strange thing that's happened lately. I mean, Michael trying to off Lucifer…then Lucifer in the clutches of an evil demon mermaid thing…hell, even Sophie deciding to come down here after all this time – "

"But the *Book of Sorrows* explained that," Sophie interrupted. "I came to give Lucas my soul, so he could go back to Heaven."

"Maybe…" Suri answered speculatively.

"It was plain as day, Suri. Get Lucifer back to Heaven, or kiss the Balance good-bye."

"That's assuming you – I mean aeon-you – knew what you were talking about."

After everything she'd been through, that riled Sophie. "Why else would I have dictated a book with those specific instructions?"

"Maybe you only *thought* you knew what you were talking about."

"What's the difference?" Sophie asked dejectedly. "Either way, I failed spectacularly to get Lucas back to Heaven."

For a few moments, they were all silent. Then Suri pinned

Sophie with sharp black eyes and said, "So, changing the subject: why didn't you tell us you still have the mojo?"

"Mojo?"

"You know – the power to smite angels and all that."

"Because I didn't know I had it," Sophie said. Suri raised an eyebrow. "Okay, I sort of knew. Something like that happened once before – in Ardnasheen, when the *Cait Sìth* attacked me. Everything went blue, and suddenly I was stronger…and I summoned Carnwennan."

"Carn what?" Angus asked.

"A legendary Iron Age dagger."

"That once belonged to King Arthur," Suri added.

"King Arthur?" Angus repeated incredulously.

"I can still wipe you, if you want," Suri offered brightly.

"Don't let her do it," Ailsa told him. "The hangover's a kicker."

To Sophie's surprise, Angus smiled – his first real smile since the attack. "Don't worry – I'd never let her wipe me. Not now."

"You mean you're okay with all of this?" Sophie asked.

He shrugged, but his eyes were bright, almost gleeful. "All my life I've loved old things, because they're a link to a time that's gone forever. Now I'm sitting at a table with a bloody *eternal being!* The only thing better would be a tardis." His eyes settled hopefully on Suri. "I don't suppose – "

"Nope," she interrupted. "No such thing as tardises and

Time Lords…no Jedis, no Superman, no Tooth Fairy…should I go on?"

"No, I get it," Angus sighed. "Fiction's fiction and this is… well, whatever it is. And yes, I'm alright with it. So what now?"

"What do you mean?" Sophie asked.

"I mean, your friend's been incarcerated by a sea witch, evil angels are on the loose stealing souls, and you might or might not have a stalker, species still undetermined."

"Rive's not a stalker," Ailsa interrupted, "or an undetermined species." All at once, she blanched. "Unless – " she gripped Suri's arm. "Please tell me he's not an angel."

Suri shook her head. "Definitely not."

"How do you know?" Angus asked.

"Because we have the Heavenly Host equivalent of gaydar – we can mark each other at a hundred paces. But," she said sternly, as Ailsa breathed a sigh of relief, "just because he isn't an angel, doesn't mean he's what he seems to be."

"Are there *any* normal people in my life anymore?" Ailsa grumbled.

"Sophie says I'm normal," Angus told her.

"No offense," she answered, "but Sophie's greatest talent is attracting freaks of nature."

Angus shrugged, sipped from his glass.

"So you really want to help us?" Sophie asked.

"Do you honestly think I could just go back to my archaeology texts after what happened tonight?" He shook his head. "Maybe all of this is normal for you, but for me, it changes everything."

"It's not normal," Suri said. "And it *does* change everything."

"Because it means the fallen can move around outside their staves?" Sophie asked.

"That," Suri said dryly, "and the fact that you almost killed one of them."

Recalling the feel of the angel's slowing pulse, Sophie swallowed hard. "She was trying to take Angus's soul," she said.

"I'm not saying you should have done different – although I'm glad we don't have a dead angel to clean up. I'm only saying, no one just trounces on an angel like that. Not even a fallen one. Other angels included. Never mind summoning Carnwennan."

"So…what does it mean that I did those things?"

"It means you aren't as human as we thought. Some part of you is still aeon. Maybe a big part."

Sophie felt ill. "And what does *that* mean?"

Suri shrugged. "Damned if I know."

"Suri!"

"Honey, I know, like, this much about aeons." She demonstrated a miniscule amount with her thumb and forefinger. "And all of that is hearsay. They just don't mix with angels."

146

"I did."

"Yeah, but most of the time you were all over Lucifer."

"Too much information," Sophie said, putting her hands to her flushing cheeks.

"It's true, though. Your superpowers didn't really see much action when you were in Heaven. Unless you were using them on him, you know, to make things more – "

"Suri!"

Suri couldn't contain a smirk. "The good news is, this self-same mojo might help us get Lucas back."

"Yeah – if I knew how to control it," Sophie said dejectedly. "Or even what makes it kick in in the first place."

"Then the first thing we have to do is find out," Angus said.

"We?"

"You saved my life, Sophie," he said, his dark eyes earnest. "I could never repay you for that. But even if you hadn't, you're my friend. You don't think I'd leave you to sort this out on your own? And I assume I speak for all of us." He looked around the table.

"Of course," Ailsa said, reaching for Sophie's hand and squeezing it.

"I live to serve," Suri added, taking her other one.

"So where do we begin?" Angus asked.

"Tomorrow," Suri said. "You all need some sleep."

CHAPTER 11

She sat high in the tree in Suriel's cemetery. Today it was an oak, its branches bare except for a faint dusting of snow. The sky above was a clear, crystalline blue. Despite the wintery scene, she wasn't cold. As in the Garden, the air in Heaven was always the same, perfect temperature. And that made her sad. It was another reminder that though Heaven could emulate the trappings of Earth and its people, it was all just a façade. It made her feel farther away than ever.

It was one of the reasons she came to the cemetery. Of course she also came for Suriel, who could always make her laugh, and who, along with Lucifer, was the closest thing to a friend she had here. But she was also compelled by the shades who passed through on their way to their ultimate fate. They were a far cry from living humans, these newly dead: shadow-grey, and more often than not, still confusedly clinging to the lives they'd left. But there was no falseness to them. There

148

couldn't be in their raw state. They were vulnerable as newly-hatched butterflies. Their eyes poured truth like burst dams.

The other reason she came was why she was now sitting in the tree. She'd found that sometimes, if she was very still and watched very carefully, she could catch images of what was happening in the living human world, on the margins of Suri's land of the dead. It seemed to happen only at times of great emotion, so it was a double-edged sword. For every birth of a prophet, there were a hundred wars or plagues or disasters. Still, any glimpse was better than nothing.

"Sophia!" someone called from below.

She looked down, and saw Lucifer's golden-brown face tipped up. Her breath skipped, and she felt herself smiling before she realized it. Since the day he had given her the tear-bottle, he had visited her frequently. They talked, or read the books he brought. He taught her the rudiments of some of the instruments he played. He always watched her carefully for signs that she was tiring of his presence, but the truth was, she relied on it more the more she got to know him.

This didn't bother her until the day she watched him reading aloud from a book of Sanskrit poetry, and realized that she hadn't heard a word of it: she'd been too busy wondering if his hair would feel as silky as it looked. Her face had burned then, like the humans' did when they were self-conscious. She didn't know why. As far as she knew, there was no reason for her not to wonder such a thing. In fact, there was no reason not to try it. Such little shows of affection – of possession – had been common among the consorts in the Garden. But it wasn't something she had ever done with her own consort, Theletos. It wasn't something she'd ever felt like doing. Besides, angels didn't form pairs as the aeons did. She knew that. It was absurd to think of Lucifer that way at all.

And yet, after that realization, she found she was hyper-aware of him: the way he moved and spoke and looked at her. The way he was meticulously careful not to touch her. She told herself to ignore her growing desire to touch him, and it would go away. There was nothing but grief to be found in feeling something he couldn't reciprocate.

Now, though, watching him climb the tree with a bag slung over his back, she couldn't stem the flood of feeling. She tried to make herself concentrate on what he was saying. "...brought you something." He settled into a crook of a branch beside her, unslung the bag from his back and held it to her. Whatever was inside it was small, but heavy. She reached in, and brought out a circle of glass, bound with silver filigree. A mirror.

"It's beautiful," she said softly, cupping it in her hands. "Where did you get it?" From the way he flushed and looked away, she knew the answer: Earth. "It's alright," she said, and it was. "These things...they don't hurt me anymore. Not the way that they did. I still long for it, but..." She shrugged, uncertain how to put into words how the deep, dull ache had

150

become a part of her; something she could live alongside of almost comfortably.

Lucifer looked up with a gentle smile. "That's good, because it's not an ordinary mirror. It's a scrying-glass."

She thought about the word. She didn't know it, but still it conjured images of people in an ancient, brutal era of the world, huddled together, deep in secret conversation. Images of Azazel and the other fallen, peering over their shoulders, whispering into their ears. "I...don't know if I should have this."

"It's alright," Lucifer said. "It was made by a priestess who worships the Garden. There's no witchcraft in it. No more than there is in whatever you see over there." He pointed to the horizon, where she could just make out a shadowy battle raging.

"How did you know?" she asked, startled. "I didn't think the angels could see it."

"We can't," he answered. "But Suriel saw you watching, and she guessed. The aeons are meant to be omniscient, so I guess it's no wonder that you can see a little bit of the human world, even from here. But..." He paused, looking up at her as if he couldn't decide whether to finish the thought, or not. "But," he continued at last, "it seems to me that whatever you see out there doesn't make you happy."

"Not usually," she agreed.

"Well...that's why I got you this. It's warded against dark visions."

She couldn't help it: she was intrigued. "How does it work?" she asked.

"You just look into it. Ask it for what you want to see."

She tipped the glass upward, and said, "Human happiness."

At first, nothing happened. Then the bright circle dimmed and flickered with yellow light. A fire. Around it, people were dancing in a ring, tiny children to the oldest grandparents. On the sidelines, men with drums between their knees beat the rhythm they moved to. Although she couldn't hear it, she could almost feel it, watching their movements. She smiled.

"It works, then?" Lucifer asked her.

"Yes," she said, clasping the mirror to her breast. "Thank you. You have no idea…"

But all at once, looking at his delighted smile, words weren't enough. She reached across the space between them, and put her fingers on his hand. His warmth rushed into her, as it had the last time their fingers touched. It was sweet, but sweeter still was when he spread his own fingers, laced them with hers, and then clasped them together.

Sophia looked at their joined hands for a long moment. Lucas's golden fingers plaited with her white ones. It was like nothing she'd ever imagined, but at the same time it seemed fundamental, and right, as if all of her life, she'd been seeking this moment. Finally, she looked up at him.

"Thank you," she said softly.
"You're welcome," he said.

*

When Sophie awakened, she lay for a long moment thinking about the dream. For the first time since she'd started dreaming of her time in Heaven with Lucas, she didn't feel sad to find that it was only a memory. Instead, she was grateful for it.

She slipped out of bed and dressed as quietly as she could, then stepped over Ailsa, who was still cocooned in her sleeping bag, and into the hallway. There was no sign of Suri, but she wasn't surprised by that. When they'd arrived home the night before, Suri had said she needed to meditate, and slipped back off into the night. Sophie could only assume that she'd reappear later, hopefully with some ideas for a way forward.

Sophie wanted to walk to work, to do some thinking of her own. She'd grabbed her jacket and bag and almost reached the door, when her mother called from the kitchen, "Love, is that you?"

Crap. She knew that her mother would want to talk about her night out and, as usual, she wouldn't be able to lie about it. She would have to come up with some very creative wording. She took a deep breath before she entered the kitchen, and then plastered on a cheery smile.

"Morning, Mum," she said. "You're up early."

Anna shrugged, sipping from a mug of tea. "I wanted to get in some work this morning. I've got that tutors' exhibition coming up."

"Right…how's that going?" Sophie tried to sound interested.

"Fine. Well, mostly fine…"

"Great. Look, Mum, I've got to get moving, they're expecting me at the café – "

"Of course! I just wanted to make sure you had fun last night."

"I…" Sophie sifted for the right words. "It was nice to see the girls," she said at last. It was the only innocuous truth she could think of.

Anna smiled encouragingly. "I'm glad to hear it. You tell your friends they can stay as long as they like."

"I will," Sophie said, "but I'm sure they'll have to go soon. Ruadhri will be going mad without help." And then, because her mother looked set to say something else, Sophie backed toward the door. "Sorry Mum, I've really got to go."

"Alright, love," Anna said, searching her face – for what, Sophie didn't really want to know. "Have a lovely day."

"Thanks," Sophie said, as she bolted for the door.

Outside it was grey, but dry. Sophie set off down the road, determined to come up with a plan of action, but for some reason her thoughts kept turning to Rive. Suri's reaction to him had touched a nerve. Whatever excuses he made, it *was* strange

154

the way he kept showing up in her life, almost as if he knew what she was going to do before she did it. But at the same time, she didn't feel threatened by him. If anything, she felt a vague warmth when she thought of him; also, a niggling sense that there was something about him that she was missing.

Aeon powers, she reminded herself firmly. That was the most important matter at hand: figuring out what she was capable of. Suri had made it clear that even sacred weapons wouldn't help in a fight against Dahud. But now Sophie knew that she had something hidden within herself that might, and she had to learn to use it.

Of course, it was easier said than done. If there were books that would help her she had no idea where to find them, and Suri, who knew more about what was going on than any of them, had been clear that she couldn't help with aeon powers. Maybe it would be a matter of trial and error – but then how would that work? Sophie couldn't very well go about looking for fallen angels to pick fights with. Maybe, she thought, Suri could be a kind of sparring partner…she rejected the thought almost as it formed. She could no more attack Suri than she could her mother or Ailsa, and besides, the one thing she did know about her abilities was that they made themselves known when she was least expecting it.

Google search it is, then.

*

Angus wasn't on that morning, and though Sophie appreciated his show of solidarity the previous night, she was glad not to have face him yet. More to the point, she didn't want anyone leaning over her shoulder when she typed "aeon powers" into one of Brewed Awakening's computers. When she finally found a moment to do it, and saw the pages of links that came up, her heart leapt with excitement that promptly shriveled and died when she began to read them. All but one of them were links to wargame wikis and blogs. The one that wasn't, was only a link to an online dictionary. She followed it anyway and read:

aeon *esp US*, **eon** [ˈiːən ˈiːɒn] *n*

1. an immeasurably long period of time; age

2. (Astronomy) a period of one thousand million years

3. (Theology) *Gnosticism* one of the powers emanating from the supreme being and culminating in the demiurge

Sophie remembered Lucas mentioning Gnosticism, but that was the most she knew about it. She typed it into the dictionary's search box. "A religious movement," she read, "characterized by a belief in gnosis, through which the spiritual element in man could be released from its bondage in matter: regarded as a heresy by the Christian Church."

Before she could begin to disentangle that, she heard voices and the thud of boots on the stairs, and then a peal of bell-like laughter. *So much for quiet contemplation,* she thought, and turned to the door just as Suri burst into the room, followed by Ailsa and Angus. They carried steaming mugs and a breath of cold outdoor air, tinged with the angels' incense smell. Despite the interruption, Sophie was glad to see them.

"How did you find me?" she asked the girls.

"Your mom told us where you worked," Suri answered, handing one of the mugs to Sophie.

"And Matrika told us you were up here on break," Ailsa said.

"And my shift doesn't officially start for another fifteen minutes," Angus said.

"Which makes this perfect timing." Suri unslung her messenger bag and dropped it with her black puffy jacket in a heap on the floor. Then she settled into a chair beside Sophie, blowing on her coffee.

"Do you actually understand that?" Ailsa asked, indicating the computer screen as she sat down on Sophie's other side.

Sophie smiled and sipped from her latte. "It's about as clear as this," she said, tapping the cup.

Suri narrowed her eyes and scanned the screen, and then made a face. "That's what you get for reading philosophy. Especially religious philosophy. Besides, do you really think you're going to find a list of your superpowers on the internet?"

"Do you have a better idea?"

"I think we should start with material evidence."

"What?" Sophie asked.

In answer, Suri opened her bag and held it toward Sophie. Angus leaned forward to look in, too. There, amidst the hair bobbles and glittering cosmetic tubes, was Carnwennan, bright as an icicle. Quickly Sophie pushed the bag away, glancing at the group of kids behind them on the sofas.

"Come on," she said, getting up.

"Where?" Ailsa asked.

"Upstairs."

They followed her up the narrow stairway to the Eyrie, where Sophie whirled on them. "Are you mad?" she asked Suri. "You can get done here for carrying a weapon!"

"That's what I told her," Ailsa said.

"That knife looked Bronze Age," Angus said speculatively. "Did you steal it?"

Suri waved their protests aside. "Angels don't get done. Or steal. The point is, I needed it."

"What for?" Sophie asked.

"To prove what I'm about to show you."

Sophie gave Ailsa a questioning look, but she shrugged and said, "Suri wouldn't tell me anything till we got here."

Suri sat down on one of the chairs and opened her bag again, while the others gathered around her. First she brought out the dagger and laid it on the table. Then she took out a piece of paper and handed it to Sophie, with a look of barely-contained excitement. Sophie looked at the page. It was a computer printout of a picture of the same knife, resting on a stand in a velvet-lined display case.

"Okay," Sophie said, "what am I supposed to be getting from this?"

Suri rolled her eyes, then took the picture back and laid it next to the knife. "Here," she said, pointing to the left side of the blade, "it's perfect, right?"

"I guess so."

"Now look at this." She indicated the same part of the blade on the printout. Sophie looked at it again. This time she saw what she hadn't before: a tiny nick in the otherwise smooth line, half way between the hilt and tip. "Do you see now?" Suri asked, nearly wriggling with excitement.

"The blade's been damaged," Angus said.

Suri nodded. "During Arthur's fight with Accolon, after the fake Excalibur broke."

"You're joking," Angus said.

"Angels don't joke, either," Suri said primly. Then, catching Ailsa's and Sophie's looks, she said, "At least not about things like this!"

"So they aren't the same knife," Sophie said, indicating the printout and the actual dagger.

"I called the British Museum just to be sure."

"No missing dagger?"

"Nope. Carnwennan is in its case, safe and sound."

"Okay…so I summoned a different knife?"

159

"You didn't summon *anything*, Sophie. You *made* this. Created it. Like, out of thin air."

"So that's a big deal, then?"

Suri shook her head in disgust. "Yes, it's a big deal! Sophie, until I looked at these," she indicated the knife and the printout, "I thought that only the Keeper and the syzygies could create matter."

"The Keeper?" Angus asked.

"Syzygies?" Sophie said, wondering why the word sounded familiar.

"Good lord, you two are hopeless," Suri sighed. She took a sip from her cup, and then said, "Okay, so, in the beginning – "

"Ooh, I know this bit!" Ailsa interrupted. "God created the Heavens and the Earth."

"Wrong. Forget Monty Python or Sunday School or whatever gave you your ideas about religion. God didn't part the darkness and make Adam and Eve out of mud pies. There isn't anyone called God at all – there's only The Keeper."

"What does he keep?" Angus asked.

"The Balance," Sophie answered. "Between good and evil. And he's not a he, he's an it." Suri raised her eyebrows, and Sophie explained, "Lucas told me a bit – but that's about it."

"Okay," Suri said. "So, before there was anything else, there were two opposing forces – what humans call good and evil. There was also the Keeper, who stood between them and kept them in balance. Then the Keeper made the first two aeons."

"Why?" Angus asked.

Suri shrugged. "That's anyone's guess."

"How?" Sophie asked.

"By considering its own nature, and naming two of its parts."

"Seriously?" Angus asked.

Suri shrugged. "That's what I've been told – remember that it happened way before I existed. Anyway, those two aeons were the first syzygy."

"Again, the vocabulary word," Ailsa said.

"It means a bound pair of spiritual consorts."

"So they were hooking up?"

Suri rolled her eyes. "Okay, sure, they were hooking up – or whatever passes for that when you have no physical substance. Anyway, those two aeons had their own thoughts, and their thoughts joined up to make the next syzygy, and so on until there were fifteen pairs."

"So…you're saying I used to have a spiritual consort?" Sophie asked.

"If you were an aeon, then you had to."

"Who was he? And what happened to him when Lucas and I got together?"

Suri only shook her head. "You never talked about him when you were in Heaven."

"And you didn't ask?"

"I didn't know about him," Suri answered. "I didn't even know there *were* such things as syzygies. None of us did – unless you told Lucifer. We weren't told about the aeons' history until after he fell, and you went back to the Garden, and even then they only told us what they thought was enough to prevent something like it from happening again."

Sophie considered this, trying to connect herself to these strange ideas, but she couldn't. She had no memories of a past life that didn't involve Lucas, and few enough of those. As far as she was concerned, he was her other half. She couldn't imagine anything else. In contrast to all of the other bizarre things she'd learned in the last few months, what Suri was telling them seemed fantastical – impossible.

"Anyway," Suri said after a moment, "your ex isn't the point here. What matters is that aeons aren't meant to be able to create stuff outside of their syzygies. Only the Keeper is meant to create on its own."

"But I did it," Sophie said, touching the tip of the knife.

"You did it," Suri agreed. "I'd call that a superpower, wouldn't you?"

"I might," Sophie answered, "if I knew *how* I'd done it… and if I could do it again."

"Which is just what we need to find out." Suri reached into her bag again, and brought out a red netbook Sophie was certain hadn't been there when she looked a few minutes before. Opening it, Suri brought up a word processing program and typed "Sophie's Superpowers" into a blank document. She began a bulleted list with "Generates Matter". "So, any thoughts on how it works?"

"Not really," Sophie said. "It just sort of – happened. I mean, one moment this huge cat demon was getting ready to rip Ailsa's throat out, and the next I had Carnwennan – or Carnwennan 2.0 – in my hands, and I was kneeling on a dead monster, and there was demon blood everywhere."

Underneath "Generates Matter" Suri typed "Life-or-death situation".

"But if it was only that, then why didn't I summon – I mean generate – something all those times I saw Revenants?"

"Maybe because they weren't trying to kill you?"

"But *I* didn't know that."

They all considered this. Then Angus said, "Maybe it's not just what you believe, but what's actually true. I mean, as I understand it, you were never really in danger from the Revenants. Maybe the Balance, or the Keeper, or the other half of your syzygy, or whoever it is holding the reins sort of… vetoed your request."

"Is that possible?" Sophie asked Suri.

Suri shrugged. "Like I told you, I know almost nothing about aeons, and even less about the Keeper."

But Sophie had thought of something even more disturbing. "What about when Lucas and I were fighting Sam? That was a real enough threat. I even started to glow, I think – but the strength bit, the knowing how to fight – that never happened."

"So…?"

"So, why couldn't I do it when…I mean, why couldn't I…" She stumbled, unable to make herself speak the question that had haunted her since that night: *Why couldn't I save him?*

"There's obviously more to it than just being in danger," Ailsa said gently.

They were all silent for a few moments. Then Suri said, "Okay, so, what other things can you do?"

"She can glow," Angus suggested.

"All Heavenly beings can glow," Suri said. "Demonic ones can too. I'd call it more of a side effect than an actual power."

"Alright, then," Ailsa said, "how about, when she glows, she goes all Sophie the Vampire Slayer."

"Good one," Suri said, and typed in "Strength, Agility, Quick Reaction Time".

"I'm a Revenant magnet," Sophie suggested.

"How is that a power?" Ailsa asked.

"It's always good to have faithful minions," Suri said. "Even if they are only the walking dead." She typed in "Revenant Whisperer". "Anything else?"

Sophie thought about it. "I don't think so." She considered the list. "That isn't really very impressive, is it."

"Are you kidding?" Angus said.

"I mean, it doesn't exactly scream 'Way to defeat sea witch and bring back boyfriend'."

They all looked at the screen for a few more moments, and then Suri said, "We can figure this out; I know we can. But not in one afternoon."

"So you're going?" Sophie asked, and she was surprised by how this saddened her, when a few days earlier she'd have done anything to avoid even speaking to Ailsa on the phone.

"We promised Ruadhri," Ailsa said. "It was the only way he'd let us come at all."

Suri gave Sophie an incisive look, and then she said, "You'll just have to come with us."

Sophie was shaking her head before Suri had even finished speaking. "Not going to happen. Mum barely lets me out of her sight since Sam almost killed me. She'd go apoplectic if I said I was going back to Ardnasheen."

"You're going to have to come, sooner or later," Suri said. "I mean, I'm assuming that's how we get to Dahud's city."

"I know," Sophie sighed, "but I need some time to think of a way to convince her."

"I'll think of something," Suri said speculatively. "In the meantime, we need a plan of action." She opened a new document on the computer and headed it, "Plan of Action". Under the first bullet she wrote, "Get Sophie to Ardnasheen".

"What about me?" Angus asked.

Sophie looked at him in surprise. "You don't have to do that."

"I know I don't," he said with a steady look, which she found she couldn't meet for very long.

"What else?" Ailsa asked, when the silence grew too long.

"What you were just saying, about Dahud's city," Angus said. "I mean, do we actually know we can get there from Ardnasheen?"

"Lucas did it," Sophie said softly.

"I don't think we want to follow his route," Ailsa said.

Suri nodded and typed, "How to get to Ker-Ys?"

"And what *about* the evil mermaid, anyway?" Ailsa continued. "I mean, don't we need to find out how to kill her or disable her or whatever?"

"Ideally," Suri answered. "But there doesn't seem to be much current information on her. I mean, how often had you heard of Dahud before all of this?"

There was another long silence. Then Sophie thought of something. "Actually, I know someone who had."

"Really? Who?"

"An old lady called Morag. I met her in the Hermitage, the day I went to try to see Dahud in the stream. I met her when I was coming home. I was really upset…she made me tea. She seemed to know a lot about faeries, and also some things about Dahud."

"Why didn't you tell us about her before?" Suri cried.

"There've been one or two things going on since you showed up," Sophie answered dryly.

"Okay," Suri said, typing "Sophie's old lady". "I guess you'll have to talk to her yourself – but you better report back right after!"

Sophie nodded. "It would also help to know what's going on with the staves," she said.

"Well," Suri said, "I can check out the ones in Ardnasheen, but as far as we know, those haven't failed. And I don't really want to go traipsing around the country looking for broken staves when all of this is going on."

"Do you want me to look for more rogue angels here in Edinburgh?" Sophie asked.

"Definitely not!"

"Then how will we find out what's happening?" Ailsa asked.

Suri stared out the window with a considering look. Then she nodded to herself and said, "We need to ask Michael about it."

"Are you mad?" Sophie cried. "After finding out he tried to get Lucas killed?"

"I know it's not cool, Sophie, but you can't take it personally."

"Not take it personally!"

"I told you, Michael's hard line. That means he'd do anything to get you back to the Garden; but it also means he's more likely than any of us to know what's going on with the fallen. And if he knows, he's more likely to tell you than me. He and I were never that tight, and remember, I'm not really supposed to be here."

"I can't talk to him, Suri," Sophie said stubbornly. "I won't."

"Fine," Suri said, sighing, and typed in "Suri: find Michael and Question re Staves." "But you can't get off that easy. If you won't talk to Michael, you need to talk to Rive."

"Rive?" Sophie asked, surprised.

"I could be wrong, but I have a feeling he's got a part to play in all of this. Maybe you can find out what it is."

"Okay," Sophie sighed, "I'll see what I can find out. But don't expect much. I don't even have the guy's phone number."

There was another long pause. "So, is that us?" Angus asked.

"I guess it is," Sophie said, wishing that the lists weren't so pitifully short.

CHAPTER 12

"I can't believe you're already going," Sophie said. She'd left work early to go with Suri and Ailsa to the train station.

"You can still come with us," Ailsa said.

"Jump the train and call your mom when you're too far away for her to do anything about it," Suri added.

"For an angel," Sophie said, "you are a very bad influence!"

Suri grinned, but Sophie was looking wistfully at the train, already filling with passengers. It was tempting to follow Suri's advice, if only to be that much nearer to Lucas. But of course, she reminded herself, it might not be nearer to him at all. She had no idea where Ker-Ys was – only that he had got there from Ardnasheen via water horse, which was a route she had no intention of following. Besides, there were things she needed to do in Edinburgh before she went back there.

Sophie hugged Ailsa, and then Suri. "I'll get there, don't worry. But we have plenty to do in the meantime. Promise to phone if you find anything out?"

"I've got you on speed-dial," Suri said. "And the same goes for you."

"Of course." The train's engines began to thrum, and it let out a whistle. "Safe journey," she said, as her friends climbed on board. A few minutes later it was pulling out of the station, Ailsa waving madly and Suri blowing kisses until they were out of sight.

Sophie turned away from the empty track. The girls' leaving had unsettled her, making her feel sadder and lonelier than she had in a long time. More than that. Bereft was the word that came to mind – cold and empty and only half-real, as if the people streaming by on either side of her couldn't see her at all.

Get a grip, she told herself. She needed to walk – to clear her head, before her mother's inevitable barrage of questions. She climbed the stairway to the overpass that let out at the bottom of the Mound, but once outside on the street, she paused again. It was cold and dark, the warren of little streets and closes leading up to the old town choked with shadows. To her right, the lights of the winter fair in Princes Street Garden shone brightly, the big wheel a gaudy windmill against the dark. That world of cheer and warmth and happy children beckoned to her, however false it might be.

Sophie turned, and began to walk. At the gate she let herself be swept into a crowd of teenagers with ice-skates slung over their shoulders. She followed them for a while, half-listening to

170

their happy banter, but she left them when they joined the queue for the ice rink. She wandered among children's fairground rides and stalls selling candyfloss and hot chocolate and mulled wine, soothed by the happy anticipation of the crowd, by their mundane chatter.

Feeling slightly better, Sophie set out for the far side of the gardens. She walked toward the open-air theatre, the unofficial boundary of the fair. As she rounded the bandstand she was alone again, the light and noise of the fairground suddenly distant. Sophie pulled her scarf tighter, and wrapped her arms around herself.

A train rumbled out of Waverly as she stepped onto the bridge over the tracks, its rumble fading away into the night. Sophie was alone on the bridge, but in the abrupt silence of the train's wake, she heard voices – two men, arguing. By the sound of it, they were underneath the bridge. Sophie quickened her pace, focusing on the light and activity of the car park on Kings Stables Road. But then she heard something that stopped her cold.

"That doesn't explain why you're still here," one of the voices said. It was a male voice, but not just that. She knew by the tinge of unplaceable accent beneath the generic British, that it belonged to an angel.

"I'm here because I don't understand why Sophia's here," the other voice replied. He, too sounded familiar, but he didn't

171

have the angel's accent. Sophie leaned over the bridge's railing, in hopes of hearing better.

"What is there to understand?" the angel said impatiently. "She's here, she's nowhere near strong enough to fight you – why not just take her and go home?"

"Because then, she would hate me."

"You don't need her to like you in order to restore the Balance," the angel said impatiently.

There was a pause, then a sigh. "Is everything really so black and white for you?"

"It is when it comes to the Balance," the angel said. "I shouldn't need to tell you that."

"No, you don't need to tell me," the other one answered in a voice full of regret. "And yet, neither you nor I know the whole story. Perhaps the little we *do* know is worse than nothing."

"Meaning?"

"Meaning, maybe there's more to her relationship with Lucifer than infatuation. It's certainly stood the test of time, not to mention numerous trials."

"You mean you would let her go back to him?" the angel asked incredulously.

A pause, and then: "Of course not. But it might soften the blow if she's allowed to save him."

"Save him!" the angel cried. "She intends to fight the sea witch for him!"

"I'm aware of that."

"She'll get herself killed!"

The other voice said softly, sadly, "How did you ever come to lead them, when you have so little faith yourself?"

Sophie waited, breathless, for the angel's answer, but if he made one, she never heard it. At that moment, a cold, slippery, claw-tipped hand closed over her mouth, and another circled her throat. She put up her hands to try to pry them off, but two more claws grabbed them and pinned them to her sides. She nearly retched at the sudden, enveloping atmosphere of sulfur and wet, rotting vegetation. A voice like a sluggish stream whispered in her ear, words that slowly penetrated the wave of terror with a weird kind of rhyme:

"From the mere, from the burn, from the weedy deep

From the slimy caves she'll wend and creep

Flesh to boil and blood to brew

Bones to grind for Jenny's stew!"

With a strength that came from a fresh surge of terror, Sophie tore one of her hands free of the creature's claws. She scrabbled for her bag, but it was slung across her back, trapped beneath the thing's slick, sinewy body. Its grip tightened on her throat as it continued to chant nonsense rhymes about all of the things it intended to do with her, before, presumably, devouring her for dinner.

Now would be a good time for super-powers to kick in. She tried to remember exactly what it had felt like the previous night in the club, to make herself feel that power again. But even though the memory was still so fresh she could almost feel it, the world around her remained stubbornly dark, her arms and legs capable of no more than an ordinary girl's.

Dragging the creature's hand momentarily from her mouth, she rasped out, "If you're still down there, HELP!" on the off chance that the angel wasn't fallen and would have to obey. Nothing happened, except that the monster clapped its claw back over her mouth. In that moment Sophie thoroughly hated this whole supernatural world she'd been dragged into. But there wasn't much time for hating anything. She began to feel lightheaded as the creature slowly but surely cut off her air supply.

Got to get it off, Sophie thought, her head spinning. Having no better ideas, she rammed her back against the side of the bridge. The creature let out a fetid gust of breath, and momentarily loosened its hold. Sophie managed to wriggle her bag around enough to get a hand into it as the creature scrabbled for purchase on her wrist. She grabbed a hairbrush and two pens before her fingers finally closed around Carnwennan. She was holding it by the blade, but enough of the tip was exposed for the monster to feel it when she jabbed it into the limb it had wrapped around her other arm.

This time, when its grip loosened, Sophie was ready. She threw the thing off, and then righted the dagger in her hand, whirling back to face it. But it was no longer coming for her. It was cowering against the side of the bridge as a sudden glow rent the darkness. It was so bright Sophie could barely look at it, swirling and shifting from golden to copper to crimson to blue, like a flame licking at a log. Squinting, she made out the shape of a man moving within its nimbus. In one arm he held a sword that seemed to be made of the same rippling light, condensed and solidified and if possible, brighter.

Next to him, the creature that had attacked her looked barely strong enough to stand, let alone throttle and eat her. Its skin was mottled greenish-grey, its limbs long and fragile-looking despite their ropey muscles, its mouth gaping over sharp teeth beneath eyes like dim yellow lamps. It shivered, cowering away from the fiery light.

"Who sent you, Jenny Greenteeth?" the angel – for it could only be an angel – asked sternly.

"Who sent me, who sent me, she sent me, my queen…" it gibbered, and continued babbling less and less intelligibly until the angel said, "Enough! Why did she send you here?"

"Bring the girl, the girl, the human girl with the immortal heart, I must find her, I must bring her, I must break her, I must grind her – "

The angel swung the sword, sending the fishy creature's head flying. Sophie stifled a scream, which turned to a gasp of surprise as the head disappeared, mid-flight. It simply turned to vapor, which dispersed on the cold wind from the Forth. Where the thing's body had been, there was only a pool of oily dark liquid, which trickled away along the gutter.

When Sophie looked up, the angel's fiery light had faded, and his sword was gone. He looked almost like an ordinary young man. Almost; but there was a tell-tale smoothness to his pale skin, a brilliance to his close-cropped coppery hair, and a spark in his green eyes that wasn't quite earthly. More than that, they were eyes she knew.

"Michael?" Sophie asked incredulously.

"Sophia," he said grimly, folding his arms over his chest. "You do have a miraculous talent for getting yourself into trouble."

"Funny thing to say when it seems you're behind most of it."

"What do you mean by that?"

"The water horse," Sophie said, enumerating on her fingers with the tip of the dagger. "The cat demon. Sam's poisoned sword – "

"None of those were meant for you," he said, his expression guarded.

Sophie smiled bitterly. "Of course not. It's Lucas you intended to kill."

He sighed. "You don't understand."

"You're right, I don't understand!" she cried, suddenly furious. "I don't understand why you still think that it's any of your business! You kicked him out of Heaven: not your problem anymore."

"Sophia – "

176

"And while we're at it, why don't you tell me who you were just talking to, and what you're plotting with him, and for that matter how you went from wrinkly Irish bar-prop to, well, *this*," she gestured to him generally, "in a few weeks' time?"

"I'll answer your questions, but first you have to – "

"No!" she cried. She was blazing now, furious about all that had happened and the part Michael had to play in it, and the fact that once, she had trusted him. "I don't have to do anything for you! And on second thought, I don't want to hear your explanations, either. No doubt they're lies, anyway. Thanks for killing that…that…whatever it was, but from now on, just stay away from me."

Sophie spun on her heel, not caring where she ran as long as it was away from him. But she found him standing in front of her again, his hands in the pockets of his long, dark coat, his face sad and implacable. "No, Sophia," he said, with a timbre to his voice that hadn't been there before. Likewise his face, while still smooth and beautiful, seemed suddenly older, full of authority. "It's time we had a talk."

"I heard you talking down there," she jerked a thumb behind her. "You have nothing new to say to me."

"You're dying," he said, and Sophie almost laughed.

"Yes, I'm very well aware of that, thank you. Eighteenth birthday, limits of the Balance, blah blah blah – "

"No, you're dying *right now*. By morning, every muscle in

your body will be paralyzed, including your heart, unless you clean your wounds of the grindylow's poison."

"The grindy-what? And anyway, what wounds?"

Michael reached out and clasped her hands before she could pull them away. He wore fingerless gloves, and the touch of his skin was hot as the light that had enveloped him a few minutes earlier. Sophie looked down, and then stared in horror. The sleeves of her jacket and shirt were shredded, the exposed skin of her forearms lacerated and bleeding. She snatched her hands away, felt her neck, her cheeks. They too were wet with blood, and something slimy that made her stomach flop. And yet, the cuts were entirely painless.

"Why can't I feel it?" Sophie demanded, beginning to panic.

"The grindylow's slime is anaesthetic. Helps it absorb more quickly, so it can kill you faster."

"How do I get it off?" Sophie cried, scrubbing at her shredded skin with the hem of her jacket.

"You come with me," he said.

"No. I'll go to the hospital – "

"There's no human cure for this. You let me help you, or you die."

Sophie stood her ground stubbornly. "Fine," Michael said. He began to walk back over the bridge, toward King's Stables Road.

Sophie took another look at her arms, and then said, "Wait."

Michael stopped, looking at her with exasperation. "How do I know you didn't make all of that up, and you really mean to kidnap me and take me back to Heaven?"

"You don't. I'm afraid it's a chance you'll have to take, if you want to live another day."

They stared at each other for a long moment. Then, wrapping her hand tighter around the dagger's hilt, Sophie followed him.

CHAPTER 13

By the time they reached Lothian Road, Sophie was beginning to feel lightheaded and sleepy. Michael gave her a critical look. "Are your hands and feet tingling yet?"

Sophie flexed her fingers. "Yes, actually. Is that a bad sign?"

Michael just gave her a grim look and hailed a cab. She watched blearily as the lights of the shops and restaurants flickered past. The drive seemed to take forever, though it could only have been a few minutes before they were turning left out of Tollcross, up toward the art college.

"You aren't taking me to Mum?" Sophie said, the words sounding thick and strange to her.

Michael gave her a quick, humorless smile. "I think not," he said, and then, to the cabbie, "just here, thanks."

The driver pulled up across the street from a derelict church, a block down from the art college. Sophie had been vaguely curious about its history the times she'd walked past, but not enough to remember to ask anyone about it. Now she wished she had, because that was where Michael was steering her. Its dark, brooding form rose up against the sky like a fortress, its ascending steeples like rows of blunted teeth.

"You don't mean we're going in here?" she asked, stopping by the boarded-up front doors. She swayed, and had to grab Michael's shoulder to keep from falling. He gave her another grim smile.

"It's not pretty, but it's consecrated ground. More to the point, it's probably the only consecrated ground in this city where no one will bother us." He led her around to the side of the building, where a broken window gaped like a toothless mouth. "Besides, for the moment it's home sweet home." He boosted himself up and through the window, then reached down to help Sophie. He had begun to glow faintly again, shedding light that swarmed with fire colors. Sophie took his hand and let him pull her up and into the church.

Once, she thought, it must have been beautiful, with its wide hall and rising galleries supported by gilded columns and arches. Now, its ruin was unsoftened even by Michael's warm light. The pews were bowed and blackened as if they'd been damaged by smoke and water. Plaster and masonry had fallen from the walls and ceiling, forming heaping mounds with half-burnt rubbish and old furniture. The pillars supporting the galleries looked frail, many of them whittled thin by fire.

Michael took her hand, his light flaring brighter as he

began to move. A cloud of pigeons rose from the railings and rafters, filling the air with wings and bubbling calls. There was something horrific about their whirring, half-seen forms. Sophie clasped Michael's hand more tightly.

"Come on," he said, pulling her toward the crumbling altar. Sophie was too weak now to protest, though she could make no sense of his bringing her to this filthy, creepy place. *Maybe,* she thought, *he means to kill me.* She didn't even have the energy to care.

She followed him through a dark, arched doorway to the left of the altar, which led down a narrow flight of steps. At the bottom he opened another door, and led her through it. He shut it behind them and turned on a light, revealing an ordinary room with dark paneled walls and a stone floor, unfurnished except for an overstuffed armchair with pink floral upholstery, a matching footrest, and an ornate Victorian desk. Like Lucas's bedroom in Ardnasheen, piles of books lined the walls from floor to ceiling.

"What is this place?" Sophie asked, working against numbing lips and tongue.

"My temporary residence," Michael said, opening the front of the desk.

"Why would you stay in a place like this?"

"Because no one in their right mind would look for me here." He took out one of several bottles of water that stood in a neat row beneath the desk's pigeonholes. "Sit there," he said, indicating the chair and handing her the bottle, "and drink this. Slow sips, or it'll make you sick."

"What is it?" Sophie asked. Though the liquid was clear and the label was that of a familiar mineral water, there seemed to be a fine sediment at the bottom of the bottle.

"Holy water."

"You're kidding me, right?"

"I am deadly bloody serious." As was his voice. "Drink the water, or forget about waking up tomorrow morning."

"I liked you better as a scatty drunken Irishman," she grumbled.

"Just drink it, Sophia."

Sophie took a dubious sip. It tasted like water – slightly stale, slightly mineral, as if it had sat for some time in a stone container – but water nonetheless. She took another sip. Her vision steadied a little bit, though the numbness seemed to be spreading, creeping up her arms and down her throat like the runners of a climbing plant.

After watching to make sure she was drinking it, Michael went back to rummaging in the desk, emerging this time with a glass cruet full of something yellowish, and a pile of tea towels. "Take off your jacket and your shirt," he said.

"Yeah, right," Sophie answered.

Michael let out an exasperated sigh. "I need to get at every place the faerie cut you. Believe me, I have no intention of following Lucifer up the garden path."

Glaring at him, Sophie put down the water and shed her jacket. Clumsily she pulled off her top, glad that she'd worn a vest that day. She saw him glance down at her jeans.

"You are *not* going there."

"Sophia."

"Anyway, it didn't touch my legs," she said. "Scout's honor."

With a faint smile, Michael tossed down the pile of tea towels and sat on the chair's footrest. He uncorked the little bottle of oil, poured some onto the corner of one of the cloths, and then took Sophie's free hand, turning it to expose the lacerated underside of her arm.

"This will hurt," he said.

"At least you're honest," she answered, and then gasped as he began to wipe at the first of the cuts with the oily towel. It was as if he were painting on all of the pain she should have felt when she was wounded.

"What is that stuff?" she asked, trying to keep her voice steady.

"Sanctified oil," Michael said, going back for more of it and a clean corner of the towel, "and angels' tears."

"It might as well be straight vodka!"

"Vodka does not possess the necessary properties to dissolve viscous demon secretions."

"That's *so* much more information than I needed."

"But you can feel your fingers again, can't you."

Sophie wiggled her fingers, and found that he was right. There was still a pins-and-needles sensation in them, but the gathering numbness was gone. More than that, the first cut Michael had cleaned had stopped bleeding.

"So, are you going to tell me what that thing was?"

"A grindylow. Specifically, Jenny Greenteeth."

"Not helpful."

"Grindylows are an order of *sìth* with female forms. They live in still water, where they lure children to their deaths and then eat them."

"Jesus! Aren't there any nice, wholesome *sìth?*"

"No. There are only Seelie and Unseelie."

"What?"

"Bad and worse."

Sophie bit her lip as he started on a new laceration with fresh oil. When the pain had subsided enough for her to speak again, she said, "There's no water in Princes Street Gardens – unless you count the ice rink. Even the fountain's off this time of year."

"True."

"So how did Jenny horrible thing get there?"

"The sewers, I imagine," he said, pulling what looked like a very long cactus spine out of one of the cuts. "She'll have come up the waterways in Cumbria – that's where she lived, last I heard – until she reached an outflow somewhere. Then she'll have followed the sewers until she reached you."

"Why would she come all this way, just to attack me?"

Michael looked up at her, his green eyes frank and more than a little exasperated. "Didn't you listen to her?"

Sophie's mind was clearing as steadily as the feeling was returning to her arms and lips. "Dahud sent her."

He nodded. "You've provoked her. No doubt all of the *sìth* who serve her – and there are many – are looking for you. She's probably offered a prize to whichever one of them brings her your head on a platter."

"Oh," Sophie said. It wasn't a comforting thought, but at least it made sense of the attack. Michael set her arm down and began to clean the wounds on her neck and chest. This hurt even worse, but as with her arm, the pain faded as he worked. When it was manageable again, she asked, "Who were you talking to, under the bridge?"

Michael barely paused before answering, but the intensity with which he watched his work told Sophie that she'd touched a nerve. "It doesn't concern you."

Sophie laughed incredulously. "It's me you were talking about!"

"Are you surprised?" he asked. "You've done plenty lately to draw attention to yourself."

Sophie reached out and caught the hand Michael was raising to her cheek. "Don't try to blame this on me," she said sharply, "and don't try to put me off. You were telling some guy to take me back to Heaven! I'd say that makes it my business."

186

Michael's eyes burned into hers, as if the flames he'd walked in when he fought the faery were still there, just beneath his skin, flaring with his anger. Still, his voice was calm when he said, "If you want me to tell you what you want to know, then you have to promise to hear me out, not just go storming off with half the story when I come to the parts you don't like."

"Okay, fine," Sophie said impatiently. She let go of his hand, and he went back to dabbing her face with the burning oil. He was silent for a time, and she began to wonder if he really meant to answer her. But then he began to speak, in a strange, low voice, full of regret.

"How much do you know about aeons?"

"Not much," she said. "Born from the Keeper's thoughts… live in the Garden…go around in pairs called, what is it? Synergies?"

He was giving her another intense, complicated look. "So you know about the syzygies."

Sophie's thoughts spun wildly toward a conclusion she didn't like at all. "Please tell me that guy you were talking to wasn't my ex."

He smiled ruefully. "Angels can't lie."

"Seriously? The other half of my syzygy is *here?*"

He gave a curt nod. "His name is Theletos."

"But what is he doing here?"

Michael's mouth set in a firm line. "Trying to clean up your mess."

"*My* mess! *You're* the one who called up demons and *sìth* and gave Sam poison to kill Lucas!"

Michael looked up at her again, and this time he looked startled. "Who told you that?"

"I'm not stupid, Michael," she snapped. "And more to the point, I heard this Theletos telling you to let me save Lucas. If even my spiritual consort thinks he should live, then who are you to get in the way?"

Michael smiled wearily. "Sometimes I think that you and Theletos deserve each other."

"What? Why? And why only sometimes?"

He shook his head. "It doesn't matter. What *does* matter is that Theletos has his own agenda, and it's not necessarily the right one."

"Because it's different from yours?"

"You know, Sophia," he sighed, "sometimes I wish that things really were as simple as you presume they are."

"God, you're a condescending arse."

He laughed humorlessly. "You wouldn't say that if you had any idea what you're dealing with."

"So now that's my fault too?" she cried, pushing away the tea towel. "If I don't know, it's only because no one will bloody tell me! Do you think I like being in the middle of this mess, with no clue how I got here or how to get out?" She shook her head. "All I want is a normal life and a normal boyfriend who takes me to the cinema or…hell, I don't know…bowling.

188

Instead I've got monsters and faeries and angels and a bloody *consort* – who by the way I can't remember at all – and in the end none of it matters anyway, because in six months time I go 'poof' and disappear!"

Michael's look turned to one of shock. "I...suppose I've never really thought about it like that."

"Well *I* have," Sophie said. "In fact, it's hard to think of anything besides this spiraling pit of crap my life's turned into." Michael looked at her for another moment, and then, to Sophie's annoyance, he began to laugh. "What?" she demanded.

"Nothing," he said, still laughing, "it's just...well, that would work metaphorically for most of the universe at the moment."

"Meaning?"

Michael shook his head. "First, the aeon history. Then, if you're still interested, we'll get into universal metaphors. And please, sit still." Grudgingly, Sophie settled back in the chair. "So," Michael began, "the Keeper created the first syzygy – Zoe and Logos – and they created the next, and so on until they got to you and Theletos, the fifteenth, and the last."

"Why were we the last?" Sophie asked.

Michael shrugged. "It could be because the Balance had set some limits. But personally, I think it's because you didn't function properly."

"What's that supposed to mean?"

"I'll get to that. But first, you need to know that the aeons weren't the Keeper's only creation. You see, the Balance works a bit like Newton's law of motion. You know it?"

"Every action has an equal and opposite reaction," Sophie recited.

"Yes. So if you create a force characterized by one thing, then there has to be an opposing force to even things out."

"So the Keeper created something evil to balance out the aeons?"

"Well, good and evil are of course relative terms…but yes, I suppose, from the human point of view, the daevas would be classed as evil."

Sophie had heard both Lucas and Suri use this word, but she realized now that she didn't know what it meant. "What are the daevas?"

"It's a Persian word…it roughly means 'the gods to be rejected'. Or, false gods. There are fifteen pairs of them, just like the aeons."

"So they aren't demons."

Michael shook his head. "The daevas are far older and more powerful than the demons."

"That doesn't sound good."

"Well, again, it's relative. As long as they were in balance with the aeons, there was no conflict."

"You're honestly telling me these two opposing forces don't fight?"

"Oh, they do now they're out of balance. But at first,

they lived in peace, each in their own realms: the aeons in the Garden, and the daevas in the Deep."

"The Deep again…" Sophie murmured, and ignored Michael's questioning look. She sipped more water, then asked, "So when did they start fighting?"

Michael tossed aside the last bloody tea towel and lifted his eyes to Sophie's. They were uncertain for the first time all evening. With clear reluctance, he said, "They started fighting when you created Earth."

Sophie choked on her holy water. When she finally stopped coughing, she said, "*I* created Earth?" Michael nodded. "And how did I do that, then?"

He smiled. "By being your own charmingly bull-headed self." Sophie opened her mouth to protest, but Michael help up a hand. "You promised to listen." She shut it again, and crossed her arms over her chest – noticing, as she did so, that the cuts there had become scabs, which were already starting to flake away.

"From the very beginning, you and Theletos were at odds," Michael continued. "You were curious, wanting to know the why and how of everything, while Theletos was content to accept what was, without question. So your thoughts never aligned into creation, like the other aeons' had."

"What does that even mean, 'aligned into creation'?"

Michael sighed. "I don't pretend to understand it, Sophia. I only know that syzygies create by the confluence of their thoughts. But because you and Theletos thought along different lines, there was no conjoining. He chose to observe, while you went poking into everything. And somehow, your imagination, working alone, made this." He gestured expansively. "The human world. Or what would one day become the human world."

Sophie was silent for a moment, trying to digest all of this. Finally, she asked, "So what happened next?"

Michael sighed. "What always happens with prime real estate: it started a war."

"Between the aeons and the daevas."

"Correct."

"Who won?"

"No one," Michael said. "They were equally matched, so they basically kicked the hell out of each other until the dust they raised killed the dinosaurs, and the Keeper called a time-out."

"You're joking, right? About the dinosaurs?"

"Do I look like I'm joking?" He looked serious, bordering on exasperated, just as he had all night. "The aeons and the daevas very nearly destroyed the Earth, and for that, the Keeper banished them all from it. None of them were happy about it, but you were devastated. You loved the world you'd made, and you couldn't be happy in the Garden anymore. You wept over your loss for a thousand years."

A faint, cold echo of despair ran through Sophie, almost – but not quite – a memory. "That must have been a lot of tears."

Michael nodded. "I suppose it's why the Keeper ultimately took pity on you. It couldn't risk giving the Earth back to an aeon, but it did give you an interest. It gathered your tears into a well, and promised that when the Earth spawned a race of beings with the intelligence to make use of them, those beings would each be given one tear from the well. One part of you – one spark of the divine – and those that lived lives worthy of it would return to the Garden when their mortal bodies died. And so your tears became the humans' souls."

Sophie didn't know what to say. Of all of the strange things that she'd heard in the last few months, this was by far the strangest. But Michael continued dispassionately, "And that's why, when Azazel and his followers corrupted the humans, the Keeper made an exception to its own rule. It sent you back to Earth, to try to repair the damage."

"But it didn't work," she said.

"No. You were recalled from Earth, and the Keeper sent the Flood to try to purify it."

"Wow, that was a resounding success."

Michael gave her another faint smile. "You were equally impressed by the effort at the time."

"Meaning?"

"You renounced the Keeper, and refused to go back to the

Garden. Since you were barred from Earth, you had nowhere to go but Heaven."

"'Her place in the midst of the angels...'" she said softly.

"Exactly."

She thought of her dreams, of the hill with the indigo grass, and Lucas with a book in his lap, eternally patient. She thought of a bottle of tears, of her hands cupped around a silver mirror.

"That's when I met Lucas, isn't it? It's when we fell in love."

"Yes," Michael answered grimly. "And that's when everything started to go wrong."

"Really?" Sophie said drily. "Because I'd say it started to go wrong when Azazel went to Earth and told everyone the angels' secrets."

"That's beside the point," Michael said, in a tone that told her he'd accept no argument.

"Fine," she said. "So after the Keeper made the angels – "

"The Keeper didn't make the angels," Michael interrupted. "The aeons did."

That silenced her for another long moment. "I thought only the Keeper could create."

"Only the Keeper – well, and you – could create *on its own*. Aeons and daevas can create within their syzygies."

"But...why? I mean, why did the aeons make the angels?"

Michael's eyes had gone distant, though his voice was

194

no less regretful. "They had to, to save the humans from the demons."

"You're losing me again. And by the way, if you're done with this," she poked at the bloody clothes on the floor with one booted toe, "do you have a dressing gown or something? I'm freezing."

"I can do better than that." Michael picked up her clothes from the floor and handed them to her.

"How am I meant to explain to my mum that they're shredded and covered in demon blood?"

"Are they?" Michael asked, with a quirk of a smile.

Sophie looked down. The jacket and top in her hands were whole and clean. "That's a useful talent – no more piles of laundry." She pulled the shirt over her head. "So, we were at aeons making angels to fight demons…?"

"Yes. Obviously, that was back before the Flood – back when humans were new to the planet. When the daevas got wind of them – intelligent creatures with free will and a touch of aeon divinity – they were furious. They charged the Keeper with skewing the Balance, and I suppose they were right. So the Keeper didn't stop them when they added an influence of their own. They couldn't affect the humans directly, since they were banned from Earth. But they could send agents – so they made the demons."

"To kill the humans?"

"No. I mean, yes, demons can kill humans, but that would

send them straight back to the Garden, and defeat the daevas' purpose."

"Which is what, exactly?"

"Corrupting them."

"Why bother? I mean, the daevas are like gods, aren't they? Shouldn't they be beyond caring what humans do?"

Michael shook his head. "Weak as humans may be, they have free will. They can choose to lead lives of good or evil, and because that's something that neither aeons nor daevas could do, it made them immensely compelling. The daevas wanted to counteract the drop of divine your tears gave the humans; they wanted to make them more like themselves. So they sent the demons to earth to tempt them, to corrupt them – and yes, sometimes to kill them.

"But the demons were a direct influence, stronger than a single, holy tear. The Balance tipped toward the Deep, and the aeons knew they had to do something to right it."

"So they made angels," Sophie said.

"Specifically, the Watchers. We were sent to Earth to try to keep humans on the right path. It's a battle we've been fighting ever since.."

Sophie thought about all that he'd said. It made sense, except for one thing: "If aeons are banned from Earth, then how is Theletos here?"

Michael shrugged. "How are *you* here? How are the fallen slipping their staves, and sea-witches taking angels prisoner?

196

Something's very wrong with the Balance, and the only thing I know for sure," he pinned her with his emerald eyes, "is that it all began when you forsook your syzygy, and took up with Lucifer."

"That's not quite true," Sophie said. "Don't you remember what I told you about the *Book of Sorrows?* How the Well of Souls is being tainted so that humans are no longer born neutral, and how it began when Lucas was banished?"

"I remember. But that was Enoch's interpretation of Sophia's words."

Sophie rolled her eyes. "It's no more an 'interpretation' than blaming Lucas and me for whatever's going wrong with the Balance."

Michael sighed. "You have to stop taking this personally."

Sophie couldn't stem a bitter laugh. "You tried to kill my boyfriend!"

"That's only because you refused to give him up!" He sighed, seeing that she was still stubbornly wary. "Sophia, this war has raged almost as long as time itself, and it will keep on raging as long as the Balance wavers. Because of your choices, the host of daevas is one syzygy stronger than the host of aeons. I can't put it any more clearly: you can't sacrifice yourself for a single angel. You *must* return to the Garden, to your syzygy."

"Which is all well and good, except that in a few months I'm going to die anyway."

"Are you certain of that?"

"The scroll spelled it out, plain as day: turn eighteen, cease to exist. So unless your friend Theletos knows how to undo whatever I did to get here, I'm not going to be much good to any of you."

Michael considered her. "Have you ever read Nostradamus?" he said at last.

"The medieval French guy who predicted World War Two?"

"My point precisely – did he? Or did he simply write something that fit a set of events well enough to be taken as the fulfillment of a prophecy?"

"I think an aeon's prophecy is a bit more credible than some medieval religious freak's."

"Maybe. But even if Enoch recorded every one of your words faithfully, prophecies are slippery fish."

"How many meanings can there be for 'your soul will be released and you'll cease to exist'?"

There was a long pause. Then Michael said, "Even if you're right, and the prophecy is literal, you aren't dead yet. In fact, you still have half a year left to do something better than moon over a lost love."

It was bitter, but it was the truth, and Sophie couldn't quite hate him for speaking it. But she also couldn't keep that bitterness out of her voice when she asked, "And in your opinion, that doesn't include saving Lucas from Dahud."

He shook his head. "All I know, Sophia, is that losing you

would be disastrous. And if you take on Dahud, that's the most likely outcome."

"Theletos didn't seem to think so."

"I told you, Theletos has his own agenda. It suits him right now to let you do what you like, but don't make the mistake of thinking he isn't interested, or that he won't try to stop you if he thinks you're putting us in danger."

Sophie looked Michael square in the eye. "Can he?"

Michael shrugged. "As aeons, you had equal power. Now…I really don't know."

"I want to meet him."

Michael smiled ruefully. "I'm afraid that's up to him."

"But you'll tell him? If you see him again?"

"I'll tell him, if you'll think about what I've said. I mean *really* think about it."

"I'll think about it," she sighed.

"Good. Now let's get you home."

CHAPTER 14

By the time Sophie got home, her cuts were faint red marks. By the following morning, they were gone. She spent far too long looking into the bathroom mirror, turning this way and that, searching for a sign, but there weren't even the faintest of scars to show that she'd nearly been ripped apart by a monster twelve hours earlier. She didn't know whether this in itself was more disturbing, or the fact that the whole event hardly even seemed strange.

Nevertheless she felt worn out, and she decided to take the bus to work. "Mum," she called, pulling on her jacket and hat, "do you have any change?"

"A bit," her mum called back. Sophie went into the sitting room, where her mother was working madly on a painting, trying to produce enough to fill the show, which would take place just before Christmas. Sophie held her breath when her mother looked up at her, wondering if there was a sign of the fight that she'd missed, but Anna only smiled distractedly and rummaged in her pocket until she came up with a handful of coins.

"Thanks," Sophie said, accepting it. She glanced at her mother's canvas, and then did a double-take. In the foreground was a kind of shanty-town populated by ragged people, all asleep. Their houses were made of rubble and cardboard boxes and broken objects from various time periods. Sophie could make out pieces of a Victorian pram, a wartime gas mask, rusted bits of a gas street-light, and many more that were difficult to identify. Behind the shanties, the spires and turrets of the Edinburgh skyline rose in silhouette against a pale blue sky. And over it all, like a hunting raptor, hung a vast, icy-white angel, its spreading wings made of dripping paint.

"What is this?" Sophie asked, trying to keep the antipathy out of her voice.

Anna looked at the painting, frowning slightly. "I don't know, exactly. I've been dreaming of angels, and a strange city where everything's almost right, but not quite. Like a parallel universe, where time didn't flow the same way as it has here..."

Sophie was staring at her mother. Anna was eminently practical, even in her art. Sophie had never seen her paint anything that wasn't figurative, let alone something so darkly fantastical. "Has this been going on long?" she asked.

Anna shook her head, but it looked more like confusion than negation. "A few weeks? It's hard to remember...but I dated all of them."

"All of them?" Sophie repeated, her concern doubling.

Anna nodded, and gestured to the wall behind her. There was a stack of canvases leaning there, covered with a dust sheet. Sophie pulled the sheet aside. With growing unease, she flicked through the paintings. Every one of them was a variation of the one on the easel.

"You know," Anna went on, in a strange, pleading voice, "with it being near Christmas, I thought, of course, angels...but they aren't very Christmassy, are they?" She shook her head, looking vaguely confused.

"Um...maybe not so much," Sophie said, trying not to let her mother know how much the paintings disturbed her. "It looks like you've been painting them since right after we got here."

"Yes, I suppose. It's the weather, I imagine. It's got me in a dreary mood."

Sophie nodded noncommittally. "Does the series have a name?"

"Well, not officially. But 'Out of Time' keeps running through my head." Anna was studying Sophie now rather than the painting. Sophie knew that she hadn't hidden her discomfort, because her mother's frown deepened. "They're a disaster, aren't they."

"No!" Sophie said. "No, I mean, they just surprised me... they're so different from your usual work..." She trailed off lamely.

Anna smiled. "Well, as your father loved to remind me, a girl can't go on painting idyllic landscapes forever…speaking of which, I had a call from him last night."

"Really?" This was almost as much of a shock as the painting. As far as Sophie knew, her parents hadn't spoken since she and her mother came up to Edinburgh.

Anna nodded, filling a fine brush with black paint and dabbing at the canvas. "He's thinking of coming up for Christmas. He feels badly that he hasn't been in touch with you much, lately."

Sophie thought guiltily of the several missed calls from his number she'd seen in her call log, and never returned. She and her father had always been particularly in tune to each other, and she'd been afraid she wouldn't be able to hide from him that something was going on. Now she realized that she'd only made their inevitable reunion that much harder.

"Where would he stay?" she asked at last – lame, she knew, but the best she could come up with as far as neutral responses went.

"Oh, we'll figure something out. There are plenty of B&Bs in the neighborhood."

The thought of her father spending Christmas Eve exiled in a B&B made Sophie sad, but she knew that it would be no use to tell her mother that. "Well…great. It'll be nice to see him." She tried to smile convincingly.

"Perhaps you could ask that friend of yours down – Suri. If she's travelling, she'll have nowhere to spend the holidays."

"Um…yeah, maybe," she said, trying desperately for nonchalance. "But I'll bet she'll be going home with Ailsa."

"Well, maybe both of them can come for a visit afterward. Hogmanay in Edinburgh is meant to be brilliant."

"Maybe," Sophie said. "Or maybe I could go up there."

She realized as soon as she said it that it had been a mistake. Her mother's face clouded, her eyes looked anxious. More than anxious: hunted. "I don't think that's such a good idea. I mean, you've only just got your feet back under you, you wouldn't want to do anything to set yourself back."

"Right," Sophie said, trying not to show her sudden anger. After all, it wasn't her mother's fault that she knew too little of the story to realize what she was forbidding. "I'd better go." She turned before she had to watch her mother attempt to smile, and pretend that everything was okay.

*

Angus was behind the counter serving a couple of pretty American girls when Sophie got in to work. She watched them flirt with him as she hung up her jacket and put on her apron, marveling at the easy nonchalance with which he flirted back. Not wanting to ruin his moment, she waited until they'd left before approaching the counter.

"You get their numbers?" she asked.

He smiled. "I didn't ask for them."

"Really? The blond one was stunning."

Angus shrugged and wiped the already-spotless counter, looking slightly embarrassed. "I'm not really a blonde kind of guy. Or in the market for a girlfriend, for that matter. At least not one who'll bugger off back to the States, come June."

"Yeah," Sophie said, watching him pour a cup of coffee. "Long distance relationships are hell."

Angus laughed, and pushed the cup over to her. "Was that an attempt at humor, or plain old irony?"

Sophie shrugged, sipping her coffee.

"So," he said in a lower voice, "have there been any more developments on the...you know..." He raised his eyebrows hopefully.

Sophie considered telling him about her adventure the previous evening, but there wasn't much to gain from it other than terrifying him, so she shrugged noncommittally. Seeing his disappointment, she added, "I was thinking of paying Morag a visit, though. You could come, if you want?"

"I do," he said, brightening. "When?"

"I don't know. I hadn't really thought about it."

Another group of students came in then, bringing a gust of cold air with them. Sophie and Angus didn't have another chance to talk until their lunch break, when he followed her up to the Eyrie. Ejecting Freyja from his favorite chair, Angus sat down and said, "So, when are we going?"

"Angus, I don't want you to get your hopes up," Sophie said, picking at her sandwich. "Morag's scatty, maybe even senile. I'm not sure how much she's going to be able to help – if at all."

"Well, there's only one way to find out," he said cheerfully.

Sophie couldn't help smiling. "Why are you always so optimistic?"

"I'm a Scot. It's the only way we survive the weather. Speaking of which, it's snowing."

Sophie looked up at the nearest window. It was indeed snowing, and not just flurries. White flakes blew diagonally across the window, obscuring even the nearest rooftops. "I didn't hear anything about snow," she said.

"Me neither," Angus answered. "But then, I haven't really been paying attention. Maybe we'll have a white Christmas."

"Maybe," Sophie said absently, and then took a bite of her sandwich. "Will you go home for the holiday?" she asked. "And where is home, incidentally?"

"Perthshire," he said, "and yes. You?"

"I think my dad's coming up."

"Is that a good thing?"

Sophie thought about it. "Of course I'll be glad to see him. But he and Mum...I don't know. They have kind of a love-hate thing going on." She didn't know why, but she found herself telling Angus all about her parents' tempestuous marriage, their obvious love for each other, challenged by his addiction to travel and her need to stay grounded in one place. The way it chipped away at the relationship until they couldn't make it work anymore.

"It must be difficult being their daughter," Angus said.

Sophie shrugged. "It's difficult being anyone's daughter – or son – if they expect anything of you at all. Don't your parents have expectations?"

Angus smiled, somewhat ruefully. "Of course. And I'm well on my way to fulfilling every one of them." He said it with a touch of bitterness.

"What does that mean?" Sophie asked.

He shrugged. "They're both academics. They've taught at Stirling since long before my brother and I arrived. Nice house, nice marriage, nice kids. They expect I'll do the same. All very predictable and boring."

"I could do with some predictable and boring," Sophie said, looking out at the whirling snow. After a few absent moments, she became aware of Angus's eyes on her, and the fact that he hadn't replied to that statement. She turned to look at him. He looked back at her for a moment as if he were trying to figure out a difficult maths problem, but he hid it quickly with a smile.

"I guess we should get back to work," Sophie said, picking up her plate and cup.

But when they got back downstairs Matrika was putting away cakes and clearing up dishes. "You two should go home," she said when they came into the front of the cafe. "The snow's meant to go on all night, and I don't want you to get stuck here. I'm going to close early – maybe tomorrow as well."

"Are you sure?" Sophie asked. "Don't you need help clearing up?"

Matrika made shooing motions with her hand. "I'll be fine. It's only a quick walk home."

"Okay," Sophie said, reaching for her jacket as Angus grabbed his.

As soon as they were out on the street he said, "So, are you thinking what I'm thinking?"

"Um – Jeez, it's cold?"

"No – that this is a golden opportunity!"

"For what?"

"Speaking to Morag."

"But…" Sophie gestured to the air full of snow.

"So she's likely to be in. And it's near your house, so it's not really out of your way."

"Well, yes, but – "

"Time is of the essence, right?"

Sophie looked at Angus's eager face. She still couldn't quite believe that he saw all of this as an adventure. Still, he was right that there was no time to waste. "Okay," she said. "But let's get a bus, or we'll be frozen by the time we get there."

As the bus trundled along the snowy streets, Sophie filled Angus in on her first meeting with Morag. When she was finished, he asked, "So how does she know all of this stuff about faeries?"

Sophie shrugged. "Who knows?"

Angus's look turned speculative. "You don't think…" He stopped, shook his head.

"What?"

"Well – could she be one of them?"

Though Sophie had considered this possibility, she'd dismissed it as quickly. Morag had seemed human enough to her, and more than that, she'd seemed somewhat frightened of the *sìth*. She thought of the grindylow, and shuddered.

"Let's hope not," she said.

They got off the bus by the clock in Morningside, and walked up Braid Road. By the time they reached the Toll House, the snow was so thick they could barely see a few feet in front of them. The windows of the house were dark. The bells on the clootie tree clashed and jangled in the rising wind.

"This is beginning to seem like a bad idea," Sophie said.

"We're here now," Angus answered, "we might as well go through with it." He opened the gate, and held it for Sophie. Reluctantly, she stepped through. Together, they walked up to the front door. There was no bell, nor any knocker, so Sophie rapped on the door with her knuckles. They waited, but nobody answered.

"I guess she's out," Sophie said, partly relieved and partly disappointed.

"Where would an old lady go in a snowstorm?" Angus asked. "I bet she just didn't hear you." He knocked again, this time more loudly. They waited, the snow whirling around them, but still there was no answer. Sophie watched disappointment cloud Angus's face.

"Never mind," she said. "We'll come back another time."

They turned to go, and then stopped. A small, dark figure was standing in front of them, shapeless under layers of clothing. She leaned heavily on a walking stick covered in carved knotwork.

"Morag?" Sophie said.

"Sophie," the woman answered, her voice surprisingly strong and clear through the wind. "Is this yer young man?"

"Oh, no…he's only…I mean, he's – "

"Angus," he said, saving her more embarrassment. He stepped toward Morag, extended a hand. Morag took his hand but didn't shake it. Instead she held it for a moment, looking at him with her cloudy eyes.

"Singular indeed," she said cryptically, and released him. "Well, what brings ye two out on such a day?"

"Actually, I was hoping you could tell us more about the sea witch," Sophie answered.

Morag studied her through the whirling snow. "Ye mean tae fight her for him. The laddie she's stolen from ye."

"Yes," Sophie said. "Do you know how to do it?"

Morag shook her head. "I know how *I* would dae it –

210

but that's no much use tae you." Morag looked off into the whitening forest for a few long moments, and then she said, "Come," and turned toward the clootie tree.

"Come where?" Angus asked.

"Out o' the storm."

"But your house is that way," Sophie said, pointing to the Toll House and wondering if Morag really was senile.

Morag looked at the house, then at Sophie, and began to laugh. "A stane box! I'd never live in such a place!"

"So this isn't your house?"

Morag only continued to chuckle, and beckoned to them to follow her. She hobbled over to the ring of stones marking the well, and then, without pause, she stepped into it. Sophie and Angus glanced at each other in horror, and then ran after her. When they reached the well, though, there was nothing there: only darkness, and the sound of running water.

"How deep is that?" Angus asked.

"I don't know," Sophie answered. "Do you think she's drowned?"

Even as she said it, a pale form emerged from the darkness below, resolving into a human face as it broke the surface of the water. Morag's face, curiously dry. She grinned at their obvious shock.

"Well?" she said. "Are ye comin' or no?"

"Ah, I'm not so sure – " Sophie began, but Angus interrupted, grabbing her hand:

"We're coming. Just tell us what to do."

"Ther's nowt tae dae. Just follow me," Morag said with another smile, and dipped back into the dark water.

"Ladies first," Angus said.

Sophie gave him a final, dubious look and then, suspecting she'd regret it, she stepped into the well.

CHAPTER 15

She'd expected to be met with icy water, but instead, after a brief push against something resistant, she felt dry, solid ground beneath her foot. "It's fine," she said to Angus, and stepped in with her other foot – which met empty air. She stumbled forward, and suddenly she was sliding down a flight of stone steps. She arrived at the bottom on her hands and knees, scraping her palms on the floor.

A moment later, Angus joined her – still standing, and with a slight smirk, Sophie was annoyed to notice. He offered her a hand, which she ignored. She stood up, dusted herself off and then looked around. The room they stood in was a kind of burrow hollowed out of the Earth, with roots trailing down from the ceiling. A fire burned blue and green in a hearth cut out of the far wall, and a round wooden table made of a single slice of a massive tree trunk stood in the center. There were shelves built into the walls, as well as a kind of dresser built from slabs of stone, all crammed with bottles and jars and pots of various substances. A small stream ran from a hole in one wall across the room to a hole in another. Morag crouched by it, trailing the fingers of one hand in the water, clutching her stick with the other.

She looked up at them and smiled as they approached. "Welcome tae my home," she said.

"Um…thanks," said Sophie.

"It's very like the houses at Skara Brae," Angus said, looking around with clear interest.

Morag chuckled gently. "Aye – they didnae get it frae the ground." Angus shot Sophie a questioning look, but she only shrugged. "So," Morag said, pinning them with that gaze that couldn't be as hazy as it appeared, "ye mean tae fight Dahud."

"Yes," Sophie said.

"And yer takin' the knight with ye?"

"Who?"

"Him," Morag said, jabbing a gnarled finger in Angus's direction.

"Yes," said Angus, as Sophie said, "No." She looked quizzically at Angus. "I mean, I didn't think that you'd want to come."

"I'd hardly let you go alone," he answered.

"Angus, you really don't have to – "

"Whisht!" Morag interrupted. "Ye dinnae yet have the key tae enter; there's nae sense in quarrelin'." Sophie opened her mouth to say something else, but Morag pointed at the table and said, "Sit!" in a tone that brooked no argument. They sat down at the table. "Good. Now I'll make the tea."

Morag opened a cupboard and brought out the copper kettle Sophie remembered from their last meeting, and filled it from the stream. She took down various jars and containers from the shelves, measured their contents into the kettle and hung it over the peculiar fire. Then she settled herself on a stool at the table with Sophie and Angus.

She studied them for a moment, and then asked, "So what dae ye know aboot the sea witch?"

"That she's half demon and half faery," Sophie answered.

"And she hates her tail," Angus added.

"And she sacrifices a human man to the Deep once a year, hoping to get rid of it."

"Aye," Morag nodded. "That's about the gist o' it."

"But none of that tells me how to get Lucas away from her."

Morag sighed, and stood up. She fetched the kettle from the fire, then mugs and a honey jar and a tea strainer, setting them all on the table before she answered. "It's a twofold thing, ken?"

"Not really, no," Sophie answered.

"Yer power must be stronger than hers over him, and the daevas' over her."

"That's all, is it?" Sophie said with a bitter smile.

"Ye could gie him up," Morag suggested with a level look,

sipping from her cup. Sophie could feel Angus's eyes on her, too.

"That will never happen," she said.

"Dinnae tempt fate," Morag said, with a seam of regret in her voice that made Sophie shiver.

Still, she said, "I'll save him or I'll die trying."

"Aye," Morag sighed, "and so ye must fight her when ye have a chance o' winnin'."

"When is that?"

"Between the langest dark and the light's return."

"Is that a riddle?" Angus asked.

"I dinnae have time for riddles," Morag said. "But its name in yer tongue escapes me. Jul…Jól…Joulu…Géol…?"

"Oh," Angus said, his eyes brightening. "Yule."

"Aye – that's it!"

"So I have to fight her on Christmas?" Sophie asked, wondering how she could possibly swing that with her parents.

"Not Christmas," Morag said, making a sour face. "The one that Christmas replaced."

"The solstice," Angus said.

Morag gave Angus an appraising look. "The knight is well up on the auld stories."

Angus shrugged. "If you're going to dig up the past, it helps to know the history."

Morag nodded. "So…the Deep's power grows wi' the fading light, frae Beltane tae Yule, and wi' it the powers o' all

216

who serve it. It's greatest just before the sun returns. When the sun rises after Yuletide, the Deep's power fades, and the Garden's grows. But there is a moment, a still point at each turnin', when all is balanced...all powers are equal, and anythin' is possible..." She looked at Sophie. "Even takin' a teind from a sea-witch."

"A teind?" Angus said. "Doesn't that mean a tax?"

"It means Lucas," Sophie said grimly.

Morag nodded. "On Midwinter's Eve, every kingdom o' the Unseelie *sìth* pays a tax tae the Deep, tae keep their power. A human is a fair price. An angel...well, in return for him, Dahud might well win back her legs, and become a full demon."

"So let me get this straight," Sophie said. "I have to take Lucas from Dahud on the night when she's the strongest – and those of us who don't serve the Deep, presumably, are the weakest?"

"Aye."

"The same night that she's planning to sacrifice Lucas to the daevas?"

"Aye."

Sophie let out a long breath, trying to ignore Angus's worried eyes. "Alright, then; do you know how to get to Ker-Ys?"

"Aye – but it's nae a matter of puttin' a pin in a map. Ye cannae get there by land or sea. You need a faery door, and tae pass through it, you need a silver bough."

"You've lost me again," Sophie said to Morag, but it was Angus who explained, the eager schoolchild look back on his face.

"The silver bough is part of the Celtic faery mythology," he said, and then, glancing at Morag, "although I suppose this means it's more than mythology." She nodded, and rewarded him with a warm smile. "The Celts thought there was a tree at the center of the world – the *axis mundi*. The silver bough is meant to be taken from that tree. Sometimes it plays music that sends you into a vision. Sometimes it's a literal ticket to faeryland for a worthy mortal. It lets him in and out, and keeps him safe while he's there."

"So how does a girl get hold of a silver bough?" Sophie asked.

"It's given to you by a faery queen – if you manage to impress her."

"But Dahud isn't a real faery queen."

"Naw," said Morag, "she stole her bough from a real one. Cut her throat for it."

"Charming. So I'm guessing that it's not something she just leaves lying around."

Morag shook her head. "I dinnae know where she keeps it. But without it, ye'll nae get into her city."

"Somehow I doubt that I'll be able to convince her to give it to me."

There was a glimmer in Morag's eyes when she answered, "Naw, you'll never. That's why ye'll have tae steal it."

"And how will I do that, if I can't get into Ker-Ys without it?"

"There are ways and ways of gettin' somewhere. Dinnae forget, ye've been tae Ker-Ys before."

"Only in a dream."

"Aye – and sae ye must dream it again."

Sophie was beginning to be annoyed by the incessant conundrums of Morag's logic. "But how will I take the bough out of the dream, if I'm not really there?"

It was Angus who answered, his eyes were lit now with inspiration. "I think I see! It's like the way you got that knife, when you fought the *Cait Sìth*. What did Suri say? You manifested it?"

Sophie shook her head. "Except I didn't, remember? I made a whole new one. A copy…" She looked at Morag with sudden hope. "I don't need a dream at all! I can just make another silver bough!"

But Morag shook her head. "It's nae that easy. Ye re-made Carnwennan because ye kenned it once. But you've never known Dahud's token. Nobody has but the fae queen she killed for it."

Sophie understood, then. "So that's why I need the dream: to learn the bough, so I can make another one, here." Morag nodded, and Sophie sighed. "That's all well and good, but I'm not one of those people who can dream of something at will."

Morag stood. "There, I can aid ye." She hobbled to the wall of shelves and began to rummage through their contents. Every now and then she took something out and put it on the table.

"The thing is," Sophie said, looking doubtfully at a jar full of pink liquid and what looked like frogs' eyes, "even if I can dream myself to Ker-Ys, how will I find what I'm looking for? I mean, my visions haven't turned out particularly well in the past."

Morag smiled. "That's because ye didnae ken whit ye were daein'."

"Pardon?"

She shrugged. "Like anythin' else, it takes knowledge and practice tae control a vision."

"Then how is this going to be any different from the others?" Sophie asked dejectedly.

"Because I'm gauin' wi' ye."

As Sophie blinked at her in surprise, Morag took a copper basin from the shelf and set it down beside the jars and bottles. She studied it for a long moment, and then she began putting things into it: splashes of liquid, pinches of powder, handfuls of dried leaves, an alarming number of the might-be-eyeballs, which she measured out with a fork to let the liquid drain, exactly as Sophie's mother drained capers for pasta sauce. Every once in a while she stopped and shook the bowl, presumably mixing its contents, and looking intently into it.

Finally, she looked up at Sophie. "Ye must draw the water yerself." She took a copper pitcher from another shelf and handed it to Sophie. "While yer fillin' it, ask the water for wha' you seek."

Sophie took the pitcher and went to the stream. She knelt down beside it, looked into its flow. At first it seemed no more than dark, empty water, but as she watched, she began to make out faint shapes beneath the surface. The longer she looked, the clearer they became, until they resolved into bodies: tiny, pale, women's bodies, eerily beautiful, with fine hair trailing behind them as they slipped and turned with the current. Sophie put out a finger to touch one of them, but it dissolved to nothing.

"Oh!" she cried, jerking her fingers back.

Morag laughed. "Dinnae fret – ye've nae done her any harm. Ye've only frightened her away."

"What is she?"

"A sylph. And they dinnae often show themselves tae humans, sae ye should think yoursel' lucky, and ask for their help."

Sophie looked down at the flowing water, dark and empty again. She tried to picture them as she said to herself: *Show me the sea-witch's silver bough.* Then she dipped the pitcher into the water and filled it to the top. She stood up and handed it to

Morag, who poured it into the bowl. She swirled the contents one more time, and then she looked up at Sophie.

"Are ye ready?" she asked.

"Yes," Sophie said, trying to make herself believe it.

"And the knight?" She looked at Angus. "Are ye comin' wi'us?"

"He'd better be," Sophie said. "This was his idea."

"Do you think I'd let you leave me behind?" he said. He came to join her, and after a moment's consideration, he took her hand.

"You don't have to – " she began, trying to pull away.

Angus just smiled and said, "It's purely practical. Remember how you got down here?" Recalling her tumble down the stairs, Sophie made a face at him, but closed her fingers around his.

Morag picked up the bowl and carried it to the fire. Sophie expected her to set it down and invite them to look into it, maybe mutter some magic words, or ask them to drink from it (her stomach churned at the thought.) Instead, the old woman picked up the bowl and flung the contents into the fire.

Rather than douse it, the liquid made the flames leap higher. They swam with all of the colors of water, not only blue and green but storm-gray and midnight, foam-white and the tannic brown of a peat bog, plus countless other shades. They emitted a steam that reached out into the room, trailing tongues that lapped and twined around them. The cloud grew thicker as it enveloped them, until the room was obscured and Sophie could see nothing but the pulsing, watery vapor. At least she could still feel Angus's hand, solid in hers. She hung on to it tightly.

A few moments passed. Then, as if with a gust of wind, the mist cleared, and they were standing in Ker-Ys. They weren't in the garden Sophie had seen in her dream, though. Instead they stood in a courtyard, with intricate buildings rising up on three sides and a road bordering the fourth. In the center was what looked like a fountain, except that its statue – a singing girl – had bubbles streaming from her mouth rather than water. They swirled with the colors of the enchanted fire, rising languidly toward the pale green sky before they eventually disappeared.

Sophie was so entranced by the bubbles, it took her a moment to realize that Morag was gone. A tall, slender girl was standing in her place – the seal girl from her first dream of Ker-Ys.

"What happened to Morag?" Sophie asked her.

The girl smiled, and her face shifted, becoming the old woman's.

"Wait – *you're* Morag?"

"Of course not," she answered, becoming the girl again. "I'm Morwen."

"But you just turned into her!"

"No – I showed you a different aspect of us."

"You mean there are more of you?"

"We one are three," Morwen said, as if this should have been obvious.

Angus's face lit with understanding. "Morag, Morwen... you're the *Morrigan*?"

"The what?" Sophie asked.

"The triple goddess," he told her, eyes alight. "The maiden, the mother and the crone. She's one of the oldest mythological deities...except I guess you aren't mythological, are you?"

Morwen smiled, turning her cool green gaze on him. "I'm glad that someone still remembers my name."

"Lots of people remember it. I spent part of last term on a dig, looking for evidence of triple-goddess worship on Skye."

Morwen laughed. "You'll be digging there a long time. Better to try Orkney."

Angus shook his head. "Bloody hell..."

"If you're the triple goddess," Sophie said, "then where is the third? I mean, you're the maiden, Morag's the crone – who's the mother?"

"If she hasn't revealed herself yet, it's not for me to do so."

"But you *are* her."

"I'll debate this with you if you like, Sophia, but you came here for another reason, and the vision won't last long."

"Right," Sophie said, shaking her head to try to clear it. "Sea witch...silver bough...do you know where to find it?"

"I don't know Ker-Ys well anymore; it's a long time since they worshipped me here. But we can be certain that the queen will keep such a powerful token close. And as every road here leads to the palace, we need only begin walking."

Morwen took Sophie and Angus's hands with her blue-patterned ones, and stepped onto the road. Except it wasn't really a road so much as a narrow lane running between high buildings, cobbled in what looked like mother-of-pearl. The buildings were varied in their architecture, some made of dressed stone while others were built of wave-smoothed pebbles and coral and shells. Still others seemed to be made of wet, dribbled sand, like the strange, dripping church Sophie had seen once on a holiday to Barcelona.

"If Dahud doesn't like Sophie," Angus asked after a few wonderstruck minutes, "how will we get into her palace?"

Morwen shrugged. "She won't know we're there."

"But in the visions in the stream, she saw me," Sophie said. "She *spoke* to me. She even tried to grab me." She shuddered at the memory.

"It's as I told you," Morwen said patiently. "You didn't know what you were doing, and so, inadvertently, you gave her the power to see and touch you."

"How?"

"By believing that she could."

Sophie groaned. "So it's like the *sìth?* Believing that Dahud can do something to me makes it possible?"

"Yes, and no," Morwen said speculatively. "In the human world, if you accept them, then you can't hide from the *sìth*.

But this isn't the human world, and at any rate we aren't really here, so there is no need to show ourselves."

"Right," Sophie said, deciding it was easier to trust Morwen than question her.

For a while they walked in silence. The road canted upward, slowly but steadily. They passed more high buildings, and also smaller ones set in gardens, which seemed to be private houses. They passed parks and promenades where the black-eyed people drifted, and never seemed to notice them.

Sophie found it difficult to keep track of time in this weird, languid place. They might have been walking for minutes as easily as hours when the cobbled lane finally let out into a vast courtyard with an ornate building at the center. It was made of pale stone that shone softly green in the watery, wavering light, built in tiers like a wedding cake, and studded with countless archways and turrets and other decorative architecture.

"That'll be the palace, then," Sophie said, trying not to feel daunted.

"Yes," Morwen answered. "Come – truly, Sophie, you are safe."

Nevertheless, Sophie was glad when Angus took her hand again. They moved toward one of several sets of white stone steps, which led upward through an arched doorway and into the palace. They came out into a window-lined corridor which led to another arched doorway, this one guarded by two green-skinned, black-eyed knights. They didn't shift as Sophie,

226

Angus and Morwen passed between them, though one of them reached up and brushed his face, as though he'd felt the breeze of their passing.

Which makes no sense, if we aren't really here, Sophie thought – and then told herself not to. She also wouldn't let herself consider how Morwen was choosing their path through the palace. The goddess walked with the same serene assurance she'd had since they came to Key-Ys, choosing doorways and corridors apparently without a second thought. And it seemed she chose them correctly, because there were more and more people around them as they moved along, as if they were coming closer to the center of activity.

Then they turned into a corridor whose walls seemed to be made of solid stone. "Wait," Sophie said, putting out a hand to stop Morwen. "I think I know this place."

"How?" Angus asked.

"In the first vision of Lucas, there was a stone wall behind him like this." She touched the wall of the corridor. There were doors cut into it, all of them shut. "Can we get in?"

"Of course." Morwen stepped through the closed door in front of her, smooth as smoke.

Just believe it, Sophie told herself, and followed her. She felt a resistance like that of the water when she and Angus had stepped into the well, a strange tugging that reached deep within her, as if the molecules of the door and her body were simultaneously rearranging themselves. Then she was through.

They stood in a small bedroom, apparently carved out of the same block of stone. A woman with hair of so pale a blue that it was almost white stood in front of a mirror, holding up each of a pile of dresses in succession. Though each one was exquisite, she discarded them all with a sour expression.

"Not here," Sophie said, and turned back to the door.

But Morwen touched her hand and headed for the wall above the bed. "It's quicker this way," she explained, and led Sophie and Angus through the wall, into the next room. They passed through several rooms this way, all of them bedrooms, all of them empty. And then they stepped through another wall, and into the room Sophie remembered. There was the bed with the ornate cover, so out of place in the cell-like space. The room held nothing else, except for a ring bolted to the wall. Sophie thought queasily of the chain around Lucas's heart.

"He's not here," she said, when she realized that she'd been staring at it for too long.

Morwen looked at her with sympathetic eyes. "Come – let's go."

Sophie didn't need to ask where.

CHAPTER 16

Sophie followed Angus, who followed Morwen, barely aware of the twists and turns she took. Her apprehension grew steadily as they neared the heart of the palace. At last they reached a pair of arched double doors, studded in silver and flanked by black-eyed knights armed with tridents.

"Ready?" Morwen asked.

"Maybe?" Sophie answered.

"It will be alright," Morwen said, stroking Sophie's cheek with a cool, blue-patterned hand. Immediately Sophie felt better.

Morwen stepped forward, through the door. It was harder to cross than the stone walls had been in the bedchambers, and as she followed Morwen through, Sophie felt lightheaded and sick. Once on the other side, though, the feeling passed, and she saw she was standing in Dahud's great hall.

It looked as it had in her vision in the stream, except that then, she hadn't got the true sense of its imposing vastness.

The room was bigger than any she'd ever stood in, and more beautiful. And yet there was an emptiness to it, a coldness to the beauty that seeped straight into her core. She saw the same vacant chill in the eyes of the knights and ladies and courtiers who stood in ranks along the walls, apparently without purpose. The light from the sconces cast no warmth, and the thick nap of the velvet carpet was frosty.

Sophie had steeled herself to see Lucas and Dahud twined together as they had been in her last vision, but the reality was worse. Dahud sat on her throne as before, her skin smooth as marble, her hair unbound and falling almost to the floor, drifting in its own swirling current. She still wore the silver filigree diadem, and ropes of pearls hung around her neck. Her low-cut gown was the deep, secret green of a sea cave. She sat idly winding and unwinding the end of Lucas's chain around one finger as a white-haired man, considerably older than her other subjects, spoke into her ear.

With difficulty, Sophie looked down. As the sea witch had flourished, Lucas had wasted. He lay at her feet, still dressed in the miserable tattered trousers. His hair had grown past his shoulders, and it was snarled with salt and bits of dried weed. He was painfully thin, every rib visible as he breathed. Despite it all, his gaze, fixed on Dahud, was one of rapture.

"Oh, Lucas..." Sophie whispered, her throat choked with tears.

"Come," Morwen said, laying a gentle hand on her

shoulder. "I believe we'll have an interest in what he is saying." She indicated the courtier at Dahud's elbow.

"Who is he?" Angus asked.

"Her father," Morwen answered. "King Gradlon."

"I thought that he threw her into the sea," Sophie said.

"He did," Morwen answered, "and he's never forgiven himself for it, or what became of her. Even now, he seeks to save her soul."

They had drawn near enough to the old man to see that more than age set him apart in appearance from the other members of Dahud's court. His clothes were coarser, his skin somehow denser, and without the greenish cast. His eyes were sad, blue-grey, human eyes.

"This one is not like the others," he pleaded, as Dahud watched him with clear disinterest. "You cannot imagine the price you will pay if you give him to them."

Dahud smiled faintly, still looking at Lucas with the fondness of a cat for a mouse it has exhausted beyond hope of escape. "And *you* cannot imagine the price we *would* pay, to be rid of your curse."

"Heaven would help you, if only you would repent."

Dahud's look turned irritable. "Help me? As they've helped him?" She tweaked the chain, and a flash of pain crossed Lucas's face. Morwen and Angus had to hold Sophie back, then.

"You cannot help him like that," Morwen said.

Unhappily, Sophie settled back between them, as Gradlon said, "Heaven would help him, likewise."

Dahud smiled. "He'll never repent, anymore than we will."

"Fallen or not, they will not look kindly on you debasing one of their own."

At that, Dahud met his eyes. Her pupils widened, and her silver irises were like a ring around an eclipse. "Heaven has already forsaken him," she said, her voice rich and velvety.

Gradlon shook his head, clearly troubled. "You have no idea what you are playing with."

"And you do?" she demanded. "Who is it that's informing you?" Gradlon looked away, as if abashed. "Ah," Dahud said, her voice bitter now. "You still grovel to that wretch, Winwaloe."

"He is a saint!"

She waved a disparaging hand. "He killed us."

"He meant to save your soul," Gradlon pleaded.

Dahud's eyes flashed with wrath. "By hurling us into the waves? The Deep saved us when you and he left us to drown. It's the Lords of the Deep to whom we owe our life, and it's to them that we will give the angel – Heaven be damned!"

Gradlon shut his eyes, as if it pained him to look at her. "Dahud…my daughter…"

"Enough!" she roared. "Guards! Take him from here!"

"No need," Gradlon said sadly. He reached a hand up, almost as if he meant to wave at somebody. But where it moved, a line of light appeared, as if he were pulling apart the very fabric of the world, opening a rent onto whatever was beyond. When it was large enough he slipped through it, and it closed behind him, leaving Dahud staring at the place where he had been, shaking with rage.

She looked around, her eyes finally settling on Lucas, who still lay, dazed, at her feet. Her lips curved then in a cruel smile, and she jerked on the chain with which he was bound. He convulsed once, his eyes wide with pain, and then leapt to his feet and stood, swaying, before the sea queen. Sophie let out a cry and fought to free herself from Morwen and Angus.

"She's hurting him!" she cried.

"And the only thing you'll accomplish by running to him is to break the glamor that's protecting us," Morwen answered, though her eyes were full of pity.

As if to confirm this, Dahud looked up and around, her smile flattening, scanning the space where Sophie and the others stood, as if she'd caught some sense of their presence. Sophie froze, and Angus touched her shoulder in warning, though she had no intention of moving again. At last, satisfied that there was nothing amiss, Dahud turned back to Lucas.

"It seems your presence is earning us attention," she said, tilting her head to look at him speculatively. "Not all of it the type we'd wish for. We wouldn't like to think that you were deceiving us."

Lucas looked mystified. "I would not deceive you, Lady."

"Why not?" she asked.

"Because I love you." The simple innocence with which he said the words was a knife into Sophie's heart.

"Remember that he's enchanted, Sophia," Morwen said into her ear. "That isn't truly Lucifer speaking."

"Isn't it?" Sophie asked, her voice unsteady. "Because it sounds like him, and it looks like he means it."

Morwen took her hand again and squeezed it, while Angus's hand remained steady and warm on her shoulder.

"You did not call on that infernal saint?" Dahud was asking Lucas, her voice icy.

"No, Lady. I call on no one. I need no one but you."

Dahud looked at him skeptically, but finally, she smiled. She took hold of the chain and pulled him toward her. "Leave us," she said to the courtiers. They turned silently and began to file out the double doors as Lucas mounted the steps, as quickly as his unsteady legs would move. When he fell into Dahud's embrace, his face a twist of pain and ecstasy, Sophie turned away.

But Morwen was watching them with a glimmer of interest. "Stay, Sophia," she said. "This is our moment."

"You can't be serious," Sophie said tremulously.

"Courage, lass," she answered, her face flickering to Morag's for a moment, crumpled with pity. Then she was Morwen again, moving briskly toward the throne. "She's distracted. Everyone else is gone. There will be no better time to find what we're looking for."

Sophie shook her head. "But where do we even begin?"

"In front of our noses, I expect," Morwen said, as she began to examine the tapestries lining the wall behind the throne.

"I'll just...ah...look over here," Angus said, glancing apprehensively at Dahud and Lucas, then moving to the nearest of the wall sconces.

Sophie joined Morwen, keeping her eyes trained carefully away from the throne. She looked at the first of the tapestries. It was made of some fabric like shot silk but far finer, undulating sapphire and sea green. Schools of fish were woven into it in brilliant colors, seeming to move through forests of kelp and coral as the fabric swayed. The other tapestries were similar in their color and subject, and in the way the figures in them seemed to move. But nothing on any of them resembled a silver branch.

When Sophie turned away from them she found Morwen and Angus examining the throne itself. Through its intricate lattice, she could also see Dahud's pale hands moving over the gold-brown skin of Lucas's back, the black of his sigil, her lips curled in pleasure as he kissed her neck. Tears filled Sophie's eyes; she felt cold and sick and simultaneously hollowed out, as if all the substance of her had drained away. Like a witness to a tragedy, she couldn't bear to watch, and she couldn't look away.

Dahud's hair fanned out around her like the tendrils of a climbing plant. Her skirt flowed on and on into the shadows. And then something caught Sophie's eye: a bright glint against the darkness. It was the filigreed crown binding the hair back from Dahud's face. At first glance, its design had resembled the fronds of some sea plant. Looking at it now, though, Sophie thought that it was also very like a tangle of twigs, the pearls scattered among them like tiny white flowers.

"Morwen," she called. "Angus – look!"

The others came and stood by her. "Have you found it?" Angus asked.

"I don't know," she said, unable to believe that it could be so obvious. "Look at Dahud's crown."

"I suppose it is a bit like a branch," Angus said.

"More like one than anything else we've found," Morwen said. Then she looked at Sophie, her eyes sympathetic, but probing deep. "You'll have to touch it, in order to recreate it."

"Fine," Sophie said.

"Sophie," Angus said tentatively, "are you really certain that you'll be able to – "

But Sophie wasn't listening. Filled with a sudden and furious determination, she strode toward the throne. Doing her best to ignore what was going on there, she examined the crown. Now she could see the bark-like texture scored into the silver. This must be the bough, but Dahud's hair was woven in and around it, keeping it fast to her head. Sophie reached out experimentally to touch it, and a tendril of hair wrapped around her arm, cold and slick as river weed. She jerked back with a cry.

"What is it?" Dahud demanded irritably, and Sophie froze, thinking that she'd heard her. After a moment, though, she realized that the sea witch was speaking to Lucas, who'd lifted his head at the sound. For a moment his dark eyes met Sophie's. For the first time since the vision in the puddle in the Grassmarket, there was something other than besotted vacancy in his gaze. Instead he looked confused, like a sleeper waking from a strange, vivid dream. He blinked, looked down at the witch in his arms, and then up again. "S–Sophie?" he said, his voice gritty, from screaming or disuse, Sophie didn't want to consider.

"Lucas!" she cried, forgetting the crown, and the glamor, and the fact that none of them were really there; forgetting everything except that he'd recognized her. She reached for him, but before he could respond, the sea witch sat up and shoved him away from her, sending him sprawling on the floor at her feet.

"How dare you!" she roared at him.

"I – I – " he began.

"Sorcery!" she cried. "Foul witchery! Tell us where she is! Show us where she's hiding!"

Sophie didn't know whether to be relieved or devastated when he said, "Where who is hiding, my Lady?"

237

Morwen was at Sophie's shoulder then, Angus behind her. "Quick, Sophie!" she said. "I can't hold the glamor long against her, now she suspects us."

"Who?" Dahud cried. "Who indeed! Stand to address us!" She jerked Lucas's chain and he stumbled to his feet, his face a rictus of agony.

Reckless now with rage, Sophie wanted only to hurt the creature that was hurting him. Ignoring the slimy cold of Dahud's hair, she thrust a hand into it, grabbed hold of the crown and yanked. Dahud howled as the thing came away, trailing hanks of hair that were still wound through it. She whirled around, and this time, Sophie knew that she could see them.

"Run!" Morwen cried, and Angus and Sophie ran back down the hall, toward the double doors. Looking over her shoulder, Sophie could see Dahud following them, but she wasn't running. Instead she moved horizontally, her bottom half undulating, as a fish moves through the water. She might have been quick, had she been unencumbered by clothing. As it was, however, she couldn't keep pace with them, dragging the heavy drapery of her gown behind her. All the while Lucas watched, dazed, still swaying on the first step of the throne's dais.

For Sophie, it was agony. She knew that she'd made Dahud furious, and it was very likely Lucas who would pay the price. Morwen seemed to have guessed her thoughts, though. She grabbed Sophie's elbow and hurried her along, saying, "You cannot free him yet!"

"I can try – "

"And die trying! Don't be a fool, Sophia!" Morwen wrenched the double doors open and shoved Sophie through them, just as Dahud caught up to them.

Sophie was already trying to work out how they'd find their way out of the palace, when she realized that they weren't standing in the stone corridor with the knights. Or if they were, she couldn't tell, because the air was swirling with mist colored blue and green and grey and brown – all the colors of water. She couldn't see her companions; she couldn't even see her hand in front of her face, though she still felt the crown, cold and solid in her hand, and Dahud's hair creeping up her arm again like a clutch of snakes.

"Morwen?" she said uncertainly. "Angus?"

Walk forward. Morwen's voice seemed to come from inside of her. *Keep walking until you can see the way…*

Sophie put one foot in front of the other and began to move, hoping that it was forward. It was impossible to tell, when she couldn't see anything. But after a few steps, solid shapes began to show through the scrim of colored mist. They resolved gradually into a table, chairs, shelves full of pots and jars and bottles – and with another step she was back in Morag's underground room, with Angus and Morwen on either side of her.

Morwen looked at the crown in Sophie's hand, shaking her head. "You don't do things by halves, do you?" There was a small smile on her face, though, rather than reproach.

"I got the branch, didn't I?"

"And half of Dahud's hair with it," Angus observed.

Sophie looked down at the crown in her hand. The silver and pearl glinted in the firelight, the lacework of twigs finer than it had seemed in the vision. The torn hair had stopped trying to climb her arm, lying now like limp, dripping hanks of water weed. With a shudder, she dropped the thing on the table.

"You've made her angry," Morwen observed, looking from the crown to Sophie. "It will make your task harder. She'll be waiting for you."

"There's nothing to be done about it now," Sophie answered. "Besides, I could never have got close enough to the crown to be able to replicate it. Not with it all tangled up in her hair like that."

"Ah, well," Morwen said, "things are as they are. And what they are right now is stormy – at least up there." She pointed to the ceiling of the room. "You'd best get home before the snow gets any deeper."

Sophie had forgotten about the storm. She had no idea how long they'd been underground. Matrika closing the shop, Angus convincing her to seek out Morag, the conversation in the Toll House's snowy garden – it all seemed to have happened years ago.

"What should we do with it?" she pointed to the crown on the table.

"Leave it with me," Morwen said, looking at it speculatively. "I'll clean it...witch's hair has its uses after all..." She looked back up at Sophie. "You'll know where it is, though, when you need it."

Sophie nodded. "Thank you."

Morwen smiled, and then crumpled and shrank and faded until she was Morag again. "You're welcome, lass. Safe home."

CHAPTER 17

By the time Angus and Sophie came out of the well, it was dark outside and the garden was barely recognizable beneath its thick blanket of snow. The streets were empty of cars, the streetlights blurred, and the lit windows of the Morningside tenements seemed worlds away.

"Crap," Sophie said. "Mum's going to have the search parties out."

"Tell her it was my fault," Angus said. "No, better still, I'll tell her."

"Really, Angus, you don't have to do that."

"Of course I do! This was my bright idea – you shouldn't take the blame."

"And what are you going to tell her? That we've spent the afternoon tripping on magic potion with an ancient deity?"

"Well, I thought that I'd massage the facts a bit."

"A bit?"

He grinned at her. "No worries – I'll think of something. Come on, it's freezing."

They battled a stiff northwest wind all the way down Braid Road, then turned into a side street. The wind wasn't as fierce there, but the snow had drifted, and Sophie felt like she was wading through treacle. At least the hard going made it difficult to talk. She needed time to process the latest developments in her life before she had to pretend to be Sophie-in-recovery for her mother.

She was surprised at her own reaction to seeing Lucas and Dahud together. There was no denying that it hurt her to hear him tell Dahud that he loved her; to give the sea witch the kisses she herself longed for. Yet none of that compared to the raw terror that Midwinter's Eve would come too late – that Dahud would use Lucas up in her reckless lust for adoration, before he even had the chance to become her teind. At the rate he was wasting, Sophie found it hard to believe that he'd last even one more week, let alone three.

"Sophie? Are you still with me?"

Sophie looked up. Angus was standing on the pavement at the edge of Comiston Road, not far from her flat. "Sorry – did you say something?"

He gave her a concerned look. "I said, where do you live?"

"Sorry," she repeated. "Come on."

She led him across the road and then, finally, out of the blasting snow and into the tenement's stairwell, which felt tropical by comparison. The sudden silence rang in her ears, but she'd barely had a moment to get used to it when she heard a door swing open somewhere above.

"Ah, crap," she muttered, and then, to Angus, "I apologize in advance."

"What for?" he asked.

Sophie didn't have a chance to answer before her mother was leaning over the bannister, calling, "Sophia Grace Creedon, do you have *any idea* what I've been through over the last two hours? I've rung everyone I can think of, I've been out scouring the streets, I was about to phone the police just this minute – "

"Pardon me, Mrs. Creedon," Angus said, stepping into view. "But please don't be angry with Sophie." Sophie's mother opened her mouth to say something and then, apparently at a loss, she shut it again. "You see," Angus continued, "I said that I'd walk her home, and we meant to come straight back, but we ran into some friends."

"Friends?" Anna repeated dubiously.

"Yes. From university."

"You're at university?" she asked, beginning to sound interested.

"Second year at Edinburgh, studying archaeology."

"I see," Anna said, the anger in her tone draining away and leaving speculation. *Here we go,* Sophie thought, mentally rolling her eyes.

"So we went for a coffee, and lost track of time, and when

we got back outside the buses weren't running, and we couldn't get mobile reception, so we had to walk – "

"You walked?" Anna interrupted. "All the way from the Old Town?"

"That's right," Angus said.

"Well come upstairs, get into the warm – you must both be frozen!"

Anna ducked back into the flat as they began to climb the stairs. "Nice," Sophie said in a low voice. "I hope you can recall what we talked about with your 'friends', all of their names, hometowns, and areas of interest, because believe me, she's going to ask."

"It'll be fine," he said with a grin. "Mums always love me."

Sophie gave him a dubious look, but when they came into the flat her mother smiled at Angus and held out her hand, as if proving his point. He shook it firmly, and Sophie groaned inwardly. Her mother was always going on about the importance of a firm handshake, and how it separated the wheat from the chaff. She was probably already planning the wedding.

"So," Anna said as she helped them hang up their wet things, "how do you two know each other?"

"I'm sure I told you about Angus, Mum," Sophie said. "We work together at the café."

"Oh, no doubt you did," Anna said, waving a hand distractedly. "You know that I'm hopeless until I have a face to match with a name." She smiled at Angus. "Lovely to meet you now, though. And I'm so glad Sophie's getting to know some people of her own age up here. Perhaps you can change her mind about university. She has a place at Oxford, you know, and another one at a music conservatory – "

"Mum," Sophie interrupted in a warning tone.

"She says she doesn't want to go," Anna continued, as if she hadn't heard. "But I think that's only because she hasn't realized how much fun it could be."

"Mum, please! Not now!"

Anna smiled indulgently, still looking at Angus. "I don't suppose you've had any tea?"

"No," Angus said, "but really I should be getting back to uni – "

"In this weather?" Anna shook her head. "This is no night for walking, and as you've already found out, the buses aren't running."

"I'll get a taxi."

"You can try – no doubt they're swamped. But you're also very welcome to stay. There's a pull-out sofa in the lounge."

"Ah…I don't know – " Angus began, glancing at Sophie, but Anna interrupted.

"Stay for tea, anyhow. Then, if the weather improves, we can try to find you a taxi." The hope on her face was so obvious that Sophie relented a little. Her mother so clearly and desperately wanted everything to be alright, and she had no idea of how very far from alright things were. Pretending was the least she could do.

"Great," Angus said, with a smile that looked entirely sincere. "Thank you."

*

Sophie had to admit, dinner wasn't as bad as she'd imagined. Anna kept Angus talking through most of it, asking about his course and the places he'd been on field trips, and what he wanted to do when he left university.

"Dig," he answered unequivocally. "Preferably somewhere warmer and drier than here."

Anna looked wistful. "That sounds lovely – doesn't it Sophie?" Without waiting for Sophie to answer, she continued, "I've often thought of packing everything in and moving to someplace warm, running painting holidays…"

"Have you?" Sophie asked. It was the first she'd heard of this rather alarming plan, and she might have pushed her mother on it if she hadn't remembered that she wouldn't be around to see it implemented. "That sounds…nice," she said lamely, pushing the end of her dinner around her plate with a fork.

"Most anyplace else sounds nice on a night like this," Anna said, standing up and peering out the small sliver of window that wasn't crusted over with snow. Clearly, the storm was still going strong. "I don't think you'll be going anywhere tonight," she said, turning to Angus. "I'll go see to that sofa."

"Don't trouble yourself," he said. "I can do it. I'll do the dishes too."

"Oh no – there's no need."

"Well then, I'll dry them. Just let me phone my flatmates first so they don't think I'm frozen to death in an alley somewhere." He went out into the hallway, ostensibly to find his phone, though he gave Sophie a covert wink when her mother's back was turned. She scowled in response.

As soon as Angus was out of earshot, Sophie's mum said, "What a lovely young man."

"Yeah, Angus is nice," Sophie said, picking up dishes and bringing them to the sink.

"There's nothing wrong with nice," Anna said, squeezing washing up liquid under the running water.

"Mum," Sophie sighed.

"I'm only saying – "

"I *know* what you're saying," she said. "But believe me, it isn't like that. Not with Angus, not with Rive, not with anyone."

"Oh, Sophie…"

"What?" Sophie snapped. "Why are you trying so hard to pair me up with someone? Didn't you hear that counselor tell me that it's normal to grieve two years for someone you loved? Lucas hasn't even been gone two months!"

Her mother was looking at her as if she'd slapped her. "You loved him?" she asked, sounding honestly stunned.

Crap, Sophie thought. She hadn't meant to say that, but now there was no taking it back. "Yes, Mum. I loved him."

Anna sloshed soapy water around the dinner dishes ruminatively for a few minutes. At last she said, "Maybe you're right. Maybe I *am* pushing you too hard to move on." She sighed, then turned to Sophie. Sophie was shocked by how exhausted her mother looked – her skin pale, her blue eyes faded and undercut by shadows. It made it all the more alarming when she said, "It's only because I don't want you to end up like me."

"Like you, how?"

"Forty-five years old and alone."

"Mum, you're not! Well, you are forty-five, but you're not alone." She put her arms around her mother's neck, hugged her. She was ashamed to realize she couldn't remember the last time she'd done so. "I promise you, I won't end up forty-five and alone," she said, wishing that it weren't so patently true. Wishing that her mother wasn't about to come face-to-face with a grief of her own.

"Of course you won't," Anna said, hugging her back. "Why would you? You're a lovely, talented girl, with your whole life ahead of you. Whatever you choose to do with it, I know that it will be brilliant. And I promise to stop interfering. Well, I promise to try."

Sophie smiled, but she couldn't quite make herself answer.

*

Anna went to bed early, after delivering a pile of sheets and blankets to the sitting room, where Sophie and Angus were sitting on the sofa, watching weather reports on the news.

"What are they saying?" Anna asked, setting the bedding on an armchair.

"The whole country's getting hit," Angus answered.

"Yeah," said Sophie. "They showed this satellite map, and you couldn't actually see anything but white."

"Well then, I wouldn't hurry out of bed in the morning. There's ice cream in the freezer, if you aren't too cold for it."

"Thanks Mum," Sophie said.

"Likewise," Angus said. "Thanks for everything."

"You're very welcome," Anna said. She seemed on the verge of saying something else, but then she looked at Sophie and shook her head slightly. "Sleep well."

"Hm," Sophie said speculatively, after she'd gone.

"Hm, what?" Angus asked.

"I just thought mums were meant to kick up more of a fuss when a guy's staying over. You know, padlock their teenage daughters in the bedroom or whatever."

Angus chuckled. "I don't think you're the typical teenage daughter. And I'm definitely not the typical guy."

"I suppose not," she said.

"Besides, I told you that mums love me."

"Well, mine certainly does. How much experience are you speaking from?"

"Now *that* would be telling." Sophie rolled her eyes. But his smile faded as he studied her. "You tired?"

"Yes. But if I go to sleep, I know I'll dream of sea witches."

"Better not go to sleep, then. Ice cream?"

"I guess. I'll get it." She went to the freezer, and found that her mother had got two tubs of her favorite flavor – the one she usually said was too expensive. With another pang of guilt, she took one of them out, microwaved it for ten seconds, then brought it back to the living room with two spoons.

Angus had switched from the news channel to one showing an old black and white film. "What is this?" Sophie said, handing him the ice cream and a spoon and indicating the telly.

"'The Philadelphia Story'," he answered. Then, seeing Sophie's blank look, "Are you serious? You've never seen it?"

"Never even heard of it," Sophie said, sitting back down beside him.

Angus shook his head. "That's a travesty. It's classic Hepburn."

"Audrey?"

"Katharine. Definitely the better actress." He handed the ice cream to Sophie and she took a little bit, sucking ruminatively on the spoon as she tried to work out what was happening onscreen. Mostly, it seemed to involve Katharine Hepburn's character arguing with everyone she came into contact with.

"Okay," Sophie said, "I'm lost."

"It's fairly simple, actually," Angus said. "See, she's a rich socialite. She used to be married to Cary Grant, but he drank too much, so she left him. Now she's about to marry John Howard, even though she doesn't really love him."

"Why would she do that?"

Angus shrugged. "I suppose because he worships her. And he's rich. And he doesn't drink."

"Right," Sophie said. "So who's the third guy?"

"Jimmy Stewart – he plays a tabloid journalist who's come to report on the wedding."

"So who's the love interest?"

"All of them," Angus said, "at one point or another. That's what makes it funny."

"Right," Sophie said. She wasn't really a fan of old films, but after a while she found herself enjoying this one. She even laughed out loud a few times, and she was sorry when it was finished.

"So," Angus asked as Sophie shut off the telly, "what did you think?"

"Katharine's character should have picked Jimmy Stewart instead of her ex."

"Seriously?"

"Yeah. Why do you say it like that?"

"I don't know. It's just, from what you've told me about Lucas, you're more into the intense, brooding type."

Lucas. She walked to the window. Outside, the sky was still full of snow, and the weird orange light it makes over a nighttime city. The wind moaned in the eaves, reminding her of Ardnasheen, and the way it had felt to lie in the circle of Lucas's arms, and know that the weather couldn't reach her. To know that she was safe.

Some of the pain must have showed on her face, because Angus said, "Sorry. I guess that overstepped a boundary."

"No, you didn't. It's just…"

What, Sophie? She didn't know. Angus's brown eyes rested on her face, sympathetic but speculative. "Don't," he said.

"Don't what?"

"Blame yourself for forgetting about him for a little while." She looked away, irritated that it was so obvious, and that she was so incapable of denying it. "It's true, isn't it? Just now, watching that film, was the first time in a long time that you haven't been completely miserable. And then it ended, and you remembered, and now you feel guilty for not worrying about him for the last two hours."

Sophie looked at Angus for a moment, and then smiled dryly. "That is just plain creepy."

"I suppose it's useless to tell you that you have nothing to feel guilty about."

"You suppose right."

He let out a sigh, leaned his head back on the sofa cushion and looked at her, as if trying to choose the right words. Finally, he said, "As far as I know, there's no rule about loving someone that says you can't have your own life too…or about grief that says it has to be constant."

"I know that," Sophie said, fiddling with the buttons on her cardigan. "But this isn't an ordinary love, or an ordinary grief."

Angus's eyes were searching. "Don't take this the wrong way, Sophie, but how could you possibly know that?"

"You've heard the story," she said irritated. "You know that Lucas and me…that it isn't an ordinary human relationship."

"In the details, maybe," he conceded. "But you're human enough now, and love is love, and grief is grief."

"There's more to it than just love, or grief," Sophie said bitterly. "More than any normal person could understand."

She'd half-expected him to be annoyed with her for saying that, but his solicitous expression didn't change. "And how many normal people have you told?"

Sophie glanced at him, and then back at her hands.

"That's what I thought. So, here's your chance."

"Pardon?"

"You heard me. Lay it all out for me – whatever it is that you're hiding from all of us normal people that makes your situation unique."

"I'm…not sure that's a good idea."

He shook his head, smiled. "Sophie, today we've climbed

down a well into someplace that properly belongs in 'Lord of the Rings', hung out with an ancient deity, and gone on a vision quest to a mythical underwater city. Do you really think anything you have to say can rattle me?"

"I think…" she began, then stopped. "It's just…" All at once, she was exhausted – so tired of hiding painful truths from everyone around her. Tired of driving herself on, when there was nowhere to go, and nothing to hope for. "Okay, Angus. I'll tell you. But you have to promise not to say anything about this to anyone."

"You don't need to ask me to promise that," he said. "I wouldn't, without your permission."

His sincerity nearly broke her heart, and it made her confession all the more difficult. It wasn't fair to burden him with the truth; but she knew that now, there was no way back. Taking a deep breath, she said, "I'm dying."

Angus blinked at her for a moment, clearly uncertain as to whether or not to believe her.

"You heard me right," she said. "You see, all of this – me being here, a human girl, in this life – it wasn't meant to happen. I did something, I don't know what…but somehow, I stole it. This life…my body, my soul. And because of that, I only get to keep them for a little while."

"How little?" he asked, his face and voice now deadly serious.

"Till my next birthday."

"Which is when?"

"The twenty-first of June."

There was a long pause, during which he looked at her as if he could excavate meaning from her face as he did from layers of earth. "Why did you do it, then?" he asked finally. "I mean, if you knew you'd have so little time here…so little time to spend with Lucas?"

"I did it to try to get him back to Heaven." Her voice shook. She clasped her hands together to keep them from shaking, too. "I still don't know why. I can't remember being an aeon, you see – well, no more than flashes. I only know that it was important enough that I was willing to die for it.

"But I failed. I lost him – or I thought I had. Now I have one more chance, but it's so slim…" She stopped, too close to tears to continue.

Angus said nothing, but he reached out, put a hand on her shoulder as he had when they'd watched Dahud toying with Lucas. They sat like that for a long time, while she fought to control her emotions. When she'd mastered herself at last, she looked at Angus and said, "So you see, there's nothing ordinary about me, or Lucas, or what I feel for him. And very soon, it won't matter."

"God, Sophie," he said after another long pause. "That's just…I'm sorry."

"I told you, you didn't want to hear it."

"That's not what I meant. I'm just sorry that it's like this. Sorry things can't be better for you…"

She shook her head, unable to answer. Tears spattered onto her clenched hands. Angus watched her for a moment, his face pained. And then he wrapped his arms around her, pulling her close, and she began to cry in earnest: silent, wracking sobs. He said nothing, but he didn't pull away. He just held her while the storm beat at the glass and the night wore on, and finally, she cried herself to sleep.

CHAPTER 18

"Put your fingers here," Lucifer said, pointing to four of the strings, "in a row."

She curved her fingers as he'd demonstrated earlier, placing the thumb and the first three fingertips lightly on the fine gold wires. "Now pluck them with your fingernails."

Tentatively, she pulled her index finger into her palm. A note rang out, pure and glasslike in the evening air, echoing among the tombstones. Thrilled, she played the others, but the sound muddied as the reverberant notes blended to dissonance.

He smiled at her look of annoyance. "With a wire-strung harp, you have to damp as many notes as you play. Cancel out the ones that clash, but leave the ones that harmonize." He demonstrated, touching his finger to two of the strings to silence them, leaving the others to ring out until the sound drifter away into the flowering branches of the tree above them.

"Wouldn't it be easier to string it with something less... well...echoey?" she asked.

"Easier, yes," Lucifer said, still smiling. "But nowhere near as beautiful."

She frowned down at the instrument in her lap. "I'll never learn how to do this."

"Of course you will."

"Not like you do."

He shrugged. "It's not a fair comparison. Angels were made with the gift of music. Aeons...well, I guess you weren't."

They were both silent for a moment, neither meeting the other's eye. It was always the same when something recalled the difference between them.

"You'll learn if you practice," Lucifer said at last, "just like the humans do. Oh, Sophia," he said, stricken eyes flying up to her face. "I didn't mean – I shouldn't have said – "

"Don't apologize," she interrupted, her own eyes calm. "It's alright." And it was. She didn't know how or when, but at some point during the time since he'd given her the tear bottle, her grief had receded. It still gave her a pang to think of the world she'd made and couldn't save, but it no longer consumed her.

She put the harp aside and took a deep breath, suddenly shy. "I...I wanted to thank you, Lucifer," she said.

"What for?" he answered.

She gestured to the harp. "For this." Finally, she met his eyes. "For all of it. You've...well, you've saved me."

She only realized that she'd reached out her hand to him

259

when he took it, his fingers closing over hers with a jolt of warmth. "I think you saved yourself," he said, holding her eyes. "But either way, it's been a pleasure."

She smiled ruefully. "I can't have been the best of company."

"I wouldn't want any other," he said, his voice low. And there was a note in it that surprised her – a note she'd heard when two aeons of a syzygy, or certain humans, spoke to each other. She looked at him, searching for evidence that she'd heard what she thought she'd heard. She didn't have to look far.

"Lucifer?" she said softly, her hand tightening around his. He pulled on it gently, urging her closer. Her heart beat, her breath quickened in response to this strange emotion she'd never felt before, and yet seemed so familiar.

"Sophia," he said, reaching a tentative hand to cup her cheek. It felt like a trail of stars. "Should I stop?"

"No," she whispered, closing her eyes. There was a moment that seemed to last forever; a moment of infinite possibility. And then his lips touched hers.

She'd seen it so many times before – her own kind with their consorts, the humans with their lovers – but she'd never thought a kiss would feel like this. Lucifer was gentle, barely touching her, and yet it was like a spark to dry kindling. Heat raged in her, and she knew in that moment that she'd do anything for him.

He began to break away, but she wrapped her arms around

his neck and pulled him close. This time, when their lips met, there was nothing gentle about it. She kissed him with a hunger she'd never known she had – with utter abandon. She kissed him as if she meant to dissolve into him, and that was how he kissed her back.

Finally, regretfully, they broke apart. Lucifer's face was stricken. The fire that had kindled in Sophia crumbled into ash. "What is it?" she asked.

"I'm sorry...I should never have – "

"Don't say it," she said, locking her arms more tightly around him and resting her head on his chest. It fit into the curve of his neck as if they'd been made to sit like this. "Please, don't tell me you regret it."

There was a long moment of silence, and then she felt his hand in her hair, gently stroking it. "No, I don't regret it. Not if you don't."

"Never," she said.

*

Sophie woke slowly, unwilling to leave the warmth of the arms that she'd missed for so long. She drifted with the beating of his heart, the steady ebb-and-flow of his breath. She remembered grief, but she couldn't remember what it was for. She could never grieve here, beside him...

Her eyes snapped open to dim grey light. For a moment, she didn't know where she was, only that she lay on something warm, and comforting…and moving. Breathing. She sat up in horror, then carefully pushed Angus's arm from where it had fallen across her shoulders, and lowered it onto his lap. She was mortified to have slept here with him, however innocently; mortified to have lost it in front of him the night before. She scuttled out into the hallway, praying that her mother hadn't woken up and witnessed the scene.

But her mother's bedroom door was shut, the flat dim and silent. Sophie went into her own room and lay down in her cold bed, pulling the covers right up to her ears. She felt far too wound up to sleep, but almost as soon as she'd thought it, she found herself waking an hour later from another dream, in which she wandered an empty house looking for someone whose face she couldn't remember.

She heard voices from down the hallway. She got up and changed her clothes, shoving the ones she'd slept in far down into the laundry basket, as if they might tell on her. Then, taking a deep breath, she went into the kitchen.

If either Angus or her mother knew her secret, neither of them showed it. Both of them smiled at her as she sat down, and her mother poured her a cup of coffee. She said, "I was just telling Angus, the BBC's reporting there hasn't been a storm like this in a hundred years. Apparently the snow's three feet deep."

Looking at the kitchen window, now dark with accumulated snow, Sophie had no trouble believing it.

"I hope the pull-out is comfortable," Anna said to Angus. "You might be staying here for a while."

Although he'd had no chance to find out, Angus smiled and said, "It is, and thanks for the invitation. But actually, I think I'd better try to get home. There are some things I need to see to."

Sophie looked at Angus. Angus looked into his cup of coffee, to which he was adding sugar in alarming proportions. She could see why he'd want to get home, but at the same time, she couldn't help wondering whether the vagueness of the excuse and his eagerness to battle the snowdrifts had anything to do with her confession, her tears, or the fact that she'd slept the whole night in his arms. *Do not blush,* she told herself, and managed it by putting her bare feet on the freezing floor.

"Well, if you're sure," Anna said doubtfully. "But if you change your mind, you're welcome to stay. Or come back, if the going's too hard."

"Thank you," he said. "You've been very kind." He included Sophie in the smile he offered Anna, making her feel slightly better.

After breakfast, Sophie walked him downstairs. When she opened the door, she saw several neighbors already busy clearing the pavements, though the snow was still falling. Beyond their activity, though, was a deeper hush, so profound it was like a background noise of its own. The silence of a city stopped in its tracks.

"Bizarre," Sophie said.

"The snow?" Angus asked.

"The quiet." She looked up at him. He met her eyes frankly. "Listen – I'm sorry about last night."

Angus frowned. "Why?"

"I shouldn't have told you all of that…and then, to start bawling like a complete idiot…"

But Angus only shook his head. "You don't need to apologize, Sophie. I'm glad that I could be there for you."

She gave him a skeptical look. "You can't still be thinking this is fun."

"No – not fun. But these things that you're involved in – they're *real*." He paused, as if searching for words. "I know it sounds strange, given everything, but it's the first time in my life that I've felt like I'm a part of something that actually matters."

"I'd say it matters a bit too much."

He shrugged. "Either way, I'm not giving up."

"On what?"

"On you."

Crap. He knows. But then, he went on, "I mean, this whole prophecy thing – I don't like to rubbish your reading of it, but isn't it in the nature of prophecies to be figurative?"

"So, you don't believe it?"

"It's not that. No doubt it means *something* – I'm just not sure that it's exactly what you think it means…or at any rate, that there's only one way of interpreting it."

"Funny, Michael said something similar."

Angus looked startled. "Michael? The one who poisoned Lucas?"

Sophie paused for a moment, cursing her carelessness, "Same one."

"You've seen him?"

She didn't know whether or not she should tell Angus about what had happened the other night. No, she decided. She'd given him enough to worry about already. "It's something we've discussed in the past," she answered, which was true enough.

Angus gave her a look, as if he knew that she wasn't being precisely honest, but he only said, "Well, there you go. If an angel says the same thing, there must be something in it."

"I hope so," Sophie answered. Catching a flash of color out of the corner of her eye, she turned to see the post man trudging up the street in bright red wellies and a Santa hat. "Unbelievable!" she said, as he stopped to hand a stack of post to one of her neighbors.

"'Neither snow, nor rain, nor heat, nor gloom of night…'" Angus said as the postman approached them.

"Isn't that the US postal service?" Sophie asked.

"The ancient Persian one, actually. Herodotus wrote that

about their mounted couriers, because nothing ever seemed to stop them."

"You do have a store of peculiar information."

"Goes with the degree." He smiled at her, sincere and apparently untroubled. She wondered if he actually believed what he'd said about the prophecy. She wished that she could. "See you soon, Sophie," he said.

"Alright," she answered. "And thanks – for everything."

He lifted a hand, then turned and trudged off down the street, saluting the postman as he passed. Sophie was still watching him when the postman reached her door. He rummaged in his bag, pulled out a padded envelope and handed it to her.

"This is for me?" Sophie asked. She couldn't think of anyone who would have sent her a package, except maybe her father, and the handwriting on the address label wasn't anything like his: bold capitals inscribed in black sharpie.

"Looks that way," the postman answered cheerfully. He handed her a bundle of smaller envelopes, too.

"Thanks," she said, and went back inside. She turned the package over as she went up the stairs, but there was no return address, and the postmark was illegible.

When she got inside the flat, Sophie put her mother's post on the hall table and then went into her bedroom with the package, a growing tingle of foreboding running down her spine. She shut the door behind her and then sat down on the bed, looking at her name in block capitals for a few long moments before she tore the seal.

Three books slid out of the envelope, onto her lap. She picked up the top one. The cover was an anime drawing of a dark-haired girl in a flowing blue coat and knee-high combat boots, holding a gleaming sword above her head as she stood above a throng of reaching monsters. The title – or what she assumed was the title – was in Japanese.

The second book's cover had the same character on it, but this time she sat on the branch of a tree in a lush, beautiful garden, throttling a snake with her bare hands. On the third cover, the same girl sat on the top of a pitched roof, with a full moon behind her and deep blue wings trailing down from her shoulders. There was a fluorescent pink post-it note stuck to this last cover, with the same black, blocky writing in which the envelope had been addressed. It read:

CALL ME!!! xxS

Sophie only knew one S who would have sent her a package like this – or any package at all – but she had no idea of Suri's phone number, or whether she even had a phone. She picked up her mobile, and pushed Ailsa's number at Madainneag. Ailsa picked up after a few rings.

"So," she said, "you got the mags."

"Hello to you, too," Sophie answered.

"Sorry," Ailsa said. "It's just that we've been waiting and

waiting for you to get them. We thought with the snow it might take ages."

"Nah. My intrepid postman put them into my hands fifteen minutes ago. So, what's the story?"

"I think you'd better talk to Suri," Ailsa said. "Hang on." Without giving Sophie time to answer, she put the phone aside and started calling for Suri. Sophie heard the sound of a door opening and closing, an unintelligible exchange of girls' voices, and then Suri picked up the phone.

"You got them!" she cried, her voice ringing with excitement.

"I got them," Sophie said, "but what exactly am I supposed to be *getting* from them?"

"Come on, Sophie: doesn't the cover girl look at all familiar?"

"She looks like a mutant Barbie doll."

"She's *you*, dumbass!"

Sophie looked at the top cover. "Even with a mind wide open, that's a bit of a leap."

"Didn't you read it?"

"Sorry, but I haven't quite got round to learning Japanese yet."

Suri let out a sigh of exasperation. "Angel Powers 101: we can read and speak any human language."

"I'm not an angel. And anyway, I'm looking right at it, and I have no idea what it says."

"That's because you're trying too hard. Remember how you saw my armor?"

Sophie looked down at the cover with the monsters, and let her focus relax. The Japanese characters shifted, wriggled and then swam into focus. They read, "Sophia 10: Double Demon." The tingle of premonition became a tide.

"Okay, you've got my attention. Where did these come from?"

"Amazon. I stumbled over them, looking for something else. Turns out it's a whole series. There're Sophia books going back to the '90s, but they only printed a couple hundred of each one. These days they're seriously rare – and worth a fortune."

Trying to maintain her calm against the certainty that her life was about to take a further nosedive into the bizarre, Sophie said, "So what are they about?"

"A type of semi-deity, called an aeon, who's named Sophia and fights the powers of darkness."

"Okay, that's weird."

"*Weird?* It's freaking *crazy!*"

"Is it?" Sophie argued. "Aeons seem to be a big deal in wargame land – why not in manga?"

"No," Suri said, sounding far too certain. "This is no coincidence."

"How do you know?"

"Look who wrote them."

Sophie looked again at the cover. The author's credit was

so small that at first she didn't see it: just a few tiny pen-strokes at the bottom left-hand corner of the image. She relaxed her eyes, and they came into focus, spelling "Tear."

"Who's Tear?" she asked.

"Jeez, Sophie, and you're supposed to be the smart one! Not 'tear' like what comes out of your eye, 'tear' like what you do with a piece of paper."

"I'm still not seeing the point."

"*Tear*, Sophie. Synonymous with rip, split, divide, dissever –"

"Rive," Sophie said, and dropped the book into her lap as if it were filthy.

"I told you there was something off about him."

"But Rive's a couple of years older than I am, at most. How could he have been writing these since the nineties?"

"Same way I can go to two parties in Edinburgh, three hundred years apart."

The premonition Sophie'd had on opening the package edged toward a truth she didn't want to face. "I thought you said he wasn't an angel."

"He isn't."

"So he's a demon?" Sophie asked, wishing she didn't sound so hopeful.

Another sigh of exasperation. "No, Sophie. He's an aeon, and not just any aeon."

"No?" Sophie murmured.

270

"No. Sophie, Rive is *Theletos*. Your consort."

Sophie paused as the words sank in. "You don't know that."

"As far as I know, aeons never leave their partners – except you, of course. Left him hanging, in fact, for several millennia. Who the hell else would it be?"

After a long moment's thought, Sophie said, "Okay, I admit, I can see how you got there…but on the other hand, it makes no sense at all! I mean, I ditched Theletos for Lucas a long time before I came down here, and back then I was right there in Heaven. Why wait till now, when it's so much harder and more dangerous, to come after me?"

"Maybe he didn't think he had a chance before. But now that Lucas is well and truly gone – "

"Lucas *isn't* well and truly gone!"

"No – but you thought he was when you first met Rive. Didn't you?"

Sophie considered it all, searching for a hole in the logic, for some way for it not to be true. But by the leaden feeling in her gut, she knew that Suri's words made sense. And when she held them against the conversation she'd overheard before the grindylow attacked her, likelihood became certainty: it could only have been Rive speaking with Michael.

"He's here to take me back," she said.

"Well, duh."

"I won't let him!"

271

"Okay…"

"Why did you say it like that? You *want* me to go with him? Are you back in league with Michael?"

"No, and I was never in league with Michael. I just think it might not be as simple as just saying no."

It might soften the blow if she's allowed to save him… "Of course it is," Sophie insisted, "and that's exactly what I'm going to do, as soon as I find him."

"Okay, but Sophie –

"Yeah, yeah, I'll be careful."

"I was going to say, be nice to him."

Sophie paused incredulously. Then: "Be *nice* to the guy who's trying to kidnap me?"

"You don't know he's trying to kidnap you. But you do know he cares about you, or he wouldn't be here."

"Cares about me? Like Michael, who sees me as a pawn in the Balance?"

"Not many of us are like Michael," Suri said gently. Remembering the overheard conversation, Sophie had to admit to herself that Rive hadn't necessarily agreed with him. "And besides, there's the way he looks at you."

"How does he look at me?"

"Like a lot more than a pawn in the Balance."

This caught Sophie off guard. Somehow, in all of the time that she'd known about her erstwhile consort, it had never occurred to her that he might still care about her. In fact, she realized with a guilty twinge, she'd simply assumed that he never had.

After a moment, Suri interrupted Sophie's rumination cheerfully: "I have some good news, though."

"Fantastic," Sophie grumbled.

"I've been doing some research, and I've found out how we get there – to Ker-Ys."

"You waited till *now* to tell me this?" Sophie cried.

"Hey, there's a lot to get through!"

"Okay, sorry. So how do we do it?"

"There are two possibilities. One, you get a selkie to loan you its skin."

Sophie thought of the bone-wrenching metamorphosis in her first dream of the underwater city. She wasn't eager to try that again. Besides, she didn't know where to begin to look for a selkie. "And the other?" she asked.

"You catch a water horse and ride it there."

"You must be joking."

"Nope. The good news is, once you get a bridle on it, it loses its power over you and has to do exactly what you want. Apparently it's been done in the past – at least, someone must have done it and lived to tell about it."

"Is that meant to convince me it's the best option?"

"Actually, I think it's the only option. We – I mean the angels, and Rive I suppose, if he really is an aeon – can shift into seal form if we choose to. But humans can't, and as far as the local faeries know, no one's ever talked a selkie into handing over its skin. Trying to steal one would be just as hard, and leaves too much to chance."

"How is this good news?"

"Well…there's one problem."

"Let's hear it," Sophie said wearily.

"It turns out you can't actually get into a faery queen's realm unless she gives you a token."

"A silver bough," Sophie said, her spirits rising for the first time since the conversation began.

"How did you know that?"

"Because I've got one."

"What? How?"

"Long story. The point is, if we can get to Ker-Ys, we can get through the faery door. Can we get to Ker-Ys?"

"Well," Suri said, "it turns out Dahud's a control freak. There's only one door to her city, but lucky for us, it's here in Ardnasheen. Apparently there's a sea cave somewhere on the promontory – "

"There is. I've been there."

"Wow…well then, I guess we're all set."

"Not quite. Dad's coming up for Christmas. There's no way Mum's going to let me leave her alone with him."

"So, we'll do it after."

"We can't," Sophie said. "You know that old lady I was

telling you about, Morag? Well, it turns out there's more to her than meets the eye." She told Suri all that Morag had told her.

"Jeez, this all just keeps getting weirder and weirder."

"No kidding. And the solstice is only two weeks away. I don't know what we're going to do."

"Don't worry, honey," Suri answered, a smile in her voice. "I always think of something."

CHAPTER 19

Everybody said that the snow wouldn't last, but the cold snap held onto Edinburgh day after day. The banks pushed up by the snow-ploughs froze solid, and the pavements were so slippery that it was easier to walk in the street. Outside Sophie's flat, the air echoed with the shrieks and laughter of the children sledging in the park up the road. The city's snow-capped roofs and spires made a picture-perfect Christmas card.

But Sophie was oblivious to it all. Every day that passed took her a step closer to her confrontation with Dahud, and she felt anything but ready. Everywhere she looked, it seemed there were loose ends; for every piece of the puzzle she had, there was another she didn't. But the one giving her the biggest headache was Rive.

Now that she actually wanted to see him, he'd left off his habit of appearing whenever she was alone somewhere creepy. A few days' aimlessly wandering cemeteries and lonely closes convinced her that he wasn't going to appear. Then she went

276

back to the derelict church, hoping that Michael would be able to help. But Michael's basement room was empty. There wasn't even a footprint in the dust to show that they'd ever been there. Likewise, when she went to the Toll House there was no old woman in the garden, and when she stepped into the well, she got nothing for it but cold, wet feet.

She didn't even have Angus to confide in. Matrika had told her on her first day back at work that he'd been offered a place unexpectedly on another dig, and he'd be gone for a week. "Where is it?" she asked.

"Egypt," Matrika said, shaking her head. "Lucky lad."

Egypt seemed a million miles away from the frozen city beyond the Eyrie window. Sophie couldn't help wondering if that had been behind Angus's decision to go: if he was avoiding her. Maybe he did know that they'd slept together on the couch that night, and thought she'd take it the wrong way. Or maybe he'd thought better of his promise to help her. She wouldn't blame him if he decided that her problems were too much to deal with. She'd even gone as far as to wonder whether she should quit her job, to spare him the hassle of avoiding her, when he returned to work.

"You're back!" Sophie cried when she walked into the café a week later, to find Angus leaning on the counter, his skin tanned dark and his eyes focused intently on a battered, cloth-bound book.

He looked up at her, his eyes wide with what looked

disturbingly like horror, and snapped the book shut. Sophie stopped, startled, until he offered her an apologetic smile. "Sorry," he said, shoving the book into his bag, but not before Sophie saw the gold-leaf image on the front: an outline of a bird with a human head, which looked vaguely familiar. "You startled me. I was miles away."

"Oh," she said. "It must be a really good book."

"Actually, not really. It's just something for my course… quite boring." But he didn't meet her eyes as he said it.

"Are you alright?" Sophie asked, as she came around the counter and took off her jacket.

"Sure. Peachy. Why do you ask?" Though he looked at her now, his eyes were skittery, evasive.

"Because you're acting weird," she said, too tired for prevarication. "And you pretty much disappeared off the face of the earth for a week. I can't help wondering if I've done something to offend you." A terrible thought struck her. "You haven't been speaking to my mother, have you?"

He laughed. "Your mother? Definitely not." When the laughter died, he seemed calmer. "But I can see why you'd think something was…I mean, I'm sorry I took off like that. I should have phoned you. But someone dropped out of the trip at the last minute, and I *really* need to impress this professor, and I had about five seconds to pack and get on the plane – "

"Don't apologize," Sophie said. "It's not as if you need my permission to go somewhere. I'm just glad – " she stopped, realizing that she didn't know how to explain to him what she was glad about. She wasn't even certain herself. "I'm glad you're back," she said at last. "Things have gotten weird." He raised his eyebrows. "Okay, weird*er.*"

He smiled, finally looking like himself. "That sounds interesting. Tell me what happened."

"I'll really need to show you."

"Does it involve trips to parallel worlds?"

She smiled. "No, thankfully."

"Alright, then. Lunch time, the Eyrie?"

She nodded, and then stepped up to the counter to serve the first of the morning's customers.

*

Angus was already in the Eyrie when business slowed enough for Sophie to take her break. He was sitting at the table, eating half a tuna sandwich. Freyja sat beside him, eating the other half.

"I don't know why she's so skinny," Sophie observed, indicating Freyja as she sat down. "She eats like a horse."

"Goddess powers," Angus answered.

"What?"

"Her namesake, Freyja. Norse goddess of love?" Seeing Sophie's blank look, he said, "Never mind. Now what have you got for me?"

Sophie reached into her bag for the books, and pushed

them across the table to him. Angus raised his eyebrows. "I didn't really take you for the manga type."

"I'm not. Suri sent them. They're all about a super-hero called Sophia, who fights the powers of darkness."

Angus shoved the end of his sandwich aside, and Freyja, having finished her half, started right in on it. He flipped through the books, and then said with a wry smile, "So how does it feel to be an action hero?"

"Distinctly creepy. Especially since Rive's the author."

His smiled flattened. "The DJ from that club the other night?"

Sophie nodded. "And that's not all. Remember how Suri got a weird feeling about him? Well, it turns out she was right." She filled him in on Suri's theory that Rive was Theletos. He listened with interest, but when she was finished he sat in silence, still thumbing through the books.

"Come on, Angus," Sophie said at last. "You must have thoughts about this."

He looked up at her, dark eyes frank. "Actually, I feel sorry for him."

"You *what?*"

"Think about it from his point of view. His soul mate falls for another guy and goes chasing him around the known universe, even after he's damned. But Rive – or Theletos – comes looking for her – you – anyway, searching Heaven and

Earth on the off chance that you just might change your mind and – "

"Alright, that's enough," Sophie interrupted. "I'm feeling properly guilty now."

Angus smiled slightly. "I wasn't trying to make you feel guilty. I just think you shouldn't necessarily assume Rive has nefarious designs on you."

"But he's stalking me!"

"That's one way of looking at it."

"There's another?"

"He's trying to help the girl he loves."

Hearing him put it so bluntly gave Sophie a strange feeling – a memory, perhaps, of something she'd felt once before, too deep and distant now to name. "You honestly think he loves me, after all this time?" she asked at last.

"I know he does."

"How?" Sophie demanded, liking this conversation less and less.

Angus tapped the cover of one of the books. "The way he draws you."

Sophie sat in silence, at a loss for words. Despite what Suri had said, she hadn't really believed that Rive's motivation might be as simple as love, until Angus said it too.

"But why?" Sophie asked at last. "Why would he want to help me – never mind love me – after everything I've done?"

Angus's eyes were direct, penetrating, and also slightly

pitying. "That's not how love works, Sophie. There is no 'why' and 'because'. It just is, and it transcends everything. Even jealousy."

He was right, of course, and once again he'd got so simply and poignantly to the heart of the matter that Sophie didn't know what to say. As they sat silent in the fading light of the cloud-veiled sunset, she wondered how she could be so certain of her love for Lucas, when she understood it so little.

Abruptly, Freyja leapt from the table to one of the window seats. Startled, Sophie looked up, and then she followed her. "God, it's snowing again?" she said, staring at the flakes falling like jewels in the silvery light.

"Must be a sign," Angus said.

"Of what?"

"Impending apocalypse?"

"Bad joke." But when she turned to him his look was strange, not remotely humorous – as if he was poised on the brink of asking her a difficult question, but couldn't quite push himself over it. "Spit it out, Angus," she said.

His eyes flickered away. "Are you going to go speak to him? Rive?"

Sophie knew that it wasn't the question he'd been pondering, and she was glad. "I would, but I have no idea how to find him."

"Have you tried the club?"

Duh, Sophie. She felt ridiculous for not having thought of it herself. Or maybe, she thought uncomfortably, she hadn't let herself think of it, because she didn't want to find out that Suri and Angus were right about Rive's reasons for being here. "I'll go after work," she said, trying to sound convincing.

"Want company?"

"Yes," she said, "but no. I don't think he'd like that."

Angus nodded. "Let me know how it goes. And Sophie... give him a chance."

*

It had been dark for two hours by the time Sophie came into the Cowgate. She walked quickly, glancing from side to side, scanning for the Revenants' tell-tale glow, but the only lights she saw were those from the pubs. She'd forgotten the name of the street where Lux Aeterna was located, but after a few wrong turns she found it. The doors were firmly shut – she hadn't really expected anything else at such an early hour – but there was a strip of light showing underneath. She knocked, half hoping no one would answer.

At first, no one did. She was about to give up when finally, she heard approaching footsteps. There was a rattle and clash as someone negotiated an arsenal of locks on the far side of the doors, and then one of them opened a crack. The blue-haired girl from the coat check peered out, her eyes sleepy and lips petulant.

"What?" she demanded.

"Sorry to bother you," Sophie said, trying not to feel intimidated. "I'm looking for Rive."

The other girl's sour expression turned to a smirk. "You and every other female in Edinburgh."

"No, I don't mean – "

"Whatever. Come back when he's spinning and get in line." She went to shut the door, but Sophie blocked it with one booted foot.

"I'm not a groupie," she snapped. "I'm a friend, and I need to find him. It's urgent."

The girl gave her a disgusted look. "If you're a friend, how come you don't know where he lives?"

"Because he prefers to meet up in dark bars and seedy hotels." The girl's eyes widened for a moment before they narrowed into a glare, confirming Sophie's suspicion that she was one of the apparent hordes of women lusting after Rive. "Just tell me where he lives," she said.

"Impossible. I'd have to show you."

"Well then…?" The girl still looked hostile. "Look, I promise, I'm not the competition."

"Fine. If you're really friends with him, then prove it."

Sophie sighed in exasperation. "And how am I meant to do that?"

"Tell me one thing about him that isn't common knowledge."

"Oh, for God's sake…okay, he's half Japanese, half Greek."

"You could have found that out with a little digging."

Crap, Sophie thought. *What's something he wouldn't want everyone to know – besides the fact that he was a supernatural being? Art student…foreign parents…likes to paint walls…* And suddenly, she had it.

"He does graffiti. His tag is 'Riven'."

The girl's smile flattened. "Look, sugar, this is my down-time. If you want me to traipse half way across the city with you in the freezing cold, there's got to be something in it for me."

Sophie looked the girl up and down, from her blue hair to her shiny vinyl boots, and all at once she had an inspiration. "Are you by any chance into manga?"

"Maybe," the girl answered with a flicker of interest. "Why?" Sophie reached into her bag, pulled out one of Suri's books and offered it up. The coat girl's eyes widened when she saw the cover. "Are you serious? An original Sophia book, in mint condition?" Then the suspicion returned. "How do I know this is real?"

Sophie sighed in exasperation. "Do you really think I'd carry around counterfeit manga on the off chance that I could use it to bribe a coat-check girl from a night club I've been to once?"

The girl rolled her eyes again, but she took the book

and said, "Fine. Give me five minutes," and shut the door in Sophie's face.

She was gone a lot longer than five minutes. By the time she re-appeared, wearing a full-length purple fur coat, Sophie couldn't feel her toes. She hoped that Rive's house wasn't really half way across town, as they started walking up the road toward the Royal Mile.

"You have a name, friend-of-Rive?" the coat-check girl asked.

"Sophie. You?"

"Kitty. What?" she snapped at Sophie's dubious look.

"Nothing."

"So how do you know him?" Kitty asked after a prickly moment.

"We…kind of go way back," Sophie said.

"Really?" Kitty asked incredulously.

"Yes. Why?"

Kitty shook her head. "Rive, he's one of those guys that doesn't seem to have a past. He never talks about anyone or anything that happened longer ago than last week."

"Yeah, well, I think his…um…childhood wasn't too happy."

Kitty snorted. "Whose was?"

After that they walked in silence. Kitty led Sophie up Old Fishmarket Close and onto the Royal Mile. They wound their way north through a series of side-streets and closes. It was still snowing, and though it was only light flurries, it made Sophie feel all the colder. When Kitty turned right instead of left at the junction with Princes Street, Sophie began to wonder if Rive lived in Leith, and whether her toes would freeze solid if they walked that far.

But Kitty kept going straight ahead. Princes Street became Waterloo Place. Far from the shops and the Christmas lights, the street was dark and deserted. Their snow-dampened footsteps echoed eerily off the dark facades of the buildings. Then Kitty turned into a narrow doorway which led up a flight of steps. The sign beside it read "Old Calton Cemetery".

Sophie stopped, uncertain. Kitty turned back to her with a nasty smile. "What – you afraid of ghosties?"

"You have no idea what you're talking about," Sophie said.

Kitty's smile didn't change. "You want to see Rive or not?"

Sophie climbed the steps after her and then stood at the top, looking around. Under the snow, the gravestones were no more than white lumps. A little way ahead, an obelisk rose like a black blade into the burgundy sky. Crypts lined the high enclosing walls, most of them missing roofs and doors, their inscriptions all but worn away by time and neglect.

But Kitty strode boldly ahead, the hem of her long coat sweeping a trail in the snow behind her. Sophie followed her toward a crypt that was bigger than most of the others, its crenelated roof pitching up toward a columned, arched doorway. The crypt's door was shut, as were the wrought iron gates outside of it. Though they were badly rusted and missing several bars, they were also chained shut and padlocked. A thin strip of light showed beneath the door.

"Good luck," Kitty said, the smirk evident in her voice, and turned back the way she had come.

"Wait – you're leaving?" Sophie called after her. Kitty hadn't been anything like good company, but her presence was better than being left alone in this desolate place, with someone living in a crypt, who might or might not be Rive. Kitty gave her two fingers, and then disappeared into the dark and blowing snow.

Sighing, Sophie turned back to the crypt. Wishing she had Carnwennan with her, she knocked on the door. Abruptly and soundlessly, it opened. Rive stood on the other side of the iron gate, long hair spilling over his shoulder, face flushed as if he were feverish. He was wearing another beat-up t-shirt – Fugazi this time. A set of iPod ear buds hung around his neck, with something abrasive pounding out of them, which made Sophie wonder how he could have heard her knock. He looked at her without the least surprise, nor any indication whether her visit was welcome or not. But he reached into his pocket and produced a rusty key, which he used to open the padlock. He unwound the chain, pushed the iron gates open, and then stood aside for Sophie to enter.

"Thanks," she said doubtfully as she stepped past him.

The crypt's single room was lit by a hurricane lamp

288

hanging from a hook in the ceiling, and a paraffin heater in the corner. Other than those, Rive's only possessions appeared to be a pile of clothes and a makeshift table constructed from an old crypt door lying on top of two broken tombstones. The table was covered with artists' equipment, some of which Sophie recognized and much of which she didn't.

Rive didn't speak until he'd shut and locked the door. Then he said, with his wry half-smile, "Given all the water roundabout is frozen solid, this is a bit of a surprise."

"Funny," Sophie said.

"To what do I owe the honor?"

Now that the moment was upon her, she felt more than a little anxious. "I…I needed to talk to you."

He gave her a twitch of a smile, and said, "I'm intrigued. I'd offer you a chair, but as you can see, I don't have any. So, feel free to sit on the floor – or not."

Sophie dropped her bag and sat down.

"Do you mind if I work while we talk?" Rive said, kneeling by the table. "I was in the middle of something."

"I can come back another time…" Sophie said, far too eagerly.

"You're here now, so now is when you're meant to be here."

"That's very zen."

"Whatever."

"I won't distract you?"

With another ghost of a smile, Rive answered, "I think I'm up to the challenge," making Sophie feel like an idiot.

The next moment, though, she forgot all about it. Rive laid his arm on the table, picked up what looked like a pen with a needle on the end, and calmly jabbed the point into his arm, then continued to jab it, slowly forming a line.

"What the hell are you *doing?*" Sophie cried, recovering her voice at last.

"Tattooing my arm," Rive answered, using a tissue to blot blood and black ink from the line he'd just made. He tilted his arm toward Sophie. She saw now that the line he'd drawn was the curling end of a vine-like tendril, growing out of one of the abstract patterns latticing his forearm. Watching in silence as he placed the pen again and then began to move it slowly, inflicting a hundred tiny pinpricks, she didn't know whether to be impressed or horrified.

"You've done all of those yourself?" she asked after a moment, indicating his other tattoos.

"All but the ones on my back."

"Your back?" she repeated.

In reply, Rive put down the pen and pulled his shirt over his head. Sophie stared. She couldn't help it: like his arms, his torso was covered in intricate black patterns, back and front. Compulsive as they were to look at, doing so gave her an uneasy feeling. Partly it was because they seemed to shift as she watched, almost resolving into identifiable images before

290

they swam again and changed subtly. But it was also that it felt as if he was showing her something too private, too intimate in a way that went far beyond his bared skin. Which in itself was confusing, because if Angus and Suri were right about Rive, then she'd more right to see that skin than anyone had.

"Why do you do it?" she blurted, though she wasn't certain that she wanted to know.

Rive pulled his shirt back on, laid his arm once again on the table and went back to work. "To remember. To forget. Now quit stalling, Sophie."

"What?" she asked.

"You didn't come here to discuss my motivations for inking myself." He said it without ever shifting his eyes from his arm. The hand with the needle remained rock-steady.

"You're right," she said, irritated, and reached into her bag. "I came to discuss these." She dropped the remaining manga books onto the table by his bottle of ink.

Rive looked at them for a moment. Then he looked back at his arm. "So, what do you think?"

"What do I *think?*" Sophie cried. "I find out some guy I just met has been writing comic books about me for years, and you ask what I *think*?"

"Well," Rive said, pausing to blot his arm again, "clearly you do have thoughts about it, and you want me to know them, or you wouldn't be here."

Sophie let her head fall back against the wall in exasperation. "Fine! I think it's time for you to tell me who you really are."

He looked up at her, his ice-blue eyes irritatingly ingenuous. "I haven't lied to you about who I am."

"Oh, come on. Athens and Tokyo?"

He shrugged. "I'm the product of both places, and many others. We are what they make of us."

Ignoring that cryptic comment for the moment, Sophie argued, "But your name isn't Rive."

"Yours isn't Sophie."

"Near enough."

"Very well, Sophia," he sighed. "If you really need me to spell it out for you, then yes, it's true, I'm Theletos, your consort."

Sophie stared at him, unable to make the words penetrate, even though she'd expected them. "Then why did you tell me you're an art student?" she said at last.

"I never said that," he answered, starting a new line on a blank piece of flesh. "You did."

"I – " Sophie began, and then she stopped, realizing that he was right. Just how much of what she thought she knew about him, she wondered, was no more than what he'd let her assume? How much of his appearance was calculated toward that end?

But neither of those was the matter at hand. "You came here to take me back to the Garden."

He didn't look up from his arm. "Obviously."

"Well, it won't work, whatever you and Michael are planning."

Now he did look at her, and the look was puzzled. "What makes you think that Michael has anything to do with it?"

"Because he does nothing but bang on about the Balance needing me, and how I should give up Lucas and do the right thing."

The smile again. This time there was something bitter in it, which made Sophie pause, wondering why.

"Anyway," she said, recalling herself, "there's no way you're going to make me go back to being your consort, or spiritual cohabitator, or whatever. I love Lucas. I'm going to save him from the sea witch even if it kills me. And if it doesn't kill me, I'm going to stay with him for as long as I live."

"That's one possibility," Rive said, watching his hand move, as steady as ever.

"Are you really so arrogant that you can't comprehend this?" Sophie cried, leaning toward him so that he had to look at her. "I'm saying I'm in love with *him,* and that's never going to change! I'll never love you!"

"And I'm saying that's fine," Rive answered, setting the pen down at last and looking her in the eye. She was shocked to see how sad his were, but not as shocked as she was when he spoke again: "Because I'll never love you either."

CHAPTER 20

Sophie stared at him, momentarily silenced. "You...you don't love me?" she asked at last.

"Well, that's not strictly accurate. I mean, you are my soul twin, flesh of my flesh and all of that...except that we don't usually have flesh..." He stopped, apparently to consider this, before he continued, "The point is, we're spiritually intermixed. That has inevitable emotional repercussions. But if it's love in the Biblical sense you mean – nope. Sorry, princess."

"You're such a condescending arse!" she snapped. "It's not as if I *wanted* you to be in love with me!"

"You sure about that?" he asked, a hint of the ironic smile in his eyes.

"What – does every girl you meet automatically throw herself at you?"

"And quite a few of their mothers."

Sophie stood up. "This is ridiculous. I'm going."

"Why? Is the truth too hard to face?"

She snorted. "What truth? That you don't have the hots for me?"

"No. That I wrecked your nice, tidy theory."

"What theory?"

"That I'm so mad for you, I risked it all to get myself a human body and try to win you back from your boyfriend. That is what you thought, isn't it? And you came here to tell me to stuff it, go home – whatever – because I couldn't possibly compete with the luscious Lucifer."

Sophie opened her mouth to reply, and then shut it again. There was nothing to say, because, of course, he was right. She'd been so certain that she understood everything, that the way forward was clear, and once again she'd been wrong-footed. On the face of it, it was mortifying. But part of her had to wonder if Rive wasn't bluffing, toward whatever inscrutable end Michael had hinted about in the conversation she'd overheard.

"Okay," she said when her thoughts had steadied a bit, "so if it's not love, then what's the story with those?" She pointed to the books.

Rive smiled – a real smile this time, though it looked more rueful than amused. "They were a way to remember you."

"Why would you want to remember me?"

"Because I missed you."

"You *missed* me?"

He nodded. "We spent a lot of quality time together after

Lucifer was damned. In some ways it was the best thing that ever happened to our relationship – you know, it kind of cleared the air. Put us on even footing. And we were both lonely…"

A shadow crossed his eyes as he said this, like a dark flush of wind across smooth blue water. Then it was gone again. Sophie had a moment to wonder what it had meant, before he was speaking again.

"You confided in me. We *got* each other, in a way we hadn't before. Hackneyed as it may be to say so, we were friends. So yes, it was a bit of a blow when you scarpered off to Earth, with no warning or explanation."

In an instant, Sophie's irritation with Rive turned to hope. "You were *there?* You know how I did it? How I made myself human?"

He shook his head. "That's the million-dollar question."

Sophie thought about this. "But *you're* here. You must have done something similar."

"Actually, no."

"Then how did you get here?"

"I asked nicely."

"Can you please be serious?"

"I *am* being serious! I asked, and I got permission from the Keeper to come to Earth and try to get you to return to the Garden."

This stunned Sophie into silence again. At last, she said, "But I thought aeons were banned from Earth – never mind that

I'm a persona non grata in the Great Beyond. Why would the Keeper want me back?"

Rive shrugged. "I guess it thinks you're important enough to bend a rule...or six."

"And you?"

He gave her a long, canny look. At last he answered, "Yes – I thought you were important enough, too."

"See, that's what I don't get," Sophie said. "Shouldn't you hate me for what I did?"

He shrugged. "No doubt I would have, if I'd ever been in love with you. But I wasn't. That's not to say I wasn't pissed off at first – not least because everyone assumed I'd been in on it, and blamed me for you skipping out. But pretty soon, I just missed you."

Sophie sat back down wearily. "Okay. So you channeled your angst into manga."

"I *am* half Japanese."

"It's still kind of weird."

"Why? Drawing's always been my thing, and I needed a distraction. Besides, I thought you might be having a rough time down here. You know, if you remembered anything about your past life...or even if you didn't. I wasn't allowed to interfere directly, but I thought you might find the books."

"You wrote them to help me?" she asked.

"Partly."

Sophie gazed at him, feeling mortified again, and also

unexpectedly guilty. Ever since she'd met Lucas, she'd been so certain that whatever they had done had been justified by their love. Besides, it was easy to feel self-righteous and defiant, pitted against Michael's hard-line morality. But Rive, for all of his arrogance and wise-cracking, was forcing her to reconsider that certainty. He'd just told her that he cared about her; that she had made him suffer. The possibility that she'd acted out of plain old selfishness was a bitter pill to swallow.

"I'm sorry," she said, feeling that the words were woefully inadequate.

"What for?"

"For whatever you've been through because of me."

"Don't flatter yourself." Then he smiled at her stricken look. "Oh, alright. Take a little credit. You deserve it. At least you keep things interesting."

"Really?"

He nodded. "You have no idea how dire the Garden is without you. All those revoltingly perfect couples…if I'd got one more sympathetic look or offer of condolences, I'd have had to start a war."

"A *war?*"

"Well, a squabble at least. Start a nasty rumor or two about some extra-syzygy socializing and they'd all be throwing punches."

Sophie laughed, but his words had made her wonder about the life she couldn't remember, in a way she never had before.

"It's funny," she said, "I can remember Heaven, a little bit. Well, I dream about it sometimes. But I don't have any memory of the Garden. What's it like?"

"It's paradise. Perfect, beautiful and eye-gougingly boring."

She couldn't suppress a laugh. "Really?"

"Really. I mean, I guess if you had a spiritual consort to pass the time with, it would be exactly what you wanted. Lots of grottoes to lie in while gazing into each other's eyes. But for you and me, it was a chintz-upholstered jail cell."

"So you and me, we were really never...you know..."

"No." There was no room in his tone for her to doubt it.

"Was there someone else for you? I mean, I had Lucas... were you with someone too?"

"No," he said again, though there was a slight hitch this time before he said it that made her wonder. Before she could push him on it, though, he began to cough. Whether or not it was because they were in an enclosed space, its rattle sounded worse than before. Rive covered his mouth with his arm and coughed into it. When the spasms finally subsided, he lowered his arm. For a moment, in the flickering light, Sophie thought that she saw a glint of wet red among the black patterns.

"Oh my God, Rive, are you alright?"

"Fine," he said shortly, wiping his eyes in what seemed more an attempt not to meet hers, than to clear them.

"But your arm – I thought I saw – "

"What?" he asked, tilting his arm toward her. Aside from the tattoos, it was smooth and clean. His look was a challenge.

"I…well, nothing, I guess. Trick of the light." Trying to force the certainty she'd seen blood from her mind, Sophie grasped at the first thought that came to mind, "So…you don't know how I became human." Rive shook his head. "What about why? I mean, from what I've been able to figure out, I came here because I was trying to get Lucas back to Heaven. But Michael thinks there's more to it than that. He thinks it all has to do with righting the wrongs in the Balance, and that I'm somehow a major player."

She said it in a way that made it clear she didn't agree, but Rive's look when he answered was speculative. "And you don't believe him?"

"It's not that…but you know how you said he had no faith?"

Too late, Sophie realized what she'd just revealed, but Rive only smiled and shook his head. "Don't go all stricken on me. I knew you were listening that night."

"You did? How?"

He shrugged. "I just know when you're nearby. I guess it's a twin thing. Anyway, I said what I said because I wanted you to hear it. I wanted you to know that I didn't come here to pull you and Lucifer apart." Again, the fleeting shadow crossed his face.

"Then why did you say what you did, about softening the blow?"

"Because I came here to bring you back to the Garden, and from your perspective, that amounts to the same thing."

She looked at him for a long moment. He met her eyes frankly, waiting for her to process what he'd said. "I didn't think it was possible for me to go back," she said at last.

"Anything's possible, if the Keeper wants it to be."

Despite what he'd just told her, for the first time in a long time Sophie felt a tiny glow of hope. "So I might not turn into foam on the sea when I turn eighteen?"

"What?"

"Sorry. It's from 'The Little Mermaid'. Horrible story."

"You don't have to be obliterated, if that's what you're asking. Not if I can get your soul back to the Garden in time."

"That can't be right. I got hold of the terms of my lease. I only get to keep this body and soul until I turn eighteen."

"No doubt that's true about the body. But a soul is a free agent."

"Not when it's a stolen human soul, apparently."

Rive looked surprised. "You didn't steal your soul."

"I thought you didn't know how I got here."

"I don't. But I've been watching you all the time you've been on Earth, and you're definitely *you*. Your aura is the same."

"What's an aura?"

301

"The energy that surrounds any living being. It's like a light…like a halo, I guess."

Sophie thought of the way the world took on a blue shimmer when she fought the *Cait Sìth* and the angel, Berith. "Mine is blue, isn't it. And Michael's is fire-colored, Suri's is silver, and Lucas's…Lucas's is like a sunset."

Rive raised his eyebrows. "You can see them?"

"Only sometimes. When they get angry, or fight. And in dreams. When I dream of Heaven, everyone has them."

"Interesting. But the point is, whatever you did to get here, you didn't unmake yourself in the process."

This information should have been a relief. Instead, Sophie felt a creeping unease. "Okay, so if the Keeper really wants me back, why didn't it just, I don't know, magic me to the Garden? Why send you?"

"Because it isn't that simple," he sighed. "Nothing is, when it comes to the Balance."

"Enlighten me." He looked at her, and the covert sadness in his eyes made her unease flare into panic. "Rive – please!"

He sighed again, then said, "I might not agree with his methods, but Michael is right about one thing: you are partly responsible for the shift in the Balance."

"Because I fell in love with Lucas?"

"No. Because you abandoned your post."

"My post?"

He studied her again, and then asked, "Do you know anything about your aeon life?"

"Not really – except that I made Earth, then cried so long when I had to leave that the Keeper turned the tears into a well of human souls."

"Then you know all you need to. See, because you made it, the Well of Souls was your responsibility. You were meant to guard it. To keep it pure, so that all human souls were neutral when they entered a body."

"How did I manage that?"

"Apparently just by being near it. But since you left to come here, other influences have been leaking in. The daevas are some of those influences. You know about them?"

"The baddest of the bad. So they're making human souls evil?"

"It's subtler than that. Nothing can turn a human's soul against his or her will. But certain influences can make it easier for them to follow pathways that take them in a particular direction. Every choice a human makes sends energy in one direction or the other. At the end, if the good energy outweighs evil, the soul returns to the Garden when the body dies. The opposite, and it goes to the Deep. Following me?"

"So far."

"Okay, so, when you left, it meant the Well of Souls was left unguarded. But also, it meant the aeons were down one syzygy, which automatically made the daevas stronger. It was easier for them to influence humans to make choices that lead them to the Deep, harder for the aeons to counteract that. The tally has been slipping in the daevas' favor for a long time. If it slips too far – "

"It's the end of the world as we know it."

He smiled ruefully. "Well, yes. But it's much more than that, too. The Balance is organic. It's an integral part of everything that is, just as everything is a part of it – including this little planet."

"So Earth matters?"

"It matters profoundly. Ever since the beginning, it's been the battleground where the aeons and daevas duke it out. Since we've been banned, the fight is more subtle, and more complicated: the humans control earth, so we fight for control of the humans."

"Using angels and demons?"

"Sometimes. But the point is, if humanity turns to the Deep, then everything encompassed by the Balance ceases to exist."

"You mean it all goes 'poof' and disappears into nothingness?"

"That would be the best-case scenario."

Sophie looked for irony, but saw only profound regret in his eyes. "And the worst?"

He sighed. "Evil thrives on chaos. And so it's possible – even likely – that with the Balance obliterated, the daevas would thrive, and make all of creation into an extension of the Deep."

"What's that like? A world overrun by demons?"

He shrugged. "I don't know for certain. I've never been. But from what I've seen of the daevas, they have a talent for warping things; for making a parody of anything that's pure and good. So yes, there'd be monsters, but worse, they'd find a way of making monsters of humans."

"And all of this would happen because I left the Well of Souls?" Sophie asked in a small, sick voice.

"It's happening already, Sophie," Rive answered. "The signs are everywhere. The Revenants. The failing staves. Never mind the *sith* and demons you've had to fight. Believe me, none of that's normal."

"The thing is," Sophie said slowly, "all of that is recent. And if you listen to Michael, the Balance started to shift when I was with Lucas. That's why he was exiled."

"Michael and I…" he began, and then stopped, running a hand through his hair. "I guess you could say, we've never seen eye-to-eye about that."

"You mean, you don't think the Balance is messed up because Lucas and I…um…" She trailed off, feeling the blood rise to her cheeks.

Rive gave her an amused half-smile. "No – as it happens, I don't. That's when the angels decided to take notice, but there were signs before that, going right back to Azazel's betrayal

305

– who knows, maybe even further back than that. Maybe the Balance never really recovered from that first war, when we fought the daevas and lost Earth…"

He stopped, catching the shine of hope in Sophie's face, and shook his head. "I know what you're thinking: that if it wasn't what happened between you and Lucifer that upset the Balance, then there's nothing to stop you being together again. But since you came to Earth, the shift in the Balance has only gained momentum. Remember, it's not just that you left the Well, it's that you broke up a syzygy."

Sophie looked at him for a long time, trying to see past the pity in his face to something she could pin her hope on. "But I've left the Garden before," she said at last. "After the Flood, when I went to stay with the angels, I must have been there for ages. We were apart then, and the Balance didn't implode – the Well of Souls wasn't tainted, either, was it?"

"Not that we know of."

"So I…I could be in Heaven, and that would be close enough to fix what's happening?"

"It might, and it might not. But that doesn't matter. The Keeper's instructions were specific: bring Sophia, and only Sophia, back to the Garden."

"It's hard to see the point. I don't have a very good track record when it comes to saving the world."

"That may be," he answered, "but it's still your creation. If you can't save it, I don't know who can."

She shuddered, premonition a leaden coldness beginning in her limbs, spreading toward her heart. "I suppose there are conditions," she said in a small, hard voice.

"Only two, actually."

"Tell me."

"First, you have to come willingly."

"Which is a no-brainer, if it means stopping Armageddon." She swallowed hard as the cold clutched at her throat. "Second?"

Rive passed a hand over his face, but when he answered, he met her eyes directly. "Once you return to the Garden, you'll never be able to leave it again."

The ice reached her heart; the world went still. "Angels can't come into the Garden," she said after a moment, in a voice that didn't sound like her own.

"No," Rive said, so softly it was almost a whisper.

Sophie was surprised at how little she felt. Maybe, she thought, it was only because her human brain couldn't begin to imagine eternity, let alone an eternity without Lucas. True, she'd faced his death not long since – but then, she hadn't expected to live long herself. She hadn't really had to face her grief.

Or maybe it was because she knew that there was no choice. It wasn't simply that choosing Lucas would be selfish; it would also be pointless. Even if Michael and Angus were right, and there was a kinder interpretation to her prophecy than the one she believed, refusing Rive wouldn't give her what she wanted. Because what she wanted was a lifetime with Lucas, years and years to love him, and in a world given over to the Deep, nothing as pure and simple and sweet as what she felt for him would be able to survive.

But even that didn't entirely explain the conviction she felt. Though it made no sense, she felt a strong push of deja-vu, as if somehow, she had been in this place, faced this choice before. And what struck her most deeply was that there was no choice to make: no possibility of not fighting for the world she'd made.

As she thought this, the room rippled in the way that it did before the aeon part of her took over. She looked at her hands. They exuded the faintest blue glow.

"Sophie?" Rive said, sounding uncertain for the first time since she'd come to him.

She looked up, and met his eyes. They seemed to draw in her fractured energy, to calm it. The room steadied around her; the ice receded enough to let her speak. "Yes," she said, and this time, she sounded like herself.

"What?" he asked, half-disbelieving.

"Yes, I'll do it. I'll go back with you to the Garden, and try to undo whatever wrong I've done."

"You will?" He seemed honestly shocked.

She smiled ruefully at him. "Do you really think I'm so selfish that I'd send the world to hell in exchange for a few months with Lucas?"

"No…no, I don't think that. I only…" He paused, clearly at a loss. After a moment, he began again. "The thing is, Sophie, I understand. I know exactly what you're sacrificing and I… well…I'm sorry. I underestimated you."

Sophie knew that he was sincere, and she wondered briefly what he meant by knowing what she was going through. She wondered if he really did understand, and if it connected to the occasional flickers of dark emotion she'd seen as they spoke. But it wasn't the time to ask. There was something else she needed to know, one thing that might make her doom a little bit easier to bear.

"Did you mean what you said to Michael? About letting me save Lucas?"

"Yes. But there's a caveat."

"Of course there is," she muttered.

"You've got to let me help you."

She looked at him, stunned speechless. After a moment, she said, "You're saying you'll help me fight Dahud?"

"Well, not physically. I don't think she's going to be willing to fight anyone but you."

"Yeah, I kind of figured that."

"But I'll come to Ker-Ys with you, and whatever happens there, I've got your back."

There was an echo to those words, too, and something about the way he looked at her when he said them made her feel, at last, like crying. Surprising herself – and, quite obviously, him

– Sophie threw her arms around Rive's neck. After a moment, though, his arms closed around her, too. She felt a surge of emotion for him that she couldn't quite name, except that it made her feel safe in a way that she hadn't since losing Lucas.

"Thank you," she said, and sat back to look at him. His face was softer than she'd ever seen it, his eyes for once unguarded.

"For telling you exactly what you didn't want to hear?" he said with gentle bitterness.

"You didn't. You've given me a chance to save him – and that's all I ever wanted."

Tentatively, he reached out, brushed back the hair that had fallen across her face. "I wish it could be different, Sophie," he said. "And if I had the power to change it, I would."

Not trusting herself to speak, Sophie could only nod her thanks.

CHAPTER 21

Sophie was so cold and tired and dejected by the time she got home, she could barely climb the stairs to the flat. She hoped that her mother wasn't home. All she wanted was a hot bath and silence, so it made a certain perverse sense when she heard angry voices coming down the stairwell. There was only one person who could bring out that particular shrill tone in her mother's voice. She was too tired to decide whether he was the first or last person she wanted to see. But when she pushed the door open and saw him standing there – all rumpled suit and exasperated frown – she knew.

"Dad," she said, falling into the arms he opened to her.

"Angel," he answered, folding his arms around her. For a moment she forgot her impending fate. For a moment she was five years old, and her father's hug could cure anything.

"I thought you weren't coming till Christmas Eve," she said, when she pulled away.

He shrugged. "That architectural convention in the States

was cancelled. I booked the first ticket out of London, before anyone could think of anything else for me to do." He glanced at Anna, who was hovering beside them, clearly trying to rein in her irritation, for Sophie's sake. "I didn't realize it would upset your mother's plans."

Sophie looked at her mother. "We have plans?"

"Oh, well, you know, there's the exhibition...I'll be very busy..." She waved her hand as if trying to catch a viable reason to be angry at him out of the air. "And I only have dinner makings for two."

Sophie's father shrugged. "We'll have a carry out."

"Andrew, you can't just show up here and – " she began, but Sophie interrupted.

"Tell you what, Mum – Dad and I will go out for tea. Then you don't have to cook, and you can get some work done, and neither of you has to deal with each other."

"Brilliant plan," Andrew said, relief written all over his face. He pulled on the coat he'd been holding. "Shall we?" He offered Sophie his arm. She couldn't help smiling, though her mother shook her head in irritation and walked off toward the kitchen.

"The sooner the better," Sophie said, taking it as he ushered her out onto the landing.

"I'm sorry about that," he said as they started down the stairs. "I really thought that we were past the silly rows...but apparently I was overly optimistic."

Sophie glanced at him, and decided it was as good a time as any to ask what she'd been wondering for so long. "How did it happen? I mean, how did you go from happily married to... well...that?" She gestured back toward the flat.

Her father sighed. "I wish I knew." They reached the door, stepped back out onto the frozen street. Sophie thought that was all she was going to get in answer, but then he said, "That's not true. I do know. I always knew, really, that we weren't quite the right fit. We had so much in common, but what we didn't was, unfortunately, fundamental. But who wants to think about that kind of thing when they're twenty-four and madly in love?"

This startled Sophie, though she couldn't say why it should. Obviously her parents must have been in love once in order to get married, never mind to cope with their inability to have a child, and to go through the grueling process of adopting her. But even in her earliest memories, long before the arguments began, there was a distance between them: a discord, like an instrument very slightly out of tune.

"Earth to Sophie..."

She turned back to her father and smiled. "Sorry. Imagining you and Mum madly in love derailed me for a minute."

"I suppose that's the last thing a teenager wants to think about."

"It's alright. I'm a big girl."

"Don't remind me! It was all so much easier when you were five, and you didn't ask questions like that."

"Tell me about it," she muttered.

"So, where are we going?"

"Can you cope with pub food? There's one close by, and I'm too tired to be creative."

"Your choice, Angel."

She started. He'd always called her that, but the irony hadn't registered until now. "This way, then," she said after a moment.

They walked for a few minutes before Sophie's father broke the silence with the inevitable question, "So, how are you coping?"

"I'm coping," she answered.

"Well, you don't look quite as wispy as you did when you left London – but what's this about being tired? Are you working too much?"

"Sleeping too little," Sophie answered, knowing there was no use trying to deflect him from the truth. From that one, anyway.

"Still having nightmares?"

"Not exactly. It's just…I've got a lot to think about. Suddenly everything just seems so…" *Futile? Hopeless?* "Complicated."

Andrew laughed humorlessly. "Welcome to adulthood." He paused, glancing at her, and then said, "Your mother says you've made some friends here."

"I guess I have."

"And the job? You like it?"

"Well, a café's a café. But Matrika – my boss – she's lovely. And Angus, the guy I work with, he's great too."

There was another pause, and Sophie knew what was coming next. "You playing at all?"

"No," she said softly, unable to look at him. She knew that her father had always understood her in a way that her mother didn't. He knew how to use her music to gauge her moods.

"Have you tried?"

"I…I can't, Dad."

Though he looked like he wanted to say something more about this, he kept his silence, for which Sophie was profoundly grateful. A few more minutes walking, and they reached the pub. They chose a table in a corner, slightly beyond the noisy post-work crowd. A waitress gave them menus, and Sophie stared at hers, not seeing it. In the sudden warmth she felt exhausted, as if she could lie down right there and sleep for days. Instead, she had to convince her well-meaning father that her life was slowly returning to normal, rather than further derailing.

The waitress returned to take their orders, and Sophie chose the first thing that her eyes lighted on, not even registering the words. Apparently that was a mistake, given the way her father was looking at her. "What?" she asked, praying that whatever faux pas she'd made would be easily explicable.

"Since when do you like scampi?" he asked.

Scampi? she thought blearily, wondering if that could

315

really be what she'd ordered. She'd hated anything prawn-like since eating a bad one as a child. "Um, since…since…" She couldn't even think of a plausible lie, let alone speak it. "I thought it was time to give it another chance?" she said weakly.

Her father looked at her, his brown eyes warm and worried. "What's going on, Sophie? Honestly, you can tell me anything."

Sophie wanted to crawl into his lap, cry on his shoulder, have him tell her that everything would be alright. Instead she said, "I wish I knew how to explain it."

"Angel, are you in some sort of trouble?"

"Trouble?" she repeated, for lack of anything more eloquent to say.

His look had turned more intense, more concerned. "Was there…more to this relationship with Lucas than you've told us? Your mother says that you're barely eating. She's worried that he…that you and he…what I'm trying to say is, could you be – "

"Oh!" Sophie yelped, her father's words finally penetrating her stupefied consciousness. She felt her cheeks burning. "God, no – it's nothing like that!"

Her father looked as relieved as she felt mortified. "Well that's good news," he said, taking a grateful gulp of the pint of ale the waitress put down in front of him. He studied Sophie as she turned her glass of coke in its ring of condensation. "But I know there's something you're not telling me."

"I suppose it would be a cliché for me to say that you wouldn't understand."

"Not a cliché, exactly. The typical teenage response."

The thought of herself as a typical teenager seemed bitterly funny to Sophie. She had to stifle a smile. She knew that her father deserved a better response than she could offer. There was only one thing that she could say, and mean it. "I loved him, Dad."

"I know that, Angel. But – "

"No," Sophie interrupted. "I really, *really* loved him. I know that Mum doesn't think I knew him long enough for that. For it to matter as much as it does." She paused, her throat suddenly choked with tears. "But it was real. He was the one. And now he's gone…" She had to stop, or burst into tears. She stared hard at the ice in her glass, swirling it with the straw.

Her father leaned forward and took her hands, holding them firmly in his. It was only then that Sophie realized her own were shaking violently. "I know," he said.

"What?" she asked.

"I know that he was the one. You wouldn't have chosen anything less."

Sophie had to pause to digest that. After months of her mother trying to sweep it all under the rug, it seemed impossible that her father could accept it so easily. "Mum thinks that I should be over him by now," she said at last. "But I can't forget him. It's as if he's still here, somewhere…"

Her father sighed. "For all we have our issues, your mother is a kind woman. But she's practical. Too practical, sometimes. She still thinks of you as a child."

"And you don't?"

He laughed gently. "Sophie, I think you were born thirty-five."

"Um…thanks?"

"I only meant, I trust your judgment. If you need to grieve for years over this, I won't try to stop you." His eyes were troubled, though, when he raised them again to hers. "And I know that this isn't the right place for that. I wish that I could tell you to come back to London with me. But I can't."

"I know," Sophie said, secretly grateful for it. She knew that her father would see through the evasions as her mother didn't. "All of the travel…"

"That's right. It would be terrible for you to be on your own with all of this. At least here you have your mum always about. And these new friends – do they know what happened?"

"Yes. They know everything."

"And they're there for you?"

"More that I realized new friends could be."

He nodded. "I'm glad to hear that. Angel, I know it's another cliché, but time really will make this better."

Sophie nodded, and tried to smile. After all, there was no way he could know that time was the one thing she didn't have.

After walking her back to the flat, Sophie's father gave her a card with the name and address of the B&B where he was staying. "Meet for breakfast?" he asked.

"Sure," Sophie said. "I don't have to work till lunch time."

"I'll pick you up at nine. Unless you want a long lie on your day off?"

"No. I always wake up early now."

"Maybe tonight will be different. Tell your mum to phone me if you decide to sleep in." She smiled at him, because she knew that he really thought she might. "Good night, Angel," he said, and kissed her forehead.

Sophie stood at the street door until he was out of sight, and then she climbed the stairs. When she got into the flat, she found her mother painting: another bleak angel-scape which she couldn't bear to look at. She ran the bath she'd been longing for earlier, and afterwards she got into bed. She knew as soon as she turned out the light, though, that she wasn't going to sleep. Despite being exhausted, she was still wound up from her conversation with Rive.

She sat up, picked up her bag and dug in it for her phone. No doubt Suri and Ailsa would both be working, but she wanted to speak to a friend, even if she couldn't tell them the whole truth. Even if she could only say it to an answering service. As the phone rang, she thought out what she would say. *It's him, but it's not like you thought.* **Nothing's** *like we thought, nothing is going to be alright, and now my dad's here, and he knows something's wrong, and I feel like a liar. Like a traitor. Please please please tell me how to make it go away…*

She couldn't leave a message like that. She couldn't even say it to their faces. She couldn't burden her friends with more unsolvable problems. She was about to push the button to end the call, when someone picked up.

"Okay, okay, I'm here!" the someone croaked.

"Who is this?" Sophie asked uncertainly.

"It's Ailsa, ding dong," the voice cracked and grated. "You called my phone. Who did you think it would be?"

"You sound – "

"Sick," Ailsa said, and then sneezed. Sophie listened to her blow her nose, and then she came back on the line. "Sorry," she said. "This must be the worst cold, ever, in the history of the world."

"No, *I'm* sorry, for waking you up. You should go back to sleep. I'll talk to you later."

"Nuh-uh," Ailsa said, sniffing wetly. "No way you're hanging up without telling me what's going on."

"How do you know something's going on?"

"Because you never phone unless something's going on. Besides, in your world there's *always* something going on."

Sophie sighed. "Alright, something's going on."

"Ha!" Ailsa said, but the triumph was dampened by a fit

of coughing. "Let me guess," she said when she'd recovered. "Rive fell on his knees, begging you to forget Lucas and come back to him."

"Wrong."

"But he declared his undying love, didn't he?"

Sophie snorted. "Rive told me in no uncertain terms that he doesn't love me, and never did."

There was a long silence at the other end. Finally, Ailsa said, "Huh. I didn't see *that* coming. Suri and I were absolutely convinced he was mad for you."

"Yeah, and thanks to you two I went and accused him of it, and ended up looking like a complete idiot."

"Sorry," Ailsa said. There was a pause for more nose-blowing, and then she asked, "So what's his story? I mean, why's he here, if not to win you back?"

"Actually, he *is* here to get me to go back with him. But it's not about love – it's all about me Doing the Right Thing."

"That sounds dreary."

"Ailsa, he told me that if I don't go back with him, the world's going to end."

"Oh." Ailsa paused, sniffling. "Do you think it's true?"

"Angels can't lie. As far as I know, that goes for aeons too."

"But he can edit the truth, right? Maybe you only thought he was saying he wasn't in love with you, and the world's going to end, so that you'd go back with him. And once he got you to the Garden, he'd be all clear to win you over."

"You know, at this point I'd actually love to believe that."

"But?"

"But he told me I could save Lucas before I go."

"He did?" Even through the congestion, Ailsa sounded shocked.

"Yeah – not really the words of a jealous love-rival."

"So what are you going to do? I mean, you can't seriously be thinking of scarpering off with Rive once you have Lucas back?"

Sophie paused. As much as she wanted to confide in Ailsa about the prophecy and the rest of what Rive had told her, she knew that it wasn't fair. There was nothing Ailsa could do to change any of it, and she'd only end up worrying pointlessly about it.

"There won't be any scarpering till Lucas is safe," Sophie said at last. "After that…I guess we'll see what happens."

"And Rive's really alright with that? He's not even a little bit worried you'll run off with Lucas once the deed's done?"

"Apparently not. He even said he'd help."

Ailsa let out a long breath. "I will never, ever understand how you get all of these guys to do your bidding."

"He's not! I mean, there was no bidding. I said I'd go with him but first I was going to Ker-Ys to get Lucas back, and Rive said if I was going, he was going too."

"Well," Ailsa said after another moment's thought, "I guess having an aeon to back us up can only be a good thing."

"That's true…but there's a problem."

"Of course there is. There's always a problem, just like there's always something going on. What is it? You're grounded? You've met yet another hot guy with an earth-shattering dilemma that only you can solve?"

"My dad's here."

"Ah."

"Which means it's going to be even harder to get away – two parents watching me, instead of one. And my dad's a whole lot more vigilant than my mum. And now it's only a few days till Solstice."

"Oh, that won't be a problem."

"How can you say that?"

"Because Suri's got a plan that's absolutely guaranteed to work."

"Oh, Lord," Sophie sighed, and sat back to listen.

CHAPTER 22

She awakened to luminous blue twilight sifting through the arched, mullioned window. On Earth, it would be hundreds of years before humans made such windows, but time was fluid in Heaven, and Sophia had developed a taste for the nineteenth century. She loved re-creating its trappings. It was the kind of thing she'd never have been allowed to do in the Garden, and one of the reasons she had no desire to go back.

But only one of them. She smiled to hear the knock on her door, on the heels of that thought. Lucifer could always sense when she was thinking of him – when she was about to come looking. She opened the door and flung herself into his arms, although she'd promised herself that this time she would be more dignified. She'd made herself countless such promises since the night they'd pledged themselves to each other. They always dissolved in the face of his warm smile, his dark eyes with their slight look of amazement, as if he couldn't believe, even after so much time, that she was real, and she was his.

He had something in his hands, but he let it fall to the floor, wrapping his arms around her as they fell back onto the bed, his lips on her throat. She wore nothing but a short blue shift, and she could feel every nuance of his body through the thin fabric. His hands slid up to her waist, almost circling it, and she pulled at his own shirt, trying to feel where it fastened. But he caught her hands, pulled away from her enough to say, "Wait."

"Why?" she asked, her voice rough with frustration.

"Because I want..." He hesitated, a flush climbing his cheeks, which only made her want him more. "I want it to be perfect, when it happens."

"This is perfect," she said, tracing his high cheekbone with one finger. "Every moment I'm with you is perfect."

He smiled, and sat up. "I brought you something."

"You don't have to bring me gifts," Sophia said, though she sat up too, curious.

"I know I don't. But I love the way you look when I do."

"How do I look?"

His smiled widened. "Just like that."

He reached for the thing he'd dropped on the floor earlier, and handed it to her. It was an awkwardly-shaped bundle in a white fabric bag, but it weighed almost nothing. Sophia opened the bag, and shook out the contents. She couldn't contain a gasp of delighted amazement.

It was a dress – the kind a human girl who lived in a

room with a mullioned window might wear. It was made of silky fabric the same shade as the sky beyond the window. The bodice was embroidered with hundreds of tiny forget-me-nots, the skirt billowing out from the pointed waist.

"Lucifer...it's beautiful," she said, hugging the dress to her chest. "Thank you."

"Don't thank me," he said. "It was mostly Suriel's doing."

"But it was your idea, wasn't it?"

He shrugged, suddenly embarrassed. "Just put it on. No, wait!" he said, flushing and flustered as Sophia reached to pull off her shift. "I'll go. Meet me on the hill when you're ready."

Sophia smiled, slightly puzzled as she always was when Lucifer reacted this way. She could never quite understand his modesty when it came to their bodies. He was like a human that way – all of the angels were. Proud of their physical forms or embarrassed by them, but always aware of them. Maybe, she thought, because they belonged to their corporeal bodies in a way that an aeon didn't. In their own realm, aeons were air and light. To Sophia, the solid form she took on in Heaven was no more a part of her than the blue dress. It was simply something she wore, to suit the circumstances.

But she didn't want to torment him, especially not when he'd brought her such a beautiful gift. "Alright," she said, and kissed him quickly, then let him out the door. When he was gone, she shed her shift and pulled the dress on carefully, conscious of the fragile lace that made up the overskirt and the *cap-sleeves. When she had it on, she made a mirror from the light coming in the window – she didn't normally keep one, but she wanted to make sure that she'd put the dress on correctly.*

She almost didn't recognize herself. It was partly the dress – she never normally wore anything so elaborate, though some of the angels delighted in making outrageous outfits. But her face had changed, too. Her hollow cheeks had filled out, her dull eyes regained their luster. Her hair fell in a mahogany sheet down her back, longer and smoother than she remembered. It was him, she realized with a kind of awe. Lucifer had brought about this change in her. It was the first time she realized that he had saved her.

She opened her hand, and a sprig of forget-me-nots appeared on her palm. She tucked it behind her ear, and then she went outside. The evening was a stunning one even for Heaven, and she sensed Suriel's hand in it. The angels took turns choosing the weather, and Sophia doubted that her dress precisely matching the sky was a coincidence.

She walked across the grass – long and indigo today, Sophie's favorite, and another sign of Suri's hand at work. Her long skirt rustled among the swaying fronds, and brushed against her legs. It was a strange, but not unpleasant sensation.

As she approached the hill where she'd first spoken to Lucifer, a mist began to rise. Soon it enveloped her, but there was nothing menacing about it. It brushed against her skin like feathers, swirling with tinges of blue and lavender. Then, as quickly as it had enveloped her, the mist let her go. She was standing on a black-and-white marble floor, cool against her bare feet. The mist bounded it on all sides, marking it off as walls mark off a room. Making it private.

A hand touched her shoulder. She turned, smiling already, to find Lucifer standing behind her, wearing a black suit that looked like it belonged in the era of the blue dress. His face was radiant as the sun as he smiled down at her. He held out his hand. She took it, and stepped forward, into his arms.

She placed her hand on his shoulder as she'd seen the dancers do in her scrying-glass. His arm came around her waist. There was music then, though she was certain that there hadn't been before. It was beautiful, and hauntingly familiar, but she couldn't place it. Nor did she particularly care, because, a moment later, Lucifer began to move in a dance, guiding her along with him. She knew this dance, too, from her solitary watching. She wondered how he knew it. Then he smiled at her, and it didn't matter.

When the music ended, Lucifer dropped her hand and wrapped his other arm around her. He looked down at her, and she looked back. She couldn't have torn herself away from the love and warmth she saw in his eyes for anything.

"Sophia," he whispered, his hands sliding to her waist as he leaned down to kiss her.

She closed her eyes. His lips touched hers gently, but she didn't want him to be gentle. She thrust her fingers into *his hair and pulled him closer, crushing her mouth to his, sliding her tongue past his teeth as he opened himself up to her. A few moments later he pulled away, and she moaned in disappointment. But then he began kissing her neck, his lips sending fire running through her, his tongue in the hollow of her throat like a drug. They slipped together to the floor – except that it wasn't a floor any longer. It had grown more of the indigo grass, and the purple mist had cleared to reveal a dark blue sky, blazing with more stars than Sophia had ever seen.*

Lucas pulled back again, resting his head on one extended arm. "Is this perfect?" he asked.

"Yes," she breathed. "It's perfect."

"Promise you'll love me always," he said, running a finger down her breastbone, sending chills through her, until it rested over her heart.

"There's no need," she answered. "I couldn't be, and not love you."

He smiled again, so sweet and radiant it would have broken her heart if he hadn't been hers. And then he lowered his lips to hers, and everything else ceased to exist.

*

The door buzzer jerked Sophie awake. It was half past eight – her father must be early. Even with her eyes closed, she could see the lights at the sides of her vision that meant a headache was building. Sophie shut her eyes and burrowed into the covers, hoping to hold on to the beautiful dream, to push back the pain in her head and heart for a few more moments. Then the buzzer went again. Sighing, she sat up. She swallowed four painkillers, then slipped out of bed and pulled on her dressing gown, to get the door.

"Sorry Dad, I overslept – " she'd begun, when she realized that it wasn't her father at the door. It was a woman roughly in her early forties, dressed in a neatly tailored grey suit, her pale hair swept smoothly back into a bun. It was her face, though, that riveted Sophie. It was Suri's face – or rather, the face Suri would have had if she'd been human, and twenty-five years older. She smiled at Sophie, making crows'-feet around her dark eyes. If Sophie looked hard, though, she could make out Suri's real face underneath the disguise. They rested together, but not quite perfectly, like an image from a film projector that's slightly out of focus. Sophie felt vaguely sea-sick.

"Good morning," Suri said in a perfect public-school accent, holding out her hand to Sophie, though this was undoubtedly meant for the benefit of her mother, who'd just come out of her bedroom. "I'm Evelyn White, of White and Starr, solicitors. And you must be Sophia Creedon."

"Sophie," Sophie answered, shaking Suri's hand dazedly.

"I'm sorry, is there some kind of trouble?" Anna asked, coming to stand at Sophie's shoulder.

"Oh no, nothing of the sort," Suri said with a reassuring smile. "And please, forgive me for calling so early, but I only just finished gathering all of the necessary paperwork for your case, and we've a train to catch in two hours."

"What case?" Sophie said.

"What train?" Anna asked, looking dubiously between Sophie and Suri.

Suri's look turned to surprise. Sophie could see that she was enjoying this charade, whatever it was about, which made her nervous. "Why, the inheritance, of course. Didn't you receive my letter?"

"I've definitely not received a solicitor's letter," Anna said. "Sophie?" Sophie shook her head mutely.

"Oh dear," Suri said, her look shifting seamlessly to professional concern, "it seems there's been some mix-up. You should have had a letter about it weeks ago. May I come in? It's going to take a while to explain."

"Explain what?" Sophie's father asked, climbing the last few stairs to the landing.

"Mr. Creedon?" Suri said, looking at him.

"Yes," he answered doubtfully.

"Excellent. You'd have had to be informed anyway; this will save us some time."

"Informed of what?"

Suri sighed with studied exasperation. Anna said, "Come in Andrew…and Miss White."

"Thank you," Suri said, with a studied smile.

Anna led them all to the sitting room. As soon as they were seated, Suri opened her briefcase and pulled out a stack of papers, setting them on the coffee table in front of Sophie. On top was a sheaf of heavy cream paper, the top page reading, "Last will and Testament of Lucas, Lord Belial of Ardnasheen." And Sophie began to understand, just as her head began to pound.

"When Lord Belial's papers were examined after his tragic and untimely death last month," Suri said, "they were found to contain a codicil to his will. It's a bit complicated, but in short, it leaves everything to you, Miss Creedon."

"What exactly does 'everything' entail?" Sophie's father asked.

"The estate, with its house and outbuildings, of course," Suri answered, looking Andrew in the eye with the utmost sincerity. "There were also a number of other assets which are detailed in the paperwork here." She tapped the pile she'd put in front of Sophie. "But to put it in the simplest terms, Lord Belial has left all of his earthly possessions to your daughter."

Sophie heard the suppressed laugh when Suri said "earthly possessions", but her parents only stared at Suri with wide-eyed wonder. "Why would he do something like that?" her mother asked.

Suri shrugged. "I wasn't the signatory on the codicil,"

she said. "But generally these things stem from matters of the heart."

Seeing that her mother was about to challenge this, Sophie said quickly, "I just don't know what to say. I never expected something like this!"

Suri smiled indulgently at her. "You needn't say anything, Miss Creedon. All you need to do is sign the requisite paperwork, and then accompany me up to Ardnasheen to formally take possession of the house and sign off on the inventory."

"What – now?" Andrew asked.

"The sooner, the better," Suri answered. "It's never the thing to leave these big places unattended, especially after a well-publicized death."

"So you're suggesting Sophie go to *live* there?" Anna asked, her voice shrill with incredulous horror. It drove a spike of pain into Sophie's head above her right eye.

"That's up to Miss Creedon – "

"Absolutely *not!*" Anna cried. "My daughter is still a minor, and it's up to me – " she glanced at Andrew, and then added reluctantly " – and her father to decide where and how she lives."

"With all due respect, Mrs. Creedon," Suri said, her calm unruffled, "I didn't mean to suggest that your daughter should move to Madainneag immediately. Only that she come for a few days, to take care of business and make herself known as a presence in the village. After that, she can appoint an appropriate caretaker to oversee the property, until such time as she chooses to live there – or to sell it."

"The answer's still no," Anna said sharply. "Do you have any idea what trauma the death of Lucas Belial has caused my daughter? And now, just when she's beginning to recover, you come with…with *this!"* She gestured to the stack of papers in front of Sophie. "It's beyond insensitive. It's…it's – "

"A matter of legal necessity," Suri answered, still serene, but with the steely edge to her tone that Sophie had heard the night she banished the fallen angel, Berith. "Unfortunately, Mrs. Creedon, legal necessity and emotion aren't always compatible."

"Fine," Anna said, with a look in her eye that didn't give Sophie much hope of this meeting ending in her favor. "I'll take her up myself." Another stab of pain drove into Sophie's skull.

To Suri's credit, she showed only the faintest twitch of annoyance – too slight, no doubt, for her parents to have seen it. "Very well, we can arrange for that. I'd hoped to leave this morning, in order to make the afternoon boat. That will give you a few hours to pack – "

But Anna was shaking her head. "I can't possibly go today. I have the exhibition to put up, and students' work to mark… perhaps in the New Year…"

There was a tiny flicker of triumph in Suri's eye as she listened to Anna Creedon list all of the reasons why she couldn't accompany them to Ardnasheen. But it disappeared when Andrew looked up at them and said, "I'll go."

"What?" Sophie asked, not quite managing to keep the alarm out of her voice.

Her father shrugged. "Why not? I'm here, and I've nothing else to do."

"But…but Christmas – " Anna began.

"I don't imagine that Ms. White intends to keep us there that long."

Anna looked at him for a moment of shocked silence, then she cried, "I don't believe this! After all that she's been through, you want to take her back to that place?"

"Maybe it would be a good thing," Andrew answered. "Help her put it to rest."

Anna was shaking her head, furious. "You have no idea, do you? *I'm* the one who's been here, watching her waste away. I'm the one who listens to her wake up crying, and worries when she's out, and lies awake at night wondering if she'll ever recover. And then you, you just waltz in here and try to turn it all upside-down – "

"Clearly, you need to discuss this further," Suri interrupted. "Here's my card. It has my mobile number. I'll stay in Edinburgh until you decide what to do."

Sophie's battling parents didn't seem to have heard her. She took the card and said, "Thanks. I'll show you out."

"Thank you, dear," Suri answered, gathering up her things. Sophie led her to the door, and shut it gratefully behind them.

"Sorry about that," Sophie said, as they started down the stairs.

"Don't be," Suri answered. "You should see angels bicker!"

"One thing I don't get."

"What?"

"You can't lie."

"No. But we can impersonate humans by special dispensation."

"But all of that about the will – "

"Is true. Ailsa and I dug it up in the secret study – thankfully, before any real lawyers could get at it."

Sophie was so stunned, she forgot about the migraine for a moment. "So Lucas actually left everything to me?"

"He sure did. That'll come in handy when he miraculously re-appears – the house and all the rest will still be in the family, so to speak."

Sophie mulled all of this over for a moment, then she asked, "So what are we going to do now? I mean, I can't let them come with me, and that's the only way they'll ever let me go."

Suri chewed a fingernail thoughtfully. "We could probably work around them if it's absolutely necessary. But I don't think it will be."

"Why not?"

"Oh, you know me. I always think of something."

"Yeah – that's what worries me," Sophie said.

Suri smiled ironically as she opened the street door. "No need to worry. Everything's going to plan."

The headache had built to the point that it was difficult to think clearly. "I don't know…" Sophie said, putting up a hand against the bright light.

Suri's look turned to one of concern, and she let the door fall closed again. "Is it another headache?"

"Yes," Sophie answered.

"They're getting more frequent, aren't they."

"I don't know. I suppose so."

"Hmm."

"Hmm what?"

"Hmm, I don't like this headache thing. I get an unnatural vibe about it. Anyway," Suri passed a hand across Sophie's forehead. Immediately, the pain faded. "Is that better?"

"Yes," she said, taking Suri's hand and squeezing it. "Thank you."

"It's the least I can do," Suri answered.

"You don't think this has anything to do with…with my birthday, do you?"

Suri gave her an inscrutable look, then said, "Take it easy today," and let herself out the street door.

*

By the time Sophie got back upstairs, the flat had fallen silent. But she'd seen her parents go too many rounds to believe that they'd come to a mutual understanding. Taking a deep breath, she opened the door.

"Mum?" she called cautiously. "Dad?"

She found them still in the sitting room, but now her mother was gazing absently out the window, and her father was speaking irritably to someone on his mobile phone. She walked over to her mother. "What's going on?" she asked, glancing at her father.

"Oh, the usual," she said with a bitter smile. "His work's calling him away again. Honestly, can you believe – "

"Mum," Sophie sighed, "don't start."

Anna opened her mouth to retort, and then shut it again. She shook her head, and went back to looking out the window until she heard Andrew end the call. "Well?" she asked.

He sighed, and looked up at Sophie. "I'm sorry, Angel, but your mum's right. It was work calling. There's been a cock-up at that hotel in Shanghai, seems someone's started building a wing where there ought to have been a garden and – "

"You're going to Shanghai?" Sophie interrupted, trying to decide whether this was a positive or a negative development, and how much Suri had to do with it.

"No – fortunately not. But they need me back in London for a few days. I'll have to catch the first flight down. Don't worry, though – I promise I'll be back for Christmas Eve."

"So you won't be able to go with me to Ardnasheen," she said.

"I'm afraid not. But we could go just after Christmas – "

"If it's after Christmas, I can take her," Sophie's mother jumped in.

"Maybe we should let Sophie decide."

"Haven't I just been telling you that she's in no position to…"

Sophie didn't stay to listen. It was the same argument she'd already heard a thousand times. She went to her room and shut the door, wondering how far an angel's powers stretched. With her parents fighting over it, getting to Ardnasheen in time for the solstice would take nothing short of a miracle.

CHAPTER 23

"What's wrong?" Angus asked when Sophie came into the café.

"What isn't?" she muttered.

"Uh-oh. Want to tell me about it?"

Sophie looked around. The lunch rush hadn't started yet, and though she could hear signs of life from the mums-and-babies space at the back, the front of the café was deserted. "Suri showed up," she said. "Only she was forty-five, and a lawyer."

"Pardon?"

"I mean, obviously not a *real* lawyer – or really forty-five. She just made herself look that way."

"So what did she want?"

"To get me to Ardnasheen. She had Lucas's will with her. Apparently he…he left me everything." The enormity of it still stunned her. After a moment she shook her head, trying to clear it of all the questions that revelation raised. "Anyway, she said I had to come up to Ardnasheen right away to claim it."

"And your mum agreed?" he asked, eyebrows raised.

"What do you think?" Sophie answered. "She said I couldn't go without her, and that wouldn't be till the New Year. Then Dad said he'd take me right away, which started world war seven hundred and forty five, and it wouldn't have helped even if it hadn't because, well, then my *dad* would be there. Then he got a call telling him to come back to London, which may or may not have been Suri's plotting, and...well, that's about it, actually."

"So basically, nothing's changed."

"Not really. I don't know, maybe if I got Ailsa to come down and collect me, Mum would rethink it...hey, are you even listening?" She nudged Angus, whose eyes were fixed on the grey street beyond the window.

"I'm listening," he answered, looking back at her. Almost as quickly, his eyes flickered away. "I just...I've been thinking."

"That sounds ominous," Sophie said.

But Angus didn't smile. "I hope you won't think so when you hear what it's about."

"Okay, now you're freaking me out."

He looked at her again, and this time there was something pleading in his eyes that made Sophie forget her problems for the moment, and wait for his words with trepidation. Just as she began to think that she'd scream if he didn't speak soon, he said, "I didn't really go to Egypt for a dig."

She wasn't sure what she'd expected to hear, but it definitely wasn't that. Her old fears about him avoiding her came rushing back. "Oh, God, I *knew* it. It's about that night, the snowstorm…look, I might have given you the wrong idea about me…and you…I mean, I should never have – "

"Sophie," he said, putting a hand on her arm, "it has nothing to do with the snowstorm, or what you told me, or you falling asleep on the sofa."

Sophie's cheeks burned. She wanted to look away, but his expression had gone deadly serious again. "Well actually, it is a bit about that, but not in the way you think." He stopped, shook his head, and then began again. "Right, so…there really was a dig in Egypt, and I really did go on it, but it wasn't to impress the professor. I went to look for something."

"What?" Sophie asked, her spine tingling in a way that told her she was about to hear something that would change everything.

With one more level look at her, Angus turned away, rummaged in his backpack, and then pulled out a small jar of cobalt glass, hexagonal in shape, the blue too dark to show what it held. The bottle had a cork stopper sealed with gold wax. An image had been pressed into the wax while it was still hot: what looked like a jug with two handles. Angus put the jar into her hand.

"Um…thank you," Sophie said. "It's lovely."

Angus gave an unexpected laugh. "Don't you want to know what it is?"

"I don't know," Sophie said, turning the little jar in her hands. "Do I?"

"I think so. I hope so." His look was indeed hopeful – but also skittish, as if it walked a tightrope between grief and joy.

"Okay – I'll bite."

"Right, so…what do you know about ancient Egyptian religion?"

Sophie shrugged. "Mummies. Pyramids. Pulling brains out through noses…actually, that's where I went off the whole thing."

"Aye, that bit seems to hang everyone up," he laughed. "But all of the spells and wrappings and rituals – scrambled brains included – had one purpose. They were meant to preserve the body after death, so that it could be reunited with its soul in the afterlife."

Sophie felt suddenly cold. She looked from the bottle in her hand to Angus's steady brown eyes. "Go on," she said, pitching her voice low in an attempt to keep it from shaking.

"Right…well, reuniting the soul and body isn't quite as simple as it sounds."

"No?"

"No," Angus said, clearly missing the irony in Sophie's tone as his ideas took hold of him. "These days, we think of the

343

soul as one entity. But the ancient Egyptians believed it was made up of five: the *Ren*, the *Ba*, the *Ka*, the *Sheut*, and the *Ib*."

"Which mean…?"

"Roughly translated – name, personality, vital spark, shadow, and heart. That," he pointed to the seal on the blue bottle, "is the hieroglyph for *Ib*. The heart."

Sophie studied the imprint in the gold wax. "Now that you say it, it does look a bit like a heart…but not the Valentines kind."

Angus nodded. "The symbol is based on a drawing of a sheep's heart."

"Please tell me there isn't a sheep's heart in here."

He smiled. "It's a bit small for that."

"So what is it – some kind of love potion?"

As soon as she said it, she wished she hadn't, but Angus only laughed. "There's no such thing. And anyway, in ancient Egypt, the heart wasn't about love. It was more like what we think of now as the brain – where emotion comes from, but also thought and will and intention. The heart was the body's driver's seat, if you like."

"Distilled and bottled for your convenience," Sophie said, turning the glass in her hand. This time, though, Angus didn't laugh. His eyes, when she looked up at him, were deadly serious. "Wait – you're saying that this bottle is actually holding a fifth of someone's soul?"

He held her eyes, and now his own were full of an intensity that frightened her. "Not just someone's, Sophie. Yours."

"Which is far less disturbing," she said, dropping the bottle onto the counter and taking a step away from him.

"Listen, I know that this sounds mad," he said.

"Terrifying, actually," Sophie answered, looking around. They were still alone in the front of the café. In fact, even the noises from the back had died out. The silence was so deep, there might not have been another person around for miles.

"More terrifying than 'I'm a semi-deity and my angel boyfriend has been kidnapped by a sea witch'?" Angus asked, not unkindly, but with a challenge in his tone.

"Well…yes, actually. I mean, if human souls were made of my tears, and it was my job to watch over them, you'd think I'd have heard by now that they come in five pieces."

"Not necessarily. How many parents know everything about their children? Once something's created, it no longer belongs to the creator. It belongs to itself."

"Fine, then," Sophie said. "Maybe the human soul has five parts, and they're called the name and the shadow and whatever. But that doesn't explain why you think my *Ib* is in a glass bottle from Egypt."

"I don't think it."

"Thank God."

"I know it. I know it's in there, because I watched the priest put it in."

Sophie put her hands to her head. "Alright, mad I can work with. But if you're going to start going religious on me – "

"Not that kind of a priest," Angus interrupted. "More of a shaman. A wise man. Or that thing they call the three kings, what is it? Magi? So, yeah – a magus. Anyway, the point is, he's someone who's spent his life studying and practicing the old religion."

"And did he tell you why I'm missing part of my soul?"

"No. I worked that out on my own. See, the *Ib* is formed at the moment of conception, from a drop of the mother's heart's blood. So you can't have an *Ib*, because you don't have – "

"A mother," Sophie finished for him, as it began to come clear. Angus nodded. "Okay. No mother's blood, no heart…but going with this theory, if I have no *Ib*, then how come I can still think and feel and all the rest?"

"I don't know for certain," Angus answered, "but Anok Sabé – the priest – he thinks it's because your soul and your body aren't bound together, at least not the way a human's are. And that accounts for all that business about ceasing to exist. Whatever way you found to hold your body and soul together – to replace the *Ib* – it's not strong enough to last a full human life-span. At some point they'll be torn apart – "

"Riven," Sophie said softly.

"Yes, if you like. But if you have an *Ib*, then your body and soul will knit together, like a human's."

"And so I won't die," Sophie said.

346

"Of course you'll die. But hopefully after a long and happy human life."

"So how does it work?" Sophie asked, indicating the bottle. "I drink it? I put it in the bath?"

"You breathe it in," Angus said, "after performing the proper ritual."

"Which you know how to do."

"As much as anyone does," he said, shrugging. "Obviously, it's theoretical. It can't be often that an Earthbound aeon needs a part of her soul replaced."

Sophie gazed at the bottle through a few long moments' silence. Then she said, "How long have you been working on this, Angus?"

Now he looked away, coloring. "Since…um…the night of the snowstorm."

"And this priest shaman guy – how did you find him?"

Blushing more deeply, he answered, "The internet."

Sophie didn't know whether to laugh or cry. It was absurd, and yet it was one of the loveliest gestures anyone had ever made her. "You really believe this will work," she said gently. "The internet priest, the ritual, and whatever-the-hell's in the bottle."

His eyes were steady. "I'd rather believe that, than that you'll die this summer."

Sophie shook her head. "I know that I'm the last person on

Earth who ought to be skeptical, but honestly, Angus – a Magi who makes soul parts? How much did he charge you for this?"

"Nothing."

"Nothing?"

"He only asked that if it works, you bless him."

"Bless him?" Sophie repeated dazedly.

"You're a deity, after all."

Sophie gave him a long look. She couldn't help wondering whether he'd done all of this out of kindness, or if there was something more to it.

"And if I do this...this ritual," she said, "and it works the way you think it will, what will I be, then?"

"Human, I guess," he answered after a pause that was long enough to tell her he hadn't actually thought about that until this moment.

"And what about everything else? Lucas, and Dahud, and the Revenants, and my aeon responsibilities, and...I don't know, *everything?*"

"That's the thing, Sophie," he said, an unreadable expression on his face, and a tremor in his voice. "If you were a human, 'everything' wouldn't be your responsibility anymore. You could have a normal life. Go to college, get married, have two-point-three kids and a dog and a cat and an African Gray parrot – whatever you wanted. You could...I could..."

He trailed off, looking down at his hands, though both of them knew exactly what he'd been about to say. For a moment she let herself consider what it would be like to go to university, or the conservatory. To date Angus. To meet his parents in Perthshire, and sneak into his room once everyone was asleep. To walk up the ailse in a white dress, and carry his children. It was more tempting now than she'd ever have thought it could be: to lay down all of the strange burdens she carried, and be just one more person among billions. To be ordinary.

Of course, she couldn't do it. She knew that even as that possible future fanned out in front of her. Even if she could stop loving Lucas, there was the certain doom Rive had described if she didn't go back to the Garden with him. And even if Rive had overstated his case – as she'd wondered more than once since their talk – breaking her promise to him would still mean turning her back on the world she'd made. Even thinking about it gave her that strange, detached, shivery feeling. Her fingers were tingling. She looked down at them at the same moment that Angus said, "Ah, Sophie, is there a reason why your hands are glowing?"

Oh God, not here! But even as she thought it, she began to understand. This reaction, this calling up of her aeon powers, wasn't random at all. In fact, if her idea was right, it made perfect sense. But this wasn't the time or place to test it. She made herself think of the present, not that future threat. Slowly, the room steadied and the tingling left her fingers, along with the blue glow.

She looked up at Angus. He was watching her with hope

and trepidation, and after all that he had done for her, she couldn't break his heart. "You know that I can't let Dahud kill Lucas," she said.

"I know," he answered, though there was dejection in his tone nevertheless.

"But the solstice is only a few days away, and if we all get through that..." She drew a deep breath. "Then I promise to think about this." She picked up the bottle, and then slipped it into her bag.

CHAPTER 24

Angus didn't say anything more about his idea, and for a while they were too busy to talk about anything other than steamed milk and espresso shots. But in the late afternoon lull, he said, "It's only four days till Solstice. Well, three, since this one's mainly spent."

"I know," Sophie answered, as she collected dirty cups and plates from the tables.

"So, do we have a plan?"

"Suri assures me she's taking care of everything."

"You don't sound convinced."

"That's because so far, all she's managed is to freak out my mother and get my father sent back to London."

Angus laughed. "Sorry, I know it's serious, but still – I'd have given anything to see Suri as a lawyer."

"Actually, I'm hoping lawyer-Suri stays away, or I'll have no chance of giving Mum the slip."

"Is that what you mean to do?"

"I'm not sure I have a choice," Sophie answered, dumping her load of dishes into the sink at the back. "But it's a crap plan. It would take her five minutes to figure out where I'd gone, and send the entire Highland police force after me."

Angus was looking at her speculatively. "What if you could convince her to let you go?"

"Her 'no' was distinctly unwavering."

"Maybe she felt threatened by the lawyer. Maybe I should talk to her."

"You?" Sophie asked, raising an eyebrow.

"I mean, maybe she'd feel better about it if I told her I'm going with you."

Sophie studied him. She knew that her mother was keen on Angus, but she doubted she was *that* keen. *Still*... "Ah, what the hell? All she can say is no – again."

"That's the spirit!"

Sophie gave him a wan smile. "So, tonight, my place, for tea and schmoozing?"

"I can't imagine anyplace I'd rather be," he said, and grinned.

*

Anna Creedon's "no" to Angus was delivered with a smile and an apology, unlike the earlier one, but it was equally firm.

"Mum, you're treating me like a child!" Sophie complained.

"Sophie, enough," her mother answered wearily. "I'm not

going to change my mind, and Angus shouldn't have to listen to us argue."

Angus and Sophie exchanged a glance across the table, but Sophie kept her silence. She knew that pushing the point would get her nowhere. All she could do now was hope that Suri came up with a feasible way around her mother's vigilance. As such, she slept that night with her phone under her pillow, set to "vibrate", hoping for a revelation. She kept jerking awake from confused dreams, thinking that she'd felt it go off, but every time she checked the call record was blank.

Morning dawned grey, the low, charcoal clouds threatening more snow. Though the radiator in Sophie's room was hot to the touch, the warmth didn't penetrate the deeper cold that had crept in overnight. She took a shower to try to warm up, but it only made the air seem colder when she got out again. Worse still, she heard arguing. Two women, no doubt her mother and lawyer-Suri. Sure enough, she came out of the bathroom to find her mother ushering Suri toward the door, her face white and furious.

"Good morning Miss – " Suri began, and then Anna shut the door in her face.

"I sincerely hope," she said, turning to Sophie, "that that is the last we see of that woman!"

"She's only doing her job," Sophie said, trailing behind her as she went to the kitchen.

Anna shook her head. "There's something odd about

her. She's too pushy – reminds me of an American." Sophie clamped down on a smile. "At any rate, I've told her in no uncertain terms that you will *not* be going up to that place until I can go with you, and that won't be until the New Year – if at all."

"If at all?"

"Mother's intuition." Anna tapped her head. "That place isn't good for you."

"But Mum, the inheritance – " Sophie began.

"You see, that's what doesn't make sense to me," Anna said, switching on the kettle. "Why on earth would that young man name you in his will when he'd known you only a few weeks? Never mind that – how would he even have had time?"

"It was longer than – "

"And what kind of twenty-year-old makes a will, anyhow?" Anna interrupted again, as if she hadn't even heard Sophie speak.

"A wealthy one," Sophie answered coldly.

Her mother gave her a look that promised a sharp retort, but then she seemed to change her mind. "There's just something funny about it," she said, shaking her head.

"But Su- the lawyer had all those papers…"

"Yes, and I'd like a solicitor of our own to look at them." The kettle had boiled, but Anna had forgotten it, staring into space.

"And?"

Finally her eyes settled back on Sophie. "And then, if the offer is genuine, we can speak to Miss White. Here. On *our* terms."

Sophie had to bite her cheek to keep herself from arguing. She tried not to show her desperation and anger at all, knowing that it would only make her mother dig her heels in further. She left for work earlier than she needed to, but once there, she couldn't concentrate. She kept checking her phone in case she'd missed a text; checking the clock, only to confirm that time was passing exactly as quickly and fruitlessly as she felt it was.

Then, when she thought she couldn't stand another moment of waiting, Suri breezed into the café. Thankfully, she was young Suri, wearing her black puffa jacket and a knitted hat open at both ends, so that her dreads spilled out in a brilliant fountain. Sophie leapt out from behind the counter, and hugged her.

"Please tell me you've thought of a way out of here!" she cried.

"I have," Suri said when Sophie released her. She produced a handful of train tickets. She counted them off: "Me, you, Rive and Angus. We leave at nine tomorrow morning."

Sophie's spirits plummeted. "We can't take the train," Sophie said. "Mum will figure it out before we even get to Mallaig."

"Not if you pretend that you're out to work," Suri answered.

"Matrika will notice that I'm not here, and no doubt phone my house."

"Not if you call in sick first."

"I never get sick."

Suri cocked her head, looking at Sophie. "You really didn't get out much in high school, did you?"

Sophie smiled. "I suppose I *was* a model child."

"Yeah. It took an angel to corrupt you."

"Don't flatter yourself."

"I wasn't," Suri said with a smirk. "I had nothing to do with it. Well, except maybe that first time, on the hill, what with the come-hither dress and all…"

Sophie turned to the sink to hide her flush. "So what happens when Mum *does* find out that I've gone?" she asked, running water over a squirt of washing-up liquid. "She's bound to guess where, and catch the next train north."

Suri shrugged. "We'll get there first. And once we're in Ardnasheen, there'll be plenty of places to hide you."

"But we need a boat to get there, and do you really think Ruadhri's going to go along with this? He's such a stick in the mud, he'll never lie to my mother. I mean, I'm a minor. He could get arrested. *I* could get arrested – "

Suri took hold of Sophie's arms, and looked her in the eye. "Honey, stop. Take a deep breath." Sophie breathed. "Now practice saying to yourself, 'It's going to work.'"

"Is it?" Sophie asked, her voice faint with worry.

"Of course it is," Suri said, squeezing her arms. "It has to."

"Goodness, you two girls look like you're plotting murder!" Matrika said gaily, gliding into the room in a forest-green *salwar kameez* with a pair of battered jeans underneath.

Sophie and Suri leapt apart.

"Aha – you *were* plotting murder." There was laughter in Matrika's voice, but her eyes were too keen for Sophie's liking.

"No," Suri answered. "Just a train journey."

"Oh? Where are you going?" She looked at Sophie rather than Suri as she said it.

"Not me," Sophie said quickly. "Her. She's going…" She looked at Suri, suddenly unsure of how much to say.

"Home," Suri answered. "It was just a flying visit."

Matrika nodded and smiled and continued back behind the counter, Freyja following at her heels, leaping for the trailing ends of the *salwar.*

"What did you say your boss's name was?" Suri asked, watching her go.

"Matrika."

"Hmm," Suri mused, still looking after her. "Means 'mother' in Sanskrit. I wonder if – "

"Oh no," Sophie said wearily, "please don't. If she's Cinderella's fairy godmother in disguise, I'd prefer not to know."

"Really? Fairy godmothers can be useful. The tame ones, anyway…"

"Suri!"

Suri smiled. "Oh, alright. I'm sure she's a perfectly normal Indian woman with an Irish accent and a triskelion tattoo."

"A what?"

"The mark between her eyes. It's an ancient Celtic symbol, stands for a triplicate. You know, mind, body, spirit; past present, future; whatever. They used to carve it on stones in sacred places, and…Sophie? What's the matter?"

Sophie shook her head, clearing the image of the linked spirals that she'd seen at the Toll House, and on Morag's walking stick, and Morwen's hands. Even if there was a connection, she couldn't afford to be sidetracked. "Nothing."

"So we're good for tomorrow? Meet at the station at nine?"

"Nine sharp."

Suri handed her three of the tickets. "For Angus and Rive," she said.

"Rive? Can't you take his to him?"

"Sorry – I've got a date. Drummer with a new band. He's totally hot."

Before Sophie could imagine how to reply to this, Suri had slipped out the door and into the shadows of the falling night.

*

Angus insisted on walking with Sophie to the cemetery to give Rive his ticket. "Really, I'm fine," she said for the tenth time, as they passed the old Scotsman newspaper building, now a plush hotel.

"I know…but it just doesn't seem right, letting you creep around graveyards by yourself in the middle of the night."

"It's early evening," Sophie pointed out, "and I can hardly creep in these boots." They were her favorite black biker boots, which her father had given her last Christmas. She stomped her feet on the icy pavement to prove it.

Angus laughed. "Okay, you win. I just want to witness for myself a guy who lives in a crypt."

"Please tell me you're not going to be weird about it," Sophie said.

"*Me* weird? He's the one that lives in someone's grave!"

"Right – just don't freak him out."

"Right. I'll try to rein in my tedious normality."

When they finally reached the crypt, though, they found it dark and silent, the iron grate padlocked. Sophie banged on the door a few times, in case Rive was only sleeping – if aeons slept – but there was no answer. So she wrote a note about their plans, and slipped it under the door with the train ticket.

"I guess that's the best we can do," she said, and they turned back toward home.

CHAPTER 25

The first thing that Sophie noticed when she woke the next morning was the silence. No traffic noises, no schoolchildren's voices, no chatter of early shoppers. She got out of bed, opened the curtains and then stood looking out the window, paralyzed by despair. All she could see was a wall of whirling snowflakes, so thick that the shapes of the buildings across the street were faint as ghosts. There was no way trains would be running in such a storm.

She stood staring at the snow until her ringing phone jerked her out of her reverie. It was Suri. "We've got a problem," she said.

"No kidding," Sophie muttered. "Maybe it'll stop soon?"

"Nope. I saw the news. It's meant to last all day."

"How come no one predicted it?"

"No doubt your friend Dahud has a hand in it."

"Seriously?"

"She's part demon and part faery – why not part storm witch?"

"What's a storm witch?"

"They can command the weather – but that's beside the point. We need to come up with a new plan ASAP."

"You don't have one already?"

"Not exactly…"

"Suri!"

"I'm only an angel, honey – there are limits!"

"Right," Sophie said. "Well, what do we do, then?"

"Can you get to the café?"

"I doubt Matrika's opening today."

"She is. I'm sitting here as we speak."

"Then I'll find a way to get there." She didn't know how, but she knew that she had to. There wasn't any other choice.

*

By the time Sophie got to the café – after convincing her mother and trudging through the snow, as no buses were running – Angus had joined Suri. They sat in gloomy silence at the table by the window, their hands wrapped around steaming mugs and not a customer in sight. Neither was Matrika.

"So," Sophie said, dropping into the free chair, "I take it from the funereal looks that no one's come up with a Plan B."

Suri shook her head, poking despondently at what appeared

to be clouds floating in her cup of coffee. "I called the station, but everything's cancelled."

"Angus? You're from up north. You must know how to deal with snow."

"Yeah," he answered. "Turn up the heat and batten down the hatches until summer."

"That's not funny," Sophie snapped.

He shrugged. "It wasn't meant to be. Up north, when it snows like this, they close the roads and you just deal with it. I did try and borrow a car off a friend," he added. "He laughed at me. And he's right – the ploughs aren't even making a dent."

"What about Rive?"

"There's no sign of him," Suri answered.

This worried Sophie, given their last conversation. "We need to find him. Maybe he can magic us there, or something."

Suri smiled humorlessly. "I don't think teleporting humans is in the aeon arsenal. And besides, where would we even begin to look for him?"

"Well then, maybe there's a way to stop the snow," Sophie said, wishing that she sounded less desperate. "I mean, if Dahud's causing it unnaturally, there must be an off switch or something…"

Suri shook her head. "This close to Solstice, she's far too powerful. And water is her element. Snow is just frozen water."

"So basically, we're screwed," Angus said.

They all sat in silence for a few long moments. Then

Sophie stood up, dragging her fingers through her tangled hair. "No," she said emphatically.

"No, what?" Suri asked.

"No, this is not how it ends! Giving up means Lucas dies, and I'm not going to let that happen!"

"I can go to Ker-Ys alone," Suri suggested. "See if she'll deal with me – "

"She won't. It's me she wants to fight." Sophie turned, and started toward the back of the café.

"Where are you going?" Angus asked.

"The Eyrie," Sophie answered. "Matrika has books on everything else, she must have something about stopping magical snowstorms." She stalked to the stairway, not looking back. But she could hear, after a few moments, that the others were following.

When she got to the Eyrie, however, she stopped short. Matrika was sitting at the table, a large book open before her in a pool of yellow light from a reading lamp. In one hand she held a cup of the curiously-scented tea she favored, and with the other, she stroked Freyja, who was also gazing intently at the open book. Matrika looked up at Sophie and her friends, and offered a warm smile.

"Goodness, Sophie," she said, "you certainly are a dedicated worker, to come in on a day like this."

Abruptly, and to her utter mortification, Sophie began to cry. It was as if all of the frustrated hope and determination of the last few weeks culminated here, with Matrika sitting at that table, making it impossible to carry out their plan. How, after all, could they possibly explain what they were doing? Sophie felt Angus and Suri hovering behind her, but it was Matrika who stood up and came toward her with open arms. In her eyes, Sophie saw all of the love and compassion of all of the mothers in the world. She fell into those arms without question, weeping her heart out into Matrika's woolly green cabled tunic.

"Come in, children," she said to the others, who stood uncertainly in the doorway. "Sit down, and tell me what's happened."

She led Sophie to the chair next to hers, guided her into it, and handed her a tissue, as the others sat down. Freyja sat calmly watching them, her cornflower eyes half-lidded. "It's nothing," Angus began. "Sophie's just upset because…ah, because – "

"No," Suri interrupted. "We don't have time for any more lies. And anyway, I think Matrika might be more open to weirdness than you think." Suri turned her incisive black eyes on the older woman. "Am I right?"

Matrika gave her a knowing smile. "Try me," she said.

Sophie wiped her eyes one last time, took a deep breath, and said, "Ker-Ys – that place in the picture I drew, and the book you gave me – it's real. Dahud is real too, only she's turned into a half-demon. And my boyfriend, the one I told you about that first day…I found out he isn't really dead. But

Dahud is keeping him prisoner, because she wants to use him as a teind. That's a kind of – "

"Tax, yes," Matrika said. "I'm well acquainted with teinds."

"You are?" Sophie asked, blinking at her.

"Unfortunately," Matrika answered. "They're one of the uglier aspects of the faery realm. No, you don't need to say any more," she added, as Sophie took a breath to begin again. "You don't need to cry, either. It's not Solstice yet. There's still time to save him."

"But how – "

"Wait, who – "

"Why do you – " They all spoke at once.

Matrika only smiled. She never moved – not, at any rate, that Sophie could see – but suddenly she was gone, and Morag was sitting in her place. "Eh, lass?" the old woman said. "Do you see now?"

"Oh, my God – it's you!" Sophie said, feeling a tiny shoot of hope press up through her despair.

"*Matrika's* the third aspect of the Morrigan?" Angus asked. "How come I didn't see it?"

"Because you didn't need to see it," the Morrigan said, becoming Matrika again. "We appear as we're needed."

"Does that mean you can stop the snow?" Sophie asked.

Matrika frowned into her tea cup. "Unfortunately, no. Even

if Dahud weren't so strong right now, there are boundaries to the old magic. I have no power over water."

"Then nothing's really changed," Sophie said dejectedly. "We're stuck here till it stops snowing."

"Don't be silly," Matrika said, in what struck Sophie as too flippant a tone, given the situation. "Just because *I* can't help you, doesn't mean that you're beyond help."

"So who will help us, then?"

"Freyja," she said.

"Ah…Freyja's a cat," Angus said.

Matrika smiled. "And I'm a middle-aged café owner." She touched the cat gently on the forehead, and said, *"Dróttning, hitta!"*

For a moment, Freyja remained still. Then she stood slowly, and stretched. But the stretch didn't end. She didn't leap to the ground or curl herself up to sleep. Instead her limbs grew and lengthened, her golden fur gradually dissolving into creamy skin, her eyes lengthening and face changing shape until it wasn't a cat but a beautiful, golden-haired woman sitting on the table.

Except when Sophie thought about it, Freyja didn't look human at all. She had a woman's form, but her eyes were of too deep and pure a blue, her hair a shifting mass of gold and red, her limbs reminiscent of birch branches in their length and delicacy. She wore a plain white dress, but it was cinched at her waist with what looked like a silver rope, and around her neck she wore a jewel whose facets glinted with all the colors of fire.

Smiling a cat's knowing smile, she said, "Well, Morrigan? Why have you called me?"

"Your help is needed." Matrika nodded to Sophie.

Freyja studied Sophie for a few long moments, and once again, her unblinking gaze reminded Sophie of a cat's. "Sophia," she said at last. "I never thought to meet you, though we are both keepers of the light of wisdom." Sophie had no idea what to say to that, but Freyja wasn't finished. "Your need must be great, to have taken a mortal body."

"The greatest," Sophie answered, hoping that her voice wouldn't shake.

"Of course. What's greater than love?" Sophie shook her head, dazzled. Freyja smiled her catlike smile. "I am a keeper of love, as well as wisdom. I've heard your story – the earlier bits of it, anyway. And if this is all for the sake of Lucifer," she gestured to Sophie's body in general, "then I can only think that it is a love worthy of my attention. So, how may I be of service to you?"

Sophie took a deep breath, and looked the goddess in the eye. "Lucas has been captured by the sea-witch, Dahud. She'll make him a teind to the Deep on Midwinter's Eve, unless we can save him. But the entrance to her city is far from here, and she's sent this storm to keep us away."

"I am the daughter of a sea god," Freyja said. "I, too, can make the water do my bidding."

"Well, that's great," Sophie said. "But it's not the only problem. There are people who will try to stop me going, or come after me once I'm gone." She stopped without giving more detail. She couldn't quite bring herself to tell a deity that she had an overprotective mother.

But Freyja only smiled her lazy smile again. "Is there more?"

"Um…yes, unfortunately. The door to Ker-Ys is under water. Apparently we need either a selkie skin or a water horse to get us there. But I wouldn't know where to begin to find a selkie skin, and the last time I dealt with a water horse, it nearly killed me."

Freyja ran the fire-colored jewel along its chain, watching Sophie. "And that's the final obstacle?"

"Aside from actually fighting Dahud, yes. But I think I'm going to be on my own with that one."

Freyja glanced around at the others, and said, "Perhaps." Then, after another pause, she said, "Very well, Sophia. I will help you."

For the first time since she'd woken up, Sophie brightened. "Really? You'll make it stop snowing?"

Freyja shook her head. "No need. Besides, it's a good alibi for your mother." Freyja reached up, made a motion like someone unhooking a jacket from a peg, and suddenly she was holding a long garment. It was made of feathers speckled in shades of cream and brown. She shook it out and let it drape over the table; it nearly covered the whole thing. The feathers quivered gently, as if in a breeze.

"With this cloak, you will have the power to fly as far and fast as the wind that lifted the wings of the sacred falcons whose feathers it was made from." Then she unwound the silver rope from around her waist, and laid it on the table. "With my girdle, you may catch and bind any creature which succumbs to magic." Next she took the chain with the jewel from around her neck, and hung it around Sophie's. "The stone is Brisingamen, the jewel of fire, whose power cannot be resisted. You will know how to use it when the time comes."

"What about Mum?" Sophie couldn't help asking.

"As far as she's concerned," Matrika said, "you're here with me. And you'll stay the night with me when you're unfortunately snowed in. Here," she reached into the air as Freyja had, and drew out Dahud's silver crown, thankfully free of the torn-out hair. "You'll need this, too." She handed it to Suri.

Likewise, Freyja picked up the silver girdle and handed it to Angus, who couldn't stop staring at her, dumbstruck. "For the valiant knight." Then she lifted the feathered cloak, holding it toward Sophie. Sophie took it. It didn't feel magical. If anything, it felt slightly creepy, too warm for an inanimate object.

"You'd best be off," Freyja said.

"I don't quite understand," Sophie answered.

"Wrap the cloak around yourself and those you would take with you, and then tell it your intention. It will do the rest."

Sophie looked at her friends. "Right. Ready, guys?" Suri and Angus joined her. Matrika, however, hung back with Freyja. "Aren't you coming?" Sophie asked her. "You…I mean Morwen…is the one who knows Ker-Ys."

Matrika gave her an enigmatic smile. "I have one or two things to take care of here. But don't worry – I'll be there when you need me."

Sophie nodded, and then spread the cloak out so that it would wrap around Suri, Angus and herself. She'd thought that it wouldn't fit, but either she'd misjudged the size, or it grew to accommodate them. She looked at them: Angus wide-eyed, Suri glowing with the anticipation of adventure. Then she put her mind to the matter at hand.

"We…ah…intend to go to Ardnasheen," she said, feeling slightly silly, and moreso when nothing happened.

Suri rolled her eyes. "You've gotta say it like you mean it." She cleared her throat, then said in what Sophie had come to think of as her angel-with-a-flaming-sword voice, "Flying cloak: Ardnasheen! Now!"

There was a sudden sound of howling wind, the vertiginous feeling of falling from a great height, and then everything went dark.

CHAPTER 26

Sophie hit the ground as if someone had flung her there. She lay for a moment, winded, until she realized that she was lying in a very cold puddle. Then she sat up and looked around, and found she was in the front garden at Madainneag. A fierce wind was blowing sleet into her face from a sky full of low, bruised cloud. Angus was sitting a few feet away, looking pale and shaken. Only Suri seemed unfazed by the violent landing, though she stood with her hands on her hips, glaring at the dark, damp pile that could only be the flying cloak.

"There was no need for that!" she snapped at it. Sophie thought that Suri had hit her head in the landing, until she saw the cloak's feathers ruffle up, like those of an angry bird.

"It can *hear* you?" Sophie asked.

"Of course it can hear me," Suri answered, as if this should have been obvious. "That's how we got here, remember? But apparently, it didn't like the tone in which I asked. That landing was its revenge." She poked the wet feathers with the toe of her boot, and the cloak drew back resentfully, bristling once again. "Fine," she said to it, "if you're going to be like that, you can stay right here." She turned toward the house.

The feathers flattened again, and the cloak lay still. "Thank you," Suri said with a self-satisfied smile. She picked up the cloak and threw it over her shoulder. "Come on," she said to the others, "let's get inside."

Sophie, already shivering, was happy enough to follow her, though it felt surreal to be walking through the stained-glass front door again. It seemed she'd been away a hundred years, rather than a few weeks.

Suri didn't lead them up the grand staircase, but down a corridor and then a much plainer set of stairs, twisting and turning through the house's basement level, toward the kitchen. As they neared the room, Sophie could hear voices. They arrived to find Ailsa and Rive sitting at the table, drinking tea. Ailsa was wearing a fluffy pink dressing gown. Rive looked exactly as he had when Sophie had seen him last – slightly flushed, slightly distant, but none the worse for the weather.

He looked Sophie up and down with a smirk, and said, "Glad to see you've made your usual entrance."

Sophie glared at him, squeezing water from her hair as Angus asked, "What does he mean?"

Rive shrugged. "Sophie seems to revel in watery misadventure."

"It wasn't my fault this time," Sophie muttered, taking

three more cups from the cupboard and filling the electric kettle.

"No?" Rive asked.

"The cloak got in a huff," Suri explained, draping it over the back of a chair, where it shook water from its feathers. "It dumped us in the front yard."

Ailsa laughed, and then coughed. "Still sick?" Sophie asked her, putting the mugs of tea on the table.

"How'd you guess?" she answered, reaching for a tissue. "Anyway, you will be too if you don't go change into something dry. You can borrow whatever's in my room."

"It'll never fit," Sophie said, sipping her tea. "And anyway, Angus is going to look a bit daft in your clothes."

Suri rolled her eyes and said, "When are you going to learn that human rules don't apply when I'm around?" She rummaged in her messenger bag, pulled out a pile of folded clothes, handed it to Sophie, and then took out another for Angus. Looking through them, Sophie realized that they were her own: her favorite jeans, a layered tee-shirt, a warm pair of woolen socks, and Lucas's crimson jumper. By the look on his face, Suri had given Angus his own favorite things, too.

"How did you – " Sophie began, but Suri made a face, waving her hand.

"I forbid you to ever ask me that question again," she said. "Now go change, before you catch Ailsa's disease."

"I'm not diseased!" Ailsa cried, then sneezed several times.

Smiling to herself, Sophie took the dry clothes into the laundry room and changed, then hung her wet ones to dry. When she returned to the kitchen, Angus had also changed, Suri had miraculously dried, and someone – no doubt Ailsa – had opened a packet of custard creams.

"So," Sophie said, sitting down and taking a biscuit, "what's the plan now?"

"It seems to me there's not a whole lot we can do until tomorrow," Angus said.

"Speak for yourselves," Suri said, grabbing a handful of biscuits. "Some of us have to work."

"Honestly?" Sophie said. "Tonight?"

"Honestly, tonight. Ruadhri won't let Ailsa near the pub in case she infects all of the customers."

"Jesus, you'd think I have leprosy the way everyone goes on!" Ailsa cried.

"If you had leprosy, we wouldn't be sitting here. Don't wait up for me – no doubt I'll be late."

When she'd left, Angus said, "It must be near tea time."

"You'll have to go to the pub if you want anything more than custard creams," Ailsa said. "We haven't been able to get to the shops in days."

"You can't go to the pub," Rive said, before Sophie or Angus could reply. "We can't risk anybody seeing you or Sophie here."

"I suppose not," Angus said, looking balefully at the packet of biscuits.

"Actually," Sophie said, "I know where there's a lot of frozen pizza."

Angus brightened. "Really?"

She nodded. "In the tower. Lucas's – " she paused, swallowed and finished " – Lucas's place. I'll go get them."

"Sophie," Ailsa said, giving her a level look, "are you sure you want to do that?"

"Yes," Sophie said firmly. Though half of her was screaming that she was mad, that to set foot in that place again would unravel her completely, the other half felt the strong need to see it again.

"I'll go with you," Angus said.

"No," Rive answered firmly, "I will." He stood up, his eyes steady on Sophie. Though Angus looked like he wanted to argue, he kept his mouth shut. Sophie followed Rive out of the room.

Once they were far enough away from the kitchen not to be overheard, Rive said, "Are you really okay?"

"Peachy," Sophie answered. "Why?"

His face was serious, his eyes worried as he studied her. "Why would you want to go back to Lucas's place?"

"Because we need to eat."

"Sophie."

She stopped walking, looked at him. "Alright, fine. I just…I need to remember what it was like to be with him."

Rive frowned. "Is that really a good idea? I mean, won't it make tomorrow more difficult?"

Sophie smiled bitterly. "I don't think there's anything that could possibly make tomorrow more difficult." She began walking again – climbing the stairs to the second floor, and the door to Lucas's bedroom. "What about you?"

"What *about* me?"

"Why did you come up here with me? Afraid I'll do a runner?"

"No. I know you keep your promises."

She didn't know why she was being snarky with him, when he was trying to be decent. Still, she couldn't stop. "So why *did* you come with me?"

He paused, then said, "Because you might find this harder than you think."

She looked toward the old wooden door at the end of the corridor. By the sudden clutch in her stomach, she knew that he was right.

"I can go, you know," he said. "If you've lost your nerve. I won't say anything to the others."

Sophie frowned. "My nerves are intact, thank you."

She walked up to the door, pressed the hasp on the rusted iron handle, and pushed it inward. Inside it was pitch dark, but Rive walked in as if he could see perfectly, and turned on a lamp. As its light flooded the room, Sophie realized that he'd been right. Nothing had changed in the room since the day she left it to go home with her parents. The towers of books still climbed the walls, the duvet was still turned back from the last time she'd got out of bed. The room around her blurred and swam as a wave of emotion pushed at her.

"Rive," she said, sounding very young and scared, and hating herself for it. But she was glad when his only answer was to reach out and take her hand. She was surprised, as she had been the night she hugged him, by how normal and natural it felt. How it made her feel safe.

"Do you want a moment up here alone?" he asked. "I can get the pizzas."

"No," she said emphatically. "I don't want to be alone."

He nodded, and then led the way down the narrow, curving staircase to the room below. He turned on some more lights, and then went to rummage in the freezer, as Sophie turned in a slow circle. Here, too, everything had been left exactly as it was on the day she left. She even saw her water glass in the sink.

"How come no one's been in here?" she asked, as Rive piled pizza-boxes onto the worktop.

"They're afraid, no doubt," he answered, with his back still to her.

"Of what? I mean, he's dead – or they think he is. He's not

exactly going to walk in on them snooping. Or do they think he's haunting the place?"

"Maybe," Rive agreed mildly. "This is a superstitious place, and the fallen never quite blend, no matter how hard they try. Humans can always sense the difference, even if they don't know what it is. The people here will no doubt have been suspicious of Lucifer, even before the whole dramatic death. Now, well," he shrugged. "He could be anything, as far as they're concerned. A ghost is probably the least of their worries."

Sophie thought of the old man, Niall Aitken, who'd pressed the talisman into her hand on the walk she'd taken into the valley, when she first came to Ardnasheen. She knew that Rive was right.

"I guess it's better this way," she said. "I don't think I could have survived coming in here to find it empty."

Rive gave her one of his direct, unblinking looks. "You'd have survived. You're a lot stronger than you think."

That surprised her. She didn't feel strong, and she certainly hadn't done anything that would make her seem that way to Rive. But he had already moved past the comment, picking up the pizzas and asking, "You ready to go?"

I'll never be ready. "I suppose so."

"Good. Wait – is that whisky?" He pointed to the decanter on the worktop beside the fridge.

"It was last time I tried it."

"Great. Bring that too."

Sophie picked up the decanter and was about to follow Rive up the stairs, when her eyes fell on the painting of the angel slaying the sea serpent. She went over to it, pulled it back from the wall and looked into the recess behind it. She thought that Lucas had taken everything out of it when he'd left to fight Sam, but she put her hand into it anyway, and felt around. She wasn't quite surprised when her hand came to rest on something cool and solid.

"Sophie?" Rive asked from the top of the stairs.

She pulled it out. It was the blade of a sword, apparently broken off from the hilt. It was so old, tarnish had turned it black. "Do you know what this is?" Sophie asked, turning to Rive, who'd come back down the stairs when she pulled out the blade.

There was a strange, speculative look on his face. "Something that shouldn't be possible."

"We really don't have time for cryptic."

"It's Lucifer's sword," Rive answered, running one finger along the blackened blade.

"But he had his sword when he fell into the sea."

Rive shook his head. "That was a different one – a faery gift. This is an angel's blade. All of them have one, but they lose them along with their armor if they fall."

Sophie thought of the crumbling armor she'd found in

Suri's cemetery; the bladeless hilt among it. "How did he keep it, then?" she asked.

Rive shook his head. "I don't know. But we ought to bring it with us."

"Why? No one will be able to fight with it, without a hilt."

"Swords often have uses beyond battle. Lucifer would have to have fought hard to keep this." He looked up at her. "So there must be a reason why."

CHAPTER 27

By the time they'd finished dinner, the storm was raging beyond anything Sophie had seen in her time in Ardnasheen. Sleet ran down the windowpanes and then froze there, until it was impossible to see out of them. The wind crashed and raged against the old stone walls, and Sophie was certain that she heard them groaning in protest.

"It's stood against worse," Suri said, reading the anxiety in Sophie's face. Ruadhri had called earlier to tell her not to try to come to work.

"I don't think we've seen Dahud's worst, yet," Sophie answered. Nobody contradicted her.

Though the house was full of empty bedrooms, no one was keen to sleep on their own. So they gathered bedding for Sophie, Ailsa and Angus, then lit the fire in the entry hall, shut the heavy velvet curtains and bolted the outer doors. Night settled over them, but though no one spoke, Sophie knew that no one slept. Ailsa and Angus tossed and turned restlessly, while Suri and Rive passed the whisky bottle back and forth, twitching the curtains aside every few minutes to look out.

At last, Sophie fell into a fitful doze. She dreamed that she was in Dahud's palace, and she was alone. Though she searched frantically through the endless rooms and corridors, she could find no sign of another being, human or otherwise. When she reached the great hall, she found the carpets rotted and the banners in rags, the lamps long since burned out. But there was something pale among the shadows.

With a bounding heart and a cold, sick feeling in her guts, Sophie walked toward it, until she could make out the bleached white bones of a skeleton, a fine gold chain woven through the ribs, shackling it to the throne. A whisper of cruel, watery laughter swirled around her, and she woke screaming, her friends in a white-faced ring around her.

"Sophie, you were dreaming," Ailsa said.

"We couldn't wake you," Angus added.

"We have to go!" she cried, ignoring them and leaping to her feet. "We have to help him!"

"It isn't time yet," Rive said, laying a hand on her shoulder, which calmed her a little.

"But I saw…I saw…" She couldn't make herself say it, couldn't make her mind reconcile that bleached skeleton with the Lucas she loved.

"Whatever you saw," Suri said, "was what *she* wanted you to see. She's trying to provoke you."

"Provoke me to do what?"

"Fail," Rive said.

Sophie dropped her head into her hands. She knew that her friends were right, but she couldn't master the panic that was telling her to run to Lucas, now, no matter what. "What time is it?" she asked at last, looking toward the windows. Someone had drawn the curtains back, but it was still dark as night outside.

"Nine," Rive answered.

"But I'm sure I didn't go to sleep until long after midnight," Sophie said, confused.

"Nine in the morning," Ailsa said, and then sneezed, and pulled a blanket tighter around her shoulders.

"Why is it so dark?" Sophie asked.

Her friends exchanged a look that Sophie didn't like at all. She got up and went to the door, jamming back the bolt and then shoving it open. But it would only move a few inches. Snow was piled up against it, at least three feet high. Between the weird, white snowscape and the dim grey sky, the sea was black and furious, flinging waves high up onto the shore. Sophie stared at it in despair until Angus shut the door.

"How are we ever meant to get to the sea cave through that?" she asked, collapsing dejectedly back into her pile of blankets.

"Freyja's bird cloak?" Angus suggested.

"I don't know if I'd trust it to fly straight in that wind,"

Suri said. "If we could even convince it to try in the first place, which I doubt – it's been in a sulk ever since I told it off yesterday."

"Maybe Matrika would have an idea. I mean, she helped us get here, right? And she *is* one of the most powerful goddesses of all time."

"Matrika's not here," Ailsa pointed out.

"She said she'd come," Sophie said.

"Maybe she wasn't expecting the weather to be this bad," Suri answered. "Or maybe she's coming later. But Ailsa's right – if she's not here now, we can't rely on her to help."

Rive, who had remained silent during this exchange, now had his head cocked slightly, as if he were listening to something. "I think we should go to the pub," he said abruptly.

"The *pub?*" Sophie cried. "Do you really mean to drink at a time like this?"

"I was thinking more in terms of breakfast. We're going to need our strength."

"But then Ruadhri will know I'm here."

Rive shrugged. "Do you really think your mum's going to be able to come after you it this?" He gestured to the snow-darkened windows.

"He's right," Suri said. "And anyway, it's better than sitting around here, fretting."

*

The walk to the pub seemed to take hours. Sleet and sea-spray needled their faces, the snow was wet and deep and difficult to walk through, and all the way the wind seemed to be trying to push them back. Finally, though, they saw a dim yellow light through the whirling snow – the first of the village houses. Ten minutes later, they were piling into the pub's coatroom.

Apparently they weren't the only ones to have had the same idea: the room was full of dripping rain gear and sodden boots. With nowhere left to hang their own things, they went on into the pub as they were. Ruadhri looked up from behind the bar, and when he saw Sophie, his face darkened.

"You!" he thundered. "Do you know I've just had your mother on the phone giving me five kinds of hell, and here I swore to her up and down that you couldn't *possibly* be in the village – "

"I know," Sophie answered wearily, "and I'm sorry. But since you didn't know, you didn't lie, right?"

Ruadhri's frown only deepened. "I have half a mind to phone her back right now, and let you explain yourself!"

"You can if you want to," Sophie said. "But it would mean a lot to me if you didn't."

"Why? Are you running away from home?"

"No. I just have something I have to do here." Ruadhri still looked dubious, but she could tell that he was wavering. "I'll phone her afterwards. Promise."

Ruadhri's look turned speculative. "And what might you be thinking of doing in this storm, then?"

"At the moment, looking for breakfast."

Ruadhri's eyes narrowed as he scanned their bedraggled lot. "Ach, well," he said. "As long as you really mean to phone your mum."

"I will," Sophie said. "As soon as I can."

"Right, then – stop dripping on my floor. Go hang your things by the fire." He waved them away, and Sophie breathed a sigh of relief.

Rive led the way through the crowded tables to one at the back, near the fire. It was a large, round table, but only one person sat there, with a pint of Guinness and a newspaper shielding his face. "Mind if we join you?" Rive said with a wry twist to his mouth that Sophie didn't understand, until the man lowered the paper, revealing Michael's in his old-man disguise.

"Now, who could say no to that face?" He folded his paper and patted the seat beside him. "How lovely to see you all this fine morning!"

The others began to shed their wet rain-gear, but Sophie stood still, watching Michael warily. "What are you doing here?" she asked.

"Drinking my breakfast," he said, nodding to the Guinness, "thank you for asking."

"The truth, Michael. And by the way, your Irish accent's worse than ever." Michael glanced at Rive, who raised his eyebrows. "Wait," Sophie said to Rive, "you knew he was here?"

Rive gave her a grave look, and said, "I asked him to come."

"What?" she cried, causing several heads to turn toward them.

"I would think, given the situation, you'd prefer to avoid making a fuss," Michael said mildly.

"Fine," she said in a low voice, looking between Rive and Michael, and settling on Rive. "But what the hell were you *thinking?* He wants Lucas dead!"

"No, I don't," Michael answered.

"Do I really have to lay out the facts again?"

"The situation has changed."

"Right, so just like that, you've changed your mind? Why would you do that?"

There was a pause, during which Michael's green eyes caught Rive's blue ones. She read that look easily: Rive had told him about her promise to return with him. *But why?*

"Sophie," Rive said, as if he'd heard her thought, "I wouldn't have asked him if we didn't need him."

Sophie was set to argue further, but Angus pre-empted her. "Why do we need him?"

Another unspoken exchange passed between Rive and Michael. This time Michael answered, "Because without me, there's no way you're going to cross that." He pointed out the window at the raging water.

They all looked out the window in silence. It was certainly true that there was no question of reaching the cave by ordinary means. Suri was the first to speak, saying dryly, "I don't think even your Heavenly Glory is enough to squash that storm, Michael."

"I don't need to squash it," he retorted. "I only need to subdue a boat-shaped portion of it for a half hour or so."

"Can you really do that?" Ailsa asked, wide-eyed.

"When I was made, the aeons gave me sovereignty over nature. Rain, snow, thunder, lightning, wind – "

"Okay, we get the picture," Suri said, tipping her chair back, her expression impatient. "But that was all about *normal* nature, not sea-witch-induced, raging tempests."

"Do you have any better ideas?"

Suri sighed. "No."

"So does that mean we're all about to see a miracle?" Angus asked, a hopeful note in his voice.

"It means we're about to *be* a miracle," Rive answered.

"Do you really think this is going to work?" Sophie asked.

"Only one way to find out," Michael said, and gave her his beatific smile.

Chapter 28

They spent the day in the pub, passing the time playing cards as the storm raged ever fiercer, until even Rive began to look worried. "I think we'd better start out," he said, eyeing the evil black clouds scudding low over the water.

"It's not even three yet," Angus said.

"No. But it'll be dark soon, and miracle or not, I don't want to face that water in the dark."

Nobody contradicted him. They filed out of the room, still packed with villagers huddled together in knots, their faces white and anxious. Even in Ardnasheen, none of them had encountered a storm so bad.

"You're not thinkin' of goin' out in that?" Ruadhri said, as Rive reached for the door handle.

"We've got to get…back," Suri told him.

"To the big house? Never, in this weather! Besides," he continued, seeing that she meant to protest, "the generator's down. We're running off the pub's private one here, but there'll be no electricity over there."

"We have oil lamps," Ailsa told him.

"It'll be an adventure!" Suri added, with a flashbulb smile.

They hurried out the door before he could protest further. As Sophie reached to shut it behind them, though, Ruadhri caught her eye. His face was serious, even sad, making her wonder if he guessed more than he let on. His pub did have a rune of protection on the door, after all. He couldn't be oblivious to all that went on beneath Ardnasheen's tourist-town veneer.

"Be careful, lass," he said. She could only nod in response.

Outside, the wind had grown so strong that they had to cling together in a group to make any headway. Even so, it was unbearably slow. Snow and frozen rain battered at them, and within moments, Sophie's face and hands were numb. She leaned toward Michael, who had changed to his young-man's form again. "Can't you do anything about this?" she yelled into his ear.

"I'm trying," he called back. "Suri was right – this isn't any ordinary storm. It's not even an ordinary magical storm."

"Here," Suri said, giving him her hand.

He looked at it as if it were a rotten fish, and said, "It's forbidden."

"What's forbidden?" Angus asked.

"One angel taking power from another," Suri answered. Then, to Michael, "I think we can assume the rules have gone

390

out the window. Besides, we all know the Keeper doesn't give a damn."

Michael's mouth tightened at that. He looked at her hand for a moment longer, but in the end, he took it. There was a glow where their palms met, and subtle lines of light flowed up from there, into their arms. Suri seemed to fade a bit, while Michael suddenly seemed larger and brighter than any of them. He spoke some words into the wind, in a language Sophie didn't recognize. It screamed louder for a second – very much like a woman's cry of defeat – and then it eased. There seemed to be a barrier now around their little group, deflecting the worst of the elements. It was transparent, and pliant as air, but it gave everything a strange, wavering quality, like looking through heat waves rising off of hot asphalt.

"Thank you," Rive said to Suri with his formal half-bow.

"Anything for you, sugar," she answered, but she sounded a bit breathless.

Michael looked at her with worried eyes. "Let's hurry. You'll need to hold onto your strength for when we…"

He trailed off, and no one supplied the words that all of them were thinking. But Suri nodded to him, and they set off again along the road, this time moving much faster. They still felt the push of the wind and the spray kicked up from the sea, but it was dampened, tempered, as if it reached them through wadded cotton.

Nevertheless, by the time they reached the old rowboat, it was so dark they could barely see it.

"You aren't seriously thinking of using *that*," Ailsa said.

"I don't know that we have an option," Michael answered. "We can't take one of the boats from the harbor – it's too near the pub, everyone will be watching."

"Will it really hold all of us?" Angus asked, looking as leery as Ailsa sounded.

"Doubtful," a woman's voice answered out of the shadows.

They turned to see who'd spoken. "Morwen!" Sophie cried, as the girl stepped forward. "We thought you weren't coming."

Morwen looked at her in surprise. "I said that I would. It just took me longer than I'd hoped to get the boat."

"What boat?"

Morwen pointed in the direction she'd come from. There was a white fishing boat bobbing on the waves a few feet from shore, half-hidden by the flying sleet.

"Where did you get it?" Suri asked.

"From a fisherman in Mallaig."

"He just *gave* it to you?"

Morwen smiled sweetly. "Of course. I asked him nicely. Now come, we haven't much time."

They waded into the surf, which seemed to pull and drag at them like hands, and then climbed aboard the boat by a ladder hanging over the side.

"So who knows how to drive this thing?" Ailsa asked.

Morwen only smiled, and the boat began to move forward, apparently steering on its own. "How did you – " Ailsa began, but Angus interrupted.

"She's the Morrigan," he said. "Anything's possible." Morwen beamed at him.

Sophie stood near the stern of the boat, gripping the gunwale with one gloved hand. Though Michael and Suri were shielding them from the worst of the waves, the little boat was still battling hard. Worse still, it was moving into darkness, as the poor grey light of the year's shortest day was swallowed by its longest night.

Rather than imagine the rocks and shoals waiting for them within that darkness, Sophie looked down at the water rushing by below. At first it was just dark water laced with the pale foam of the boat's wake. As she watched, though, she began to make out shapes moving within it. They grew brighter and more detailed as the daylight failed, until they looked as solid as her own hand.

It was a parade of monstrous forms and faces, and though she wished she could look away, they held her mesmerized. A mermaid crested the surface, her delicate, pearly face splitting into a grin full of sharks' teeth. A weird, goggle-eyed fish reached up to her with human hands. A black-flippered monster swam in its wake, trailing a white horse's tail, its walrus-tusks a good meter long. A woman with fangs and hair made of coiling snakes flipped and turned in the troughs of the waves. A beautiful blue man surfaced just below Sophie, reached up and grabbed the gunwale, and smiled at her. His eyes were a bright, hypnotic silver, not unlike Dahud's.

"A riddle, my sweet, to pass the time?" he said.

"Pardon?" Sophie answered, and then Rive pulled her back, speaking angry words to the blue man in a language that sounded like the one Michael had used to still the storm. The man screamed and howled, his face blackening as if it were on fire, until he sank without a trace.

"Why did you do that?" Sophie asked, appalled.

"If you'd accepted his challenge, he'd have killed you," Rive told her.

"Oh," Sophie said. "Thanks, then. What was he? And all of those other...things?" She indicated the swarming forms below.

"They're sea demons," he said.

"Are they always here?"

"No," he said, his hand tightening on her shoulder. "They've come tonight to join Dahud's festivities."

"Will we have to fight them?" Sophie asked, thinking of the shark's teeth and walrus tusks.

"I hope not," Rive said. And then, as if he knew how his words had chilled her, he put his other arm around her. He felt hot – too hot for human – but Sophie leaned into him, grateful for the warmth and the feeling of peace his touch always brought her. Then she looked up, and caught Ailsa and Angus staring at them: Ailsa sadly, Angus with a more complicated expression. She wished she could tell them both that it wasn't what they were thinking; that it wouldn't matter even if it was. That nothing she did would matter to them after that night, at least not in any way that they would ever know.

Instead, she gently pulled free of Rive's arms, and looked toward the black mass of the looming headland. "There it is," she said, pointing across the dark water to the patch that was darker still. The boat didn't slow as they approached the rock where Lucas had tied the rowboat on the day he'd taken Sophie there, but carried on, right into the dark cavern.

"Alright?" Michael said to Suri, who was sitting near the bow of the boat, knees drawn up to her chest. Though the line of light no longer ran between them, Michael still looked larger than life, and Suri diminished.

"I will be," she answered, but without her usual bravado.

A light flared behind Sophie, and she whirled, heart pounding. But it was only Morwen, lighting storm lanterns and hanging them at various points around the boat as it continued its steady journey up the channel. Nobody spoke. The silence was churchlike in that weird world of still water and static rock-flows. Thinking about how far underground they were made Sophie feel claustrophobic, so instead she looked into the water. She remembered it as being so clear she could make out every detail of the stones at its bottom. Now it was black, sluggish and opaque, with a faintly iridescent sheen.

"What's wrong with the water?" she asked.

"It'll be another of Dahud's tricks," Michael answered.

As Sophie watched, a dark tentacle broke the surface of the channel, turning this way and that, as if surveying the scene, before slipping silently back below the water.

"And it's working," Ailsa said in an unsteady voice, backing away from the gunwale.

"Try not to be afraid," Rive told her. "She wants us frightened, but unharmed."

"Why would you say that," Angus asked, "when she's been doing her damnedest to keep us away?"

Rive shrugged. "It's all part of the game." No one contradicted him.

The channel began to narrow, the twisting forms of stalactites and stalagmites closing around them like the teeth of a massive jaw. Sophie, Ailsa and Angus instinctively drew together, away from the menacing forms, but the others looked unperturbed. Michael and Rive stood still as sentinels at the bow and stern of the boat. Suri was looking a little better: she stood peering contemplatively into the dark water. Morwen sat with her eyes closed, rocking gently to the rhythm of the boat until, abruptly, it stopped. Her green eyes opened, and she said, "From here, we walk."

The boat slid up to the rocky path that followed the channel, and they all stepped out. "Stay," Morwen said, pointing a stern finger at the boat, as if it were a dog. And the boat stayed, resting up against the side of the channel where it had let them off. Sophie looked for a rope to tie it off with, until Morwen said, "There's no need. It will do as it's told."

Of course it will, Sophie thought dazedly, and turned to follow the others, already making their way up the path by the light of Morwen's lanterns. She tried not to think about the last time she'd made this trip: how happy she'd been then, and how simple everything had seemed. And yet, at the same time, she couldn't quite feel surprise at how much had changed. It was as if a deep-buried part of her had always known where a relationship with Lucas would lead; as if it had remembered their star-crossed past, even in her innocent elation.

Stay in the present. Their shadows danced along the glistening walls. The oily liquid in the channel threw back the lanterns' light, as if it were too thick to penetrate. Sophie tried not to consider the fact that they were about to enter that water. She tried not to worry that it wouldn't let them pass, or worse, it would admit them only for them to lose their way, and flail forever in its viscous darkness. But as they neared the end of the path, the water began to clear. By the time they reached the beach where seals had once come to bear their pups, Sophie could make out stones on the pool's bottom again.

Ailsa sneezed. "What happens now?"

"Now," Morwen answered, "you call the *Each Uisge*."

"How?" Sophie asked, realizing for the first time that she had no idea how this was to be done.

"Just as you call any of the *sìth*. You speak its true name."

"But we don't know even know their fake names," Ailsa said.

"Actually," Suri said, "I do. Well, I know one…its real name, I mean." She gave Sophie a sidelong glance, which Sophie didn't like at all.

"How did you get a faery to tell you its name?" Michael asked, sounding as dubious as Sophie felt.

Suri shrugged. "It lost a drinking game."

Michael looked horrified, while Rive gave her a half-smile. "I'd have thought a faery would know better than to get into a drinking match with an angel."

"Well, she was kind of upset, on account of losing her boyfriend."

"Oh, no," Sophie said, finally understanding the look Suri had given her. "We can't call *that* water horse!"

Suri shrugged again. "It's the only one whose name I know. Once we have command of her, it won't matter what she thinks of us. Plus, we can make her call up others."

"Let me do it," Angus said. "Freyja gave me the girdle, after all." He reached into his coat pocket and pulled out the silvery coil.

"No," Sophie answered, reaching for it. "I can't let you

do that. This is my fight; I'll take the risks." Angus looked at her for a moment, clearly wanting to argue. "Angus – please."

Sighing, he relinquished the girdle to Sophie. "Thank you," she said. Then, looking at Suri: "But I have no idea what to do with it."

"As soon as the water horse appears, get the girdle around her neck. Once the ends connect, you've caught her."

"That's all, is it?" Sophie asked grimly, remembering how the *Each Uisge* on the mountain had fought and thrashed against Lucas's iron chain.

"It'll be fine," Suri said, squeezing her hand. "I promise." She stepped to the edge of the water and spoke in her mountain-top voice: "Swamplily Tickseed, show yourself!"

"Swamplily Tickseed?" Sophie repeated incredulously.

"Shush!" Suri hissed. "If you offend her, it'll be much harder."

The group stood in silence, watching the water for any sign of the faery, but its surface remained unbroken. After a few minutes, Angus asked, "When is something meant to happen?"

"Five minutes ago," Suri said, her irritation clear. "Okay, does anyone have any meat?"

"Of course," Sophie answered. "I regularly go round with a pound of mince in my handbag."

"This is no time for sarcasm," Suri told her. Then she turned to Michael, who was standing by Rive, speaking to him quietly. "Hey, guys, do you think you can help us out here?"

Michael looked up at Suri, blinked at her for a moment as if trying to recall what she'd asked, and then said, "Meat? Why?"

"An *Each Uisge* can't resist raw meat, especially if it's bloody."

"Right. Bloody meat." He picked up a large-ish stone and gave it a hard look. A moment later, he was holding a large-ish steak, dripping blood onto the sand at his feet. "Now what?" he asked.

"I'll call her again. Better put it down, unless you want her to bite your hands off." Michael put the steak down and stepped away from it. Suri called the faery's name again, adding, "We've brought you a gift."

Something broke the pool's surface and began moving toward them. At first Sophie could only make out two flaring nostrils, two eyes of a fiery red peering from behind them. But as the creature came closer and gained solid ground, it took on the shape of a black horse. It looked far bigger to Sophie than the one she and Lucas had killed on the mountain; then again, she hadn't had a chance to get a good look at it once it had changed from its lost-pony disguise.

The black horse shook herself, spraying water that smelled like decaying pond vegetation. Then it caught sight of Sophie and let out a terrible sound, somewhere between a whinny and a roar. "Michael!" Suri shouted.

Recovering himself, Michael kicked the steak toward the

horse. It paused for a moment, its nostrils flaring, and then it bared its wolf-like teeth and tore into the meat.

"Sophie!" Suri cried, and with shaking hands, Sophie uncoiled Freyja's girdle and tossed it over the horse's neck. As soon as it felt the touch of the metal, the water horse gave another furious roar, looking up at Sophie with blood dripping from its mouth. Before fear could overwhelm her, she reached for the ends of the girdle and twisted them together. With another cry of rage, the horse lunged for her neck. But it seemed to hit some invisible barrier. Sophie held onto the girdle with both hands, and met the monster's burning eye as it stilled, peering down at her.

"Very well, human," it said in a weird, watery voice. "You have caught me. Now what will you do with me?"

"I want you to take me to Ker-Ys," Sophie said, still holding the creature's fiery eye.

The horse gave her what looked very like a malevolent smile. "You'd trust me to take you there, after you killed my beloved?"

"As I understand it, you don't have a choice, now I've caught you."

"True, you've caught me. But if you would ride me, then first you must bridle me."

"Fine." Still watching the water horse carefully, Sophie took the ends of the silver girdle, and looped them into a makeshift bridle and reins. She was wondering why it had succumbed so easily, when it answered her thought aloud.

"Come. Dahud awaits you."

This time, there was no doubt that its bared teeth were a menacing grin. Shrugging off a cold runnel of fear, Sophie looked it in the eye and said, "Not yet. First you'll call two more horses – one for each of my friends." She indicated Ailsa and Angus.

"And why would I grant the wish of a murderess?"

"Because I have your name, Swamplily Tickseed, and we both know that means you have no choice."

The water horse narrowed its eyes and blew, spraying Sophie with a mist of murky water. It was all she could do not to retch, but she held her ground, and after a moment, the creature lowered its head a fraction. "Very well, I will call them. But they, too must be caught and bridled, if your mortal friends would ride them."

Sophie looked in despair at the short length of silver rope left in her hand. The water horse laughed coldly. But Rive's voice cut across it, clean and unyielding as steel: "Remember who you are, Sophia."

Sophie knew then what he meant for her to do, but she doubted that she was capable of it. "The whole me making things from nothing," she said. "I think that only works when a human is in danger."

402

"That's irrelevant," said Rive. "You don't need to make something. You only need to modify what you already have."

Sophie looked back at the silver rope, fastidiously avoiding the water horse's evil smile. She thought about making it longer. She tried to remember what it had felt like to make Carnwennan, but that night had become a blur. Besides, as Rive had said, that had been making something out of nothing. This was only changing the nature of something already made.

She'd seen Lucas do it effortlessly, when he turned a cobweb into the silver bracelet she still wore. Surely if a fallen angel could do it, she could too. She closed her eyes and ran her hand along the length of rope, imagining it stretching, playing out like yarn from a spindle. And then she could feel it happening, the miraculous weight of it, the gentle rasp as new coils joined the others at her feet. It was hypnotic, and she became lost in it until she heard someone calling her name.

Sophie opened her eyes. Suri was standing with her hand on Sophie's shoulder, shaking her gently. "Sophie – I think you've got enough."

Sophie looked down. There was a pile of silver rope at her feet, almost knee high. "Um…yeah." She broke the connection with the horse's bridle, and held the reins toward Suri. "Can you hold this while we catch the others?"

Suri took the bridle, looking warily at the creature. It glared back, no longer grinning. But Sophie's fear had gone.

"Swamplily Tickseed," she said, "please call up two more of your kind."

The water horse glared her for a moment, and then, reaching its neck over the water, it uttered another bone-chilling cry. This time it only took a second for the two *sìth* to appear, swimming quickly toward their captured mate. Sophie barely had time to register what they looked like – one iron-grey, the other a peaty brown – before she was looping the girdle around their necks. They danced and pulled, but they could not break away. Angus came and took one end of the rope, and Sophie broke it in the middle. They tied them into simple bridles and reins, as she had the first one.

"Ready?" she said, handing the grey horse's bridle to Ailsa.

Ailsa looked at the fierce, dripping creature, and sneezed. "Not especially," she said unhappily.

"It'll be fine," Sophie assured her, wondering if any of them actually believed that. But when she turned back to the others, Rive, Morwen and the angels had already turned to seals. They kept their own eyes, as Morwen had in Sophie's first dream of Ker-Ys, and so she could tell them apart. Morwen took to the water first, her awkward land-bound shuffle becoming a fluid grace as she swam to the center of the pool. The other seals followed her.

Sophie turned back to her horse, whose reins Angus was holding now along with those of his own. Its slick back looked impossibly high, and she wondered suddenly how she was meant to mount, with nothing to stand on. There was no way that she would stoop to asking the horse what to do.

With another chilly laugh, the horse began pulling her toward the water. At first she resisted, thinking it meant to try to escape, but then it stopped and looked back at her with a cold, supercilious smile. "You may try to mount from there," it said, "but you'll find my way far easier." It tugged the rein, pulling her toward the water. Then, Sophie understood. She followed the horse out into the pool until her feet no longer reached the sandy bottom. Then she slipped easily onto its back.

"Did I mention that I hate horses?"Ailsa said, as she pulled herself, shivering, onto the grey one. "Plus, I'll probably get pneumonia."

"If that's the worst that happens, we'll be lucky," Angus said from the back of his own horse.

Though she wanted to, Sophie couldn't muster words of encouragement. She couldn't muster any words at all. She was shivering, but not from cold; in fact, she hardly felt the icy water. She could think of nothing now but the nightmare of a skeleton chained to an empty throne, and the desperate hope that it hadn't been prophecy.

Ailsa and Angus and the seals were looking at her. It took a moment for understanding to penetrate: this was her mission. They were waiting for her orders.

"Swamplily Tickweed," she said as clearly and steadily as she could, "take us to Dahud's palace."

"With pleasure," the horse answered, and with a huge leap, it dove into the shadowy depths of the pool. The last thing Sophie heard, before the water closed over her head, was a peal of frigid, watery laughter.

CHAPTER 29

For a few moments she saw only darkness, felt only the rush of tremendous speed and the panicked sense that she needed to draw breath, and couldn't. Her only conscious thought was that she had to hold onto the reins at any cost.

Then a faint light trickled into the darkness, and she sensed something close to her – a sleek black shape, slipping along beside her. It didn't speak – it *couldn't* speak – but all the same she heard it say to her, *Breathe.* It needn't have bothered. She couldn't resist the burning pressure in her chest any longer. She opened her mouth, felt it fill with water, waited to lose consciousness – and then the pain in her chest eased, as she took the water deep into her lungs.

After a few more faltering breaths, she could pull the water in an out of her almost as thoughtlessly as she breathed air. Slowly, she calmed, and it was then that she saw the sky-blue eyes of the seal swimming beside her, the faint blue glow that shone like a halo around him. And though he didn't touch her, she felt the deep peace that Rive always seemed to be able to impart to her. Peace, and an intense gratitude.

You're welcome, he whispered into her mind, and then he turned in a graceful circle around her and fell back with the other shape-shifters.

Yet his leaving didn't abandon her to darkness. Just as in the dream when she, too had taken a seal's form, she could make out a greenish glow coming from below. She could see the dark shapes of Ailsa and Angus on either side of her, their horses bounding through the water like thoroughbreds on a racing green, but faster than she'd ever seen a mortal horse run. Before she knew it, the city was rushing up to meet them, and the seals had stopped, hovering around the square of light that marked the door to Dahud's realm.

It was only then that she remembered the silver bough. But just as she looked despairingly at Suri, wondering where she could possibly have hidden it in her seal form, Ailsa reached into her jacket and pulled it out. It blazed now with silver light, the white dots of the pearls too bright to look at. Ailsa cast it toward the door. It spun through the dark water, connecting with the bright square in a brilliant flash that slowly faded, until it was the clear, watery green of the sky above Ker-Ys.

The seals were the first to drop through the door. Sophie guided her horse toward it, and once Angus and Ailsa were safely through, she followed. Just as in her dream, the element around them changed as soon as they were through. There was no longer the resistance of water, only the sense of falling, slowly, toward a field of swaying aqua grass. And then the black horse landed with a jolt, and Sophie toppled gracelessly to the ground, which was harder than it had appeared.

Ailsa and Angus managed to stay on their horses as they landed, but both looked relieved to slide off of their backs. Ailsa was about to let go of the silver rein when Suri, back in human form, pushed herself out of the meadow grass and said, "Wait."

They waited, holding the reins of their horses as Suri approached the black one. "Swamplily Tickseed, you and your companions will wait here for us until we return."

The black horse glowered. "You are sentencing us to an eternity, then."

"Stay here until I tell you otherwise!" Suri snapped.

The black horse made a gesture very like a shrug, but it said, "Very well."

"Can I let go now?" Ailsa asked.

"Yes," Suri said, still glaring at the horses.

Ailsa dropped the reins as if they burned her, and stepped away from the grey horse, which watched her with clear contempt. "Now I remember why I never wanted riding lessons," she said, shuddering.

"It's over for now, anyway," Angus said, giving her a squeeze around the shoulders.

"What time is it?" Sophie asked anxiously. She had no idea how long the journey to Ker-Ys had taken.

"Time," Michael said grimly.

"What? We'll be too late!"

"Not if we hurry," Rive said, exchanging a sober look with Michael, which Sophie didn't like at all.

"Come," said Morwen, "I know a short-cut."

The idea of Ker-Ys having short cuts, let alone anyone knowing them, was somehow more bizarre to Sophie than anything that had yet happened that day. Nevertheless, she fell into step beside Morwen, who was striding purposefully across the field. Sophie didn't see how she could possibly navigate the featureless landscape. Nevertheless, only a few minutes had passed before a line of swaying cobalt-blue trees appeared on the horizon, and only a few more before they were among them.

Morwen plunged on into the forest, apparently without a second thought, and though there had been no sign of one before they entered, now there was a clear path running between the trees. It was carpeted in something like pine needles, though they were pale blue, and fell like snow flurries from the trees above. In a different situation, Sophie would have thought them beautiful. Now all she could think was that they would arrive too late.

But again, Morwen moved them through the wood so quickly that it seemed they'd barely entered when the trees started thinning again. Sophie wondered how she was doing it: whether it was time or matter that the goddess nipped and tucked to shorten the distances, or only her own, limited human perception of them. Considering it made her head spin – as did looking too hard into the depths of the woods, which seemed to shift and swim, like the borders of Suri's cemetery. But it was better than thinking about Lucas's skeleton.

A few minutes later, they were leaving the trees behind for a street paved in colored sea-glass, which ran uphill between two rows of houses with steeply-pitched roofs. Sophie looked into the houses' windows as they passed them, but they were dark and lifeless in a way that felt like long abandonment, rather than temporary absence. At first she thought this was just because they were on the outskirts of the city, but as they continued toward its heart, and the buildings grew bigger and grander, the sense of abandonment didn't change. The silence felt like a held breath; the stillness seemed to hide horror in its margins.

At last, Sophie couldn't stand it any longer. "Where *is* everyone?" she asked. She'd meant to say it loudly, defiantly, but it came out as a muted whisper.

"No doubt they've gathered for the paying of the teind," Morwen said. "It's a feast-day, here."

"Do they know that we're coming?"

Morwen shrugged. "They will soon enough."

411

"How much longer till we're there?" Ailsa asked apprehensively.

Morwen smiled joylessly. "We're there."

She turned a corner, and they emerged into the courtyard of Dahud's palace. It was as silent as the rest of the city, but the stillness was somehow sentient. It felt to Sophie as if every dark orifice of the building was full of watching eyes. She looked around at her friends. They, too stood looking up at the palace unhappily. Only Rive's face remained inscrutable.

Because if this goes well, he gets what he wants. Sophie knew that it wasn't a charitable thought, but she wasn't feeling particularly charitable. She'd focused so long on saving Lucas, she'd managed not to think about the flip side of success. Now, so close to her goal, she was overwhelmed by the thought of what success would mean. She'd barely survived losing Lucas the first time. How would she face it again?

"I can't."

Sophie was only aware that she'd spoken aloud when Ailsa said, "Can't what?"

"I can't...I can't believe we're here," Sophie recovered hastily. Now everyone was looking at her, their eyes worried. She couldn't meet them. "Come on," she said, turning away, "let's go." She started up the nearest staircase without looking to see whether anyone followed. But she sensed them behind her as she ducked beneath an ornate archway, and into a shadowed, cloister-like corridor.

As her eyes adjusted to the dimness, she stopped short. What she had thought was just another shadow had detached itself from the wall, and lurched into the weak light coming from the archway. For a moment everyone froze. Then Ailsa let out a strangled shriek and grabbed Sophie's and Angus' hands, as the others drew protectively around them.

Aproaching them was the most bizarrely disfigured creature Sophie had ever seen. It was taller than any of them by at least a foot, with a man's torso and powerfully muscled arms, and spindly legs clothed in tattered trousers. Its face was vaguely human, but its yellowed teeth protruded from behind its lower lip up and over the top one, and where its eyes should have been there was a single, lidded orifice. The lid itself was shut, and painted with strange symbols. To Sophie's horror, it turned its blind eye on her, and bowed low.

"Greetings, Sophia," it said, in a voice like breaking stone.

"Ah…likewise," she answered after a moment's hesitation. "Have we met?"

"I am Balor, your guide. Come with me." Without waiting to see if she followed, it turned and hobbled off down the corridor. hopped off down the corridor on its single leg.

"There is *no way* I'm following that thing!" Ailsa hissed.

"That thing," Rive told her, "is the Celtic God of Death. So you might want to do what he says."

"What happens if we don't?"

"He opens his eye."

413

"And then?"

"You really don't want to know."

"COME!" Balor roared then, realizing that none of them had yet moved to follow him. Half-dragging a whimpering Ailsa, they went.

Considering his blindness, Balor moved remarkably quickly through the maze-like corridors of Dahud's palace. They passed through hallways and up and down flights of stairs, some of which Sophie thought she remembered from Morag's vision, but they were moving too quickly to be sure.

At last, the murky light of the corridors gave way to a brighter, blue-green one, but it was cold and comfortless as an iceberg. Sophie's heart beat faster, her head spun, and she fought down a wave of nausea. *Please be alive...please be alive...* Her head was full of the single mantra, though she was barely conscious of it, just as she was unconscious of clenching her hands together so tightly that they'd turned white.

Balor stopped a few yards before an arched doorway. Sophie could hear the sound of many voices, and a strange, plangent music beyond it. "You," he said, turning his blind face toward her friends, "stay here. You," he nodded to Sophie, "come with me."

"I don't think so," Michael said, beginning to shimmer with flame-colored light.

"Do you question me?" Balor rumbled menacingly.

Morwen stepped in front of them then, her eyes blazing like

sun through church glass. And then, in a blink, she was Morag, leaning on her walking stick, whose carved spirals glowed with deep blue light. "Move aside, Balor!" she commanded.

"This is *my* realm, Morrigan!" he roared back.

Morag shook her head and said, "It's Dahud's realm, and a halfling cannot deny entry to the Morrigan, or to those under her protection."

"Indeed, we can't," came a crystalline voice from within the hall, silencing all of the others. "Please, Morrigan, enter with your companions. You are welcome in our court. Balor! Stand down."

Grimly, Balor stepped aside. He bowed again to Sophie and her companions, indicating for them to move past him, though it was clear he didn't want to. Sophie didn't like the thought of his deadly eye at their backs, but Dahud had left them no choice other than to pass him and enter the room. Taking a breath which she hoped wouldn't be her last, she stepped through the door.

This time, the hall was crowded. There were many of the black-eyed sea faeries who made up Dahud's court, but there were also creatures like the ones Sophie had seen from the boat, and others both more beautiful and more terrifying. They sat at long banquet tables which had been set out in rows on either side of the velvet runner that stretched up the middle of the room. The tables were loaded with bowls and dishes, though much of what they contained didn't resemble anything Sophie would have called food. A troll-like creature with tusks in place of his lower canine teeth shovelled what looked like lengths of blue hair into his enormous mouth. A mermaid gnawed daintily on what might have been a human foot, if it hadn't been a deep, wet purple. When Sophie saw another creature delving into a bowl of what looked like eyeballs, she turned her gaze firmly ahead, toward the sight she'd been dreading.

It wasn't what she'd feared, but it wasn't much better. Dahud sat placidly on her throne, leaning her head on two fingers as she watched Sophie's band approach. Lucas sat at her feet as he'd done in the vision, but otherwise he was almost unrecognizable. He was so thin, his ribcage was like a xylophone. His hair reached below his shoulders now, matted with knots, as if someone had deliberately tangled it. The velvet trousers were little more than shreds, and his eyes were vacant above his hollow cheeks.

Though it stung Sophie to see him in such wretched condition, she had the strong sense that something else was wrong with the scene – something more than Lucas's suffering. Looking from Lucas to Dahud, who glowed with supernatural health, she realized what it was: Lucas didn't look like an offering. He didn't look like he'd survive the next hour.

Before Sophie could consider what this might mean, Dahud drew herself upright, placed both long hands on the arms of her chair and said, "Welcome, Sophia." Her silver eyes flickered with disdain over the others, and she added, "And to your companions. State your purpose."

"You know very well what my purpose is," Sophie answered sharply.

"Say it for the benefit of my court."

"Fine. I'm here to win Lucas back from you."

"Mmm," Dahud said, fixing Sophie with her languid, unblinking gaze. "That word, 'win'…it rather implies a fight."

"I'd happily take him without one," Sophie answered.

"No doubt; but where's the fun in that? You've challenged us to a fight, so a fight we shall have."

"But I didn't – " Sophie began.

"Silence!" Dahud cried. "This is *our* kingdom, and *our* word is law. You have challenged us to a duel, and since the challenge was yours, it is our right to choose the weapon."

A brace of courtiers, both *sìth* and demon, emerged from the shadows with an array of hideous-looking weapons. Sophie swallowed hard, and felt for Carnwennan, still stuck in her belt-loop. But Dahud didn't choose any of the offered arsenal, only waved them away impatiently.

"Sophia has little experience of warrior's weapons," she said as the courtiers bowed their way back into the shadows. "I'd kill her far too quickly. No…I'm thinking of a different type of duel altogether." Once again, she was studying Sophie with unblinking eyes, and an intensity Sophie didn't like at all.

"Your kind, Sophia, have a great talent for music, have they not?"

Suddenly apprehensive, Sophie answered, "It's the angels who are gifted in music."

Dahud waved a hand dismissively. "I've read his memories. I know that Lucifer shared his gift with you, and it's one your human form has kept. You play the *clarsach*."

"I..." Sophie began, glancing again toward her friends. They looked on with varying degrees of anxiety, but none of them offered help. She knew that they couldn't, but it was still discouraging. "Yes," she said, trying to sound more confident than she felt, "I do."

"A lovely instrument," Dahud mused. "One of the oldest of our tradition. We learned to play as a human girl...as all noblewomen did, in those times. And there was no waffling about with airs and dances. We played the *Ceòl Mór*."

"Pardon?"

"Your knight will translate."

Angus said, "It's Gaelic for 'great music.'"

Dahud smiled at him. "Very good. But it's also called *pibroch*. That's a word we'll wager you know."

Sophie knew. It was an ancient type of music, a series of variations on a theme with a drone running under it, much like the drone of the bagpipes that had overtaken the genre in more modern times. But *Pibroch* had first been played on the harp, so long ago that no record of those original versions survived.

Nevertheless, a few modern harp players had tried to recreate it from the pipe notation. Sophie had been working her own arrangement of a *pibroch* when she first came to Ardnasheen. She remembered playing it in the valley behind Madainneag, on a warm sunny day that seemed to belong to another lifetime. She couldn't even remember now how the music sounded. But she couldn't say so to Dahud.

"I know it," she answered, her voice thin but hard.

"Perfect," Dahud said with a smile, and then she cried, "Magnus!"

Another courtier stepped forward, a man with pearly skin, long, lapis-colored hair and his people's ubiquitous black eyes. He carried a small harp in each hand. They were nothing like the harps Sophie had learned on. In fact, they most closely resembled the ancient lap-harps she'd seen in the national museum in Edinburgh: wide, with thick sound-boxes and gracefully arched necks and pillars. Unlike those museum pieces, though, these were brightly painted with twining animals and symbols, and strung with gold wire. Magnus bowed deeply to Dahud and handed one of the harps to her. The other he put into Sophie's cold hands, the faint turn to his mouth suggesting contempt.

"So," Dahud concluded, "we are equally armed. And because you are my guest, I will allow you to choose the theme."

Sophie looked dismally at the harp in her hands. Not only

had she not practised in months, she had never played a wire-strung harp, except in that one dream of Heaven. From that, she remembered Lucas telling her that the strings were meant to be plucked with the fingernails and damped with the pads. That was the most she knew. She looked down at her hands: nails cut short, fingertips rough with calluses from years of playing.

"But – " she began, wondering how she could talk Dahud out of this. When she saw the triumph dawning on the witch's face, however, her words deserted her. She drew a breath, and said, "It's not a fair duel unless the judge is impartial."

Dahud gave her a feral smile. "Indeed. That is why the judge will be the prize."

"What do you mean?" Sophie asked, her eyes darting in confusion to Lucas's wasted face.

"We play for Lucifer's life. Let him decide who earns it."

Sophie opened her mouth to ask how this was possible, when he was clearly beyond reason – perhaps even beyond hearing. Seeing Dahud's leer, though, she swallowed her protests and said, "I'll need a seat."

The courtier, Magnus, was at her elbow in an instant, setting down a three-legged stool. Numbly, Sophie lowered herself onto it. As she settled herself, though, Sophie heard Rive's voice saying, *You can do this. You've done it before.* She was poised to ask him how he knew that, when she realized that his lips had never moved. He gave her a tiny smile.

"Theletos," Dahud said sharply, "and the rest of Sophia's

420

entourage, please sit." She pointed a finger – equipped with a long, strong, silvery nail, Sophie noticed – toward the nearest of the banquet tables. There were seven empty places which Sophie would have sworn hadn't been there a moment before. They were set with plates and glasses and cutlery, and an array of delicacies. As her friends filed toward it, however, Sophie heard Suri whisper to Angus and Ailsa, "Don't eat or drink *anything!*"

"Well, Sophia?" Dahud fixed Sophie with her eerie eyes. It seemed the whole hall watched her, waiting to see whether she would rise to the challenge, or crumble. Even Lucas's empty, wandering gaze paused on her for a moment.

Sophie lifted the harp, set it between her knees and drew the soundbox back to balance on her shoulder. She looked down at her short fingernails, felt Carnwennan cold against her back. *If I can kill a demon and ride a water horse, I can do this,* she told herself. *And if I can grow Freyja's girdle, I can damn well grow my own fingernails.* She shut her eyes, pictured them growing long and strong as Dahud's. When she opened them and saw that she had succeeded, she couldn't stifle a small smile.

But Dahud looked at her coldly, her own smile gone. "Play," she said, "before we lose our patience!"

Slowly, deliberately, and keeping her eyes on Dahud, Sophie played a scale to test the instrument's tuning, and to get a feel of its action. It was very different from the harps she was used to, but the deep resonance of the metal strings lit those buried memories of Heaven, of Lucas teaching her to play a harp like this. She caught herself thinking that if she won, he could teach her again; then she smiled bitterly, and damped the strings.

It was time to choose her theme. The melody of the *pibroch* she'd been arranging had come back to her, but she'd struggled too hard to make it her own to be willing to give it away to the sea witch. She looked at Lucas, hoping for inspiration, but his eyes wandered on restlessly, flickering over her as if she were no more than a shadow.

A deep sadness welled in her, far beyond the grief she'd felt when she thought that he'd died. All at once she hated Dahud for taking the little time she and Lucas might have had together. She knew that it was irrational – that if it wasn't for Dahud, there wouldn't be a Lucas here to save. It made no difference. She hated her – for taking him, for kissing him, for hurting him – and she wanted to hurt her back.

Sophie looked Dahud in the eye as she plucked out the melody, and felt a petty satisfaction when she saw the witch recognize it, and recoil. But the harp rang out sweet and true across the hall, which had fallen deathly silent. *Good,* Sophie thought fiercely. *They know it, too.* The final note of the melody died on the silence. Once again, Lucas was looking at her, but it was without curiosity, or even any particular interest. *Don't think about it,* she told herself, waiting for Dahud's response.

"*Oran na Maighdinn-Mhara,*" the witch said at last. *The*

Mermaid's Song. That was all she said before she took up her own harp and played the melody back to Sophie, with a few grace notes and embellishments. But Sophie could feel the cold fury radiating from her, and it filled her with bitter triumph.

She answered Dahud's challenge with another variation full of trills and triads. And so they played on, the audience watching and listening greedily for one of them to make a mistake, to show the strain, to balk at a variation that was just too difficult to better. But the music had taken Sophie now: she was its vessel. She understood by some deep intuition – or perhaps an ancient memory – exactly how to pull the sounds she wanted from the instrument in her arms. She could tell by the look on Dahud's face, by the concentration with which she now met each new challenge, that the witch hadn't expected her to keep pace. That perhaps she was even struggling.

Yet no matter how brilliant the music was, Lucas didn't seem to hear it. As Dahud played a variation so elaborate it seemed barely related to the original, simple theme, Sophie spared a look at her friends. Ailsa tried to smile. Angus watched with a set face. Rive looked on with preternatural stillness, his eyes hard and gem-like, almost as remote as Lucas's, while Michael's eyes were burning with buried fire. Morag leaned heavily on her stick as she swayed to the music.

But Suri's black eyes cut straight across the distance between them, clearly trying to tell her something. Sophie shook her head slightly. Suri looked away, raised a hand and ran it down her throat. Her throat…her neck…*oh!* As soon as Sophie remembered it, Freyja's jewel, Brisingamen, flared with heat, burning against her breast like a coal. *Jewel of fire, whose powers cannot be resisted…* Could it really be so simple?

Sophie looked at Dahud, still intent on the music she was playing. With as little movement as she could manage, Sophie slipped the pendant up and out of her shirt, so that it lay now in the open. She chanced another glance at Suri. Her faint smile told her she'd guessed correctly.

But that wasn't all. Sophie had the sudden, strong sense that she was being watched. She looked up at Dahud: the sea witch was still intent on her own flying fingers. But Lucas was sitting up straight now, leaning slightly away from Dahud, toward Sophie. He was looking at her, studying her, and though there was not yet any recognition in the gaze, there was interest.

Dahud finished her variation and looked up at Sophie with a grim smile. She hadn't yet noticed the change in Lucas, but as Sophie began to play, and Lucas leaned still nearer to her, she saw realization dawn in Dahud's narrowed eyes. Sophie barely even thought about her fingers running over the strings, letting whatever buried knowledge was guiding them take over completely. She kept her eyes on Lucas, repeating a silent prayer: *Please remember…please remember…*

Lucas's expression changed again – changed to dismay. Like a man waking after a long, drugged slumber, he looked up and around, first with bafflement, and then, when he saw

Dahud, and the chain running from his chest, with horror. He tugged at it, but it stayed in place. He stood up, stumbled down the steps of the dais toward Sophie. She put the harp aside, caught him as he collapsed to his knees, gripping her arms, his face anguished.

"Sophie, what's happened? What is this place? We were fighting...where is Azazel?"

Sophie didn't realize that she was weeping until she tried to answer him, and her voice hitched on a sob. She struggled to pull herself together, then she said, "Gone. It's over now." She kissed his hands, clasped in hers, and only then did she realize that the room had erupted into furor. Her friends surrounded her and Lucas, as Dahud looked down at them from her throne. Though it was a cold look, it was oddly lacking in anger. *Why?* Sophie had begun to wonder, when Suri interrupted:

"Lucifer's chosen! Now free him!"

"She used sorcery," Dahud answered, her eyes on Brisingaman, which glowed like an ember on Sophie's breast.

"You never said she couldn't," Rive said in a steely voice. "By your rules, she won. Free the angel."

A languorous smile worked its way across Dahud's face, which Sophie found infinitely more frightening than any threat she could have made. "Very well," she said, and jerked the gold chain. Lucas cried out, clutching at his chest where the chain had entered it, and where a wound now gaped, raw and red. He collapsed into Sophie's arms. She looked up at Dahud in horror and fury.

"Oh, don't look like that," the witch said. "He's healing already."

It was true – the wound was already closing. Shakily, Lucas stood, still clinging to Sophie for support. She laced her arms around him, wondering how she would ever bear to let go. "Sophie," he said, gazing down at her with the eyes she remembered – warm, and full of love. "I've been so far away...I thought I'd lost you..."

"Never," she said, trying to keep her voice from breaking. But when he leaned down to kiss her, she couldn't stop the tears. She hadn't let herself remember what it was like to feel his arms around her; to feel his lips on hers. After so many cold, sad weeks, it was like catching fire. Warmth flooded her, sweeping everything else away.

"Um, guys," Suri said, "I hate to break up the reunion, but it's almost midnight."

Sophie and Lucas broke apart, but kept hold of each other as they looked around. Dahud's hall was chaos, the faeries and demons arguing, some physically fighting. Dahud herself, though, remained calm. She looked down at Sophie and Lucas with a smile that had grown peculiarly indulgent.

"Leaving already?" she asked.

"Our business with you is finished," Sophie said, clutching

Lucas's hand firmly, and turning to look for a path through the crowd.

"Oh, no," Dahud answered. "It's only just begun."

"By your rules," Sophie said, looking distractedly back at her, "I won the duel."

Dahud smiled. "A conclusion we wouldn't dare to dispute. And as you see, we have set the angel free."

"Then tell your people to let us go," Sophie answered.

"*Lucifer* is free to go," Dahud answered, "as are your other companions. But we're afraid, Sophia, that the terms of our duel made no provision for you." And her face split into a predator's grin.

CHAPTER 30

"Don't test us, witch," Rive said, coming to stand at Sophie's side as the others pulled in around them. "You have no hold over her."

"We have precisely the hold on her we sought all along," Dahud answered. "We couldn't have wished you to play the game more perfectly. Or should we say, lose it?"

"What are you talking about?" Angus asked.

Dahud looked at him, as if at a particularly tiresome child. "We are talking about the teind."

"But you set Lucas free!" Sophie cried.

Dahud's eyes were a parody of sympathy. "Did you truly believe that the daevas would accept a ruined angel for a teind? An aeon, on the other hand – still pure, and so very pretty – now *that's* something they don't come across every day. They have promised to reward us richly for such a prize."

"What is this all about?" Lucas asked, turning stricken

eyes on Sophie. And Dahud's nonchalance toward the duel finally made sense.

"We thought you were supposed to be the teind," Sophie said to him miserably. "The tax Dahud pays to the daevas, to keep her power. But it looks like it wasn't you she was after at all."

Suri had begun to shimmer with silver light, and Michael with red-gold. Rive was glowing too, the same blue light Sophie had shed herself the few times she had been provoked to it. But it was different from the way the angels glowed. While they kept their forms, Rive seemed to be dissolving into his own brilliance.

"You cannot have Sophia," he said, with a steely resonance that shuddered into Sophie's core. "She made a vow to return to the Garden with me after Lucifer was freed, and it cannot be broken."

"What?" Lucas whispered, his expression dangerously fragile. "Sophie, is this true?"

Sophie couldn't answer; she could only nod, as tears streamed down her cheeks. Slowly, Lucas let go of her, his eyes filling with pain, and worse – the dawning realization of betrayal. "The witch called him Theletos," he said. Once again, Sophie nodded. "Theletos is your consort. You're going *back* to him?"

"No!" Sophie cried fiercely, clutching his hands like a drowning girl. "I love *you*, Lucas! I'll only ever love you."

429

"But…this vow…"

She bowed her head, unable to look at the raw pain in his eyes. "I had no choice. If I don't go with Rive – with Theletos – it will mean the end of this world."

Once again, the hall had fallen deathly silent, as Dahud's court waited eagerly to see which new turn this drama would take. Angus spoke into it, his voice tremulous: "How long have you been keeping this from us?"

Sophie looked at him. It took a moment for his question to penetrate. Then she faltered, "Not long…a few days…"

"A few *days?*"

She looked up at him with tear-blurred vision. "I don't have a choice!"

"I offered you a choice," he said, with quiet regret and infinite hurt. "I gave you back your soul."

"Has the entire world gone insane?" Ailsa cried, putting her hands to her head.

"Not quite yet," Rive answered grimly.

"As entertaining as this little drama is," Dahud said wearily, "the daevas will be here any moment. Sophia, you must be ready to meet them."

"No!" Michael thundered. "The Keeper has claimed her!"

Dahud shrugged. "Then the Keeper should have taken her when it could. In our realm, on this hour of this night, no such claim is valid."

"You can't cross the Keeper," Suri said, but without conviction.

Now the Morrigan, who had remained silent through this exchange, stepped forward in her old-woman's form and faced Sophie's friends. She looked sadly at each of them in turn, before settling on Sophie. "I'm afraid that she can."

"It won't be midnight for long," Sophie answered.

"No," said the Morrigan sadly. "But the spell you wove with her binds you to her will."

"What spell?"

"The music, of course," Dahud answered with a smile. "You put your soul into it, and gave it to me. You're as much my minion now as Lucifer ever was."

"Why didn't you tell me?" Sophie demanded of the Morrigan.

"You called the challenge," Morag answered tiredly. "By then it was too late. But I would implore you, Daughter of Gradlon," she continued, turning to Dahud, "to reconsider, for all of our sakes."

Before anybody could respond to that, there was a sound of stone grating against stone. The floor trembled beneath their feet, and Dahud's court began a whole new chorus of shrieks and wails and curses. A long crack split the floor in front of the dais. Faeries and demons fled from it, crying and gibbering in terror, but Dahud looked on, imperturbable as stone.

The rift widened and rounded until it was roughly elliptical in shape. Peering into it, Sophie could see the top of a spiral staircase, elaborately built of what looked like bent metal bridge girders. A figure was moving up the staircase, but in its deep shadows, it was difficult to make out any detail.

The next moment, the figure stepped out of the chasm. He was tall and imposing, with an austere white face framed with lank, pale, chin-length hair, and penetrating eyes of no clear color. He wore an old-fashioned military jacket with tarnished brass buttons over a tattered t-shirt and combat trousers. His right arm was a bizarre construction of brass cogs and gears and plates, held together with studded leather straps.

It was so arresting that for a moment, Sophie didn't even register the figure beside him. But once her eyes shifted to the woman, she couldn't look away. She, too was dark haired, with a pale, delicate, doe-eyed beauty that seemed to belong to an earlier time. She wore what might once have been a wedding dress, its white lace frail and yellowed and cut away at the front to show knee-high black combat boots. Around her neck was a string of bones, and on her back a pair of gossamer wings, iridescent and veined like a dragonfly's.

The couple stepped aside to make way for others coming up the stairs behind them, all equally beautiful and bizarrely attired. Their faces and costumes shifted and blurred as they gathered, so that it became difficult to see them as individuals, and their distinctions appeared to Sophie as momentary flashes. An Asian man in a pin-stripe suit and aviator glasses, his long hair plaited with silvery wire. A woman in a Victorian gown with mahogany skin and what looked like dark tree roots splayed across one smooth cheek. A man with white skin and black hair and a monocle made of steel and cobalt glass.

At last they stopped coming. Dahud smiled and bowed low to them and the truth finally dawned on Sophie: "*Those* are the daevas?" she said.

"Pretty things, aren't they?" Rive said grimly.

"Beauty," the Morrigan said with soft regret, "can hide a multitude of evils."

They all watched in awestruck silence as Dahud conversed quietly with the man with the clockwork arm. At length he turned, his wide, water-colored eyes coming to rest on Sophie. Looking at him, Sophie was filled with horror. He was smitingly, painfully beautiful, but there was a remoteness to that beauty, as if he were carved of ice – cold, and hard, and very far from human.

"I am Abaddon," he said in a voice like a churchbell on a frozen winter morning. "I've waited a long time to meet you, Sophia."

"Sorry if I can't say likewise," she answered.

He shrugged. "It makes no difference to us. Come." He unfolded his metal-and-leather arm, unfurled its long fingers and beckoned to her. Sophie shrank back against Lucas. The daeva frowned, and turned to Dahud. "I thought you said that she had been told."

"She *has* been told," Dahud said, giving Sophie a contemptuous look. "But we haven't the power to make her like it."

"You have no choice, little aeon," Abaddon said, stepping toward Sophie. The woman in the ruined wedding dress slipped after him, silent as a ghost despite her heavy boots. "You are the teind." He touched Sophie's cheek with one metal fingertip. She flinched at its frigid bite, but didn't drop her eyes.

"If you take her, you destroy the Balance," Rive said, pushing Abaddon's hand away from Sophie's face. His blue shimmer had become a light that was almost too bright to look at.

Abaddon smiled a feral smile. "Precisely."

"Would you really condemn all of Creation to chaos?" Michael asked.

"Chaos is the perfect medium from which to build a new balance of power."

"There's nothing to say that you'll even be able to control it, let alone bend it to your will," Rive said, still coldly calm.

"It's a chance we're willing to take," Abaddon answered, no longer smiling. "We've been confined to the Deep long enough, and as it's by *her* hand," he nodded at Sophie, "then it's her hand that must free us. Midnight is almost upon us! It's time to go." He took firm hold of Sophie's arm with his metal fingers, and jerked her away from Lucas.

But Sophie planted her feet and wrenched free. "I won't

go with you!" she said fiercely, as her friends pulled in around her again.

For a moment the daeva looked surprised; then he smiled. "You can't mean to challenge us."

"Can't we?" Michael said. He reached into the air in front of him, and suddenly he was holding his flaming sword. Suri held one too, its light the piercing white of sun through ice. The Morrigan's staff was glowing, and she, too radiated an aura of ancient strength.

The daeva looked at them for a long moment. Then he said, "Very well. If it's a fight you want, it's a fight you shall have."

He waved his hand, and abruptly, every creature of Dahud's court was rushing at Sophie and her friends. For the first, confusing moments Suri and Michael kept the creatures back, their swords blazing brightly, monsters falling away from the deadly blades. Rive had disappeared into a blur of blue light, spinning and diving almost too quickly for Sophie's eyes to register. The Morrigan stood still and impervious, leaning on her staff, but any creature that threatened her fell dead at her feet.

Angus and Ailsa huddled, dumbstruck, by Lucas and Sophie. "Think you can make us some weapons?" Lucas asked her.

"I have this," Sophie said, pulling Carnwennan from her belt. It was as painfully bright as the angels' blades.

Remembering the drag and crunch of that knife driving into the *Cait Sìth,* Sophie swallowed hard.

"Good," he said. "But that's yours."

"I have this, too," she said, taking the piece of sword she'd found in Lucas's house from inside her coat.

He smiled ruefully, touching the corroded metal. "I don't think that will do us much good now. It was broken when I fell."

As he spoke the words, Sophie saw it: not the blackened hilt in the grave in Suri's cemetery, not the pieces of shattered metal from the long-ago dream, not even the stunted, tarnished blade in her hands. In her mind's eye was a weapon whole and perfect, glowing with deep red light, inscribed with intricate golden symbols. Even as she thought it, she felt a humming warmth in her hands. She didn't know whether she or Lucas was more shocked when she looked down to find the exact sword she'd been imagining in place of the broken one. Wordlessly, she handed it to Lucas. He held it for a moment, testing its balance. Then, with the first smile since he'd awakened from his enchantment, he plunged into the fight.

Sophie looked at Ailsa and Angus. "Well, guys, what'll it be? Swords? Knives? Light sabres?"

"Well…I *have* always fancied a claymore," Angus said.

"A what?"

"A really big sword. Did you ever see 'Braveheart'?"

"Okay," Sophie said, and shut her eyes, trying to imagine

Mel Gibson skewering English mercenaries. In a moment, something fell at her feet with a heavy, metallic clunk. She opened her eyes to see Angus beaming as he picked up what was, indeed, a really big sword.

"Do you know how to use that?" Ailsa asked dubiously.

"I've read all about it," he answered, just as a green thing with wolfish teeth and long, clawed fingers launched itself at Ailsa. Angus hefted his sword as she screamed, and whacked it aside. It fell to the ground screeching, and slowly disintegrated until it was no more than an oily puddle on the floor. "See?" he said, beaming, and turned to find something else to fight.

"Ailsa?" Sophie said, brandishing Carnwennan at something that looked very like the grindylow, which was creeping up on Ailsa from behind. "Can we move this along?"

"Can't we just hide or something?" Ailsa whimpered.

Sophie looked around. Not only was there nowhere to hide, there was nowhere to run. The demons and Dahud's *sith* surrounded them, pressing them slowly but surely toward the chasm in front of the throne. The staircase was gone, replaced by impenetrable darkness. Already, Michael and Suri were standing on its lip, though both still parried with the expert grace of cavaliers. Lucas fought with grim determination, though every sword-stroke visibly depleted his emaciated body. Angus was surrounded by fork-tailed devils armed with tridents, and Rive's blue light was ringed with daevas. If something didn't change soon, not only Sophie but all of them would succumb to the Deep.

And then something did. Ailsa's eyes widened in horror, and Sophie had a moment to wonder why, before something small and wiry with cold, vice-like limbs attached itself to her back. One clawed hand held a dagger, pressing it to Sophie's throat. "Think you can kill my sister, and walk free?" it hissed.

Wondering if it would forever be her fate to be pursued by vengeful *sith,* Sophie said, "I guess 'sorry' doesn't really cover it?"

"I'll drink your blood," it chanted, "grind your bone, tear your flesh, stew your heart – "

"Leave her, Peg," spoke a dreamy, crystalline voice.

Grumbling, the creature let her go. Sophie looked up to find the daeva in the wedding dress and wings standing before her, a faint smile on her purple lips. "Pretty," she said in a high, childlike voice, reaching out to stroke Sophie's cheek with one black-gloved hand. Even through the glove's leather, Sophie felt the creature's searing cold. "Like a china dolly. I've never had a china dolly. Abi says I would break it. But he's promised you can be mine to play with…"

This time when the daeva smiled, she showed rows of pointed teeth. Involuntarily Sophie took a step back, and then tottered for a moment as her heel met empty air. She stood at the edge of the rift. *The mouth of Hell.* The breath that rose from it held an arctic cold and a sulfurous reek. Her head swam with half-formed images of monsters she knew she could never have thought up on her own. She wondered if the daeva was somehow putting them into her mind. The thought made her long to take another step away from her – which was, of course, exactly what the daeva wanted. *Don't think,* she told herself.

She realized then that the room had fallen silent. Every eye in the place was focused on her, to see what she would do. But there was only one option left to her. Looking resolutely away from the wedding-dress daeva, she said, "I'll go willingly, if you let my friends leave unharmed." Her voice cut through the clustered silence like a knife-edge. For a moment, nothing else broke it.

And then Lucas spoke with soft conviction: "Leave her alone. I'll be your teind."

Abaddon, who'd come to join his consort, gave him a deprecating smile. "A tarnished angel in exchange for the Keeper's own child? I don't think so."

"Then have an untarnished one," Michael said, coming to stand at Sophie's other side.

Abaddon looked at him contemptuously. "A noble offer," he said, "but even an angel of as pure a heart as yours, Michael, is no match for an aeon." He reached for her hand, his metal fingers closing over hers with cold finality. "We accept Sophia's terms," he said. And then, to Sophie, "Come."

"No," Rive said, his voice quiet but implacable.

"Don't test my patience!" Abaddon snapped.

"Dahud promised you an aeon?"

"As I have told you already!"

"Very well," Rive said. His words were directed at the daeva, but his eyes had locked with Michael's. He took Michael's hand in his. An entire, unspoken conversation seemed to pass between them in the few seconds before he broke away, turned to Sophie. "Get back to the Garden, Sophia – at any cost." He pulled her roughly into an embrace, kissed both of her cheeks. And then he flung himself, head-first, into the chasm.

If she hadn't understood before what Theletos was to her, Sophie knew it now. It felt as if her heart were being ripped from her chest. She might not have loved him the way she was meant to – the way she loved Lucas – but she loved him just as much. As she watched him fall, their whole strange history exploded across her vision, quicker than thought, quicker than light. And then he was gone, swallowed by the frigid blackness of the Deep.

Blue stars exploded across her vision, and pain drove a red-hot needle into her skull. Blinded, Sophie fell to her knees, feeling for the edge of the rift, every instinct telling her to follow her twin into it. Then there were hands pulling her back. She screamed and fought against them, but they were too strong for her, and so she collapsed into the arms that tightened around her, wracked by wrenching sobs.

Through the pain and overwhelming grief, she was aware

of voices arguing. She took in their meaning slowly, dully. "This was not our agreement!" Abaddon cried.

"It was precisely your agreement," answered another male voice, cold and hard and still somehow fragile, like a stone wall holding back a flood. "You have your aeon: you have your teind."

"The hour turns," said a female voice. "We cannot stay…"

There was a pause, and then a rush of motion as the daevas lept into the chasm where Rive had disappeared. With a rumble of stone, the gap closed over them. But the deep, grating sound didn't stop, even after the floor was whole again. Abruptly it buckled, sending them all sprawling as stones began to rain from the ceiling. Dahud was screaming orders at her servants, who ran every which way, clearly at a loss as to what to do.

Sophie wrapped her arms around herself as the room juddered again, almost senseless with the pain in her head. "Sophie!" she heard someone cry into her ear – a warm voice, one she knew and whose tone offered comfort, though she couldn't place it through her confusion. "We've got to run!"

"Leave her to me," said another voice – the one like the dammed river. "You're too weak to carry her."

Sophie felt herself being lifted in arms that were strong and certain and far too warm. As the person holding her began to run, the pain drove deeper into her skull. "Come on!" he cried, raising his voice to be heard over the increasing roar of rending stone. "This place is coming to pieces!"

They moved through falling stone and flickering green light, into someplace darker and colder. Slowly, the cool air began to disperse the pain in Sophie's head. The neon confetti at the edges of her vision thinned out. By the time they emerged from Dahud's palace, both had subsided enough that she knew that it was Michael carrying her, and she recognized Lucas beside him, peering down at her anxiously.

"Stop," she said. "Put me down."

"We can't waste time," Michael said sharply.

"I'm alright!" she insisted. "And I'm slowing you down like this." It was true. She could see the others far ahead.

"Very well," Michael said, and put her down. The ground wasn't shaking here, but the buildings around her swam and fuzzed, like a projection that's slipped out of focus.

"Why do they look like that?" she asked.

"I don't know," Michael answered grimly, and with a steeliness that told her he guessed, and didn't much like what he was guessing. "But we need to get out of here."

Lucas took her hand and they began to run. They didn't reach the others until they were back in the field where they'd left the water horses. Good as their word, the *sìth* were still there. "Double up on the horses," Michael said, and then, to Suri's questioning look, "We need to stay together."

Lucas helped Sophie onto the black horse, and then got up behind her. Michael got up on Ailsa's horse with her,

442

Suri shared Angus's. It was then that Sophie realized that the Morrigan was missing.

"Where is Morag?" she asked.

"She can look after herself," Michael answered. "Now let's go!"

But the horses didn't move. "What now?" Sophie demanded.

"*Sìth* do not deal with angels," the black horse answered, the derisive humor clear in its tone, "let alone carry them."

"Swamplily Tickseed," Sophie said through gritted teeth, "you and your companions will take the six of us back to Ardnasheen."

The horse bucked and twisted, but Sophie and Lucas hung on. Now the ground around them was trembling, and as they watched, the forest they'd just left collapsed with a whoosh that was nothing like breaking wood, and very like the fall of a theater curtain. Beyond the flattened trees, Sophie could see the buildings of Ker-Ys falling too. Then a crack opened in the ground in front of them, tearing across the turquoise field like a ripped seam.

"Swamplily Tickseed," Sophie yelled, driving her heels into the horse's side, "you'll do as you're bloody well told, or we're all going to die!"

With a squeal of frustration, the water horse flung herself into the air at the moment the ground gave way beneath them. Looking around quickly, Sophie saw that the others had taken to the air as well. They moved skyward in great bounds. Sophie wound her fingers grimly in the horse's dank, wet mane, feeling Lucas's arms tighten around her. She saw the faery door, burning brightly against the green sky. With a lurch and a tug that almost unseated her, the horse leapt through it.

Sophie had thought that they would leave the destruction behind them in Ker-Ys, but as they surged through the dark water she realized that this wasn't the case. As the horses swam, they were buffeted by opposing currents, clearly struggling to make headway. Worse still, great dark shapes loomed around them, lit dimly by the dwindling green glow of Ker-Ys and the angels' muted auras.

Sophie drew back instinctively from a massive form that swam up from the shadows, only for it to reveal itself as a bi-plane, moving through the dark water on tattered wings, flown by a skeletal pilot glowing a ghostly grey. Another winged shadow resolved into a skeletal pterodactyl, which dove, screeching soundlessly at them before wheeling away into the dark. A sinuous shape slipped past, twice the length of the water horse, turning to reveal an eel's flat, dead eyes and a rack of teeth before it was gone again.

Everywhere Sophie looked, the dark water swarmed with monsters, as if the earth's shuddering had dislodged all of the sea's buried horrors at once. She wished that she could ask Lucas what was happening. She wished that she could scream.

Instead, the heavy water forced her to watch the unfolding horrors in silence.

Then, abruptly, they were gone. Sophie had only a moment to wonder why, before a current stronger than any she'd felt yet was dragging her backward. It reminded her of the way a retreating wave on a seashore would pull the sand from beneath her feet, except that it was far more powerful. Even the water-horse was unable to make headway against it. The rhythm of its legs stuttered, and then fell still.

The backward-flowing current slackened and then stilled, but Sophie knew that it wasn't finished. Every muscle in her body tensed. Lucas's arms tightened around her. Then the horse gave a violent shake, freeing herself of her passengers. Sophie was left clinging to Lucas in the darkness, unable to breathe. She began to panic as her chest squeezed painfully, desperate for air.

At the same time, a roar was gathering in the distance; a roar that she felt rather than heard. A moment later the current inverted, shoving them forward as quickly as it had drawn them back. The world disintegrated into a dark blur, a searing pain in her chest, a deafening roar in her ears. And then she was lying on wet sand as hard as concrete. Sea-water spewed from her lungs, and she retched it up in painful spasms. When they passed, she sucked in a breath: it felt as if she'd tried to swallow sandpaper. But she drew another, and another. She lay like that, trying to remember how to breathe, too exhausted

445

even to lift her head from the cold, hard sand, until a voice began to sing. It came from nowhere and everywhere, high and cold and plangent as a child's:

Hush, little dolly, don't say a word,
Mama's going to love you till the end of the world...

Sophie tried to scream. Everything went black.

EPILOGUE

Sophie surfaced slowly from the dream, trying to remember what it had been about. Something horrific. Something urgent, which still pushed at her, trying to make itself heard. Harp music and bitter laughter. Monstrous angels and cold black water. A pain in her head, and in her heart, an agony of loss. But that made no sense. She had the only thing she could ever want. The only mark on her happiness was the feeling she had sometimes that it was too sweet to be real.

She was fully awake now, but she didn't open her eyes. Instead she pressed herself closer against Lucas, shivering despite the warmth as his skin touched hers, at once soft and smooth and hard with muscle. She buried her face in his neck as he ran a hand up the curve of her waist, feeling her face heat as it travelled further up, gentle and maddening, until he pushed his fingers into her long hair, tilted her head up so that he could kiss her.

As their lips met, Sophie was suddenly, keenly awake. She

kissed him with abandon, her hands moving over his body as if she'd never have enough of it, her legs tangling with his. At the same time, though, the memory of the dream pushed more insistently against her. Reluctantly she pulled away, opened her eyes. The familiar shapes of the room materialized in the grey, early morning light: the stacks of books, the dresser, the sconces of the gas lamps. The table with the victrola, its horn opening like a tropical flower, and the accompanying box of records beside it.

Finally she looked at Lucas. The color was high in his face, his dark eyes soft. The look in them wrung her heart. "Why did you stop?" he asked, tracing her collarbones with the tip of one finger.

"I had such a strange dream," she said, moving her hand so that it rested over his heart.

"What kind of dream?" he asked, taking the hand in his and kissing each finger.

"It was cold. There was a woman…a witch, with eyes like ice. She'd kept you prisoner and made you forget me. And when I came to win you back, she killed my brother."

"Sophie," he said, smoothing back her hair, "you don't have a brother. There are no such things as witches, and you will never, ever be cold as long as we're together."

"No," she agreed, closing her eyes again as he ran his hands over her body. She reached for him, but this time he was the one who pulled back.

"Wait," he said.

"Why?" she asked.

"Because I have something for you."

"I told you I didn't want Christmas presents."

"I hope you'll want this one," he said, offering her his closed hand.

Smiling, Sophie peeled back his fingers. But when she saw what was lying in his palm, the smile faded and she sat up. It was a ring, made of two twists of gold, set with a bright blue stone. From the lustre of the metal and the slight irregularity of the design, she knew that it was very old. Carefully, she touched it with a fingertip, as if it might disintegrate.

"It's survived two thousand years of battering," Lucas said, as if reading her thought. "I doubt you'll be able to break it."

Sophie picked it up, looked into the winking blue depths of the stone. "Two thousand years?"

"More or less. It belonged to a Roman empress." He paused for a moment, and then added, "It was her engagement ring."

Sophie looked at him, her eyes wide and her hands suddenly trembling. "Was?" she asked softly.

"And is…I mean, if you want it to be."

She blinked at him for a moment in disbelief, and then she flung her arms around his neck. "Yes!" she said. "I want that more than anything."

He kissed her, and she melted all over again, forgetting the ring in her hand until he pushed her gently away, took it, and slipped it onto her finger. It fitted as if it had been made for her. Sophie looked at it, turning her hand this way and that.

"God, what will my parents say?" she said.

"We'll find out in a few hours," he said with a smile, running his hand down through her hair, until it ended at her waist.

"They'll say we're too young. That we've only known each other a few months."

Lucas shrugged. "You said they got married right out of university, and look at them – still going strong."

"True," Sophie answered.

"Anyway, we don't have to do it right away. I just wanted…" He stopped, looking at her, suddenly shy. "I just wanted you to know that there will never be anyone else for me. I'll love you until the end of time."

"That's terribly melodramatic," Sophie said, slipping her arms around his neck.

"Sorry," he answered, not sounding at all sorry.

"I didn't say there was anything wrong with that," she said, kissing him. "In fact, nothing has ever seemed so right."

"Good," Lucas said. "Because we still have a few hours before your parents get here." He pulled her down into his arms. "And I know exactly how I want to spend them."

Preview Morningstar, the exciting sequel to *Bound*, coming 2013. For more information go to www.sarahbryant.net

MORNINGSTAR

Sarah Bryant

"Between two worlds life hovers like a star..."
Lord Byron

May 21

Dublin, Ireland

1

Esther woke screaming, her cries drowning out the bells ringing the call to Lauds. The eyes of the demon blazed in her mind like sun through seawater. He hadn't said a word. He hadn't needed to. In his eyes, Esther could see every city he'd raze, every sea he'd set to boiling and the rivers of blood that would flow from the clenched fist of his metal arm, while the girl in the tattered white dress and gossamer wings danced gleefully on the margins.

"Stop it!" Sister Agnes roared, slammed through the door. Faced with the nun's florid, furious countenance, Esther's screams faded to whimpers. Sister Agnes took Esther's shoulders in a vice-like grip and shook her until she was silent, but Esther couldn't suppress the shudders that ran through her body.

Sister Agnes was peering closely into her face, looking, no doubt, for some sign of the evil she was certain Esther harboured. "More dreams of murderous angels, I suppose?" the nun said. Esther didn't answer, but she was sure that the nun read the truth in her eyes. *Eyes like an open book*, her father used to say, in a time so distant, a world so different from the one in which Esther now lived that sometimes, like the others, she could almost believe that it had never been.

Don't, she told herself. *You'll go mad that way.*

"I don't think they're angels, Sister," she answered softly.

"White robes?" Sister Agnes sneered. "Wings on their backs?" She shook her head. "No, Esther Madden: you are a wicked girl with a wicked soul, and your dreams are sacrilege."

Esther knew that there was no answer to that. She'd tried and failed to explain the dreams, the doom they portended and whose path she and everyone she knew were all blindly treading. It wasn't particularly surprising that her mother hadn't believed her: she saw only what suited her, and if she could tune out the nine children who went hungry while she drank, it was hardly surprising that she'd ignore the end of the world.

But the nuns' disbelief had been a bitter blow. Esther had

been certain that an order that called itself the Sisters of Charity would at least hear her out, and possibly afford an explanation. Three months on, it was hard to believe she'd ever had such naïve certainty. Telling the truth had got her nowhere but the cell where she was now locked; prayers and pleas had earned her nothing but beatings. So, now, she kept her mouth shut, looking down at her hands clenched in her lap, thin and purplish with the room's sepulchral chill.

The bells had fallen silent. Sister Agnes looked at her for another long moment, then she said, "Get up – get dressed, or you'll be late for mass." She turned to go and shut the door behind her, but Esther breathed no sigh of relief. She knew that the nun would be waiting outside, listening for any suspicious sound or silence.

Esther got out of bed. She pulled the flimsy nightgown over her head and shoved it under her pillow, quickly tidying the bedclothes afterward. Then she pulled on the knitted, one-piece undergarment which still felt like a form of torture three months on, and dropped the ugly grey dress over her head. She couldn't have come up with a less attractive design if she'd tried: shapeless bodice, short sleeves, wide waist and a hemline that hit just under the knee, like something straight out of a Dust Bowl photo. She pulled on white knee socks and black, lace-up shoes, and a black cardigan that did little against the chill. Last, she picked up the comb form its place next to the battered Bible on the table beside the bed. They'd forbidden her a mirror (though whether to discourage vanity or some occult experiment, she had no idea) so she combed her hair by the faint reflection in the window.

In the glass, her long, light-brown hair and pale blue eyes were as grey as the sky beyond, and as insubstantial as she felt. Esther set the comb on the window sill and looked down at the street below. It was grey and slicked with the past night's rain. A couple of rusted cars of mid-twentieth-century vintage went past, followed by a black-and-white horse with tufted legs pulling a rickety wagon loaded with potatoes. Modern technology had disappeared with the Change.

The Change. She wished she had a better name for it. She wished she had even an inkling of an explanation. All she had, though, was the memory of a life that had been very different from the one she was now living, and the certainty that this strange new reality was the precursor to something horrific. The demon with the mechanical arm and the eyes full of ruin had convinced her of that.

A hard rapping on the door made her jump. Esther's heart fluttered in response. Sighing, she popped two tablets from the bubble pack on her bedside table – one more thing that hadn't changed with the rest – and swallowed them. Then she picked up her black plastic rosary, dropped it over her head, and opened the door. Sister Agnes' eyes snapped, as if she were furious merely at the necessity of being in Esther's presence.

She said nothing, however, giving her only a quick once-over before she turned down the corridor toward the chapel.

They met no other students in the hallway. This was the nuns' wing. Each of the sisters had her own small cell of a room, like the one where Esther slept. Esther's cell was part punishment, but mostly practicality. At first she'd been put in one of the dormitories, but her screams had woken the other girls, and they were too curious about the cause of them for the nuns' liking. Bad enough to have one girl spouting blasphemy; the Sisters couldn't risk an epidemic.

Likewise, when they reached the chapel, Sister Agnes turned away from the centre pews where the other girls were assembled, leading Esther to the row of little wooden benches along the left wall where the nuns sat, each separated from the next by a carved partition. Esther sat down, focusing again on the hands in her lap so that she wouldn't have to look at the altar's painted saints. They looked far too much like the demons for her comfort.

When the priest began to speak, Esther relaxed slightly. Although she now knew that the rituals were empty, the familiarity of the morning and evening masses was soothing. They were one of only a handful of things that hadn't changed from the world she remembered, and they made reality feel a little less awful, her task a little less hopeless. Because Esther was in no doubt that she had been tasked. She had to make the others see what was happening, make them stop it before the demons came and destroyed them all.

How, though, remained beyond her. She thought about it as she went through the motions of the service, mouthing the words of the hymn and letting her mind drift during the readings of the psalms and the canticle. Part of the problem was that there had been no warning, no time to prepare. The day before had been an average one, beginning with waking her mother from her fractious alcoholic doze, ending with trying to soothe the baby, Peter, who was teething.

Finally, exhausted, Esther had taken him into her own bed. She'd fallen asleep to the baby's gentle breathing, underscored by a Northside cacophony of traffic and sirens and drunken men shouting as they left the pubs. She'd awakened to a world gone mad. Peter was no longer beside her, but wailing in a funereal black perambulator with large, spindly wheels, parked in a corner of the room. The digital clock-radio on her bedside table had become an old wind-up alarm clock with two metal bells, and her cheap fibreboard bed had turned to chipped wrought iron. Her little sisters were buttoning each other into drab, smock-like dresses as if they'd worn them all their lives, and brushing their short bobs, which had been long plaits when they went to sleep the evening before.

For a long time Esther just started at them, wondering if she was dreaming, or insane, or if she'd died in the night and wakened somehow in purgatory. She lay back down, shut her eyes tightly and prayed, but when she opened them again nothing had changed. Whatever had happened to the world she knew, this new one was apparently here to stay – at least for the time being.

Her first mistake had been assuming that everyone else would remember the other one, as she did. When she asked the other children what had happened in the night, they looked at her with varying degrees of puzzlement. Nine-year-old Martha, always the most practical, finally said, "Well, dad came home – but you were there."

Esther blinked at her in shock for a moment before blurting, "Dad is dead!"

Martha's look grew wary. "That isn't funny, Esther." At which point Esther leapt from her bed and ran into the kitchen. He mother stood at the stove frying bread and apparently sober, humming a hymn and wearing a dress and head-scarf that reminded Esther of posters from the Second World War. But that wasn't what stopped her in her tracks, and had her reaching for the work top for support as the room tipped and wheeled around her. Because her father was sitting at the table, with a mug of black tea in one hand and a newspaper in the other. He looked up at her with the blue eyes she'd inherited, and smiled a soft, warm smile.

"Daddy?" she choked out, her throat tight with tears.

"Esther, *mo chroí*," he said. "Why are you crying, my girl?"

462

"I thought...I thought..." She couldn't speak the words, couldn't tell him that in a cruel and distant world he'd been dead three years, killed when a section of scaffolding collapsed on a building project where he worked as a foreman. "I had a terrible dream," she answered at last.

"Well, that's no excuse to be standing there in your underclothes!" he mother said, frowning at her as she put a plate of breakfast in front of her father.

Esther looked down at herself, and found that the t-shirt and tracksuit bottoms she'd gone to sleep in had been replaced by a kind of vest top and shorts. The sight of the strange clothes jolted her back to the present. "Mum...Dad...has something happened?"

Her father looked at her, surprised and puzzled. Her mother muttered, "Not unless you mean the bloody king putting up the price of tea again."

"What king?" Esther asked, puzzled.

"Charles," her father said, his smile gone and his eyes worried. "King of Britain and Ireland."

"Ireland has a king?" Esther said, the world reeling again.

"What's wrong with you, girl?" her mother asked.

"Are you ill?" her father said, pushing his plate aside and coming to feel her forehead.

"I..." Esther began, knowing she had to make a difficult decision, and quickly: tell the truth and hope it jogged her parents' memories, or play along until she figured out what was going on and how, hopefully, to reverse it.

She'd chosen wrong. Telling the truth had done nothing but convince her parents that she'd lost her mind, and in the end even her father's love couldn't save her. He had continued to believe that she was suffering a sudden madness that might at any point dissipate, but her mother had become convinced that her problem was more sinister than that. When Esther had told her about the demon with the water-coloured eyes, her mother had called in the priest. He had examined her, then spoken to her parents in low tones about possession and a soul compromised by evil, and the danger it posed to the other children. In the end her father had broken down and signed the papers releasing her into the care of the Sisters of Charity, and their School for the Rehabilitation of Wayward Young Women.

The title still made Esther smile, if bitterly. Her entire life she'd been nothing but a good girl. The things her classmates had done to earn their places here horrified her. And yet she was the one who was kept under lock and key, as a danger to the others. She had a nun to guard her every moment of the day – from chapel to classes to the hard hours of "remedial" labour in the laundry – to make sure she didn't so much as look askance at the other students.

Someone jabbed an elbow into her ribs, interrupting her reverie. Esther flinched, glancing up at the hard eyes of the nun beside her. The woman shook a prayer book in her face, letting

Esther know that she was aware her attention had lapsed. They'd moved on to the responsory. Hastily Esther fumbled for the correct page in the book, and then mumbled the responses to the priest along with the others. She managed to pay attention through the rest of the service, and then she turned toward the door as the nuns and students began to file out.

"Not you, Esther," Sister Agnes said sharply, grabbing her arm.

Esther turned back, wondering what she could possibly have done wrong this time. "Yes, Sister?"

"The priest has asked that you make confession this morning," the nun answered, with a glint in her eye that told Esther she'd had something to do with this request.

"But I confessed after Vespers last night – "

"Aye, and you woke screaming blasphemy. Go." She pointed toward the confessional booths at the other side of the chapel. Esther had hated confession even before the Change, but now she despised it. She could feel the priest's eagerness through the screen, as if he wanted her to be acting out the will of a demon. He certainly found it easy enough to twist her simple words into something sinister, and make penitence into a misery.

Reluctantly, Esther opened the dark wooden door of the confessional, and sat down on the hard, narrow bench. She could hear the priest breathing on the other side. She could feel him waiting. With a trembling hand, she crossed herself and then, taking a deep breath, she said, "In the name of the Father, and of the Son, and of the Holy Spirit. My last confession was last night."

There was a long silence on the other side of the screen. She knew that the priest hadn't left – she could still hear him breathing. But it had become stilted, erratic. There was a knock against the wall that separated them, hard enough to make the booth shudder. Suddenly frightened, Esther stood up to leave. Her hand was on the door when a strangled whisper came from the other side of the screen: "Wait!"

The priest still gasped and wheezed as if he had been running, or fighting. And yet, something in the choked word made Esther pause. Something that sounded like a plea, rather than an order. Reluctantly she sat back down, poised on the edge of the bench to run if her instinct proved false.

"Father?" she asked softly.

The priest pressed his hands against the dividing screen. "Sophia?" It was the priest's voice, but it was so low, so close to both hope and despair that she couldn't believe she was speaking to the same crotchety man who doled out her daily penance.

"No, Father," she answered. "It's Esther."

"Esther?" he asked confusedly. "What's your surname?"

"Madden, Father," Esther answered, beginning to wonder whether the priest had lost his mind.

"No relation of a family named Creedon?"

"Not that I know of."

The priest let out a jagged sigh, and lowered his hands from the screen. Esther knew that she should leave, that the priest had had some kind of turn, and that it might well be blamed on her. On the other hand, that would no doubt happen whether she left now or stayed, and besides, she was curious. Because a part of herself – the part she had tried so hard to suppress over her months with the Sisters of Charity – was whispering to her: *What if he isn't mad at all? What if this is the chance I've been waiting for?*

His next words seemed to confirm it. "Well, Esther Madden, can you tell me where I am?"

"You're in Northside."

"The north side of what?"

"Dublin," she answered, settling a little further back onto the bench. "This is the convent of the Sisters of Charity. Ah... specifically, you're in a confessional booth in the chapel."

To her surprise, the priest let out a low, bitter, laugh. "Of course I am. They'd have never let me manifest where someone might believe me."

Manifest? "Believe you...about what, Father?" Esther asked, barely able to form the words in her sudden hope.

"I'm not your 'Father', Esther," the priest said suddenly, in a rush. "My name is Theletos. I'm an aeon – although I don't expect you to have any idea what that means – and I'm trying to save the world. But I'm finding it a bit difficult, as I'm currently incarcerated in the Deep, at the mercy of the daevas."

Most of it made no sense to Esther, but one phrase stood out, gleaming like a beacon on a night-shrouded sea: "Save the world from what?" she asked, barely above a whisper.

"From hell, Esther," he said bitterly. "Because that's where it's headed, though no one appears to notice."

She swallowed, shut her eyes, and willed her voice to be steady. "*I've* noticed," she said.

There was a pause, and then another jagged breath. "You mean…you know that everything's changed?"

"Yes."

"You…do you remember the time before?"

"As clearly as I remember yesterday."

The priest – or Theletos – let out the breath he'd drawn. "Then I might just be able to save the world after all."

"Fath- I mean, Theletos – I have no idea what you're talking about."

"It doesn't matter. You have to deliver a message for me. You have to find a girl called Sophie Creedon, and tell her that unless she goes back to the Garden immediately, the world will end and the human race will be exterminated."

"Sophie Creedon – does she go to this school?"

"I very much doubt it."

"Then how am I meant to find her?"

He paused, then said anxiously, "I don't have much time. Am I right in assuming that you have psychic talents?"

"I…I don't know. Sometimes I dream things, or know them before they happen, like. But you'd be the first to call it a talent."

"Good enough," Theletos answered. "Touch your hand to mine, Esther."

"But the screen – "

"Allows a bit of contact." He put his hand up against it. Slowly, Esther placed hers against it, and then she gasped as a surge of energy flowed through her, along with a string of images. They moved so quickly that she only caught a few of them: a woman with green hair and silver eyes, a hole in the ground with a curved stairway leading into it, the face of the metal-armed demon and the one in the wings and wedding dress, and then a pretty girl of about her own age.

Here the flow stopped, giving her a clear view of the girl's face. It was heart-shaped and sweet, with a soft, sensitive mouth and wide grey eyes that seemed to hold all of the sadness of the world, framed by thick dark hair that hung just shy of her shoulders. But there was something about her more striking than her beauty: a light that surrounded her, a faint wash of pure, clear blue which Esther recognized as the light she saw sometimes around her own face in the mirror. An aura – she knew that's what they were called, having once seen a man at a street fair who claimed to be able to photograph them.

She knew that good Catholic girls weren't supposed to believe in them, let alone admit to seeing them, and so she didn't. But despite that, she'd seen enough of them to know that they were as individual as the people they belonged to. No two were ever quite the same colour. No two except hers, and the one belonging to the dark-haired girl with the heart-shaped face.

"That's Sophie Creedon," she said. Somehow, seeing the aura had convinced her of the truth of what Theletos had told her, as nothing else could have.

"Yes."

"If she's not at this school, is she at least in Dublin?"

"I don't know for certain, but I think she's more likely to be in Scotland – a village called Ardnasheen."

"Scotland! The nuns don't even let me out the front door."

In response, a key clattered onto the bench beside Esther. She picked it up. It was an ordinary-looking key, the type that fit a Yale lock. "That will open the front door," Theletos said. "The rest, I'm afraid, you'll have to sort out for yourself."

"But how did you just – "

"It doesn't matter. There isn't time to explain. Just find Sophie, and tell her what I said."

"And she'll believe me?"

Theletos sighed. "I truly don't know. But if she doesn't, you'll have to make her believe."

"I haven't had much luck with that, so far."

"There's no choice. You have to try. There's no time left – they're coming – "

Abruptly, the man slumped against the screen. His face was clearly the priest's, and it was grey and lifeless. Esther looked at him for a moment, wondering if he was dead. Either way, she knew that she had to get out of the chapel immediately.

Slipping the key into the pocket of her dress, she stood up, took a deep breath, and then opened the door. The chapel was empty, except for Sister Agnes, snoring in one of the back pews. Esther was tempted to walk right past her, but the practical part of her knew that she needed more of a plan than that. At the very least, a set of clothes that didn't obviously belong to a convent schoolgirl. So, composing herself, she shook the nun's shoulder. She started awake.

"You were long enough about it," the nun grumbled, heaving herself to her feet.

"I suppose I had more to confess than I thought," Esther answered blandly.

"I don't doubt it."

If only you knew, Esther thought as she followed her out of the chapel. And despite what Theletos had told her – despite the fact that she had no idea who he really was, or if he could even be trusted – for the first time in months, she felt hope.

About the Author

Sarah Bryant was born and raised in Maine and Massachusetts, before attending Brown University to study English and American literature. After that she moved to the UK to do a masters in writing, where she met and married her Scottish husband. After fifteen years in southern Scotland, Sarah and family have moved to the wilds of Washington State, USA, to the horse farm she's always dreamed of. *Riven* is her sixth novel for Snowbooks, and her second for young adults.